More Praise for *KILL THE FATHER*

"Outstanding . . . [an] unrelenting, adrenaline-fueled novel, with a final twist serving as a setup for a sequel. Don't be surprised if *Kill the Father* becomes the next Big Thing in international crime fiction."
—*Booklist* (starred review)

"Dazzling . . . told in brutal, often wrenching detail."
—*Publishers Weekly*

"One of the nastier crimes in recent memory . . . There are twists aplenty as Dante and Colomba track down the Father, even as he spins an ever finer trap for them. . . . A dark treat for mystery buffs."
—*Kirkus Reviews*

"Simply a masterpiece: for the poignancy of the story, the creation of characters you can never forget, and the way the author grabs the reader by the throat and doesn't let go, even when the book has ended."
—*La Lettura/Corriere della Sera*

"The best of this season's thrillers. It's a sinister and terrifying dream, and lurking within it, in the most hidden corner, barely accessible, is something that emits the cold light of absolute evil."
—*Sette/Corriere della Sera*

"A hunt without mercy. Full of surprising special effects but also flashes of sheer literary gold."
—*Krimiblock.d...*

"Dazieri rewards his readers with ... socks off. *Kill the Father* is a compellir... ...acters have the potential to go on to big...
—*Krimicouch.de*

KILL THE FATHER

KILL THE FATHER

SANDRONE DAZIERI

**SIMON &
SCHUSTER**

London · New York · Sydney · Toronto · New Delhi

A CBS COMPANY

First published in Great Britain by Simon & Schuster UK Ltd, 2017
A CBS COMPANY

1 3 5 7 9 10 8 6 4 2

Simon & Schuster UK Ltd
1st Floor
222 Gray's Inn Road
London WC1X 8HB

www.simonandschuster.co.uk

Simon & Schuster Australia, Sydney
Simon & Schuster India, New Delhi

A CIP catalogue record for this book
is available from the British Library

Hardback ISBN: 978-1-4711-5410-2
Export Trade Paperback ISBN: 978-1-4711-6326-5
Australian Trade Paperback ISBN: 978-1-4711-5411-9
eBook ISBN: 978-1-4711-5413-3

Printed and bound by CPI Group (UK) Ltd, Croydon, CR0 4YY

Simon & Schuster UK Ltd are committed to sourcing paper
that is made from wood grown in sustainable forests and support the Forest
Stewardship Council, the leading international forest certification organisation.
Our books displaying the FSC logo are printed on FSC certified paper.

For Olga, who held out

– I –

BEFORE

The world is a curving wall of gray cement. The world has muffled sounds and echoes. The world is a circle two times the length of his outstretched arms. The first thing the boy learned in that circular world were his new names. He has two. Son is the name he prefers. He has a right to it when he does the right things, when he obeys, when his thoughts are clear and quick. Otherwise, his name is Beast. When he's called Beast, the boy is punished. When he's called Beast, the boy goes cold and hungry. When he's called Beast, the circular world stinks.

If Son doesn't want to become Beast, he has to remember the right place for the things he's been given and take good care of them. The bucket for his excrement and urine must always be hanging from the beam, ready to be emptied. The pitcher for the water must always stand at the center of the table. The bed must always be clean and tidy, with the covers nicely tucked in. The tray for his meals must always sit next to the hatch.

The hatch is the center of the circular world. The boy fears it and venerates it as a capricious deity. The hatch can open suddenly or remain shut for days at a time. The hatch can give him food, clean clothing, books, and pencils, or it can dispense punishment.

Mistakes are always punished. For minor errors, the punishment is hunger. For bigger mistakes, there's atrocious heat or cold. One time he was so hot that he simply stopped sweating. He fell to the cement, convinced he was about to die. He was pardoned with a stream of cold water. He was Son once again. Now he could drink again and clean the bucket, abuzz with flies. Punishment is hard in the circular world. Implacable and precise.

That's what he always believed until the day he discovered that the circular world is imperfect. The circular world has a crack. The length of his forefinger, the crack appeared in the wall, right where the wooden beam the bucket hangs from fits into the wall. The boy *didn't dare look closely at the crack for weeks. He knew it was there, it impinged on the boundaries of his consciousness, scorching it like flame. The boy knew that looking at the crack was a Forbidden Thing, because in the circular world everything that isn't explicitly allowed is forbidden. But one night the boy gave in to his impulse. He transgressed for the first time in a long time, the unchanging time of his circular world. He did it cautiously, slowly, planning out each move in advance. He got out of bed and pretended he'd fallen.*

Stupid Beast. Incompetent *Beast. He pretended he had to lean against the wall to support himself and for just an instant he brought his left eye into contact with the crack. He didn't see anything, only the darkness, but the enormity of what he'd done made him sweat in fear for hours. For hours he expected punishment and pain. He awaited cold and hunger. But nothing happened. This was an extraordinary surprise. In those hours of waiting, which eventually became a sleepless night and a feverish day, the boy understood that not everything he does can be seen. Not everything he does is weighed and judged. Not everything he does is rewarded or punished. He felt lost and alone, in a way he hadn't experienced since his very first days in the circular world, when the memory of Before was still strong, when the walls didn't exist and he had another name, different from Beast or Son. The boy felt his certainties shatter, and so he dared to take another look. The second time he kept his eye glued to the crack for nearly a whole second. The third time he looked for a full breath. And he saw. He saw the green. He saw the blue. He saw a cloud that looked like a pig. He saw the red roof of a house.*

Now the boy is looking again, balanced on tiptoe, his hands spread out against the cold cement to support himself. There's something moving outside, in a light that the boy imagines to be the light of dawn. It's a dark silhouette, and it grows bigger and bigger as it comes closer. Suddenly the boy realizes he's making the most serious mistake, that he's committing the most unforgivable transgression.

The man walking over the meadow is the Father, and he's looking at him. As if he'd read his thoughts, the Father speeds up his pace. He's coming for him.

And he has a knife in his hand.

- II -

THE STONE CIRCLE

1

The horror began at five in the afternoon on a Saturday in early September, with a man in shorts waving his arms, trying to flag down a car. The man had a T-shirt draped over his head to ward off the hot sun and a pair of ravaged flip-flops on his feet.

Watching him as he pulled the police car over to the side of the county road, the older officer classified the man in shorts as a "nutcase." After seventeen years on the force and several hundred winos and other delirious citizens calmed into docility with various carrots and sticks, he could spot a nutcase at a glance. And this was one, beyond the shadow of a doubt.

The two officers got out of the car, and the man in shorts crouched down, mumbling something. He was wrecked and dehydrated, and the younger officer gave him a drink of water from the bottle he kept in the car door, ignoring his fellow officer's look of disgust.

At that point the words of the man in shorts became comprehensible. "I've lost my wife," he said. "And my son." His name was Stefano Maugeri, and that morning he'd gone with his family for a picnic, a few miles farther up, in the Vivaro mountain meadows. They'd eaten an early lunch and he'd fallen asleep, lulled by the breeze. When he'd woken back up, his wife and son were gone.

For three hours, he'd moved in a circle, searching for them without success, until he found himself walking along the side of the county road, completely lost and on the verge of sunstroke. The older officer, whose confidence in his first impression was beginning to waver, asked why he hadn't called his wife's cell phone, and Maugeri replied that in fact he had, but he'd heard only the click of the voice mail, over and over until the battery of his cell phone ran out.

The older officer looked at Maugeri with a little less skepticism. He'd racked up quite a collection of emergency calls concerning wives who'd gone missing, taking the children with them, but none of those callers had dumped their spouse in the middle of a mountain meadow. Not still alive, anyway.

The officers took Maugeri back to his starting point. There was no one there. The other day-trippers had all gone home, and his gray Fiat Bravo sat alone on the lane, not far from a magenta tablecloth strewn with leftover food and an action figure of Ben 10, a young superhero with the power to transform himself into an array of alien monsters.

At that point, Ben 10 would probably have turned into a giant horse-fly and flown over the meadows in search of the missing wife and son, but the two policemen could only radio in to headquarters and turn in the alarm, triggering one of the most spectacular search-and-rescue operations the meadows had witnessed in recent years.

That was when Colomba got involved. It was her first day back at work after a long break, and it would be, beyond the shadow of a doubt, one of her worst.

2

A little older around her eyes than her thirty-two years, Colomba never went unnoticed, with her broad, muscular shoulders and her high, prominent cheekbones. The face of a warrior, a boyfriend had once told her, a woman warrior who rode stallions bareback and cut her enemies' heads off with a scimitar. She had laughed in response, and then she'd leapt astride him and ridden him furiously, leaving him breathless. Now, though, she felt more like a victim than a warrior, sitting on the edge of the bathtub, holding her cell phone, and staring at the display, where the name of Alfredo Rovere kept blinking. He was the chief officer of the Mobile Squad of the Rome police, technically still her boss and her mentor, and he was calling for the fifth time in three minutes: she'd never once answered his calls.

Colomba was still wearing a robe after stepping out of the shower, already horribly late for a dinner party at the house of friends, a dinner party to which she'd finally accepted an invitation. Since being released from the hospital, she'd spent most of her time alone. She rarely ventured out of her apartment; she usually went out in the morning, often at dawn, when she put on her tracksuit and went running along the Tiber River, which flowed past the windows of her apartment, just a short walk from the Vatican.

Jogging along the banks of the Tiber was a challenge to her reflexes, because, potholes aside, she had to avoid the dog shit, as well as the rats skittering suddenly out of the piles of rotting garbage, but none of that bothered Colomba, any more than she minded the exhaust fumes from the cars roaring past overhead. This was Rome, and she liked it precisely because it was dirty and nasty, even if that was something the tourists would never understand. After her run, every other day, she would do her grocery shopping at the corner minimart run by two Sinhalese immigrants, and on Saturdays she'd venture as far as the bookstall on Piazza Cavour; there she'd fill her bag with used books she would read during the week, an assortment of classics, detective novels, and romances that she almost never finished. She'd get lost in the plots that were too intricate, and she'd get bored with the ones that were too simple. She really couldn't seem to concentrate on anything. Sometimes she had the impression that it was all just sliding over her.

Aside from shopkeepers, Colomba spent days at a time without uttering a word to a living soul. There was her mother, of course, but she could just listen to her without having to open her mouth; then there were her friends and coworkers, who still called every now and then. In the rare moments that she devoted to self-awareness, Colomba knew she was overdoing it. Because this wasn't a matter of being comfortable on her own, something she'd always been able to do very well; she now felt indifferent to the rest of the world. She knew that she could blame it on what had happened to her, that it was the fault of the Disaster, but no matter how hard she tried, she couldn't pierce the invisible film separating her from the rest of humanity. That was another reason she had made a special effort to accept tonight's invitation, but with such scant enthusiasm that she was still trying to make up her mind what to wear while her friends were already on their third aperitif.

She waited for the incoming call to time out, then went back to brushing her hair. At the hospital they'd cut her hair extremely short, but now it had grown back to something approaching its normal length. Just as Colomba was noticing that some gray had begun to appear, someone rang the buzzer from downstairs. She stood there with her hairbrush in her hand for a few seconds, hoping there'd been some mistake, but then it rang again. She went and looked out the window: there was a squad car parked downstairs in the street. *Fuck*, she thought to herself as she grabbed the phone and called back Rovere.

He picked up on the first ring. "So the squad car arrived," he said by way of greeting.

"Yes, goddamn it," said Colomba.

"I wanted to tell you, but you wouldn't answer your phone."

"I was in the shower. And I'm late for a dinner party. So I'm very sorry, but you'll have to tell your man to go back where he came from."

"And you don't even want to know why I sent him out?"

"No."

"Well, I'll tell you anyway. I need you to come take a hike around the Vivaro mountain meadows."

"What's there?"

"I don't want to spoil the surprise."

"You've already sprung one on me."

"The next one's more interesting."

Colomba blew out her cheeks in impatience. "Sir . . . I'm on leave. Maybe you forgot."

Rovere's voice turned serious. "Have I ever asked you for anything during all these months?"

"No, never," Colomba admitted.

"Have I ever done anything to try to get you back before you were ready or to talk you into staying on the force?"

"No."

"Then you can't deny me this favor."

"Like hell I can't."

"I really need you, Colomba."

From his tone she understood he meant it. She fell silent for a few seconds. She felt she'd been cornered. Then she asked, "Is this absolutely necessary?"

"Of course."

"And you don't want to tell me what it's about."

"I don't want to influence you."

"So thoughtful."

"Well? Yes or no?"

This is the last time, thought Colomba. "All right. But tell your officer to stop ringing my buzzer."

Rovere hung up, and Colomba sat for a brief moment staring at the phone. Then she informed her resigned host that she wouldn't be coming to dinner after all, imposing her will over a series of half-hearted objections, and put on a pair of tattered jeans and an Angry Birds sweatshirt. It was clothing that she would never have worn while on duty, and that's why she'd picked it.

She grabbed the keys from the dresser by the front door and

instinctively checked to make sure her holster was fastened to her belt. Her fingers brushed only empty air. All at once, she remembered that her pistol had been in the police armory since the day she was admitted to the hospital, but it came as a deeply unpleasant sensation, like stumbling over a step that wasn't there; for a moment she hurtled back to the last time she'd reached for her weapon, and the feeling triggered an attack.

Her lungs immediately clamped tight; the room filled with fast-moving shadows. Shadows that were *screaming* as they slithered along the walls and floors, shadows she couldn't look straight at. They were always just outside her field of vision, visible only out of the corner of her eye. Colomba knew they weren't real, but she could feel them with every fiber of her being all the same. A blind, absolute terror took her breath away and was steadily suffocating her. She reached out sightless for the corner of the dresser and hit it hard, intentionally, with the back of her hand. Pain burst into her fingers and jolted up her arm like an electric shock, but it vanished too soon. She hit the dresser again and again, until the skin of one of her knuckles was torn and bleeding and the shock got her lungs working again, like a defibrillator. She gasped and swallowed an enormous mouthful of air, then started breathing regularly again. The shadows vanished, dissolving into a patina of icy sweat on the back of her neck.

She was alive, she was alive. She went on telling herself that for the next five minutes, kneeling on the floor, until the words seemed to mean something.

3

Seated on the floor, Colomba controlled her breathing for five minutes more. It had been days since her last panic attack, *weeks*. They'd begun right after she was released from the hospital. She'd been warned that they were pretty common after the sort of thing that had happened to her—but she'd expected just a little shakiness and some insomnia. Instead, the first one had been like an earthquake that had shaken her to her foundations, and the second one had been even more powerful. She'd passed out from lack of oxygen, convinced she was dying. The attacks had become frequent, sometimes three or four a day. It took only something as small as a sound or an odor like the smell of smoke to set them off.

The hospital psychologist had given her a number to call if she needed support of any kind. In fact, he'd urged her to call him. But Colomba had never told him or anyone else what was happening. All her life, she'd made her way in a world of men, many of whom would have been happier to see her serving coffee than packing a firearm, and she'd learned to conceal her weaknesses and troubles. And after all, somewhere deep down inside, she thought she deserved it. A punishment for the Disaster.

While she was bandaging her injured knuckle, she thought about calling Rovere back and telling him to go to hell, but she couldn't bring herself to. She'd limit their meeting to a minimum, the shortest time civil decency would allow, then she'd return home and mail in the letter of resignation she kept in a kitchen drawer. Then she'd decide what to do with the rest of her life, hoping she wouldn't wind up like those cops who'd taken retirement but kept hanging around police headquarters to make themselves feel they were still part of the family.

Outside, a cloudburst seemed to shake the world. Colomba threw on a lightweight K-Way windbreaker over her sweatshirt and went downstairs.

A young man was at the wheel of the squad car, and he stepped out into the rain to greet her. "Deputy Captain Caselli? Officer Massimo Alberti."

"Get back in the car, you're getting drenched," she said, climbing into the passenger seat. A number of neighbors sheltering under umbrellas were watching the scene curiously. She'd only moved into that apartment building recently, and not everyone knew what she did for a living. Maybe no one did, actually, given how seldom she talked to anyone.

For Colomba the squad car was like a whiff of home: the reflections of the flashing roof lights on the windshield, the radio and mike on the dashboard, the pictures of wanted men taped to the sun visors were all like so many familiar faces she hadn't seen in far too long. *Are you really ready to give this up?* she asked herself. No, she wasn't. But what choice did she have?

Alberti turned on the siren and started down the street.

Colomba snorted. "Turn that off," she said. "We're not in any hurry."

"My orders are to hurry, Deputy Captain," Alberti replied, but he obeyed.

He was a young man, about twenty-five, fair-skinned, with a light sprinkling of freckles. He emanated a scent of aftershave that she found agreeable, though out of place at that time of day. Maybe he carried a bottle of the stuff around with him and had sprayed some on to make a good impression on her. For that matter, his uniform was a little too clean and tidy. "Are you new?" she asked.

"I graduated from the academy a month ago, Deputy Captain, and I first enlisted as a cop a little over a year ago. I come from Naples."

"You got started late."

"If I hadn't passed the admissions exam last year I'd have been too old. I squeaked through just in time."

"Well, break a leg," she muttered.

"Deputy Captain, can I ask you something?"

"Go on."

"How do you get onto the Mobile Squad?"

Colomba smirked. Nearly everyone on patrol duty wanted to get onto the Mobile Squad. "You need a recommendation. You file a request with your commanding officer, and then you take a justice police course. But if you do get in, just remember, it's nowhere near as much fun as you think. You have to forget about the clock."

"Can I ask how you got in?"

"After passing the police admission exam in Milan, I served two years at police headquarters; then I was transferred to drug enforcement down in Palermo. When Captain Rovere was sent up to Rome four years ago, I came with him, as his deputy."

"In Homicide."

"Let me give you a piece of advice, don't call it Homicide unless you want everyone to think you're a *penguin*." "Penguins" were newly minted cops. "That's strictly in the movies. It's the third section of the Mobile Squad, okay?"

"Excuse me, Deputy Captain," said Alberti. When he blushed, his freckles became more noticeable.

Colomba was sick of talking about herself. "How come you're out driving around solo?"

"Normally I make my rounds with my older partner, but I volunteered for the search-and-rescue effort, Deputy Captain. My partner and I found Maugeri earlier today, on the county road."

"Just assume I don't know what the fuck you're talking about."

Alberti complied, and Colomba found out about the vanished picnickers and the guy in shorts.

"Actually, I haven't done any searching. I just went to the apartment and then stood guard outside," Alberti summed up.

"The family apartment?"

"That's right. If the wife ran away, she didn't take anything with her."

"What do the neighbors say?"

"Nothing helpful, Deputy Captain, but they did have plenty to say," said Alberti with another smile. The fact that he didn't make an effort to keep an expression of granite solemnity on his face, the way most penguins did, was a point in his favor.

Colomba smiled back in spite of herself and it almost hurt her face, she was so out of practice. "Where are we going?"

"The search coordination center is at the Vivaro riding stables. There's us, the carabinieri, the firemen, and civil protection. And a bunch of civilians who mostly just get in the way. Word's gotten out."

"Word always does," said Colomba, discontentedly.

"There was a little activity three hours ago. I saw two Land Rover Defenders heading out toward Monte Cavo with several officers and a magistrate. Judge De Angelis. You know him?"

"Yes," and she didn't like him. Prosecutor Franco De Angelis was always far too pleased to appear in the press. He had only a couple of years before he'd be eligible to retire, and everyone said that he had his sights set on the Superior Council of the Magistrature. They also said he'd do anything to land a seat on that exalted panel. "How far is Monte Cavo from where they were picnicking?" she asked.

"A mile and a half through the woods, six miles by road. You want to see the report? There's a printout in the glove compartment."

Colomba got it out. It featured two photos of the missing persons, taken off Facebook. Lucia Maugeri had dark, wavy hair; thirty-nine but she looked older. The boy was plump, with Coke-bottle glasses. The picture had been taken at his desk at school, and he wasn't looking into the lens. Six and a half. His name was Luca.

"If they wound up on Monte Cavo, they certainly took a nice long hike, him and his mother. And no one saw them, is that right?"

"That's what I was told."

The rain started coming down again, and the traffic ground to a halt. Still, with their flashers on, they cut through the line of cars like Moses through the Red Sea. They reached the turnoff for Velletri in half an hour. Colomba began to see official cars and civil protection vans coming and going; soon there was a solid mass of emergency vehicles as they reached the fences surrounding the riding stables. The stables were a compound of one-story buildings, modest in appearance, built around a harness track.

At walking speed, they drove along the county road cluttered with squad cars, civilian automobiles, carabinieri troop buses, ambulances, and fire trucks. There were also mobile news vans from two television networks, with satellite dish antennas on the roofs, and a field kitchen on wheels that was sending up a dense plume of smoke. *The only things missing are sideshow attractions and a shooting gallery*, thought Colomba.

Alberti pulled up behind a camper. "We're here, Deputy Captain," he said. "Captain Rovere is waiting for you at the operations center."

"Have you already been there?" asked Colomba.

"Yes, Deputy Captain."

"Then show me the way, and we'll save time."

Alberti pulled the hand brake and then escorted her past buildings that seemed to be deserted. Colomba could hear horses whinnying inside and just hoped she wouldn't run into a runaway horse, panicking in the rainstorm. They were heading for one of the buildings, guarded by two uniformed officers who saluted Alberti brusquely and ignored her entirely, taking her for a civilian.

"You wait here," she said and, without knocking, pulled open a door on which hung a piece of paper that bore the warning STATE POLICE—WAIT TO BE ANNOUNCED.

She walked into an old records room with metal filing cabinets lining the walls. Half a dozen police officers, uniformed and plainclothes, sat at four large central desks, making phone calls or talking on radios. Colomba spotted Alfredo Rovere, standing over a map spread out on one of the desks. He was a short man, about sixty, with thinning hair carefully combed back. Colomba noticed that his shoes and trousers were spattered with mud up to the knee.

The officer sitting by the door looked up and recognized her. "Deputy Captain Caselli!" he exclaimed, getting to his feet. Colomba couldn't remember his name, just the handle Argo 03, which he used when it was his shift at the operations switchboard. Everyone in the room stared at her, and for a moment all conversation ceased.

Colomba forced a smile onto her face and gestured with one hand for them all to go back to work. "Please, don't make a fuss."

Argo 03 gripped her hand. "How are you, Deputy Captain? You've been missed."

"You haven't, that's for sure," she answered, pretending to kid around. Argo went back to his phone, and soon the sound of multiple conversations resumed. From what they were saying, Colomba understood that checkpoints had been set up all along the county road. Odd. That wasn't standard practice in disappearance cases.

Rovere came over. He gently squeezed her shoulders and looked her in the eyes. His breath reeked of cigarette smoke.

"You're looking good, Colomba. For real."

"Thanks, Captain," she replied, thinking to herself that he actually looked aged and weary. There were bags under his eyes, and he needed a shave. "What's going on?"

"Curious?"

"Not in the slightest. But as long as I'm here . . ."

"You'll see in a minute," he said, taking her by the arm and steering her toward the door. "Let's go find a car."

"Mine's parked at the front entrance."

"No, we need a jeep."

They walked out, and Alberti, who'd been leaning against the wall, snapped to attention.

"Are you still here?" asked Rovere.

"I asked him to wait," said Colomba. "I'd hoped I'd be heading home soon."

"Do you know how to drive an off-road vehicle?" Rovere asked Alberti.

"Yes, Captain."

"Then go to the front gate and requisition one. We'll wait for you here," Rovere ordered.

Alberti rushed outside. Rovere lit a cigarette in open defiance of the sign that said NO SMOKING.

"Are we going to Monte Cavo?" asked Colomba.

"I try to keep things from you, and you figure them out anyway," he replied.

"Did you think I wouldn't talk to my driver?"

"I'd have preferred it."

"And what's up there?"

"You'll see with your own eyes."

A Land Rover Defender reversed toward them across the courtyard, narrowly missing a highway patrol motorcycle.

"About time." Rovere took Colomba by the arm and started to lead her out.

She wriggled free. "Are we in a hurry?"

"Yes, we are. In an hour, or possibly less, we won't be welcome anymore."

"Why not?"

"I'll bet you can figure it out all by yourself."

Rovere opened the door for her. Colomba didn't get in. "I'm seriously thinking of just going home, Captain," she said, "I didn't like riddles even when I was little."

"Liar. You'd have picked another line of work."

"That's exactly what I'm planning to do."

He sighed. "Have you really made up your mind?"

"I couldn't be more determined."

"We can talk about that later. Come on, get in."

Colomba slipped into the backseat resignedly.

"Good girl," said Rovere as he got in front.

With Rovere giving directions, they left the stables and turned onto the Vivaro county road, following it for a little less than three miles; then they took the lake road until they reached the state road toward Rocca di Papa. They drove past the last few homes and a trattoria where a small knot of police officers were drinking coffee and smoking under a pergola. It seemed the civilians had all gone to ground and only uniforms and military vehicles remained. They traveled another three quarters of a mile and turned off onto the road up to Monte Cavo.

When they stopped, there was no one else in sight. Beyond the trees at the end of the trail, Colomba glimpsed the glow of floodlights breaking the darkness.

"From here we're going to have to continue on foot; the trail is too narrow," said Rovere. He opened the trunk and pulled out two Maglite flashlights.

"Will I be looking for hidden notes?"

"It would be nice if they left such easy clues, wouldn't it?" said Rovere, handing her a flashlight.

"Clues to what?"

"Be patient."

They started up the trail, shielded on both sides by trees whose branches twined together to form a sort of green corridor. The silence was practically absolute, now that the rain had stopped, and the air was redolent with the scent of dampness and rotting leaves that Colomba associated with mushrooms. The smell stirred up memories from when she was small and used to go mushroom hunting with an uncle who'd been dead for years. She couldn't remember whether they'd ever actually found any.

Rovere lit another cigarette, though his breathing was already labored from the hike. "This is the Via Sacra," he said.

"What's that?" asked Colomba.

"A road that once led to a Roman temple. You see? The original paving stones are still there," said Rovere, playing the beam of his light over the gray, time-worn basalt slabs. "Three hours ago one of the search teams took this trail and followed it out to the overlook."

"What overlook?"

Rovere pointed the flashlight at the line of trees straight ahead of them. "Behind there."

Colomba ducked her head and stepped under a tangle of branches and out onto a broad flagstone terrace bounded by a metal railing. The overlook surveyed a clearing about thirty feet beneath it, at the center of which was a stand of pine trees, holm oaks, and tangled underbrush. Parked between the narrow road and the trees were two Defenders and a police van used to transport technical equipment. The muttering roar of the diesel generator powering the floodlights could be heard, along with the echoing sound of voices.

Rovere puffed up beside her, panting like a pressure cooker. "The team halted here. It was pure luck they spotted them at all."

Colomba darted the flashlight beam over the edge, following Rovere's pointing finger.

There was a bright reflection on a solitary boulder at the edge of the darkness that at first looked to her like a plastic bag caught in a bush. When she trained the beam directly on it, she realized that it was a pair of white-and-blue gym shoes dangling from the branch of a bush, slowly twisting in the air. Even from that distance, she could see they were small, a child's size nine or ten at the most.

"So the boy fell down here?" Colomba asked.

"Look closer."

Colomba did, and then she saw that the shoes weren't simply tangled in the bush, the laces had been knotted together. She turned to look at Rovere. "Someone hung them there."

"That's right. Which is why the team decided to go down. Go this way," he said, pointing to the lane. "But be careful, it's steep. One of the men twisted his ankle."

Rovere went down ahead of her and Colomba followed, her curiosity piqued in spite of herself. Who'd put those shoes there? And why?

A sudden gust of wind sprinkled her with drops, and Colomba jumped, her lungs contracting. *That's enough panic for today, okay?* she told herself. *When I get home, I can have a nice fat attack, and maybe another good cry to go with it. Just not now, please.* Who she was talking to, she couldn't say. All she knew was that the atmosphere of that place was starting to twist her nerves; she wanted to get out of there as quick as she could. They made their way past the line of trees until they emerged onto a steep embankment, dotted with thorn bushes and underbrush, and surrounded by a number of large rocks arranged in a semicircle. Standing around one of the boulders were a dozen people, including Franco De Angelis and Deputy Chief Marco Santini of the Central Investigative Service. Two guys in white jumpsuits were photographing something at the base of the boulder, but Colomba couldn't see what it was. Their chest patches displayed the emblem of the Violent Crime Analysis Unit, and suddenly Colomba understood everything, even if deep down she'd known it the whole time. She didn't work on missing persons cases, after all; she worked on murders. She went over. The rock cast a sharp, dark shadow over a shape huddled on the ground. *Please don't let it be the boy*, Colomba thought. Her silent prayer didn't go unanswered.

The corpse belonged to the mother.

She'd been decapitated.

4

The corpse lay facedown, legs folded and one arm tucked under the body. The other arm lay stretched out flat, palm turned upward. The neck ended with a cut that sparkled wine red in the glare of the floodlights, with the white of the bones gleaming damp. The head was about a yard away, resting on a cheek, with the face turned toward the body.

Colomba looked up from the cadaver and found that the others were all staring at her.

Santini was evidently pissed off. He was an athletic man of about fifty with a narrow mustache. "Who invited you?" he asked.

"I did," Rovere replied.

"And why, if I might ask?"

"Professional enrichment."

Santini threw both arms into the air and walked off.

Colomba shook hands with the magistrate. "Very good, very good," he said distractedly. He moved away almost immediately on some pretext, dragging Rovere with him. From a distance, Colomba saw that they were arguing in an undertone.

The rest of the small knot of people—some of whom knew her by sight while others had only heard of her—stood around watching her until Mario Tirelli emerged from the shadows and came to her aid. He was a medical examiner, a tall, skinny man wearing a fisherman's cap. He was chewing on a stick of licorice root; he always carried a supply with him in a silver cigarette case as old as he was.

"How are you?" he asked, gripping her hand with both of his, which were chilly. "I've missed you so much."

"And I missed you," Colomba replied, and she meant it. "I'm still on leave, so don't get too excited."

"Then what are you doing out here in the cold and the damp?"

"Apparently it's something Rovere really wanted. But why don't you tell me what *they're* doing here."

"Are you referring to the CIS or the VCU?"

"Both. They're supposed to work on organized crime or serial killers. And there's only one corpse here."

"Technically they can work on lost cats if a magistrate asks them to get involved."

"And De Angelis is a friend of Santini."

"And they're happy to scratch each other's backs. Of course, Santini couldn't count on the Forensic Squad, so he decided to pull the clowns in white jumpsuits in on it. If he brings home a prize of some sort, he won't have to share with anyone."

"And if he doesn't pull it off?"

"Then he'll blame you guys."

"Nice piece of shit he is."

"The usual. You ought to be at home resting up, instead of out here stepping in it."

"Same goes for you. Weren't you retired?"

Tirelli smiled. "Yes, in fact, I *work* as a consultant. I don't like sitting at home reading detective novels, and I don't know how to do crossword puzzles." Tirelli was a widower and childless; the day he died, it would be with a scalpel in his hand. "Do you want me to tell you about the woman, or do you want to go on pretending you don't give a damn?"

"Go ahead."

"Decapitation with a semicurved bladed weapon. The murderer took at least four or five chops to separate the head from the torso, between the C2 and the C3. The first blow was in all likelihood fatal, delivered right below the occipital bone, while she was still on her feet."

"From behind."

"Yes, judging from the direction of the cut. She died in no more than a minute, instantaneous loss of consciousness. It happened this afternoon, judging from the rigor mortis, but with the rain and everything the exact time is hard to establish. Sometime between one and six in the afternoon, I'd say. Wait and see, the guys from the VCU will give it to you down to the second," he added sarcastically.

"There are no signs of a struggle," said Colomba. "She trusted the murderer, otherwise she would have turned around at least three-quarters of the way before being killed."

"He caught her off guard and finished decapitating her on the ground."

Taking advantage of the fact that Santini and the others had moved away from the corpse, Colomba went back to take a look at it. She did it instinctively, practically without realizing it. Tirelli followed her.

"The clothing wasn't removed and replaced," Colomba said. "No postmortem rape."

"I thought the same thing."

She examined the head from up close. The eyes were intact. "No signs of penetration to mouth or eyes."

"Thank God . . ."

"Do you think the boy watched?"

"No way of saying. They haven't found him yet."

"The murderer took him?"

"That's the most likely scenario."

Colomba shook her head. She didn't like it when kids were involved. She went back to look at the scene of the crime. "Sex has nothing to do with this. And he didn't ravage the body."

"You don't call cutting the head off ravaging?"

"There are no other marks on her. Not even a bruise."

"Maybe he was satisfied with what he did," said Tirelli.

Before Colomba had a chance to reply, the technician in the bushes stood up. "Hey! Over here!" he shouted.

Everyone headed toward him, including Colomba, once again a victim of her mechanical instincts. The technician pulled a pruning hook out from under the bush, holding it by the blade with gloved fingers. Santini bent over to examine it closely. "There are little notches that could have been caused by the bone."

"You might have a future as a knife sharpener," said Colomba.

Santini clenched his jaw. "You still here?"

"No, you're hallucinating again."

"As long as you don't touch anything. The last thing we need here is another one of your messes."

Colomba felt the blood surge into her face. She took a step forward, balling her fists. "Just try saying that again, dickhead."

The technician with the pruning hook held up a hand. "Hey, what is this? Are we in high school?"

"She's the one who's out of her mind," said Santini. "Don't you see that?"

Tirelli put a hand on Colomba's arm. "It's not worth it," he whispered to her.

She let the air out of her lungs with a long sigh. "Fuck off, Santini. Just do your job and pretend I'm not here."

Santini fished around for a snappy retort, but nothing came to mind. He pointed to the pruning hook and looked at Tirelli. "Doctor, could that be it?"

"It could be," he replied.

The forensic technician ran a cotton swab over the blade. The cotton turned dark blue: blood. He bagged and labeled the farm tool. At the lab they'd compare the blood residue with the victim's DNA, but as far as Colomba could see, the odds that they'd made a mistake were practically nonexistent. Tirelli followed the technician, while Santini, summoned by a uniformed officer, disappeared in the direction of the access road. Colomba was left standing alone by the bush. As she was thinking about heading back to the car and saying to hell with all of it, there was a rustling sound from the trees nearby; then the glare of the floodlight reflected off Alberti's pale, sweaty face. He was wiping his mouth with a paper tissue.

Colomba realized that he'd stepped away to vomit and regretted having left him alone. "Are you okay?"

He nodded. "Yes, Deputy Captain," he said, but in a tone of voice that clearly stated the opposite. "I just had to . . ."

"I can imagine. Don't sweat it. It happens. Is that the first dead body you've seen?"

Alberti shook his head. "No. But never like this . . . How long did it take you to get accustomed?"

Before Colomba had a chance to reply, Rovere called her. "Come on over, you're about to miss the last part of the show."

Colomba patted Alberti on the shoulder. "Just stay here for a few minutes." She caught up with her former boss next to one of the boulders farthest from the corpse, which couldn't be seen from where they stood. "What show?"

The group of investigators had gathered around the dead woman again, and they seemed to be waiting for someone. De Angelis especially, who was smiling nervously into the empty air.

"The husband's on his way," said Rovere.

A few seconds later the engine of an off-road vehicle fell silent, just beyond the line of trees. Santini reappeared, walking alongside two uniformed officers and a man wearing only a pair of shorts and a dirty T-shirt and looking around him in confusion.

Stefano Maugeri. From the shape he was in, Colomba understood that he hadn't left the search area since his wife had disappeared. "Are they idiots, bringing him here?" she said. "He could have identified the body at the morgue, after they'd put her back together."

"They're not interested in identifying anyone," Rovere replied.

Still being guided by Santini and the two officers, Maugeri was led over to the boulder. Colomba could see him hesitate and then balk for a moment. "What's behind there?" she heard him ask.

Oh, Christ, they haven't told him, thought Colomba.

Santini invited Maugeri to walk forward, but like an animal that can sense the ax, the man wouldn't budge. "No, I'm not going over there unless you tell me what it is. I won't go. I refuse."

"It's your wife, Signor Maugeri," said Santini, staring at him.

Maugeri shook his head as the realization dawned on him. "No . . ." He looked around, more and more bewildered. Then he covered the last few yards at a dead run, until he was stopped by the cordon of officers around the body. Colomba turned her face away when the man burst into sobs.

5

"Let's head back," Rovere said a few minutes before eleven. Maugeri had been led away, held up and half-collapsing, and just then the woman was being put into a body bag by attendants from the morgue. Colomba, Rovere, and Alberti followed the trail back to their car.

Once they were in the moving jeep, Colomba was the first to break the silence. "That was a filthy trick," she murmured.

"But you know why they did it, don't you?" asked Rovere.

"It doesn't take a genius," said Colomba. She was starting to get a headache, and she felt tired in a way she hadn't experienced in months. "They were hoping for a spontaneous confession."

Rovere tapped on Alberti's shoulder. "Stop here."

They'd arrived at the trattoria they'd passed on the way up. Under the canopy the owner stood alone, pulling in tables and chairs.

"You want an espresso, don't you, Colomba?" asked Rovere. "Or maybe you'd rather have something to eat."

"Coffee's fine," she lied. What she really wanted was to go home and forget about the whole thing. Pick up the book she'd left lying open on the living room table—an old edition of Giovanni Verga's *Mastro-don Gesualdo*—and polish off the bottle of Primitivo wine that was in the fridge. Normal things, things that didn't reek of blood and mud.

The restaurateur let them in, even if he was closing up for the night. His was an old trattoria that smelled of bleach and rancid wine, with wooden benches and tables. It was colder inside than out. Colomba decided that, for the beginning of September, the summer seemed a long time ago. It didn't even seem like they were close to Rome.

They sat at a table by the plate-glass window. Rovere had ordered an Americano, and he turned the cup in his hands, never taking his eyes off her, but not really seeing her at all.

"Why do they think the husband did it?" Colomba asked.

"First of all," Rovere replied, "no one saw Maugeri with his wife and son at the Vivaro mountain meadows. Everyone who volunteered to give their account said that they had only seen him alone."

"It's easier to remember a desperate father searching for a wife and son than it is a family out for a picnic."

"Exactly. Still, for now, the testimony all seems to point in one direction." He tapped on his lips with the handle of the demitasse spoon. "Second, there was blood in the trunk of the car."

"Tirelli says that the woman was killed up there, on the spot," Colomba objected. "And he usually knows what he's talking about."

"It was the boy's blood. Just a few spots, ineptly washed. The father has no explanation."

"What else?" asked Colomba.

"Maugeri beat his wife. There were three calls to the local police station about the screams. She was admitted to the hospital a month ago with a broken nose. She said she slipped and fell in the kitchen."

Colomba felt her headache getting worse. The more she talked about the case, the stickier it made her feel. "It all adds up. So what am I doing here?"

"Think about it for a second. The woman showed no signs of having put up a fight."

Colomba's head cleared ever so slightly. "She knew that her husband was a violent man. But she turned her back to him, and didn't even try to run away . . ." She thought it over for a moment, then shook her head. "It's strange, I'll give you that, but not enough to let him off the hook. There could be a thousand explanations."

"How many murderers that we might classify as psychopathic or sociopathic have you dealt with, Colomba?" asked Rovere.

"A few," she said dismissively.

"How of many of those who killed a family member confessed in the end?"

"Some never did," said Colomba.

"But was there something about them that told you they were guilty, no matter how strongly they denied the charges?"

Colomba nodded reluctantly. "Lying is hard. But sensations don't look very good on police reports."

"And they're no good in court . . . Still, their reactions aren't quite natural. They say the wrong thing, they say something funny when they should be crying. Or they cry when they ought to get angry. Even the ones who've suppressed their memories of the act of murder still show voids." He paused. "Did you notice anything like that in Maugeri when he saw his dead wife?"

Colomba massaged her forehead. What was happening? "No. But I didn't speak to him. I only saw him writhing in the mud."

"I was present at the first interview, before we knew anything. He wasn't lying."

"All right. Then he's the wrong man. Sooner or later Santini and De Angelis will figure that out and they'll find the right man."

Rovere was staring at her almost lustfully. "What about the boy?"

"Do you think he's still alive, sir?" asked Colomba.

"I think there's a chance. If the father's innocent, the boy was taken by the murderer. And there's some other explanation for the blood in the trunk of the father's car."

"Unless he fell into a ravine while trying to run away."

"We would have found him by now. How far can a barefoot kid get around here?"

"In any case, Santini must be looking for him," Colomba said. "He's not a complete idiot."

"Santini and De Angelis already have their explanation. How likely is it that new and conflicting evidence is going to be taken into consideration? I mean, in the short term, not a week from now or a month."

"Not very," she admitted.

"And what's going to become of the boy in the meantime?"

"What's that to you?"

Rovere grimaced. "I'm not a robot, you know."

"But you weren't born yesterday, either." Colomba leaned toward him. "You became the chief of the Mobile Squad because you're a good cop, but also because you know how to maneuver successfully. And sticking your nose into someone else's investigation is *never* a successful maneuver."

"I never said that I'd be sticking *my* nose into it," Rovere said.

Colomba slapped her hand down on the table. "Fuck! You're planning to throw me to the wolves?"

"That's right," replied Rovere without a flicker of emotion.

Colomba had had many disagreements with Rovere in the past. There were times when they'd even fought, right down to the shouting and slammed doors. But she'd never experienced that kind of treatment from him. "You could have saved yourself the trip, sir."

"You said you were planning to turn in your resignation, so you have nothing to lose. And you could do a good deed on behalf of that boy."

Colomba couldn't stay in her chair any longer. She leapt up and turned her back on him. Through the plate-glass window, she saw Alberti leaning against the Defender, yawning so vigorously he could easily have dislocated his jaw.

"You owe me this one, Colomba," Rovere said again.

"Why are you so insistent on getting me to do such a thing?"

Rovere sighed. "Do you know who the head of the CIS is?"

"Scotti. If it's still him."

"He's taking his pension next year. Do you know who's next in line for that desk?"

"I couldn't care less."

"Santini. And you know who used to be in line ahead of him?"

Colomba turned around to look at him in horror. "You?"

"Me. But I took a little jump back in line after what happened to you. If it was going to be someone worthy of the job, I'd accept that. But Santini isn't the right man for that position."

"So you need me to screw Santini for you," said Colomba in disgust. She felt as though she were watching Rovere transform himself before her eyes, showing a face that she not only had never seen before but had never even imagined he might possess. "For your career."

"If things turn out right, you'll save a child's life. Don't forget that."

"If he's still alive now, that is, and if he doesn't die in the meantime."

"The blame, in that case, will belong to whoever screwed up the investigation."

"De Angelis is going to resent my interference."

"Under normal circumstances, he could have you suspended or

fired. But in your situation, unless you break the law, he can't do a thing to you. In any case, you can just say it was your own personal initiative because you don't like Santini, and that'll be the end of it."

Colomba sat down again and slumped back into her chair. She was disgusted with herself and with her boss. But Rovere was right about one thing: she owed it to him. She owed it to him because in his eyes alone had she never seen a glimmer of suspicion, not even a hint of mistrust after the Disaster, nothing but sorrow. "And I'd be acting as a private citizen?" she asked.

"You still have your badge, so pull it out when you need to. But don't kick up too much dust: if you need something, let me know."

"And if I find something?"

"I'll very discreetly let De Angelis have it."

"As soon as De Angelis gets a whiff of the possibility that he's backing the wrong horse . . ."

"He'll switch horses," Rovere concluded.

Colomba reached up and touched her aching temple. "But that's impossible. I can never do it alone." Rovere hesitated, but Colomba understood that he had an answer and was just pretending. *He's got everything all figured out*, she thought, *he knows just how to use me in his miserable war.*

"There *is* someone who could give you a hand," Rovere said. "Someone who, if you were a cop who cared about your career, you wouldn't even talk to and who might not even let you approach him. But in your case . . ."

"Who?"

Rovere lit a cigarette. "Have you ever heard of the boy in the silo?"

- III -

BEFORE

The young couple at the middle table in the restaurant are the ones talking in the loudest voices. They're not used to luxury, and they've decided to eat there to celebrate their first wedding anniversary. She looks around at the other tables, hoping to spot someone famous, while he tries to keep his thoughts from straying to the astronomical check that's going to arrive. He knew it was going to be expensive, this restaurant on the top floor of a boutique where they'd never dare to set foot (actually she does set foot there regularly, to see the new collections when they arrive), but not nearly as expensive as what he saw to his dismay on the menu. Still, he doesn't want to ask his wife to skimp on her order, not after she's waited all week for this night out, trying out all the best combinations of her Zara outfits, all purchased at discount.

He's twenty-seven, she's twenty-nine.

A few yards away, a German citizen is sitting alone, eating a sushi assortment. He's reading the American edition of The Bone Collector. He's slightly irritated to find that his English has gotten worse over the past few years. He's having trouble with the book, though he's already read it in German translation. He's the chief executive of a company that manufactures microcomponents, and he hasn't had many opportunities lately to practice his English. He's thinking of starting private language lessons again, though the mere idea depresses him. He feels too old to go back to school, and he suspects that his memory isn't as sharp as it once was. He loves sushi, and he eats dinner there every week, usually by himself.

He's just turned sixty.

At the large round table by the window, which is discreetly shaded by white curtains made of raw organic cotton, a deejay is sitting with his date, his agent, and the owner of a discotheque on the outskirts of town. They're listening as the waiter inquires about possible allergies *before telling them the night's specials. The deejay is about to say, "I'm allergic to raw fish," without realizing that this wisecrack is something the waiter hears about once a day and that he no longer even smiles when he does. The deejay is the former lead singer of a band that had a top ten single three years ago. He works roughly two hundred nights a year in the biggest nightclubs and discos. Music no longer sells; deejaying is the profession of the future.*

The girl holding his hand, which has as many rings as the hand of the Madonna of Lourdes (everything about the deejay's look is a little excessive, including the tribal tattoo on the back of his neck and his bleached hair), hopes that this time he's at least going to stay for the weekend or that he'll ask her to go with him. She's not his girlfriend, she's just the girl he calls when he's going to spend a night in town, but she knows that the two of them are really in tune. She can feel it under her skin. After they had sex in the hotel that afternoon, he opened up like a little boy. He laughed and joked with her. Would he have done that if he was just looking for a fuck on the fly? He even confided that he plans to replace his agent with someone new, someone more skilled and less emotional. A top secret piece of news, right?

The agent in question wasn't born yesterday, and he has a hunch about what's coming. While he dreams of a cigarette, he desperately tries to remember the name of that movie where Woody Allen plays someone in his exact line of business, someone who's always being dumped by the artists he represents. For the past month or so, the deejay has been pretty evasive about his future plans, and that, for shit sure, is a warning sign. The deejay's planning to cut the cord, now that he's finally starting to have a smidgen of personal success.

The owner of the discotheque isn't participating much in the conversation, which is by and large a monologue by the artist about the new musical directions that he was way ahead of; frankly, he just hopes this dinner will be over as soon as possible. As far as he's concerned, the finest album in rock history is The Dark Side of the Moon, and all the deejays on Earth put together don't have a crumb of the class that the old-school rockers had. But that's not the kind of thing you can say to someone you just hired, paying him 2,000 euros under the table to fill your disco for you. In the meantime the owner sits smiling at the girl and thinking that she really is one hot babe, with the physique of a fashion model and a sweet expression. He can just see her doing filthy things, with that sweet, naive face of hers. Once the deejay gets the hell out from underfoot, he's planning to give her a call and ask her if she wants to come work in his club, helping to improve the place's image. "It can be a good stepping-stone, a way of getting into the world of show business. Don't tell me it never occurred to you. Trust me."

The deejay is twenty-nine, the agent's thirty-nine, the owner of the discotheque is fifty, the deejay's date is seventeen, the waiter is twenty-two.

At the table by the door an older couple is waiting for dessert: green tea ice cream for him and an assortment of soy and red bean paste pastries for her, though she practically hasn't touched any of the earlier dishes. They were the first to be seated in the dining room, when it was still empty and silent. The husband has asked her more than once if there's something wrong, but she just smiled and replied, "Everything's fine, I'm just not very hungry tonight." They've lived together for almost half a century. He's had a successful career as a government functionary, but now he's retired; she raised two sons, who come for the major holidays. She put up with his occasional cheating over the years, by now ancient history and virtually forgotten; he's accepted her moments of emotional fragility, when she can't get out of bed and keeps the shades down so she doesn't have to see sunlight. Time has worn away their differences and sharp edges; it has intertwined them, made them dependent one upon the other. That's why she's having such a hard time now figuring out how to tell him that her test results were anything but reassuring, that they definitely reveal a tumoral mass between her breasts. What scares her most isn't death but leaving him all alone. She wonders how he can go on living without her.

He is seventy-two. She is sixty-five.

Two tables away, at another of the round tables, sit four young Albanian women and a man with a Greek profile. The girls are models and the man is paid by the agency to take them out and about. Having dinner with them before any major runway presentation is part of his job. He looks after them, he assists them, and most of all he keeps an eye on them to make sure they don't do anything stupid. That's why he bought them a gram of coke and why the girls are now just picking listlessly at their food. He doesn't like drugs. He doesn't use them, and if it were up to him, he'd line all the dealers up against the wall and execute them. But he also knows that it's pointless to tell the girls not to get high. If he didn't buy it for them, they'd get drugs from the guys parking their Porsche Cayennes in front of the model hotels with baggies ready to go. If he locked them in their room, they'd climb out the windows to get to the coke. They're always going out and getting wrecked. So they show up for rehearsals puffy-faced, with circles under their eyes. Cocaine keeps them from feeling hunger or the fear that they might not be pretty enough or good enough. He'll give them an extra gram before telling them good night, and he hopes that'll hold them.

The conversation at the table is fragmentary: the girls speak only halting English, but to make up for it, they laugh a lot. Speaking in Albanian, they wonder if he's gay or if he's planning to take one of them to bed. Both options are mistaken. He's not gay, it's just that he doesn't like models. He finds them boring and stupid. He has a hard time telling them apart. And he finds them depressing.

He's thirty-five years old, two of the girls are nineteen, one's eighteen, and one's twenty.

The maître d' ushers four Japanese businessmen into the dining room. They represent one of the best-selling companies in the West in terms of Asian style, and they've just spent the week meeting local wholesalers. An experience that they found rather demeaning. It seems that no one wants anything that varies an inch from the stereotype of white tatami mats, futons, and rice-paper lampshades.

The next day they have a flight back to Tokyo, and eating Japanese wasn't what they had in mind. But the director of the boutique has invited them out to dinner, and they couldn't turn him down. They would have preferred someplace fun, somewhere they could loosen their ties and laugh and drink wine. But that's not the way it went, so they have to resign themselves.

They're fifty, forty-five, forty, and thirty-six years old. The maître d' is fifty-five.

The woman with her back to the wall keeps staring at the restaurant's entrance. Whenever someone walks past, she moves her head to ensure she maintains her line of sight. She hasn't uttered a word since she first sat down, she hasn't touched her water, she hasn't read the menu or looked at the specials of the day. She just sits watching, with one hand on her knee and the other opened flat on the tablecloth. When the waiter asked her if she wanted to order, she replied that she was waiting for someone, lifting her eyes to look at him for just a fleeting instant. In those eyes, the waiter saw no reflection of himself. Her gaze looked right through him, as if he were air, as if he didn't exist. He thought to himself that he wouldn't want to be the person who was late for dinner. That woman didn't seem willing to forgive and forget.

She's thirty-one, the waiter is twenty-nine.

And while the woman with the cold eyes suddenly stands up, while the deejay is about to make his wisecrack, as the German citizen is about to turn to page 100 in his novel, while the young bride is about to order the twenty-course tasting menu, while the group of Japanese businessmen decline the offer of a house sake, and while one of the Albanian models starts to get up to go to the bathroom to snort one last line . . .

Time stands still.

- IV -

OLD FRIENDS

1

The man with the leather jacket was back. He was standing at the usual corner of Via Tiburtina Antica, nervously shifting his weight from one foot to the other. Dante Torre spied on him from behind the glass enclosing his terrace six stories above the street, trying in vain to catch the man's eye. He knew that the man in the jacket would wait for another hour, until 12:30, when the crowd of mothers outside the elementary school would start to grow and the man would retreat step by step. By the time the school doors were thrown open to let the kids out for the day, he'd be at least sixty feet from the other waiting parents, he'd watch the crowd of pupils charging down the steps and into waiting arms, then to be taken by the hand and walked home. Then the man in the jacket would vanish beyond the old city walls, not to reappear again until two or three days later, at the same time of day. While he waited, he'd smoke at least four cigarettes, but if he still had one going when the school doors opened, he'd crush it out immediately.

The only thing that had changed since Dante had first noticed him two weeks earlier was his clothing. The man had changed from a T-shirt to a fake-leather biker jacket, with a bear's head embossed on the back. Dante had googled it and learned that it was a low-cost Chinese-made brand.

Dante gazed out at him for a long while. "How much longer will you wait?" he asked softly. He rolled over on the bed until he lay facing up at the skylight: a small blob of water on the glass above him sketched out a skull, with small pockets of air for eyes and a tiny ripple at the center carving out a nose. He wriggled across the mattress until the reflection of his own face lined up with it. It fit him perfectly, but the illusion was shattered when a raindrop fell from the gutter above and hit the blob. He shivered and pulled the blankets up to his chin. Soon he'd have to turn on the little catalytic heater that stood unused in a corner. It was the only way he could maintain a decent temperature on the terrace, which he'd enclosed in a glass cage, turning it into his bedroom-office. The rest of the apartment had been gutted, with no regard for appearance. A number of the internal partition walls had been eliminated, and the windows had been enlarged until they almost entirely filled the outside walls. Only flimsy ivory-colored cotton curtains concealed the chaos within.

A bicycle was propped against the living room table, which was piled high with books, newspapers, file boxes, and folders, and the profusion of paper continued across the floor in teetering stacks, some of which had collapsed into piles of photographs and printouts. The only tidy part of the house was the kitchen, arranged in a corner of the large central room, and it was actually spic and span. The stainless-steel cabinets and cooktops gave the impression of an operating room, with dozens of electric utensils neatly arrayed. Atop the microwave oven a laptop computer sat charging.

Dante had a desktop computer with a thirty-inch screen out on the terrace, as well as another laptop in the guest bedroom, though no one had ever slept there and the bed was a bare mattress. He used that room for the stacks of "time capsule" boxes that had occupied every available square inch until it became impossible to open the window. Dante never even went in there anymore. He'd drag the boxes out to him with one of those retriever poles they use in shops to hang clothes up high, and when he was done he'd slide them back into place, lying flat on the bathroom floor.

He shivered again.

He often thought about moving someplace warm where he could sleep under the stars. He'd go by boat, of course. He couldn't picture himself inside the sealed metal tube of an airplane, not much bigger than a coffin with wings. But he knew that far from the world he knew, he'd wither and droop like a plant left in darkness.

Every time he sensed the onset of winter, though, he regretted that decision. In winter, outdoor restaurants disappeared, as did the already far too few outdoor venues for movies and concerts; convertible cars vanished, too. In winter everything he loved was closed up in hermetically sealed boxes, boxes he couldn't enter without suffering. The world became suffocating and confined.

Dante pulled a cigarette out of the pack and lit it, snapping the lighter into flame with his bad hand, and then went back to looking down into the street, sliding the glass open just a crack. With the wind that smelled of rain came street noises and the sound of a neighbor's radio. Dante took one last look at the man in the jacket, still standing at his corner, then ran his eyes over the rooftops of San Lorenzo. It was one of the loveliest neighborhoods in Rome, and Dante didn't mind the racket from the restaurants and bars. He rarely fell asleep before dawn anyway, and the sounds of life put him in a good mood.

The man in the jacket had taken another step back. Dante finally rolled out of the bedclothes and went to take a shower. He moved lightly, gracefully, silently. He stood almost six foot three and was as slender as an Etruscan statue. Dripping wet, wrapped in a bathrobe, he took his morning dose of drops and pills, basing the prescription on his internal thermometer; then he turned on the espresso maker and his cell phone. The cell phone immediately spat out a text from his lawyer, Roberto Minutillo. It said only: "Please look at it."

Dante sighed. A week ago Minutillo had submitted a case for his opinion. Dante still hadn't worked up the desire to look at it and had left the lawyer in limbo, pretending to himself that he'd forgotten. But now he'd have to tend to it. Sighing again, he woke the desktop out of its sleep, skimmed the documents the lawyer had sent, doing his best to keep from dying of boredom, then started the video attachment.

The scene was of a room painted in pastel colors, with a table in the middle. In the background he could guess at large colorful plastic cubes and a plush teddy bear. Sitting at the table was a six-year-old girl in a checkered pink dress; facing her was a woman about fifty, smiling from behind eyeglasses. The girl was drawing with an orange pencil.

Another woman, seen from the neck down, was standing behind the girl; her hands were resting on the girl's shoulders. The woman with glasses was a family court psychologist, and the one without a head was the little girl's mother. Dante fast-forwarded the video, skipping the psychologist's first questions and the girl's first answers, then carefully watched the rest. At minute 4:06 he hit stop, ran back, and opened the video to full screen.

The psychologist leaned smiling toward the little girl, who went on drawing. "You can tell me. You can trust me."

The girl held the pencil still for a moment. "It was Daddy," she said.

Dante hit the space bar to stop the video, then went back to minute 4:06 and ran it forward from there, in slow motion, without sound. He focused on the mother's hands. He watched them move, slightly squeezing the little girl's shoulders. Dante clicked the video off the screen and sat looking at his own reflection in its place for a few seconds. He felt icy sweat dripping down his back. *That's it*, he thought. It could have been harder. He texted Minutillo, then got up and poured a blend of Panamanian arabica into the espresso machine. The phone rang while he was on his second cup.

"Hi there, counselor," said Dante without even bothering to glance at the number on the display. The aftertaste of the coffee on his tongue was a symphony of bitter and sweet, with hints of chocolate.

"So you just spent the past week meditating, and now all you have to say to me is 'no'?" the lawyer demanded.

"Tell your client that she needs to find someone else to help her ruin her ex-husband's reputation." Dante drained the second demitasse. "That girl hasn't been abused."

"Are you certain?"

"Yes." Dante looked down into the street: the man in the jacket had almost exited his line of sight. Another twenty minutes, and he'd be gone.

"The little girl says that her father sexually molested her."

"Do we still have to talk about this?" asked Dante.

"Yes, until you've convinced me."

Dante huffed in exasperation. "Does the girl show any physical signs of abuse?"

"No. But the stories she tells are detailed. And everyone that's talked to her so far is convinced she's telling the truth."

Dante drained the cup once again, put it back under the spout, and started a third cup of espresso. He used caffeine to help manage his benzodiazepine. "She doesn't know she's lying. And that's not me saying it. It's DeYoung, von Klitzing, Haugaard, Elterman and

Ehrenberg, Ackerman, Kane, and Piaget," he said, reeling off the names in a monotone.

"Psychologists and psychiatrists. I know them. To become a lawyer, you have to study . . ."

"Then you ought to know that children the age of your *non*-client's daughter have only one way of distinguishing between the truth and lies. The truth is whatever their parents approve. Lies are whatever make them unhappy. And they're eminently capable of remembering things they never experienced; you just have to ask them the right way. In the eighties, Stephen J. Ceci—"

"That's one I don't know."

"He's a psychologist, too, a professor at Cornell University, and he studies the accuracy of children's courtroom testimony. In one study, Ceci asked a group of children to concentrate and remember *that one time* they hurt their finger, by getting it caught in a mousetrap. It hadn't happened to any of the children, but when questioned in the weeks that followed, nearly all of them remembered it and embroidered on the details. That their finger had bled, that the mouse had run away . . . Do I need to go on?"

"No. And you're saying the mother prompted her?"

"You can see it in the video."

"All you can see is her hands."

"Hands that are clutching the girl's shoulders before her answer accusing her father. And then the hands relax and caress her. First *tension*, then *reward*. The girl realizes she's doing well and continues. The expert is having the wool pulled over her eyes. Or maybe we should say, the coconut mat, since she's a vegan, just like the mother."

"How can you tell that the girl's mother is a vegan?" asked Minutillo, sincerely astonished.

"In the video you can see her handbag, a model produced by a vegan manufacturer using vegetan instead of leather. Cruelty free. It's hard to know these things even exist unless you're an insider, like me."

"Now you're just taking stabs in the dark."

"The little girl is consuming a meat-free diet. The father included that fact as a reason for his request for custody, saying that a vegetarian diet was cruel to the child, even though that's unmistakable bullshit. That was in the documents you sent me."

"And you read them?"

"As much as I needed to. Okay, then? Can I send you my invoice?"

"For ten minutes of work?"

"They'll be the ten most expensive minutes of your life."

Someone rang the doorbell. Dante said good-bye to the lawyer, went silently over to the door, and looked through the peephole.

On the landing, he saw a woman who looked a little over thirty, with a serious look on her face. She wore a pair of tight jeans and a light-colored jacket that stretched over her swimmer's shoulders. She looked strong enough to bend a steel bar. Dante shivered. He didn't know who the woman was, but he was certain of one thing: she was bringing trouble.

2

To avoid surprise visits, Dante had put the apartment in Minutillo's name and gave out the address to only a very small and select group of people. He'd made that decision after the father of a missing boy had stubbornly stood downstairs from the terrace of his old apartment, shouting and sobbing.

The woman placed one green eye against the peephole, and Dante realized that she'd seen his shadow moving behind the door. "Signor Torre," she said. "I'm Deputy Captain Caselli. I need to talk to you."

She had a slightly hoarse voice, which Dante would have found sexy if it weren't a cop's voice. He slid the chain into place and pulled the door open a cautious crack.

Colomba gave him a level look, then pulled out her ID and put it in front of his nose. "*Buongiorno.*"

"Can I take a closer look?" asked Dante.

Colomba shrugged. "Be my guest."

Dante took it with his good hand and pretended to examine it closely. He had no talent for catching counterfeit IDs, but that wasn't what he was looking for. He wanted to see how Colomba reacted. She didn't seem concerned about his examination. Most likely, she was exactly what she claimed to be. Dante gave her back her ID. "Have I done something wrong?" he asked.

"No. I just need a few minutes of your time."

"What for?"

"I'd prefer to discuss that inside," Colomba replied patiently.

"But I don't have to, do I? I could just tell you no and there's nothing you could do. You wouldn't kick down my door."

"Absolutely not." Colomba smiled, and Dante was struck by the way her face changed for an instant, losing all its hardness. Even if it was fake, it was still a nice smile. "But if I were you, I'd be curious to know what I wanted."

"I think that if you were me, you wouldn't have even answered the doorbell," said Dante.

Colomba stiffened, and Dante understood that he'd touched a sore spot. He'd done it on purpose, but he still felt oddly guilty. To get rid of the sensation, he stuck his bad hand into his pocket and let her in.

Colomba made an effort not to change her expression at the sight of the mess in the apartment, but she was unsuccessful.

Dante headed for the kitchen, zigzagging past the books. "I'll make you a cup of coffee if you like," he said.

"Thanks."

He pointed her to the table in the living room. "Clear off a chair and sit down. How do you like it? Full-bodied, rich, aromatic . . ."

"I usually drink instant, so anything's good for me."

"I'll pretend I didn't hear that." To make up for his rudeness of just a short while ago, Dante added to the blend a handful of Kopi Luwak beans, light roasted. The beans were gathered after the Indonesian palm civet ate the coffee cherries and defecated the partly digested beans. Connoisseurs considered it the finest coffee on Earth for its fruity aftertaste and absence of bitterness, and it was certainly the most expensive and the hardest to find. He had it sent to him by courier, like nearly everything else. "I don't know if you normally take yours with sugar, but this variety doesn't need it," he said, closing the lid of the machine, which started the coffee grinder. "Something not right?" he asked.

Colomba nodded. Her eyes had turned hard as marbles, and looked even greener than ever. "Would you mind taking your left hand out of your pocket, please?"

"Excuse me?"

"I noticed that you've kept it in your pocket ever since I came in. Even when you could have used it. For example, to open the can of coffee."

That was true, of course. Dante kept his bad hand hidden whenever he met someone, a habit that was something he couldn't help.

Colomba's body language was clearly expressing imminent danger. She'd instinctively pushed one foot forward and was holding her arms slightly flexed. Her right hand was clenched around the handle of her purse, as if she were ready to throw it in his face. "Please," she said again.

"As you wish," said Dante, raising his bad hand so she could see it clearly. It was a mass of scar tissue. Only his thumb and forefinger worked, while the other fingers were clasped shut, much smaller than normal, and devoid of fingernails.

Colomba had seen a hand like that once, on an ex-con who'd had it mangled in an accident in an industrial laundry facility. "I apologize," she said, looking away. "I just woke up a little on edge this morning."

"Don't mention it." Accustomed to reading even the faintest of signs in those he spoke to, Dante understand that Colomba's nervousness was anything but momentary. She'd been the victim of something. Some kind of violence, an on-duty incident? *Interesting*, he decided. He went back to working with the coffee cups. With a black robe that was too big for him and his fair hair slicked back, still wet from the shower, he reminded Colomba very much of David Bowie in a science fiction movie she'd once seen.

The aroma of coffee spread across the room. Dante took a seat across from Colomba and set down two modern-looking designer demitasses. *Just to put the finishing touch on things, I could break his cup*, she thought, but she managed to get the coffee to her lips without any further damage. Her head was spinning, and she felt terribly on display. Until two days ago, she'd avoided even her closest friends, and now she was trading idle chitchat in the home of a perfect stranger. "Good," she lied. It was too weak for her taste.

"I thank you," Dante replied, with a half smile. "I'm not ashamed of my poor hand." To prove it, he held it up and turned it in front of her face: the scars on the back of the hand formed an intricate network. "I usually hide it just to avoid having to answer the questions it prompts. Even though most people are too kind and polite to ask. Or else they already know what happened to me and don't need to ask." He smiled again. "But you belong to a third category." Dante's eyes glittered. "What do you know about me?"

"Are you giving me the third degree? Or is it just a topic you're fond of?"

Dante smiled. He had gleaming white teeth. "Let's say it helps to save time."

Colomba decided that after her gaffe, she couldn't refuse. "You're from Cremona. You were born in 1972. In November of 1978, at the age of six, while you were playing alone in a construction site behind the building where you lived, you were kidnapped by one or more unknown persons. You weren't capable of remembering what happened, and no one saw anything."

"There was a door that led from the cellar under my apartment building to the field where we used to play. I must have been taken somewhere along the way and probably drugged," said Dante.

Colomba nodded. "You were held prisoner for eleven years, most of the time in a cement silo next to a farmhouse in the province of Cremona."

"Not most of the time. The whole time. The town is Acquanegra Cremonese, a nice archaic name."

"You're right. In 1989, you managed to escape from your captor. He killed himself. His name was Antonio Bodini, and he was a farmer."

"Bodini owned the farmhouse, and he certainly did commit suicide, but he didn't kidnap me. Or at least he didn't hold me prisoner."

Colomba narrowed her eyes in surprise. "I didn't think I was wrong on that point."

"You aren't the one who was wrong. It's the person who investigated the case. I looked my captor in the face, and he didn't look a bit like Bodini."

"Why didn't they believe you?"

"Because all the evidence pointed right at Bodini, because he killed himself, because I was in a mental state that . . . let's just say was anything but easy."

"But you're still convinced of what you say."

"Yes."

"They investigated, in a hunt for accomplices," Colomba said, cautiously.

"And they didn't find any. I know. But go on with your account, I was just starting to enjoy it."

"I don't have a lot left to add. You changed your last name, taking your mother's maiden name. You traveled a bit and got yourself into some trouble. You have a criminal record for brawling, disorderly conduct, assault and battery, and unauthorized possession of a weapon."

"It was a Taser, which in many countries is sold legally."

"But not in this one. Over the past eight years, you've calmed down. No more criminal complaints." Colomba looked him in the eye. "Is that enough?"

Dante let himself slump back into his chair. He was struck by the fact that Colomba had never looked at notes. Good memory, solid preparation. "You know a lot of things about me, but you didn't know about the hand."

"Maybe I just missed that."

"You couldn't have missed anything like that. Not you. No, quite simply, the documents you read made no mention of it." Dante flashed a smile that looked more like a sneer. "You see, the hand made me too recognizable, especially in a small town like Cremona. The family court chose not to publish the detail." Dante stared at her. "Which makes me think you didn't have access to the documents in the district attorney's office. And there's another strange thing. Do you want to know what that is?"

Colomba didn't, but she nodded anyway. "Sure."

"You're on administrative leave."

"How can you tell that?"

"You're not armed. I might not see the gun if you wore it behind your back, but a person who's armed and well trained tends to keep their dominant hand next to the holster if they think they're in danger. But you grabbed the handle of your purse. And a deputy captain goes everywhere armed, unless they're on vacation or on administrative leave. Am I wrong?"

Colomba shook her head. "No."

"On administrative leave, not fully informed . . . Are you here for some personal reason?"

Colomba tried to keep her expression unchanged. "Yes."

"You're a terrible liar, which means you're slightly ashamed of it. But let's skip over that detail, for now. What do you want from me?"

"A child is missing, up at the Vivaro mountain meadows."

"A woman murdered, her husband in a jail cell. I heard the news." Dante was doing his best to conceal it, but it hit him hard. "Whoever it was that sent you to see me thinks the man's innocent, but someone else involved in this investigation disagrees, probably the investigating magistrate. And since the father has no way of knowing what's become of his son and this probably isn't a kidnapping for ransom, you want my help finding him."

Colomba's head was spinning. "You're an expert on missing persons."

"According to you."

"You've worked on at least two kidnappings for ransom, five others involving psychological abuse, and I don't know how many other cases of voluntary abandonment. You solved every one. You sometimes work on cases of child abuse."

Dante cracked his usual, humorless grin. "Can you prove that?"

"Of course not. You hide behind the law firm, which in turn hires private investigators and operates under cover of attorney-client privilege. Still, word does get around, and the people who sent me here have heard about you. And what they've heard is that you're good at what you do."

Dante shook his head. "I've just made good use of my own experience."

"As a kidnap victim?"

"You see, Agent Colomba, for eleven years, the most critical years in any human being's development, I lived in total isolation except for occasional interactions with my kidnapper. No books, no TV, no radio. When I got out, the world was incomprehensible to me. Ordinary social exchanges appeared alien, as alien as you might find life in an anthill."

"I'm sorry," said Colomba, and she meant it.

"Thanks, but spare me the condolences. While I was studying the world *outside*, I realized that I understood certain workings of that world better than people who had grown up in it. To see something clearly, you need the right distance. And I had that distance, through no choice of my own. I can summon it even now, when I need it. I can see if something's altered in a missing person's daily habits, I can sense what they love and what they fear just by observing the way they arrange their personal effects. Whether someone or something has interrupted the normal course of their lives."

"And you read body language, the way you did with me."

Dante nodded. "My kidnapper always wore gloves and kept his face covered. I tried to read his posture to tell if I was doing the right thing or if he was about to punish me. If he was telling the truth when he promised me I'd have food or water to drink. I used it to find the people you mentioned. There was always someone who knew more than they told, and I could see that. But a prosecutor isn't likely to want me as an expert witness. Aside from the fact that the last thing I want is to be in the spotlight again."

"All I'm asking for is a private consultation," said Colomba. "Your name could be kept out of it."

"No, Agent Colomba. There are two things I won't do: become involved in a case directly or work with the police. And you're asking me to do both." Dante stood up and extended his good hand. "It's been a pleasure speaking with you. Come back and see me, and I'll be glad to make you another espresso."

Colomba didn't budge, and Dante grimaced faintly. It was like a crack through which she could briefly see him for what he was. A victim who had painstakingly rebuilt a life for himself, gluing the pieces back together after experiencing the unimaginable. *I ought to leave*, Colomba thought. *That would be the right thing to do*. But she couldn't. "Signor Torre," she said. "Now please let me have my say."

Dante sat back down, reluctantly.

"I want to begin by saying once again how sorry I am," Colomba went on. "With all that's happened to you, you deserve to be left in peace for the rest of your life."

"Do me a favor and don't pity me. It's one thing I can't stand."

"I just want to be straight with you. I dislike this situation every bit as much as you do. I'm not accustomed to involving civilians in police investigations, and I don't like behind-the-scenes maneuvering."

"That comes as a surprise."

"While we're on the subject, believe me, the only reason I drank that coffee squeezed out of some squirrel's butt was to be polite. That's right, I saw the name on the bag, and even though I'm just a cop, I know what Kopi Luwak is. I know how much it costs, too, before you try and throw that fact in my face."

"I'm not that rude," he muttered.

"And I'm not that squeamish: I've been on the force for thirteen years now, and I've gulped down and witnessed more shit than you could even begin to imagine. I haven't told you everything I know about you. I know what became of your parents. Your father was in and out of prison before you turned up again. And your mother killed herself when you were . . . how old . . . ten?"

"Nine," he said flatly.

"My colleagues on the force back then failed to find you or even guess that you were still alive. If I were you, I'd be furious at the police, the prosecutors, the whole world. We abandoned you, and we took it out on your parents. You were forced to rescue yourself." Colomba gave him a level look. "But do you really want the same thing to happen to another family?"

"Do you think it's fair to come into my home and try to guilt me into working with you?"

"I'm sorry about that, too. But now I'd like an answer, please."

Dante stared at her. "Every day, about thirty thousand children die, and half of them starve to death. I can't take responsibility for all the bad things that happen on Earth."

Colomba went on staring back at him. "The Maugeri boy is closer than Africa."

"Then find him."

"You could make all the difference for that boy. You know that, don't you?"

Dante shook his head. "Until yesterday, you didn't even know I existed. Tell me who sent you here."

Colomba understood that if she hoped to get anything out of him, she'd have to tell the truth. "Captain Rovere, the head of the Mobile Squad."

"And the asshole magistrate, who's that?"

"De Angelis."

Dante shook his head a second time. "You really are in trouble."

"Well, will you help us?" asked Colomba.

Dante studied her. "Do you really think I can do anything? Or are you just dragging me into some power play between your boss and the district attorney's office?"

Colomba decided to go on telling the truth. "I'm hoping that you can pull a rabbit out of a hat, but I doubt that's going to happen."

"You've stopped believing in miracles, eh?"

"And in Santa Claus," she said, thinking back to the Disaster.

Dante nodded slightly, as if he'd just read Colomba's mind. And actually, in a way, he had. He understood that this woman with a decisive manner sitting across from him was concealing some deep sorrow. And not because Rovere, by selecting her for that assignment so unorthodox and contrary to regulation, had sent her to the slaughter, but because she had agreed to go. No one would have risked her professional future for the sake of a faint possibility they didn't even believe in, unless she was sure they didn't possess such a thing as a future. Colomba was a kamikaze pilot power-diving into her final mission, and Dante found that fact irresistible. He loved dramatic, heroic deeds, even when they were quite stupid. Or perhaps especially when they were stupid. "Let's do this, Deputy Captain," he said. "I'm willing to take a look at the documents you certainly have in that bag and tell you what I think of them."

"Thank you."

"Why don't you wait before you thank me: I want a favor from you first."

Colomba narrowed her eyes, suspiciously. "What favor?"

Dante walked her over to the balcony and pointed to the man in the street below. "Him."

3

Alberti yawned as he stood next to the squad car parked a few hundred yards away from Dante's apartment, along the perimeter of the old city walls. Colomba had asked him not to park too close to avoid attracting too much attention, and Alberti, deep down, had to agree with her. Unlike his colleagues, who seemed not to give a damn, he was painfully aware of the uneasiness that a patrol car and a uniformed cop tended to stir in civilians. All you had to do was go into a café for a piss, and it was unmistakable.

Alberti wondered if he'd eventually become like his partner, after a few years of police duty, capable only of spending time with people in uniform, maybe even married to another cop. He hoped not. He had other plans, projects that kept him awake when he was off duty, hunched over the MIDI keyboard connected to his computer running Music Maker. The pieces he wrote and posted on Facebook under the pseudonym Rookie Blue had gathered almost ten thousand "likes." They still weren't bringing in money, but it was just a matter of time.

As he was yawning for what seemed like the millionth time, his cell phone rang to the notes of the piece he'd entitled "Time." It was Colomba. Given the fact that she was still on leave, she couldn't use the radio. "At your orders, Deputy Captain," he said.

"Get out of the car and go to the corner of Via Tiburtina Antica."

"Is there something wrong, Deputy Captain?"

"Not for now. But make sure you aren't seen. I'll stay on the line."

Alberti went where he'd been told. "I'm here, Deputy Captain," he said. In the street ahead of him, the mothers were starting to head for the elementary school.

"Do you see the big vases with plants right in front of you?" asked Colomba.

"Yes, Deputy Captain." They were outside a corner café with two outside tables.

"There's a man smoking a cigarette, in a red jacket."

"I see him." The man was about fifty, huge, and looking in the opposite direction from where Alberti was. "What do you want me to do?"

"Keep an eye on him until I get downstairs. I don't want him to get away while I'm on the stairs. Okay?"

"Excuse me, though, Deputy Captain. What did he do?"

"Don't ask pointless questions," said Colomba and hung up.

Alberti thought to himself that the question didn't seem all that pointless as he stood a few yards away from the man in the jacket. What should he expect from him? Just then, the man took a look behind him and noticed that Alberti was staring at him. He didn't even try to conceal his nervousness. He just started walking at a brisk pace. Another two seconds, and he'd vanish down one of the side streets.

Alberti went after him. "Excuse me," he shouted. *"Hey!"*

The man in the jacket pretended he couldn't hear him.

Alberti picked up the pace and put a hand on the man's shoulder. "I'm talking to you."

The man turned around and in the same movement swung a fist into Alberti's face.

Alberti saw black, and his legs gave way beneath him. He fell on his ass, grabbing at his nose, which was spraying blood, filling his mouth. When he opened his eyes again, Colomba's police boots had materialized in front of him.

"Are you still alive?"

"Yes."

Colomba had already set off at a dead run after the fugitive.

"I'll call Dispatch . . ." Alberti stammered as he tried to grab a planter to hoist himself back upright.

"No!" shouted Colomba. "Don't do anything else!" and disappeared around the corner.

The man in the jacket was running as if he were on roller skates, and Colomba spotted him already at the far end of the street, galloping past a fruit and vegetable stand, bumping an old woman with a shopping trolley. She accelerated anyway, hurtling through the crowd of pedestrians and shoving the ones who didn't get out of the way. How long had it been since she'd chased anyone in the street? Years, since back when she was still assistant captain in the Drug Enforcement Division and the officers had made no secret of how much they disliked taking orders from her, a penguin and a woman, to boot. After her promotion there had mostly been indoor raids and stakeouts in cars. Lengthy stakeouts. And four gun battles, one of which had left her with a scar on her leg. In none of those cases had there been any major street chases. And now she was chasing someone, and she didn't even really know why.

She barely missed hitting a kid on a bicycle who yelled after her, while a group of young Maghrebi immigrants from North Africa scattered the minute they caught a whiff of the uniform that she wasn't wearing. Meanwhile, the fugitive had managed to put several more yards' distance between them.

The street that the man in the jacket was running down ended in a T, and Colomba knew that she had only one chance of catching him: taking side streets to one of the two crossbars of that T and hoping she picked the right street. Dodging around a granite bollard, she veered to the right, heading for the elevated rail line that ran to Termini Station and the metro stop. If she'd been the one running away, that's the direction she'd have headed, not the other way, deeper into the neighborhood.

A car honked its horn behind her, but Colomba kept running straight down the middle of the street, ignoring it. A few yards short of the intersection she saw that she'd guessed right, because the man in the jacket was heading straight toward her at a brisk pace, convinced he'd lost her. He didn't even notice Colomba until she smashed into him, shoulder first, knocking him hard against the side of a building.

"Police," said Colomba, twisting his forearm behind his head. "Hands in the air, up against the wall."

The man jabbed his elbow at her. Colomba managed to avoid the blow to her face and grabbed his elbow and wrist, doing her best to gain leverage, but it was like trying to bend the branch of an oak tree, the man was so muscle-bound. He tried to punch her again, this time in the belly. She jumped back and grabbed him around the back of the neck, smashing her right knee repeatedly into his solar plexus and testicles.

He shook her off and folded forward from the waist. "You fucking whore . . ." he muttered between miserable bouts of retching.

At that point Colomba made a mistake. She was positive she'd broken his spirit and paused to catch her breath, but in fact the man in the jacket still had plenty of energy and, with an unexpected lunge, grabbed her by the throat. Colomba felt the air choke off and her lungs emptying out. At the margins of her field of vision the buzzing shadows immediately appeared, the warning signs of an oncoming attack. *No, not now.* If she lost control, she'd be done for. She focused on the pain she felt in her throat and seized onto the discomfort as a sort of Ariadne's thread that would lead her out of the darkness. Something like two seconds had elapsed. The man kept throttling her and shouting abuse. Colomba hit him right above his Adam's apple with the blow called *nukite* in karate, a full-hand straight-fingered jab.

The man fell gasping to his knees: now it was his turn to suffocate. Colomba shoved him facedown onto the ground and climbed on top of him.

"Spread your arms! Spread them!" she said in a hoarse voice.

"I didn't do anything!" he wheezed.

"Spread them, goddamn it!"

The man obeyed. While Colomba was patting him down, he unexpectedly burst into tears. "I love him. I love him," he mumbled.

"Oh, shut up," said Colomba, without a clue of what he was talking about. All around them, a dozen or so people had gathered, emerging from the nearby shops. Colomba flashed her ID in a circle. "I'm from the police, okay? I'm placing this man under arrest."

"What did he do?" asked a young man with a black-and-white kaffiyeh scarf.

"He put his hands on me, is that enough for you?" The young man kept staring at her, and Colomba turned down the collar of her blouse, where the man in the jacket's hands had left the skin chafed and sore. "You see?"

The young man nodded. "But let him up, okay? He could suffocate. It wouldn't be the first time."

"Listen, I don't have handcuffs on me, and I'm going to keep him in this position until my partners show up." Colomba reached into her pocket in search of her cell phone but couldn't find it. *Fuck*, she thought. "Does anyone have a phone they can lend me?" she asked.

4

Colomba went back to Dante's apartment three hours later, exhausted from the adrenaline surge and annoyed at the stories she'd had to make up for her colleagues at the local police station.

When Dante opened the door, he was wearing a pair of black jeans and a spandex shirt, also black, which made him look skinnier and even more like an alien; Colomba could count his ribs.

Alberti was stretched out on the sofa with an iced compress on his forehead.

"You don't look happy," said Dante, mixing together coffee beans for his umpteenth espresso of the day. He picked them out of three different bags, counting them out like a pharmacist.

"He wasn't an al-Qaeda terrorist."

"So I imagined."

"Did you also imagine that he was a divorced father just trying to see his son?"

"Even though he wasn't supposed to, right?"

"There was a restraining order, forbidding him from approaching the child or the mother."

"Because he'd abused one or the other, I imagine. Just be proud you've done a little justice." Dante started the machine and watched as a stream of coffee filled the cup. He stopped the machine when the cup was only one-third full. "To savor this variety, you need to make it a very short black," he explained. He smelled the coffee, then took a sip. "The child will have a better shot at a decent life without a violent father around."

"Unless his mother turns out to be worse than the father or he meets someone on the street who splits his head open."

"I don't claim to be God. I just want to take care of problems in my own backyard."

"By sending me out to trade punches in the street."

Dante cracked his sarcastic grin. "You got off lighter than your partner."

"Hey, he caught me off guard," said Alberti in a Donald Duck voice.

"Of course he did." Dante lit a cigarette using his bad hand. He moved the only two working fingers adroitly, grabbing the lighter like a pair of pliers. "I'm afraid I can't turn down your requests now."

Colomba pulled a file folder out of her bag and handed it to him. "Don't you dare try."

Dante sat down at the table, opened the folder, and began leafing through the reports. "Naturally." He sighed disconsolately when he saw the quantity of paper. "You're still using paper? You do know there's such a thing as flash drives and the Internet, don't you?"

"Quit grumbling," said Colomba, sitting down across from him.

"Are you planning to stare at me the whole time?"

Colomba put her forefinger to her lips. "Sssh. Just read."

Dante obeyed with a smile on his lips.

For twenty minutes or so, the only sound was Alberti's rasping breath and the sound of pages turning. Dante separated them into small stacks, giving some of them only a cursory glance.

After checking to make sure that Dante was really reading, Colomba let her gaze wander around the living room. A few details caught her attention. The DVDs piled on the television set, for instance. They were all movies from the seventies, of various types but all of them low quality. She knew it because, to pay her way through college, she'd worked as a clerk at Blockbuster and she knew that stuff wasn't worth the plastic it was manufactured out of. And he must have really searched for them, because one of the open cases displayed the label of an American distributor who sold by correspondence. Another package delivered by courier, this one also half-opened and forgotten in a corner, contained a handful of toy figures that were surprise gifts in chocolate eggs sold many years ago. Colomba speculated that Dante was a passionate collector of pop culture trash, or perhaps he used them in some obscure research project of his.

Dante's voice made her jump. "Is this supposed to be a murder on impulse?" he asked.

"Premeditated. He took her to that isolated spot."

"Which is a rational act. But he decapitated her, which is a demented act. And he didn't cut her body into bits, which is rational. Just as it's rational to get rid of the dirty clothing and pretend to be worried. But at the same time only an idiot would discard the weapon no more than a few yards away. Contradictory, our little friend. The same thing occurred to you, didn't it?"

"People aren't always rational."

"But they aren't intermittently irrational, either. The boy. Don't you have anything from school? Notebooks, drawings?"

"No."

"Do you at least know the name of his pediatrician?"

"I know that he was contacted for information about the child's state of health."

"Well?"

"We don't believe there were any particular problems," said Colomba.

Dante snorted in disgust. "Oh, really? Look at this."

He took the stack of photographs of the Maugeris' son that had been printed out by the investigators at the VCU and laid them out on the table. They depicted the boy in various settings from the apparent age of one year to the age of six. The last one seemed to have been taken outside his elementary school.

"Notice anything?" asked Dante.

Colomba was about to say no. Then she was struck by the serious-ness of the boy's expression in the last picture. Serious and sober. She scanned the pictures, going backward in time. It was as if the child had gradually lost any desire to smile. From the first picture, which showed him running into his mother's outstretched arms, delirious with joy, to the last one, serious and sober, there was no mistaking the change. "He turned sad."

"He's not just sad," said Dante. "Look at his posture, too. In the next-to-last picture. His father wants to hug him, but he doesn't seem to care."

"Maybe it's because of the family climate. Maybe it's different in other pictures."

"No. It's too systematic. You know what autism is, I imagine."

"I know that it manifests itself in much younger children."

"Not always. In some cases, the first symptoms of what's known as Heller's syndrome can appear as late as four or five years of age."

"And you think the Maugeris' son might be suffering from that?"

"Maybe. I'd have to talk to the father about it."

"I don't think that's going to be possible."

Dante let himself slump back in his chair. "Whatever you say. This is all I can tell you. Who do I invoice?"

"At least take a look at the initial reconstruction put together by my colleagues. There's a complete transcript of the interviews."

"I've already read it. Maybe the father's lying, maybe he isn't." He shrugged.

Colomba looked straight into his eyes. Dante discovered that when Colomba's green eyes hardened, it took an effort to stare at them. "Try again," she told him.

"What'll happen if I don't find anything?"

"I hope that my colleagues have better luck," she replied.

"But not you. You'll just throw in the towel. And maybe that's what you really want, isn't it? Just to get out of it entirely," Dante said.

"I'm not the one throwing in the towel right now."

Dante gave her a hard look, as if the air around him had suddenly turned chilly. Colomba felt herself shiver. "I can't obtain anything else from photographs," he said in irritation. "To find out more, I'd have to take a walk around the scene of the crime."

"No problem," Colomba replied.

"Yes, there *is* a problem." Dante looked around. "I haven't left this apartment in two months. I hope you're a patient person, because it's going to take a while."

"I'm in no hurry."

"And you're not worried, either," Dante pointed out with a smile.

"About what?"

"You see, if the father is innocent, then someone's staged a murder to frame him and then be able to have their way with the child by making it look like an impulse murder. But they were unsuccessful, and you know why?"

"No."

"Because the killer's hand was too firm. It took him a couple of chops to take the head off, but he only hit the neck. There's not so much as a scratch on the woman's face. The murderer's hand never trembled." Dante smiled, and Colomba felt a shiver go up her back. "Whoever it was, he's used to killing."

5

Dante let Colomba and Alberti precede him out of the building, leaving him alone; then he prepared himself spiritually for the descent. His claustrophobia wasn't constant. When he was in a state of grace, he could force himself to face such difficult challenges as going into a supermarket for short periods, as long as there were very few people in the place and the store had lots of plate-glass windows. If he was tired or emotionally drained, it was practically impossible for him to leave his home.

His first psychiatrist had recommended that he rate his symptoms on a numerical scale, from one to ten. At one, he could do almost anything, but when he dropped to ten, he needed to be sedated because he completely lost control.

Right now, Dante was at level seven, at the verge of code red. He blamed it on the unusual day, but also the fact that he cared so much about making a good impression on the sad-seeming policewoman. And so it took all the willpower he possessed to face the six flights of stairs. Six stories without windows, with sharp corners and low ceilings, with other tenants who could appear without warning and fill up the already limited space, consuming his oxygen.

He knew there was no real danger on the stairs, any more than there was in an enclosed building or a dark closet, but the rational part of his mind couldn't conquer the frightened animal that was shivering inside him. Sometimes he'd break out in a cold sweat just at the sound of the winch hoisting the elevator car up the shaft on the other side of the wall: he could imagine himself inside, pounding on the walls.

He'd chosen to wear a raincoat and a pair of hiking boots that were suitable for muddy ground, and he'd put in his earbuds and set his iPhone to play a symphony of ocean waves. He set his respiration to their rhythm, then started his descent, banging the door behind him.

The first two floors went off without a hitch. He descended quickly, one hand on the railing, the sound of the ocean filling his ears and his mind. When he got to the third floor down, he made the mistake of looking up. He saw the underside of the stairs above his head, so close that it appeared to be crushing him. For a good solid minute, he stood frozen on the step; then he turned his head and looked up the stairwell, where a skylight let in a sliver of sky. He kept descending, face upturned, hand on the railing. At the fifth floor down he bumped into somebody and felt his heart leap into his mouth. He took a quick look: it was a woman, one of his neighbors, and her lips were moving as she said something to him. His immediate impulse was to return home and lock the door behind him. Once again, it was the thought of Colomba that drove him to keep going. He smiled tight-lipped at his neighbor and continued down the stairs. There was only one floor left to go when his cell phone rang, cutting off the music. He answered the phone, one hand gripping the railing.

"How is it going, Signor Torre?" asked Colomba.

"Everything's fine, I'm almost there. How long has it been?" he inquired, doing his best to maintain a normal tone of voice.

"Forty minutes."

To Dante it had seemed like five minutes at the most. Or five years. "Be there soon," he said and hung up.

One more floor. Just one more. He took a deep breath as if he were about to dive underwater and then went down the last flight of stairs. He went through the front door almost without realizing it.

He was outside. He leapt for joy on the sidewalk, filling his lungs with fresh air.

Colomba leaned against the hood of the squad car, watching him with her arms crossed. "Was it hard?"

"A little. But being outside is so *intoxicating* . . ." Dante said, dancing around a little more. He looked like he was spring-loaded.

"Have you ever thought of seeing a therapist?" Colomba asked.

"Have *you*?" Dante retorted.

Colomba didn't answer, but her green eyes turned darker and greener still. She opened the rear door of the squad car for him. "Take a seat," she said icily.

"I'm sitting in front. And I don't give a damn if there's some regulation against it. I'm not putting on a seat belt, and I'm keeping the car window open, even if it's raining. Okay?"

"Don't you own a car of your own?" Colomba asked. "You might feel more comfortable."

"I only use it in the summer. It doesn't have a top."

It was a long drive. Going fast had a disastrous effect on Dante's nerves, and Alberti was forced to pull over a dozen times or so to let his passenger get out. Each time, Dante did a few push-ups and jumped in place, then got back in, promising that would be the last time, but punctually, after a few minutes, he would turn pale and feverish again.

Still, they did finally manage to reach the stables. With the operational base dismantled, the lines of vehicles jamming the roads were gone and a couple of horses were trotting around the track. In that new and surreal quiet, Alberti managed to requisition one of the Defenders made available to the investigators, and they drove on to the scene of the crime.

Energized by the drive, Dante insisted on walking the Via Sacra on his own. Alberti stayed behind to keep an eye on the vehicle, and Colomba followed Dante, trailing a few dozen yards behind. Dante seemed fascinated by everything he saw, brimming over with energy. He poked at leaves and rocks and often left the trail to look downhill. During the hike, Colomba called Rovere to brief him. "I warned you it wouldn't be easy," he said.

"But you didn't tell me he was a complete nutcase. You should see the place where he lives."

"Is what he told you just as nutty?"

Colomba didn't answer. She hadn't entirely made up her mind. "Any news on the boy?"

"Nothing. Relatives and friends have been contacted, without results. But the first laboratory findings are reinforcing De Angelis's idea. The blood in the car trunk is the boy's, and the pruning hook definitely comes from Maugeri's home. He'd bought it himself last month, to prune a tree in the yard, but he said he's never used it."

"The only thing missing is a confession."

"There's no confession, but he's still being held."

"I'd only be surprised if he wasn't. Sir, we're wasting time. Everything points to Maugeri. You're going to have to find some other way of getting rid of . . ." Colomba stopped before uttering the name Santini. You never know who might be listening to you, legally or otherwise. ". . . you know who."

"What does Torre have to say?"

"He already thinks there's a plot."

"You see?"

Dante had gone all the way to the overlook. He peered down for a moment and then rocked on his heels; if he hadn't grabbed the railing, he would have pitched over headfirst.

Colomba hung up in a hurry and galloped over to him. "Are you feeling dizzy?"

Dante smiled and stayed hunched over, beneath the railing. "Is it that obvious?"

"I just had a hunch."

"I'll be fine in a minute." He breathed deeply for a few seconds before getting back up on his feet. "I didn't think it was so high, it caught me by surprise. What does your boss say?"

"That the husband bought the weapon."

"Were his fingerprints on it?"

"No."

Dante grasped the railing and stood up. "Well, then, our murderer could have taken it from the family's home."

"A little daring, don't you think?"

Dante shrugged. "I told you." He looked shyly over the edge of the bluff. "*He* doesn't scare easy. Where were the shoes?"

Colomba pointed to the location. Now there was a numbered card on the bush.

Dante looked without letting go of the railing. "Very theatrical." Then he turned sharply around and continued along the trail. "Let's get going while there's still light."

Colomba followed him, doing her best to keep up. Dante leapt lightly from rock to rock. "Why would a cold-blooded, clear-minded murderer decide to take it out on the Maugeris?" she shouted after him.

"Ah, that's something I don't know yet."

Dante came to a halt when he reached the police barriers

surrounding the site where the body was found. Two squad cars controlled the points of access, and an officer flicked away a cigarette as he headed over toward them. Colomba pulled out her police ID while Dante, impatient, headed out into the clearing.

The officer saluted her, and Colomba remembered running into him a few years ago. "Who's he, Voldemort?" he asked her, pointing at Dante: he was walking in circles among the boulders, careful not to step on the marks left by the technicians, flapping the tails of his black leather raincoat.

"A consultant," she replied vaguely.

"Well, that's good. I was afraid he was a cop."

Colomba caught up with Dante, who was climbing a tree. "Reliving your childhood?" she asked. She immediately bit her tongue. "I'm sorry."

"Don't think twice. I had my happy moments when I was a boy. When he thought I deserved it, the Father would give me hot food, for instance."

"The Father?"

"That's what he wanted me to call him. And since you all never figured out who he was . . ." He hauled himself up with both arms, then hunkered down on a branch about six feet off the ground. He looked like a large black crow in wait of prey.

"Do you see anything interesting from up there?" asked Colomba.

"A miniature Stonehenge. I couldn't think of a better location for a ritual murder."

"Or to stage a fake one," said Colomba.

"You took the words right out of my mouth. What do you think, did the murderer hang up the shoes before or after killing the mother?"

"Before seems unlikely," Colomba replied. "The mother would have realized that something wasn't right."

"So you kill someone, and then you start doing a little exterior decorating? I mean, cold-hearted and everything, but *that's* a little much."

"If it was your firm-handed killer, maybe it's part of the fabrication. Or else the boy lost them on the trail and someone hung them up so their rightful owner could find them."

"What do the footprints tell you?"

"Too much rain, too much mud, and too many people walking around. Even if the footprints of the murderer or the little boy walking away were ever there, it's impossible to make them out now."

"So we don't know which way he went when he left."

"If it was Maugeri, he went back to the place they had their picnic and started pretending to be looking for his wife and son."

"I thought we'd already eliminated him as a suspect, hadn't we?"

"You eliminated him. I didn't. For now, all I have are question marks."

Dante thought it over for a few seconds. "I don't think the murderer left by the route we took to get here. There are too many people on that trail, and he certainly didn't want to run the risk of being seen."

"So he hung up the shoes and went back?"

Dante shook his head. "Maybe. Which makes the act even more significant, but I don't know why." He looked around, then pointed to the trail, which continued on. He leapt lightly to the ground. "Let's go," and he headed off without waiting for an answer.

Colomba went after him, still amazed at his energy. In his home, he hadn't seemed capable of taking two steps without someone's arm to lean on.

They continued down the trail and ran into a pair of mushroom hunters with wicker baskets. Dante nodded to them as they passed. "Finding anything good?"

"Nothing much," one answered.

"People looking for mushrooms always go out after it rains," said Dante once the pair were far away. "Maybe someone crossed paths with the murderer."

"No one came in to report anything."

"Because he didn't particularly stand out. And I doubt your colleagues took much trouble to collect eyewitness accounts."

"Not after Maugeri's arrest," Colomba admitted. "But by now everyone knows about the missing boy, his picture is everywhere. If a mushroom hunter had seen him walking with someone, we would have heard about it."

"I don't think he was walking." Dante pointed to a hiker a short distance below them. He was carrying a sleepy child who had his arms wrapped around his neck. "Can you see that kid's face?"

"No," said Colomba.

"A six-year-old is a little big to be carried in someone's arms, but no one would really notice."

"That is, if this mysterious kidnapper really exists."

"Maybe the boy flew away on My Little Pony." Dante speeded up, passing the trees and forcing Colomba to run to catch up with him, thinking as she did about Dante's allusion to the popular Hasbro toy. Had his stunted childhood made him particularly tuned in to what fascinated children these days? She felt a stab of pain in her rebuilt tendon, which she'd already strained when she'd chased the man in the jacket a few hours earlier.

They emerged onto a plaza at the center of which stood a small light blue chapel dedicated to the Madonna and surrounded by enormous boulders.

"If your theory is correct, the kidnapper ought to have parked not very far from here," said Colomba. "And if he left before dark, he might not have met anyone. Day hikers usually go home at sunset."

She realized that Dante wasn't listening to her. He was staring at a metallic object hanging about halfway down the pole of a traffic sign. Colomba went over to take a closer look. It was a cylindrical metal whistle with a dull finish, tied to a frayed piece of hemp twine. She reached out to grab it, but Dante seized her by the wrist. His grip was icy and powerful, and it almost hurt.

"Don't touch it," he told her.

Colomba shook free with a brusque movement. "Well, don't you touch me either, if you don't mind." She realized that Dante was gray in the face. "What's the matter?" she asked, suddenly worried.

Dante finally answered after a number of failed attempts, his voice reduced to little more than a murmur. "When he took me . . . when the Father took me, I had something with me that I'd found in the field where I went to play. It was a Boy Scout whistle." He shifted his gaze to her. But he wasn't looking at her. He was looking at an ancient, boundless terror. "That's it," he said, pointing.

6

Dante was sitting by the side of the road, his arms wrapped around his legs. He hadn't said another word, he hadn't moved.

Colomba wasn't comfortable leaving him alone in that condition, but she had to call Rovere and she didn't want him to overhear. "How do you feel, Signor Torre?" she asked.

Dante sat mute and motionless, gaze lost in the distance.

"Signor Torre, I'm going to have to step away for just a few minutes. But I can't do that unless you tell me you're all right." Still no reaction. "Dante . . ."

Hearing the sound of his name, he came to. "I'm not going to die," he replied tonelessly. "Do what you have to."

Colomba walked a short distance away and called Rovere again. "Dante isn't doing well," she told him. "Not that he was doing all that well before."

"What happened?"

"He saw a whistle hanging from a signpost and started saying that it had been left by the man who kidnapped the Maugeris' son, who is supposedly the same man who kidnapped him. Because Torre is convinced that his *real* kidnapper is still on the loose."

"And why would he have left the whistle?"

From his tone, it seemed that Rovere was actually mulling the question over, and Colomba was amazed. "I have no idea, and if you ask me, neither does Torre. Listen, I'm going to take him back home."

"And do you intend to ignore what he told you?"

"Help me understand. What are you telling me I ought to do instead?"

"Inform the man in charge of this investigation about this discovery."

Colomba thought she must have misheard. "Captain Rovere . . . Torre is delirious! We've put him face-to-face with a situation that resembles what happened to him, and it's driven him around the bend."

"That whistle might be evidence in a case of kidnapping and murder," said Rovere stubbornly.

"Now I'm starting to think you're delirious, too." Could it be that Rovere's desire to screw Santini was so powerful that it was driving him crazy? "If I try to tell De Angelis anything of the sort, he'll laugh in my face."

"The responsibility for that will be his, not ours."

"I'm pulling out of this, Captain," said Colomba coldly.

"You're free to do that, starting this evening. But for now, wait until someone can get there. I'll alert De Angelis myself," said Rovere and ended the conversation without saying good-bye.

Well, go fuck yourself, thought Colomba. But his reaction still left a bitter taste in her mouth.

An hour later, Santini was the first to arrive. In the meantime, Dante might have said at the most three or four words, and he'd refused any offers to take him home. The CIS deputy chief's car was followed by a station wagon with the insignia of the VCU on the doors. Colomba had already seen the two technicians riding in that car the previous day.

"And we're back," said the older member of the pair as they got out of the car. "I'm starting to hate this place."

Santini walked straight over to them. "Whose idea was this bullshit?" he asked.

Colomba concealed her embarrassment by keeping her face impassive. "Figure it out for yourself, genius."

"I'm going to make you pay for this."

She pointed behind her. "The pole in question is right there. Why don't you shove it up your ass?"

Santini nodded to the forensic technicians. "Come on, let's get moving."

The two technicians, who weren't wearing the white jumpsuits they trotted out on special occasions, photographed the whistle, then placed it in a sterile evidence bag. Santini stayed glued to Colomba.

"Are you afraid I might hang up another one?" she asked him.

"You know you're going to be lucky if they send you to stamp passports when you get back from leave, right?"

"I should take lessons from you about how to kiss the asses that count. How's every little thing with De Angelis? Do you take him coffee in bed?"

Santini stared at her with loathing. "You'd better be careful what you say."

"I am. Just think if I wasn't."

Colomba sat back down next to Dante while the technicians dusted the pole with fingerprint powder and found a tangled mess of prints.

"He's back," said Dante in a low voice. "After all these years."

"We'll see what the lab has to say," she replied diplomatically.

"I've always known he was still out there somewhere."

Santini's shadow loomed over them both. "The technicians are done, Caselli. Tell your friend he has to come with us for a little chat with the magistrate."

"No," said Dante without looking at him. "And you can talk to *me*, you know. I'm not deaf or retarded."

"I know who you are, Torre," said Santini. "I have colleagues who've experienced your 'consultations.' And none of them liked it."

"Maybe that's because they didn't know how to do their jobs."

Santini leaned over him. "You care to repeat that?"

Colomba stood up and squared off. "Quit trying to be a tough guy."

"Out of the way."

"Can't you see he's not well?"

"I don't give a fuck."

"Oh, you don't?" Colomba took a step forward, and Santini was forced to retreat. "He was the victim of a kidnapping that left him severely traumatized, he suffers from claustrophobia, and he's under medical treatment. If you drag him around against his will, you'll be cited for intentional infliction of emotional distress and abuse of power."

"You're the one who got him into this, Caselli!" Santini said, clearly exasperated.

Colomba felt a stab of guilt. "That's true. But from here on in, it's entirely your responsibility."

Santini made an effort to appear reasonable. "The magistrate wants to talk to him. What should I tell him, to call on him at home?"

"And why not?"

"Because that's not the way it *works*!"

One of the two technicians laid a hand on the CIS deputy chief's shoulder. "About a mile from here there's an autogrill; the restaurant's entirely surrounded by plate-glass windows. What do you say, would that be acceptable to you, Signor Torre?"

Colomba leaned over Dante. "If you say no, I can take you home right away."

"I have to do this."

"No, you don't."

"Let me be the judge of that, Deputy Captain, if you don't mind."

"Well?" said Santini. "Are you good with this fucking autogrill?"

"I'm good with it," Dante replied.

While Santini was working out the details on the phone with De Angelis, the older technician smiled at him. "He acts like that, but he's not a bad guy," he said. "He's just a piece of shit."

"Do you know each other?" asked Colomba.

Dante shook his head and seemed to lose interest in the conversation.

"We've never met in person, but I know who he is," the technician explained to Colomba. "Do you remember the case of the nursery school in Putignano?"

"Of course." It had happened just after the Disaster, and the story had managed to penetrate through the blanket of indifference enveloping her. In spite of the fact that she'd been in bad, *extremely* bad shape, it had still struck her as incredible that anyone could have believed it. The entire teaching staff of a nursery school had been accused of abusing the children in extremely imaginative ways. With no evidence except for the claims of the parents. But in fact, a great many people had believed the charges. "Does he have anything to do with it?"

"According to legend, yes."

"According to legend?"

"Well, none of us saw him, but the word was that he was acting as a consultant for the defendants' lawyers. Tons of rumors were circulating about him . . . My instinct is that they were all true." He smiled. "He tore the plaintiffs' lawyers new assholes."

"It didn't do any good," said Dante in a sepulchral voice.

"The prosecution was forced to call off the trial," Colomba objected.

"The defendants had to move away. All of them," Dante went on. "The parents are still convinced they were right. And the children can no longer tell the difference between reality and the diseased fantasies other people put in their heads. They're going to grow up twisted and lead troubled lives."

The technician nodded. "True."

Santini finished his phone call. "Judge De Angelis is going to meet us at the autogrill in an hour." Then he added, "In any case, it's a colossal waste of time."

In the meantime, a squad car had pulled up in the plaza. When the two officers got out, Santini pointed to the pole. "Make sure nobody touches it or gets near it, okay? And if anyone asks why, say that it's special orders from the highway patrol."

"The highway patrol?" one of the two asked, perplexed.

"What's the matter? Are you deaf?" Santini snarled.

The officer jumped. "No sir."

"Your friend can ride with you, right?" Santini said to Colomba as he got in his car. "That way you can't accuse us of having mistreated him on the way over."

"Drive safely," she advised him.

7

There were already guards at the entrance to the autogrill when Colomba and Dante arrived, along with Alberti, who was complaining even more loudly about his swollen nose. The restaurant loomed above them, a futuristic bridge structure spanning the highway, overlooking the cars zipping past beneath at high speed. Customers could come in and go out, but access to the restaurant area, a large glassed-in gazebo on the large-scale retail model, had been closed off. During the drive, Colomba's sense of guilt had ballooned out of proportion. Dante was going to make a fool of himself in the presence of the pack of hyenas that De Angelis and his henchmen really were. And all because she hadn't had the courage to stand up to her soon-to-be ex-boss. When she overheard Dante calling his lawyer, she felt a tiny flood of relief: that could be the out she'd been praying for.

Dante looked at the entrance to the autogrill the way a condemned man looks at the noose. His internal thermometer was dangerously close to ten, and the two Xanax tablets that he'd popped in the car were just giving him dizziness and nausea. Images of the past flashed through his head. The Father, his silo prison, the light that had filtered through the cracks in the cement. The ice that had formed on the window high above. The stink of his own excrement. His mind echoed to the words of one of the things the Father liked to say most often: *You'll never be as safe as you are here.*

At the time, Dante had believed it. Sometimes he believed it even now.

"You're almost done for today," Colomba said. "But, for what it's worth, I'm sorry I dragged you into this. I really am."

"It wasn't you who dragged me into it, Deputy Captain. It was *him*."

"The Father."

"Yes."

This is going well, thought Colomba.

A tall, thin man in a tweed overcoat met them at the entrance to the autogrill, walking in long strides. He vaguely resembled the actor Jeremy Irons at middle age, with shorter hair and tanned skin. Colomba immediately realized that this was Minutillo.

The lawyer placed both hands on his client's shoulders. "How are you?"

Dante ignored the question. "It's the Father, Roberto," he said.

The lawyer shook his head in concern. "Are you sure?"

"Yes," Dante replied.

"Then you have to do it." He shook Colomba's hand. "Pleased to meet you, I'm Roberto Minutillo. If my client has any problems as a result of this, I'll hold you responsible."

"Can I speak to you for just a couple of seconds?"

Minutillo looked at Dante. "Go ahead," Dante said.

They walked away a short distance. "Take him away from here," Colomba said quickly.

"I can't force him to go."

"But did you hear what he just said? He thinks his kidnapper has come back."

"I've learned to respect his views, no matter how bizarre they appear."

"This goes beyond bizarre. This is madness."

Minutillo raised an eyebrow. "Really?"

"Torre was kidnapped thirty-five years ago. And it's impossible to think that he can identify the presence of his kidnapper from nothing more than an old toy he couldn't conceivably remember with any precision!"

Minutillo studied her for a few seconds, and the wrinkles around his eyes relaxed slightly. "Thanks for your concern. It's very commendable. But now we ought to go in."

Without waiting for a reply, the lawyer returned to his client, locking arms with him companionably. Colomba sighed in frustration. *All right, then.* One way or another, this would soon be over.

There were officers standing guard around the restaurant, and Colomba was obliged to show her ID before she was allowed in with the others. Dante kept his eyes focused on the outside world the whole time, until they reached De Angelis and Santini, who were sitting at a table by the plate-glass windows. With them was a third man Colomba didn't know, with a laptop in front of him.

Colomba made the introductions; Santini didn't even look at her and De Angelis shot her a suspicious glance, but everyone shook hands with the lawyer. On the far side of the room, near the serving counters, were standing two CIS lieutenants that Colomba had seen at the scene of the murder. They were chatting quietly and laughing discreetly. They stopped as soon as they noticed her staring at them.

De Angelis spoke to Minutillo. "The presence of a lawyer is unnecessary."

"It's the way we chose to do this. But if you have any objections, Judge De Angelis, we certainly don't want to waste your time. We can arrange for a more appropriate meeting at some other time."

De Angelis shook his head. "Don't even think of it, counselor. Please have a seat. In fact, everyone take a seat." He introduced the man with the computer as the lieutenant making the official transcription of the interview. He copied the details of everyone's IDs, then started a digital recording device. De Angelis stated the date, the time, and the names of those present, then pushed a four-color printout in front of Dante. It was a picture of the whistle, stamped VCU. Colomba noted that they had worked fast. "I'm showing Signor Torre a picture of the whistle found near a parking lot, some five hundred meters from the site of Signora Maugeri's murder," he said into the digital recorder. "Do you confirm that this is the same object found by you on today's date and acquired by my office as an item of evidence?"

"It looks like the same one."

"You stated to Deputy Captain Caselli, who is present here today, that this whistle is linked to the murder of Signora Maugeri and the kidnapping of young Luca Maugeri. Is that correct?"

"That's not exactly what he said," Colomba broke in.

De Angelis raised one hand. "Deputy Captain, please limit yourself to answering only when and if you are asked a question. Please be so kind."

So kind, my ass, Colomba thought, but said, "Sorry."

Dante grimaced in sympathy. "Those weren't the words I said; Deputy Captain Caselli is right. And I believe that for a while I wasn't especially coherent. What I wanted to say was that this whistle is identical to the one I possessed when I was kidnapped. A whistle that was then taken from me by my kidnapper. To find it again just a short distance from where a child went missing, a child the same age that I was when I was kidnapped, makes me think that it was no coincidence."

"Could you explain that?"

"I think that my kidnapper left it there. Therefore, I imagine that this is my whistle and that it remained in his possession."

De Angelis and Santini exchanged a glance.

"The man who kidnapped you is dead, Signor Torre," said De Angelis, and he enunciated each word distinctly as if addressing someone simpleminded. "His name was Bodini, and he shot himself in his farmhouse before the police arrived."

"It wasn't him. Bodini was just a useful idiot who became a scapegoat."

De Angelis tapped a pen against the tip of his nose. "Yes. I know that you've always maintained that version of events . . . Was the whistle in the list of items belonging to you drawn up by your parents?"

"No."

"And did you speak to the authorities about it after you were freed?"

"No. But I didn't just invent it now either, if that's what you're trying to insinuate."

De Angelis shot him a look of reproof. "Signor Torre, it's not my job to insinuate anything. I ask questions, and you are a witness and are therefore required to answer me, even in this somewhat . . . informal setting."

"Is there already a report from the forensic squad?" asked Minutillo.

"Considering the time frame, only a preliminary report," Santini replied, "which was shared with me over the phone. There are no fingerprints, no traces of organic material. Difficult to say from the degree of oxidation how long it was exposed to the elements, especially since we have no knowledge of its previous condition. Not for long, in any case. It's pretty well preserved."

"Is the year of manufacture compatible with my client's account?" Minutillo asked.

"Only in the most general terms. That model of whistle was manufactured in Italy from 1960 to 1977; it could have been any one of those years."

De Angelis smiled at Dante, but there wasn't the slightest hint of human sympathy in that smile. "Signor Torre, let's grant that the whistle is identical to the one you had." He raised a hand as if to ward off a possible objection. "But I invite you to calculate the odds. How likely is it that this whistle really is yours, placed there by some conspiratorial hand, and not a whistle lost by a hiker or perhaps by a child who was given it by his parent? And that someone then hung it up as an act of kindness, to ensure it would be found by its owner, the way we do with gloves or keys?"

"I don't need to calculate the odds," said Dante. "I know for certain."

"But we don't. There's no evidence whatsoever, unfortunately, to corroborate your claims."

"You're wrong," Dante objected.

De Angelis's smile turned icy. "So tell me. How am I wrong?"

"There are no fingerprints. Do you think that the little boy who lost it simply never touched it?"

"Perhaps whoever found it cleaned off the mud."

"So thoroughly that they eliminated all traces? Erasing any organic residues, such as any traces of saliva? Or do you think that no one ever blew that whistle? You know, it *is* what people do with whistles."

Colomba felt a swell of admiration for Dante. He wasn't coming off like the fool she'd feared.

"The rain must have washed it clean, Signor Torre," said De Angelis.

Santini leaned forward, placing an elbow on the table. "Unless whoever placed it there wanted to make sure no one could tell who he was," he said. "Because he knew that we'd check it against his DNA before anyone else's."

"Are you accusing my client of something?" asked Minutillo. If De Angelis's smile was chilly, Minutillo's glare was burning hot.

"We're just talking," said De Angelis.

"Sorry to interrupt, Judge, your honor," Santini said, looking over at Colomba. "Deputy Captain, can you tell us that you never lost sight of him for even a second when you came downhill?"

"I don't have to tell you a fucking thing, Santini."

"She's right, Judge De Angelis," Minutillo broke in again. "And if the interview of my client is going to continue in this atmosphere, we'll leave immediately."

"All right, all right, let's all calm down," said De Angelis. "But I am obliged to ask the deputy captain, present here today, the same question."

"Who are you interviewing? My client or the deputy captain?" asked Minutillo.

"Your client. But I'd like to save some time, if you're in agreement."

"No."

"Excuse me, counselor, but let's just cut this short," Colomba broke in. "There's no way I lost sight of him."

"Now are you satisfied?" asked Dante. "Or do you think that the deputy captain is lying, too?"

"Signor Torre, you can understand that any skeptical observer would find the coincidence highly suspicious?"

"There's no coincidence," said Dante. "*He* put it there on purpose."

"Your kidnapper."

"Yes."

"But what motive would he have for doing it? To send a message? Lay down a challenge? Establish his signature?"

Dante hesitated, and Colomba had the distinct impression that he wasn't telling the whole story. "I don't know what he might be thinking. I didn't know thirty years ago, and I don't know now."

"Mightn't it have simply gone unnoticed, your whistle? Stayed there until it rusted? Wound up in the trash?"

"I'm hardly the best person to judge his intentions. I'm . . . influenced, I'd say, by the fact that he taught me to think of him as God as long as he held me prisoner. And it's difficult to understand the mind of God."

Another glance between De Angelis and Santini. "All right, Signor Torre . . . I thank you. I'm done," said De Angelis.

Until that moment Dante had spoken in a low voice, without moving, practically. Suddenly he lunged forward, and De Angelis shot back, pressing his shoulders against the back of his chair. "Do you know what's going to happen to that child now?" said Dante. "Years of imprisonment, if not the rest of his life. Psychological violence, physical violence. And the risk of being killed if he fails to learn or disobeys."

De Angelis scrutinized him. "Just like what happened to you, isn't it?" he said.

"Yes. Just like what happened to me."

"You do see, then, why that makes you a witness who can easily be influenced by events?"

"Is that another way of saying unreliable?"

"I'm very sorry."

Dante nodded slowly. "Well, I had to try. Can I go?"

"Yes, we're done," De Angelis announced. "You'll be asked to sign the transcript when your interview is typed up."

"Let us know, and we'll come in," said Minutillo, getting to his feet along with Dante.

Colomba stood up, too.

"Do you mind waiting for a minute, Deputy Captain?" said De Angelis.

"As you like."

Minutillo and Dante left. De Angelis rubbed his chin, then took Santini and the lieutenant in at a single glance. "I need to have a private chat with the deputy captain."

The lieutenant shut the screen of his computer and stood up. Santini reached out to shake hands with De Angelis. "Well, I'll just swing by police headquarters and then back to the office, if you don't have anything else for me."

"No, go right ahead. I'll call you tomorrow."

Santini headed for the exit; the lieutenant went over to an open window and lit a cigarette.

"You know what I want to ask you, don't you?" said De Angelis once they were alone.

"No. Give me some help."

"If you really want to make it as hard as possible . . . What were you doing on the scene of an investigation you're not involved in?"

"I wanted Signor Torre to see the place," she replied impassively.

"For what reason?"

"He's an expert consultant on missing persons."

"He's an unhinged individual, and law firms hire him to muddy the waters so they can make money."

"That's your opinion. It's not mine."

"Is Maugeri Torre's client?"

"No."

De Angelis put his fingertips together. "If he was, you might not know it. And this thing with the whistle could be the first brick in their defense theory."

"I came to *him*. Torre isn't working for anybody right now."

"In what capacity, seeing that you're on leave?"

"As a private citizen. I happened to come into contact with the investigation, I tried to offer my small contribution . . ."

De Angelis let himself slump back in his chair, looking her in the eyes. Colomba held his gaze.

"You aren't under oath right now, but I demand you tell me the truth, given the position I occupy. And you're lying. It was Rovere who sent you. He didn't like being shoved aside, proving once again how right I was not to involve him in the first place."

It would have been fair to put the blame on Rovere after what he'd forced her to do, but Colomba wasn't the type to go over to the other side. "Absolutely not," she replied. "He knows nothing about what I'm doing in this context."

"I don't believe you, Deputy Captain. You're intimate, the two of you, aren't you?"

"What do you mean by 'intimate'?"

De Angelis threw both arms wide. "Don't take it the wrong way! I only mean to say that he was your boss for many years. And that he was very close to you during your convalescence. And he did a great deal for you; he didn't turn his back on you when many others would have, after what happened to you."

Colomba dug her fingernails into the palms of her hands. "Is it really necessary to talk about it?"

"Only to explain to you why I don't believe you. You'd never operate behind Rovere's back. Behind my back and Santini's, no doubt. And you wouldn't betray his trust by revealing the fact to me."

"If you know it, what's the purpose of this interrogation?" she asked.

"I just wanted to give you a chance. I'm sorry you didn't take it."

"Can I go now?"

De Angelis dropped his eyes to the papers lying in front of him. "Have a good evening, Deputy Captain."

Outside, in the meantime, with the excuse of a cigarette, Dante was waiting to say good-bye to Colomba after having strategically sent Minutillo to make a phone call in the parking area. After that night, he'd never see the green-eyed policewoman again, and he was sorry about that. Partly because she was an attractive and unconventional woman— and he'd seen far too few attractive women for quite some time now— and partly because he'd feel even more alone now in the presence of his phantoms and specters. Just then, Santini emerged from the restroom, wiping his hands on his trousers. He saw Dante standing alone, and in an instant his expression turned predatory. He galloped the few yards separating them and grabbed Dante by one arm.

"What the fuck do you think you're doing?" said Dante, dropping the pack of cigarettes. Santini clapped one hand over his mouth and shoved him into one of the bathrooms. It was small and windowless. It reeked of shit.

Santini closed the door behind him. It was dark. Dante could only see the black outline of the other man against the gray background and the eyes that appeared to glitter. The darkness seemed to weigh on his consciousness, beginning to crush it. Santini took his hand off his mouth, but Dante didn't yell. His voice stuck in his throat. It seemed as if the walls were wrapping around him, and his legs gave way beneath him. He'd have fallen if Santini hadn't held him up by the collar of his raincoat.

"You're afraid of being in confined spaces, aren't you? And I'll bet you're afraid of the dark, too. Do you keep a night light on your bed-side dresser? Shaped like a ducky?"

Dante said nothing and concentrated on remaining conscious. Now the past was gleaming like a lightning bolt and echoing. Santini's voice reached him, muffled, as if from behind a cement wall.

The cement wall of the silo.

"Let go of me," he tried to say again, but his voice stuck in his throat.

"*Me* is who you need to be afraid of. If you come around busting our chops again with this fairy tale about the whistle or anything else that has to do with the investigation, I'll dig a hole and throw you down it. A hole in the ground. So you have to breathe through a pipe. You understand?"

Dante did not understand. The Father's voice drowned out everything else. It came down from on high and dictated the Law to him. It told him that he had once again made a mistake in parroting back what he'd been taught and that he would therefore need to punish himself. And that he must take the club and beat his bad hand with it. Keeping time with the Father's count.

Dante grabbed a wooden club made of air and tried to lift it, but Santini gripped his arm. "Stop flailing around. Just tell me that you understand. Tell me!"

In the darkness of the silo, Dante found a window into the present and hooked onto it, bringing himself back into that foul-smelling bathroom standing face-to-face with the cop. He came back there, or a small part of him did, just enough to let him move his lips and say that he'd understood. Even if he didn't know what that was. Or he'd forgotten it. He felt light. Rarified.

Santini released him and threw open the door as he left. The burst of light whipped Dante like a jolt of electricity. He fell to his knees on the wet tiles, then threw himself on all fours and slithered through the filth to the main door.

Outside, Colomba saw Santini get into his car, his tires spraying gravel. She wondered what had happened until she saw Dante crawling out of the bathroom.

Colomba kneeled down to lift his head; at the same time, Minutillo interrupted his phone call and came running toward them, cursing himself for his carelessness.

"Are you all right? What happened?" asked Colomba.

"Nothing. Just leave me alone," Dante murmured.

"You heard him, leave him alone," said Minutillo, behind her, pushing her aside none too gently. He leaned over Dante. "Can you get to your feet?"

"Give me a hand."

Minutillo pulled him up, practically lifting him bodily. Dante's trousers and raincoat were dripping and filthy. Minutillo took off his coat and wrapped it around him. "I'm taking you home now."

"Signor Torre," said Colomba. "Wait a second."

Dante turned his eyes toward her.

"I saw Santini running away. Did he do something to you?"

Dante shook his head. "It doesn't matter."

"It does to me."

"Just words and without witnesses." Dante pointed at the restaurant from which De Angelis was emerging at that exact moment, pretending not to see them. "Considering the way they reacted today, do you think that anyone would believe me?"

"I believe you."

"But not about the most important things, apparently."

Dante let himself be dragged off by his lawyer. Colomba kicked a rock, but it did nothing to rid her mind of bad thoughts. Which increased, if anything, until she finally decided to get them off her chest and jumped into the car. Alberti snapped out of it.

"Where am I taking you, Deputy Captain?"

"To police headquarters. And this time put on that fucking siren."

Alberti drove fast, and every time he dared to slow at an intersection, Colomba urged him on.

They got to Via San Vitale just as Santini's car was pulling through the police headquarters security barrier.

Colomba jumped out and waved her police ID in the guard's face. When Santini opened the car door to get out, she was standing in front of him.

"Caselli? What the fuck do you want?"

She kicked him in the face. She caught him square on the chin with the tip of her boot, and Santini fell back into the car, literally seeing stars.

"Get near Torre again, and I'll hurt you," Colomba said.

"Have you lost your mind?" he demanded, slurring the words as he grabbed the door frame and tried to get back on his feet. But he was like a punch-drunk boxer; his hands weren't responding.

"You heard me."

Two uniformed officers came running on the double, even though it had all been so quick that no one really knew what had happened. Colomba was already walking toward the front entrance. From behind her, Santini started shouting, but she didn't stop to listen to what he had to say.

8

Minutillo drove Dante home and went upstairs with him, because he knew his presence would make it easier for him to face the stairs. The whole long way up they talked about trivial topics, keeping Dante's mind as far as possible from the forest and from the silo. Dante refused to tell him what had happened in the bathroom, and Minutillo knew that it was pointless to insist.

As they went up the stairs, Dante's mood improved, and once they reached his apartment he seemed to be his usual wry self. What struck Minutillo was the chaos. A functional chaos, with paths clearly marked out between the objects piled on the floor and reasonably clean, but still a sign that Dante had been living as a recluse for too long. The lawyer made a mental note to check on his friend's living conditions more frequently, no matter how witty or relaxed he might seem over the phone. "Don't you think it's time to tidy up a little?" he asked.

"I haven't exceeded the warning level yet. See? The clutter hasn't reached the stove." He went into the bathroom, closing the door behind him, stripped his clothes off, and took a shower. They spoke through the bathroom door.

"Make yourself an espresso if you want," said Dante.

"Never after five in the afternoon. I need my sleep. What happened to the cleaning woman?"

"She's gone. She was a woman of narrow views."

"You could have told me and I'd have found you another one."

"I hate to make you look bad with the agencies." Dante scrubbed his skin. He could still detect the reek of piss, but maybe that was just a trick of his mind. He turned off the water. "It's not the first time."

"I always tell them that you're an eccentric . . ."

"Then find me one who doesn't know Italian. That way I won't have to hide my documents."

"What about that girl you were seeing? What's her name . . ." the lawyer asked, though he'd already guessed the answer.

"She's gone, too. And you can't contact the employment agency to find me another one of those."

"I'm sorry to hear it. What went wrong?"

"She was a woman of narrow views."

"You've already used that excuse."

"Oh, really?" Dante opened the bathroom door in a charcoal gray bathrobe and tossed his dirty clothes into an overflowing laundry hamper. "Maybe I should burn them." He sprawled out on the sofa, legs propped over the armrest. Remembering that Alberti had assumed that same position just a few hours earlier, he sat up straight again. Alberti seemed like too much of a loser for him to think of imitating him.

Minutillo remained standing. "I'm worried about you," he said. "You don't go out and you never see anyone. And now this thing . . ."

"What thing?"

"Don't be a fool."

"Roberto . . . I was already pretty sure that the Father was still alive, and now I just have proof. It doesn't change a lot as far as I'm concerned."

"It changes everything, actually."

"I've survived so far, and I'll go on living. Every now and then, I admit, I'll think about that boy, who's going through what I went through, but maybe he'll be luckier."

"Why don't you take a trip somewhere? You don't mind traveling by train. Or else hire a driver."

Dante giggled. "Or maybe just post two armed guards outside the door?"

Minutillo didn't bat an eye. "I can arrange that."

"I'm not a child anymore, I no longer constitute his type of prey."

"We don't know what constitutes his type of prey."

"Everyone thinks I'm the only one he kidnapped and that now he's dead."

"You don't. So neither do I."

Dante waved a hand. "Time for you to go, I want to mix up some pharmaceuticals and alcohol. And I can't do it with you watching."

"What about the cop who assaulted you?"

"He'll get off, the way cops always do when they step over the line."

"Especially when you don't bother to file a complaint."

"I'll get even with him sooner or later, even if I don't yet know how. I never forget, and you know that."

Minutillo picked up his overcoat from the floor, where Dante had dropped it, and folded it. "I saw the scattered packages. New items for your collection?"

"It's not a collection, it's an homage to things past."

"Make sure you don't get buried in it."

Dante waited for the horrible sound of the elevator winching down its shaft, then promptly shed his relaxed demeanor. He shot to his feet and switched off the light. The wall of glass turned brilliant, sketching arabesques on the floor. Beyond the glow of the streetlamps loomed the silhouette of the building across the street. Dante waited for his eyes to become accustomed to the darkness, then pulled the curtains, leaving only a narrow crack, and stuck his head through that. Now he could see a slice of the neighborhood spreading out behind the reflected image of his own face.

The Father was out there, somewhere.

Dante was still his prisoner, and now the cage was as big as the world.

9

While Dante was turning out the light and hoping that a monster would gaze back at him, Colomba had just been dropped off outside her mother's apartment building. She'd called her on the way back, and her mother's tone was so unmistakably wounded at not having received so much as a phone call in the previous two days that Colomba had decided to move up their weekly dinner together.

Alberti looked at her like a dog that's been beaten as he opened the car door for her. "I'm calling in sick tomorrow, Deputy Captain. I really feel wrecked."

"Inform your superior officer."

"*You're* my superior officer."

"Not since I stepped out of the patrol car." *And that's to say nothing of the fact that I kicked a fellow cop in the face*, she thought to herself. "Give my regards to Captain Rovere."

"Well, see you around, Deputy Captain," said Alberti.

Colomba smiled, and Alberti realized what a good-looking face she had. "Be a good boy," she told him. "Otherwise you'll wind up like me."

Colomba's mother lived in an eighteenth-century palazzo right behind Piazza dell'Orologio, in the heart of the historical center. The apartment was a bequest of her husband, who'd died many years before, and he had in turn inherited it from his father, one of the remaining relics of a family with quarters of nobility that had been squandered along with almost the entire family fortune.

Her mother was sixty years old, had the same eyes as Colomba, and was heavily made up, with blue highlights. When she opened the door, she was wearing a pair of jeans and a white polo shirt, as well as a pair of earrings that Colomba had given her for Christmas. She pointed to them after kissing Colomba hello. "Did you see that I wear them?"

"I saw, thanks."

"But you're filthy . . . Have you been out in the fields?"

Colomba unlaced her muddy police boots and took them off, along with her damp socks. Ignoring the slippers her mother was holding out to her, she walked barefoot over the marble floor. Something she'd loved to do ever since she was a girl. "Yes."

Her mother's face lit up. "Have you gone back to work?"

"No, Mamma. I'm still on leave."

Her mother grimaced in disappointment and unsubtly shifted her gaze to the photograph of Colomba taking the oath that hung by the front door. "Do you see how good you looked that day?"

"Young and foolish."

"Don't say such a thing," her mother said in a scandalized voice. She led her to the kitchen, where the table was set for one. "I've already eaten."

Colomba sat down. "Hey, wait . . . if you're going to invite me over for dinner, you could at least eat with me, don't you think?"

"I've been snacking all day, I'm not hungry." She set a glass down in front of Colomba and poured her some wine from the same bottle she'd opened for her the week before. "I got you something from the deli that just opened downstairs. It's really good. Unbelievably expensive but good."

"Thanks."

Her mother served her some veal with tuna-caper sauce from an aluminum tray. A solitary caper bobbed in the watery sauce. Colomba ate in silence, and her mother stood watching her.

"I was just thinking, though, that you look good. You seem to be in good shape, don't you? You're not limping anymore."

"Every so often my knee still hurts me," said Colomba.

"But I can *see* that you're better."

Colomba put down her fork, not actually banging it on the table but almost. "So?"

"So if you run into a colleague, what are they going to think?"

"That I'm a lucky girl. It's not like in the movies, Mamma. If the cops I work with can get out of anything, they do."

"All of them?"

"No, not all of them. But it's a job, it's not a calling." Colomba started eating again. *And*, she added mentally, *if I ever had that calling, I've lost it*. "And most of the time it'll bore you to tears."

"What you do isn't boring."

"If winding up in the hospital is the price you pay for interesting work, then long live boredom."

"Still, you can return to duty whenever you want, can't you?" Her mother said "return to duty" as if she were reading a script from a cop show. "All you have to do is tell them you're better."

"It's a little more complicated than that."

"But you *could*, couldn't you?"

Colomba sighed. "Yes, I could. But I'm not going to."

"And when are you planning to *return to duty*?"

"Never. I'm turning in my resignation."

Colomba had planned to tell her in some more diplomatic way, but it just came out that way. Her mother turned toward the stove, where the greasy paper sack from the deli sat on the cold burner. "Ah."

Colomba knew that the best thing she could do was ignore her, but still she demanded, "Ah *what*, goddamn it? Mamma?"

Her mother turned to look at her again. She had the disappointed expression she saved for special occasions. Like the time when Colomba was fourteen and said she wanted to stop competitive swimming, at sixteen when she'd given up piano lessons, and at twenty-two, that she wanted to take the civil service exam to become a police inspector instead of continuing her doctoral studies. "It's up to you," she said. "If you want to throw away everything you've built so far, I can't stop you. Though your father and I made sacrifices so you could study."

"Look, I finished school, I took my degree. And you didn't even want me to take the police exam. You said, 'That's gross, you'll be putting tickets under windshield wipers!'"

"Then I realized that it's a job you like. I saw you were happy!"

"You saw me in the newspaper. And you thought it was cool."

"And what's wrong with that?"

"What's wrong is that my job almost killed me, Mamma. Does it really not worry you?"

Her mother started tearing up. "How can you say such a thing to me?"

Colomba lost her temper, stuck the dishes into the dishwasher, put her police boots on her bare feet, and left, slamming the door behind her. She walked home with a knot in her stomach and the desire to have some filthy pig try to molest her so she could cut loose on him. She intentionally chose the most dimly lighted alleys, slowing her pace hopefully every time she crossed paths with any human being of the male gender, but the black cloud enveloping her was sufficient to keep them at a distance. When she got home, she was even more frustrated than before and was almost tempted to knock at her downstairs neighbor's door, the neighbor who had once brought back the thong that had fallen off the clothesline (the next day she'd had a dryer delivered) and had stood at her door with X-ray eyes. "I'll bet you look good in it," he'd said. All she'd done at the time was yank it out of his hand and tell him to leave, but she'd have been happy to find herself face-to-face with him now, him and his knowing little grin.

Instead, she found Rovere sitting on the top step.

10

Colomba felt a sequence of impulses: to ignore him and step around him, to grab him by the ankle and yank him down the stairs, to shout into his face. She chose the fourth option and sat down beside him.

"Santini has a bruised chin, and he's out for blood," said Rovere.

"He can file a complaint."

"That wouldn't make him look very good, being beaten up by a woman. It's in his best interests to play it down." He lit a cigarette. "Was he the one who left those marks on your neck?"

Colomba rubbed the place; she'd forgotten all about it. "No. It was a guy on the street under Torre's window."

"Apparently he made a big impression on you."

Colomba didn't reply. "Take the cigarette butt with you after you're done. I don't want the concierge to blame me for it," she said instead.

"Can we talk inside?" Rovere asked.

"No."

"As you like." He opened the briefcase he'd set down on the step below. He pulled out a belt holster and a Beretta that looked like a scale model of the police-issue handgun. A PX4 Compact. Ten bullets in the standard clip, one in the barrel. Easy to conceal.

"You must be joking," said Colomba.

Rovere set the gun down between them, along with two boxes of 9 mm ammunition and a clip. Atop the little pile he laid a brand-new firearm permit. The picture on it was of Colomba, from five years ago. The same picture she'd used to renew her police ID. "Concealed carry license, for personal defense," Rovere explained. "The weapon is registered in your name. I can't give you back your department-issued handgun as long as you're on leave, as you can imagine."

"That would mean until tomorrow. I'm going to bring you my let- ter of resignation."

"You can't give up now."

Colomba slammed her hand down on the railing, which rang like a gong down the stairwell. "If we ever had any chance to weigh in on this investigation, we've pissed it away now. Torre's flipped out!"

"What if he was right?"

Colomba stood up. "As long as it'll let you screw Santini, sir, you're willing to clutch at any straws that come floating past! But sorry, I'm not. Sit right here, and I'll go get you that fucking letter."

Rovere reached out and grabbed her arm. "Torre was telling the truth about the whistle."

"And just how do you know that?"

Rovere opened his briefcase again and pulled out some papers in a clear plastic sleeve. "Today Torre was confronted with the fact that he'd never mentioned the whistle, and he admitted it. Actually, he never talked about it to the investigators, but he *did* say something to a woman who interviewed him for a newspaper. Read it. His one and only interview."

He handed her the plastic sleeve: it held a color Xerox of an article from the newsweekly *Oggi*. The heading bore the date of August 1991. Two years after Dante was freed. There were three pictures of him illustrating the article. He was sitting on a park bench, many years younger and a few pounds heavier. The overambitious goatee and the self-consciously pensive pose, with his good hand propping up his chin and the ravaged hand in his pocket, made him look like a little boy posing as a grown-up. He wore a pair of corduroy trousers, the kind you never see anymore.

The interview barely touched on the topic of his captivity and focused on Dante's new life. His relationship with his father, his return home after so many years . . . The journalist explained that Dante had asked her to meet him in the public park of Piazza Roma in Cremona because he tried to spend as much time as he could outdoors. "I've been locked up indoors for far too long," he'd said, and Colomba wondered if he had already been suffering from claustrophobia or whether the symptoms had manifested later and he was just pretending. The whole thing was sugary and fake. Dante confessed his secret hopes to attend the university after taking the entrance exams as an outside candidate, his yearning to bike along the banks of the Po River to feel free. "I'd like to finish school and apply for the police academy. To keep what happened to me from happening to others" was how the interview ended. And in fact the headline read "The Boy Who Was Held Prisoner in a Grain Silo for Eleven Years Wants to Become a Policeman." There was even a picture of the silo. It was cement, twenty feet tall by fourteen feet in diameter, blackened by the smoke from the fire Bodini had set in the farmhouse before killing himself, and for a moment Colomba imagined herself locked up in it.

Rovere had highlighted in yellow one of the things that Dante had said, the only one in which Colomba glimpsed a bit of the wit that she knew so well. "The police recovered most of my school things. Unfortunately that didn't include a metal whistle that I'd always thought of as my good-luck charm. It turns out I was wrong about that."

Rovere pointed at the line of text. "It seems unlikely that Signor Torre came up with this line just so it would come in handy more than twenty years later."

"All that proves is that he didn't lie about his past, not that he's right about the present. And his kidnapper is dead and buried."

"But what if the investigators before us got it wrong back then? What if Signor Torre has been shouting the truth for years and no one ever believed him?"

"There must be a reason, don't you think?" asked Colomba, pretending to be more confident than she was.

"Can you swear that he didn't put the whistle there?"

"Yes."

Rovere gesticulated with the dead cigarette butt. "Look at the printout attached to the article."

Colomba slipped the sheet of paper out of the paper clip. It was a photo of the piazza next to the highway.

"The men from the VCU are what they are," said Rovere, "but they did check all roads leading away from the scene of the crime. And since they enjoy snapping pictures, this morning they also photographed the pole you found the whistle hanging from."

"That tears it. It wasn't the murderer on the run," Colomba observed.

"The whistle showed up later, you're right about that. But it wasn't the rain that washed away all organic traces, since it didn't rain today."

Colomba eyed him suspiciously. "Sir, you know a lot of things about what De Angelis said today, and I doubt that it was him or Santini who told you. Was it the lieutenant taking down the transcript?"

"An old friend," said Rovere, faintly embarrassed. "In any case, the murderer came back after the VCU came through, and that's when he hung it up."

"At the risk of being seen."

"Maybe he had a good reason."

"Like leaving a signature?"

"Yes, and doing so just a short while before the only person capable of reading it passed right by there."

"But that's insane," murmured Colomba, feeling a chill spread inside her. "Flat-out insane, no two ways about it."

"Certainly. It might be a coincidence. Torre might have finally lost his mind. Or else . . ."

"Or else the kidnapper was still close by," Colomba said softly. "And he recognized him."

"Decide for yourself which version you want to believe."

Colomba grabbed the gun and hurried inside

11

Dante had chosen his ideal observation point. He was sitting on the floor with his back against the front door. From there he could see through the crack he'd left open between the curtains on the central living room window. By moving his head he enjoyed a good view of the surrounding buildings, while no one could see him from outside, protected as he was by the darkness and the shape of the table. He was still in his bathrobe, and his butt was freezing from the cold floor, but he was too enervated to get dressed. The mere thought of getting up to do anything other than watch was enough to send his internal thermometer rocketing to astronomical levels.

Twice now, he had lost awareness of where he was. The first time he'd thought he was back in the silo, the second time in the clinic where he'd met Lodovica.

She'd been his first girlfriend, two years and six months after his liberation. She was in the clinic recovering from amphetamine addiction; he was there at the advice of his father's lawyer after having lost control in a crowded place. Dante found the clinic boring and Switzerland horrible in general. He couldn't know that he'd be in there for the next four years, incapable of going home and just as incapable of choosing a better place to go.

According to her birth certificate, Lodovica was a couple of years younger than him, but her knowledge of the world was immeasurably broader and deeper than his. Dante had spent the days following his liberation researching the present, but the things he'd learned as abstract information, she carried carved into her flesh. A diplomat's daughter, Lodovica had changed city and nation at least ten times before finishing middle school, each time starting over from scratch, establishing friendships, and finding her footing. At age fourteen she'd started taking cocaine occasionally, when her older friends gave it to her, and getting drunk almost every night, discovering that bad girls had a much easier time getting invited to parties. At age fifteen she'd lost her virginity to an ambassador's son her age, the same boy who had taught her how to freebase by putting cocaine in acetone nail polish remover and then putting it in the freezer. At sixteen she'd been hospitalized for a methadone overdose, and after that she started checking into and out of clinics. This was her fourth.

They'd had sex the first time in the rec hall; she'd managed to get her hands on the key. Afterward, Lodovica had caressed his bad hand and had asked him whether the Father had ever molested him sexually. Dante had been so scandalized at the thought that he'd been unable to speak. Nothing of the sort had ever taken place between him and the Father. But to explain what their relationship had been like, to express the love he still felt for him in spite of everything he'd done to him, had been simply impossible, and he'd broken into tears. She'd comforted him, holding his head in her lap, until dawn.

They'd been inseparable for three months. Even after Lodovica was released, she came to see him every day and sometimes stayed overnight to sleep in his bed, tucking her head under the covers and laughing like crazy whenever a nurse went by. Then her father had received a new posting—his government had sent him to some African country—and Lodovica had gone with him. The day she'd left, Dante had had such a bad attack that he'd been unable to leave his room, and he hadn't gone to tell her good-bye. The psychiatrist had talked about psychotic abandonment issues.

Dante now wondered whether Lodovica had continued damaging herself until she finally succeeded in killing herself, or whether instead she'd married some diplomat's son. He hoped for the second option, even if he'd have been faintly disappointed.

Someone rang the doorbell, and Dante froze in the middle of a thought he was unable to retrieve. The doorbell rang once more, and this time it was accompanied by Colomba's voice. "Signor Torre. It's me, Caselli! Open the door, please."

He didn't move. Colomba rang the bell again.

"Signor Torre. If you're all right and can hear me, please say something."

Dante reached up his hand and snapped the lock open, moving as if caught in molasses. A draft pushed the door partway open.

Colomba pushed it lightly. "Signor Torre?" She couldn't see anything past the doorway.

Mechanically, without shifting her gaze, she unholstered her new handgun and held it out straight in front of her with both hands; the pistol felt unfamiliar and too light. With her right index finger, she flipped the safety off; then she extended it parallel with the barrel to prevent accidental discharge. She pushed the door open with one foot. The door came to a halt before it was half open, bumping into something.

That was the last straw for Colomba, already tense well beyond measure. Suddenly the darkness in front of her seethed with shadows and her ears erupted with screams and hisses only she could hear. She began to tremble violently, her lungs clenched tight as a fist, while in her head she kept repeating just one word: *Run!* Instead, she walked through the doorway on unsteady legs and aimed the gun at the shape on the floor that had halted the swinging door. Only then did she realize it was Dante, huddled in his bathrobe.

Colomba felt a burning desire for oxygen, and her legs sagged. She slammed her injured knuckles into the wall, and, as always, the electric shock dissolved the clamp of panic. She heaved a deep breath and coughed, looking at the giant shadow her backlit silhouette with outheld gun cast into the room. "Are you all right, Signor Torre?" she asked in a choking voice.

"Yes," he replied without moving.

"Are you alone?"

"Yes, but come in out of the light." Dante pointed to the window. "He's out there . . ."

Colomba reholstered her gun and, groping at the wall, found the switch to the halogen light. Dante blinked as the stream of light made the phantoms fade away.

Colomba helped him to his feet. The lighted apartment looked to Dante like a faded memory. Colomba snapped her fingers in front of his nose. "Are you with me, Signor Torre?"

"Yes, yes." Dante let himself drop onto the couch. His internal thermometer was dropping to an acceptable level. "I just got lost there for a minute."

"Does that happen often?"

"Not anymore."

Colomba brought him a glass of water, then dragged a chair out of the kitchen area, turned it around, and placed it in front of him, straddling the back rest and placing her chin on her hands. "You think the Father is spying on you."

"He left the whistle for me. That means he knows I'm working on the case."

"Why didn't you say that if you're sure of it?"

"Say it to who? To those two comedians when they were interrogating me?"

"To me."

Dante trotted out a pale imitation of his usual sarcastic grin. "It didn't occur to me."

"Did you mention it to your lawyer at least?"

"He's already too worried." Dante drained the glass and set it down on a stack of travel magazines. "What made you start to have doubts?"

"I saw the VCU report. The whistle wasn't there until a couple of hours before we got there."

"And you think that was more than just a coincidence."

"I don't believe that your kidnapper has come back, Signor Torre. In fact, as of now, I have no reasonable cause to doubt that Maugeri is guilty."

"Then why are you here?"

"Because I'm *unreasonably* afraid I might be wrong. And if I am wrong, then you're in danger."

Dante smiled at her, and it finally looked like his usual smile. "Thanks for coming to my aid. I know how much that must have cost you."

"Only the gas in the tank."

"That's not what I'm talking about."

Colomba eyed him suspiciously. "Then what instead?"

"You're suffering from something that, considering the work you do, is probably post-traumatic stress disorder. Panic attacks, sensory disorientation . . . When you came in I was afraid you were going to shoot me in the face. That would explain why you're not on duty."

"You weren't yourself. And I'm perfectly fine."

"You just scratched your nose, you're lying."

"Cut it out."

"Why? It's interesting to talk about noses. Did you know that the length of your thumb is exactly the same as the length of your nose?"

Colomba resisted the temptation to check. "All right then, can you give me anything that can transform my fear into concrete doubt? Something I can take to the magistrate?"

"Do you know what the Father was trying to tell me with that whistle?"

"He's dead, Torre. And he has been for years."

"He was telling me 'Steer clear of my territory.' And that's exactly what I intend to do."

"Let's just say, ridiculous though it is, that it *was* the Father . . . You can't really know what he's thinking. Do I need to remind you of what you said about his inscrutable mind?"

"What alternative would you suggest?" asked Dante.

Colomba hesitated. She was about to commit herself to something she didn't want to do. But she was already involved, and she knew it. "I can help you to do some digging. You'd have access to all the documentation on your case and on the Maugeri case," she said.

"And what am I supposed to do with that?"

"Prove what you're saying. That the boy wasn't kidnapped by his father, that there are certain commonalities with your own kidnapping. I'll get the material to whoever needs to see it, the boy might have a chance of being rescued, and you'd be safe."

"But what if I can't do it?"

"Then that means that the child was taken and probably killed by Maugeri and there's no one out there who has it in for you. I'll go back to my life, you'll go back to yours."

Dante let himself sink back into his chair. "What happened to you?"

"Excuse me?"

"What is it that makes you worry so much about me and that little boy? We mean nothing to you, but you want to help us, even though it makes no sense."

"Maybe I'm sick and tired of scratching my ass."

Dante narrowed his eyes, and for a second they looked merciless. Predatory. "Or maybe you have sins to expiate. The ones that keep you up at night and take your breath away."

This time Colomba didn't move a muscle. "I sleep fine."

"You're asking me to work with you, yet you keep lying to me about your condition. Does that seem right?"

Against her will, Colomba looked away, and Dante understood that she was ashamed. The same thing used to happen to him.

"If you really want to help me, I need to be able to trust you," Dante continued. "And I need to know the truth. The truth about you. Otherwise I'd just have looked it up on the Internet."

Colomba leapt to her feet, and Dante decided with a stab of regret that she was about to leave and that he'd never see her again. But she was just getting more comfortable. She slipped off her police boots and massaged her icy feet. Dante wondered where she'd left her socks, since she hadn't changed her clothes since that afternoon.

"You wouldn't have found what you were looking for on the Internet. My name was never mentioned. Cop secrets." She turned her gaze back on him. "Let's do this, Signor Torre; when I feel comfortable around you, which is something that may never happen, but one day that I'm in an especially good mood or especially sad, I'll tell you the whole story. But for now, why don't you just settle for the knowledge that I know how to keep my condition at bay."

"Without psychotropic drugs."

"I don't like to put crap into my body. But whatever my mental state, I'll never use my gun unless it's genuinely necessary. And I'll never put you in danger."

"How many people have you shot, CC?"

"CC is an idiotic nickname. And I have no intention of telling you that either. You're going to have to take me as I am."

Dante looked her in the eyes, which now had a vague hazel highlight. And that was what made him say yes. The most rational of men, or at least that's how he liked to think of himself, undone by a woman's eyes. He stood up. "I'll make you an espresso before you go back out into the cold and damp."

Colomba stood up. "I have no intention of going outside. But I'm going to need the coffee because I have work to do. I'm going to have to search your apartment."

Dante blinked. "I must still be out of it. I could have sworn you just said *search*."

Colomba was already looking around. "If there's someone spying on you, they're not doing it with a pair of binoculars. Or not just that way. I'm going to search for microphones and microcameras."

Dante looked uneasily at the lights in the building across the way. "Do you really want to go through my stuff?"

Colomba raised an eyebrow. "You can get rid of anything you don't want me to see."

"Huh? No . . . you don't understand. I don't have anything illegal in my home, except for some medicines I bought on the Internet. It's that I don't want you to mess up my archives." Dante closed his bathrobe, went over to the guest bedroom, and opened the door. "Take a look."

Colomba stopped in the doorway.

The room measured ten feet by thirteen, and it was stacked to the ceiling with cardboard boxes. There was a narrow central aisle that lined up with the window overlooking the courtyard; over the center of the aisle hung a bare bulb that barely illuminated the room.

"The archive of lost time," said Dante.

"I'm sorry?"

"What do you remember about 1984?"

"Right here, right now? Nothing."

"Alphaville hit the Top Ten with their song 'Forever Young.'" He sang the refrain.

"Oh, right," Colomba replied. *The guy's got a voice*, she thought.

"And *Red Dawn* by John Milius came out. It's a great movie. In comparison, the remake is horrible."

Colomba remembered it vaguely. "So?"

"I don't know what it is that makes us who we are, CC."

"Stop calling me CC."

"But at least in part it's our memories, even the ones that seem trivial." Dante opened a box by the door and pulled out a blue plush toy. "Like this one."

Colomba recognized it immediately. "Judge Brainy Smurf."

"They came in the Kinder eggs. In the ones from 1989, to be exact. Did your folks get them for you?"

"Yes. And I'd trade my doubles at school for others I wanted."

"For the whole time the Father held me prisoner, he never gave me sweets. Only what he considered healthy food. He never let me listen to music, he never let me watch a movie. I discovered the existence of Judge Brainy Smurf on eBay, where I bought him for forty euros." He smiled. "According to collectors, I got a bargain."

"You're trying to get back what you lost in the silo," said Colomba, and she was touched. *Poor guy*, she thought. Not even in the toughest high-security prison would you be cut off from the world the way he'd been. The fact that he'd recovered, even if not in full, still struck her as nothing short of miraculous.

Dante nodded. "I started when I realized that sometimes I didn't get the references people my age would make. They'd talk about a movie or go into ecstasies about a song that meant absolutely nothing to me."

"And do you collect everything?"

"No. Just Western pop culture. You can study official history in books, but you have to watch TV shows and you have to play with toys to understand anything about them. And music, too, unless you listen to it, it's worthless to you. Though I've stopped buying CDs now that Spotify exists."

"Half of the things you find, no one even remembers anymore."

"They *think* they don't remember them. How long has it been since you thought back to the Smurfs you used to trade at school?"

"A long time."

"But they came back to you immediately. The way you act, speak, laugh at a joke, or make a decision is influenced by your experience. I couldn't have done my job without my boxes of lost time. Last year I found a bipolar girl who ran away from home because I understood what she meant when she said, 'She went away with Scooby-Doo.'"

"What did she mean?"

"A Volkswagen Type 2 van. A microbus. The members of Mystery, Inc., have one covered with flowers, the Mystery Machine, because they're hippies. Did you know that there's a theory that Scooby is actually just a collective hallucination of his friends, who are all tripping on LSD?"

"There's a theory about everything," said Colomba, uninterested. She pointed at the room. "May I?"

"Absolutely."

Colomba went in, while Dante remained cautiously at the door. She opened a box at random. It contained videocassettes. The first one was of a taped television show. "*Non Stop*?" she read out loud.

"An Italian variety show that was on the air from 1977 to 1979. You can find old movies on TV from time to time, but if you're looking for old programs, you have to go to the broadcasters or to collectors."

Colomba closed the box back up, unconvinced. "You have your whole collection here."

"No, these are just the things I haven't examined yet. The complete collection is in a storage unit, and there's a guy I pay to dust it off once a month. When I die, I'll leave it to a foundation in my name."

They'll just set fire to it, thought Colomba. "Then I'll start here, if that's all right with you. This seems like the hardest part. I promise I won't get things out of order."

Dante nodded. "But if you're going to go through my things, do you mind if we address each other in the informal? I'd find it less embarrassing."

She nodded. "Of course I don't mind."

Dante extended his good hand. "Dante."

She shook it. "Colomba."

"CC."

"Fuck yourself."

He laughed. "I'll make you a first-rate espresso."

For the rest of the night, Colomba opened boxes and drawers, moved furniture, tapped at tiles, dismantled electric plugs and lamps, doing her best to work quietly so she wouldn't wake the neighbors, even though Dante had soundproofed floors and walls. She staggered with exhaustion once or twice, but it was hardly the first time she'd gone the night without sleep, and rummaging through Dante's things was more interesting than a stakeout in a police van, with an eavesdropping headset over her ears.

Dante's archive contained many references to, and memories of, happier times; she even found a bottle of the patchouli perfume she'd worn in high school. Sniffing it, she was amazed to discover how much her tastes had changed.

Dante accompanied her for a couple of hours, singing the praises of this object or annotating that one—for each one he seemed to have a bottomless store of anecdotes—then his voice grew muddled and Colomba found him facedown in the bed on the balcony. She was glad. In the past few days Dante had talked to more people than he had in the past six months, and he needed some rest.

At seven in the morning Dante opened his eyes and saw Colomba emerge from the bathroom with her wet hair in a ponytail and a soup mug in her hands. Her T-shirt stuck to her damp skin. She was done with her work, and she'd taken a shower. "I didn't want to wake you up," she said.

Dante slid over to the edge of the bed, wrapping his naked body in the sheets. He'd forgotten who she was, and for a moment he thought she was his ex-girlfriend. "What's in the mug?"

"Caffè latte."

Dante shuddered. "What kind of coffee did you use?"

"I don't know, just some kind that was lying around."

"I don't have *just some kind of coffee lying around* in here," Dante muttered.

"Take a shower, and then we can talk," she grunted.

"Yes, ma'am." Dante slithered into the bathroom and emerged half an hour later with the occasional drop of water still beading his skin, dressed in a black suit, with a shirt and tie in the same color.

Colomba was waiting for him at the kitchen table, picking at a piece of stale bread. "Do you always dress like an undertaker?" she said grimly.

"More like Johnny Cash, actually."

"Who's that?"

"Never mind. Well?"

"Nothing. I even took the television set apart. Maybe your paranoia is nothing but paranoia."

"Maybe he's listening to what I say with a laser that can detect the vibration of the window panes," said Dante.

"You read too much crap. Anyway, you can't stay here."

Dante sat with his cup in midair. "Are you kidding?"

"This morning I called Rovere. He'll give us anything we ask for, on the current investigation as well."

"What's he gain by putting his career at risk like this? Aside from making the magistrate look like an asshole?"

Colomba hesitated, then shook her head. "Maybe that's worth it to him. Well, where are we moving to?"

"Together, you mean?"

"You don't have a gun. I do. Until I'm sure that your fears are strictly paranoia, I'm going to be glued to you. Believe me, I'm no more thrilled than you are."

"There just might be a place where we can go," he said with a smile. "Let me make a couple of phone calls."

"Which would be where?"

"It's a surprise."

"I hate surprises."

"I can't imagine why, but I expected that."

While Dante went to get the phone and Colomba stretched out for a nap, down in the street a man, unseen, stopped beneath the balcony. He was wearing a raincoat buttoned to the neck, and he was carrying a plastic shopping bag with enough food for a week's balanced diet for a six-year-old boy. A boy who refused to eat and kept crying for his parents. The man in the raincoat knew that the boy would soon become more tractable. That was the way things worked. As long as someone didn't stick their nose into things and ruin it all. The man in the raincoat looked up to the seventh floor. He didn't like what was going on behind Dante's window right now, not one bit.

He was going to have to take care of that.

- V -

BEFORE

Inside the counterfeit Invicta backpack sitting on the floor of the teak and rice-paper coat check booth, there's a pressure cooker that contains roughly two kilos of a mixture of cyclotrimethylenetrinitramine, also known as RDX, and polyisobutylene. It's a very stable compound commonly known as C-4. It can be shaped like Play-Doh, which it closely resembles in terms of its consistency—the color is an opaque white, however—it can be mashed, it can get wet, it can even be burned with relative safety. But it can't be set on fire and compressed at the same time or raised to temperatures greater than 250 degrees centigrade. In that case, it detonates with great power. C-4 is a high-power explosive, very popular with the military. During the Vietnam War, the soldiers used to burn it to keep warm. Or they'd eat it so they'd be sent to the sick bay. It's relatively simple to make, even in a fairly crude laboratory, though the process does present its risks. That's why it's also very popular with terrorists.

At 9:30 p.m. a digital timer, originally part of a Swedish-made hot-water heater, sends an electric impulse from four penlight batteries to a small steel capsule. That's the detonator, and it contains twenty grams of black powder. The detonator goes off, producing the temperature necessary to trigger the bomb. The C-4 explodes, transforming itself instantaneously into a gas that travels at a velocity greater than the speed of sound: to be exact, 8,550 meters per second. The pressure cooker bursts, shattering into fragments and displacing a substantial mass of air, which turns red hot from the velocity.

Shrapnel, fragments of the coat check, cement dust, and scalding air hit the elderly couple sitting at the table by the door. The first to be hit is the man, who is literally lifted into the air. For an instant he assumes the position of a crucified man, his pelvis in contact with the table; then his limbs are torn from their sockets and ripped from his body, while shrapnel, fragments, and dust pass through him.

The shock wave continues until it hits his wife. She still has her head hanging over the table, lost in her gloomy thoughts, and she's shoved into a semifetal position. It's as if she were rolling backward, but with each turn her body loses consistency. It crumbles, so to speak. Fragments of her body, her husband's body, their table, the glasses, and the bottle of Chardonnay, whose content is vaporized, are absorbed into the cloud of fragments. They hurtle into the recently married couple sitting behind the elderly couple.

The young bride is the first to be hit. Her left eye socket is traversed by her elderly neighbor's dessert spoon, while her body hurtles over the table and hits her husband, who starts to slide backward while still seated in his chair, as the menu in his hands starts to catch fire. But the flames haven't yet caught when the shock wave and the fruit cocktail of fragments hit the microcomponents manager and his novel. The bones of the older woman's ulna and humerus pierce his chest and skull like javelins. He falls backward, grazing with what remains of the back of his head the feet of the young husband, who's continuing his backward slide across the room.

The shock wave expands to the group of Japanese businessmen and the maître d'. The kinetic energy is uneven; there are differences of pressure and direction due to obstacles encountered and air resistance. Therefore, the five men are not simply lifted but dragged in many directions at the same time, as if they'd been sentenced to death by being tied to horses and drawn and quartered. Three of the Japanese lose their upper limbs. The back of the fourth businessman is ripped open from shoulder blades to tailbone, stripping the spinal cord bare. The maître d', partly protected by the four Japanese businessmen but taller than they, is hit in the back of the head by a chunk of cement the size of a bar of hotel soap. The chunk of cement passes through bones and soft tissue and shoots out of his mouth. The maître d' falls forward, while the shock wave, the fragments, and the shrapnel all reach the windows and shatter them. Part of the blast disperses into the outside air, but not enough. Shrapnel, fragments, and red-hot dust continue hurtling through the room.

They machine-gun the waiter who's waiting for the deejay to make his wisecrack. They perforate his back, reducing heart, lungs, liver, and intestine to mush; they exit from his body and riddle the face of the agent, who's still trying to remember the name of that movie he has on the tip of his tongue; they hit the deejay and his besotted friend, smashing them both into a load-bearing column. The deejay's left hand and the girl's right hand, still intertwined, are torn off and sail all the way to the four Albanian models and their chaperone, arriving just before a hail of chunks of reinforced concrete. A flaming piece of the coat check room, about a foot and a half long, lodges in the spinal cord of one of the girls, just above a tattoo of two butterflies kissing, and exiting through the belly button. The shock wave knocks down the group like tenpins, and the five of them slide across the dining room floor, burning from the friction. The chaperone's sternum snaps inward, crushing the muscle of his heart.

While the deejay's head bends farther and farther back, snapping his cervical vertebrae, the young husband passes through what is left of a window. He starts to tumble to the street below at the same instant that one of the models, the one who was about to go snort another line of coke, impacts another load-bearing column, shattering her pelvis. The surface of the table where she and the others were sitting has now lifted into the air. It flies like a sixty-five-pound frisbee.

The shock waves keep spreading. While part of them are hitting the dining room, another part is wedging into the staircase. High-pressure air is shrieking like a train in a tunnel, growing scorching hot. It uproots a section of handrail, rips the plaster off the walls, and thunders down to the floor below. A bartender winds up on the floor, legs in the air, while the shaking of the walls, comparable to a magnitude 5 earthquake, knocks shelves and bottles to the floor, shatters the glass display cases holding the pastries, and knocks the espresso machine off the counter and onto the bartender, leaving her with six broken ribs and a fractured vertebra. The shock wave expands toward the boutique. The ceiling in one of the bathrooms collapses, taking down with it all the electrical wiring and cutting the power to the bottom floor. Mannequins and chests of drawers tumble over. The plate-glass shop windows of the bar and the boutique explode outward, covering the parked and standing cars in the street with shards of glass. It is atop one of those cars, a Smart car, parked illegally with the running lights on—the owner is enjoying an aperitif just a short distance away—that the young husband ends his long trajectory. He slams into the car's roof with the upper part of his body. At the moment of impact, his face is almost entirely devoid of nose, lips, and eyelids.

The table that's been sailing along like a Frisbee also ends its flight. It's heavy, and before it's gone more than a few yards it's lost most of its initial momentum. All that would be needed is for it to glance off one of the columns or for a new funnel of hot air to shove it off course and render it harmless. But this isn't a day for miracles, and the Frisbee continues along its trajectory unhampered. The woman with the penetrating gaze really doesn't see it at all, though afterward she'll feel sure that she at least sensed it, the shadow of a hurtling object wobbling out of the corner of her eye. The table lands flat on her, pinning her to the floor, knocking her senseless and breathless.

Three seconds have passed since the explosion. The roar echoes off the facades of the buildings all the way to the piazza, where it startles the pigeons.

Then the screaming starts.

- VI -

HOUSE CALLS

1

The Hotel Impero was a potpourri of modern, vaguely Japanese design and ecocompatible architecture, with tiny waterfalls in the hallways and grass growing on the fifteenth-story roof. It had been built into an early-nineteenth-century office building on a small cross street of Via del Corso, the central Roman shopping street, just a short walk from the Ara Pacis, or Altar of Peace. The bar was a transparent veranda located to one side of the interior garden, which also featured a Japanese touch in the path of white Zen river stones.

Colomba walked through the marble-clad lobby feeling decidedly out of place with her backpack and her jeans. When she was on duty, she used her police ID to get in everywhere, but as a civilian she faced a certain uneasiness in her social interactions. She should have paid closer attention when her mother was trying to teach her how a well-behaved young lady was supposed to act.

"There should be a room in the name of Signor Torre," she said to one of the two concierges working at the reception desk, as a harem's worth of women in chadors escorted by two bearded bodyguards went streaming past her.

The concierge typed into his computer, and his smile broadened. "Of course, madame. The manager will join you immediately to see you to your suite."

Colomba pretended that nothing had happened, but thought to herself: *Suite?* She pulled her ID out of her wallet, as required by law, but the clerk waved his hand in mock horror.

"There's no need. If you'd care to make yourself comfortable . . ."

"I'll be in the garden."

"Very good, madame. Can I have a drink brought out?"

"No, thanks. I'm fine."

She went out, still somewhat dazed, and joined Dante at one of the little tables scattered under the dwarf palms and the oleanders;

he was smoking a cigarette and sizing up a heavily retouched blonde at the neighboring table. He'd stuffed himself with Xanax to deal with the stress of moving house, and his eyes were at half-staff. "Hey, listen, just how rich are you?" she asked him.

"If you turn me upside down and shake me, you won't get a cent. I live from one consulting job to the next."

"Bullshit. Unless you have an American Express Centurion card, they won't even let you rummage through the Dumpster in this place."

"Do you remember when I told you about the girl who disappeared with Scooby-Doo's van?"

"I'm not suffering from senile dementia."

"It was the owner's daughter, and I agreed to take my payment out in trade. Now all I have to do is pick up the phone and I can have a suite, even if they're overbooked. No charge."

"And what good is it to you if you never leave your apartment?"

"It impresses girls."

"Like the blonde right behind me? Even a Centurion card wouldn't get you anywhere with her."

"Let me dream."

The manager came to their table and practically bowed at their feet, while two porters loaded Dante's matched set of suitcases onto a luggage cart, along with Colomba's backpack, and then vanished in the direction of the freight elevator. The two of them, in contrast, were accompanied to the top floor in the glass elevator that rose from the center of the lobby. It was transparent from floor to ceiling, and it moved so slowly that Dante agreed to take it, even though he couldn't conceal a hint of unease. "The only elevator I've taken in the past ten years," he said with a foolish grin.

Colomba took advantage of the slow ascent to study the security situation beneath her. She identified at least four members of the hotel security staff in the lobby, dressed in dark suits, with earpieces and the broad shoulders of ex-military. Given the rank of the clientele, she assumed they'd be efficient and accustomed to noticing any anomalies. It was no accident that they'd all zeroed in on her when she entered the hotel. If she hadn't kept her handgun in her pocketbook—it was too hot that day for a jacket—they'd have certainly spotted it.

The elevator stopped across from the door to the suite, which the manager opened, stopping short at the threshold. "Signor Torre is very familiar with our hotel, so I'll spare you the guided tour. If there's anything you need, please don't hesitate to call me," he said.

Colomba tried to hand him her ID; the manager pretended not to see it and stepped back into the elevator with a smile.

Colomba put her ID away, once again embarrassed. "Why don't they want my ID?" she asked Dante. "It's the law in this country, a hotel guest has to show ID and the hotel is required to register it."

"I'm already registered, and my guests have a right to their privacy. It's a side benefit."

"It's against the law."

"What a pain in the ass you are, *mamma mia*!"

"The next time you see him, tell him that I'm not one of your girl-friends."

The suite was divided into two bedrooms, each with a truly sybaritic bathroom, and a large living room with a fireplace; before five minutes were up, two maintenance men came in to install a café-quality espresso machine and an electric coffee grinder.

"Let me guess," said Colomba. "Another side benefit."

"Well done."

"Is there someone to wash your back in the shower?"

Dante displayed his sarcastic grin. "Only upon request."

Dante assigned Colomba the smaller bedroom—so to speak; after all, it was half the size of her whole apartment—and kept the big room for himself, but he explained that the reason he was doing it was that it had so many more windows, as well as a terrace with a Jacuzzi and a sauna. "Where I'll sleep."

"Aren't you going to use the round bed in the room?" asked Colomba, who'd only ever seen anything like it in movies.

"Not to sleep on . . ." he winked. "If you get what I mean."

Colomba snorted. "No, I don't." She checked the view from the terrace: it overlooked the rear garden, and there were no other buildings nearby. Of course, she couldn't be one hundred percent certain, but considering Dante's needs, it was either this or they'd have to move into the open countryside. "Pull the curtains when you go to sleep, okay?" she said. "And keep the light turned off in the bedroom, otherwise your silhouette will be visible."

"Are you worried about snipers?" he asked, uncertain whether or not to kid around.

"I'm not worried about anything, you just do it."

"Yes, Mamma."

Colomba went to put away her things. The bed was a standard bed-shaped rectangle, but it was a king, covered with a fluffy white quilt. On one wall was a plasma-screen television set, and on the other was a burnished metal armoire and a set of shelves. She wondered, for the hundredth time that day, whether it even made sense to move someone with a few screws loose on the basis of such a vague threat or if she'd been infected with his paranoia. She hoped she'd be able to figure that out soon, before she got tangled up in an even bigger mess. She put her change of clothes in the dresser drawers and her shoes in the bathroom, then returned to the living room.

Dante noticed that she'd clipped her holster back onto her belt but said nothing. He was extracting his bags of whole-bean coffee from his suitcases, placing them in alphabetical order on the bar counter behind the espresso machine. Blue Mountain, Mérida, Vintage Colombian . . . The aroma of roasted coffee was spreading through the room. "There's a magnificent heated pool right above us and, just think, with a transparent roof. We could take a swim and drink an aperitif up there," he said.

"I have an even better idea. Let's get to work."

Dante sighed. "You really just don't like to enjoy life, do you?"

Alberti had been standing by, and less than half an hour later he delivered two large boxes of documents in the lobby; Colomba went downstairs to take delivery. Alberti was in plain clothes.

"You used your own car, didn't you?"

"Actually, I don't own a car. I borrowed one from a friend."

"That's just as good."

The swelling had gone down, and his nose looked almost normal, even if it was clear that it would never be the same. It didn't look bad though, thought Colomba. It made him look a little more grown up.

He gave her a hand carrying the boxes up to the floor and looked around the suite with unguarded curiosity. "Do you really live here now, Deputy Captain?"

"Only for a few days. And I'm not paying for it," she replied, shutting the door in his face with a hint of sadistic glee.

"Santa Claus came early!" Dante exclaimed as he looked at the file boxes. "Why on earth don't you archive things in digital versions?"

"Nearly everything on the Maugeri case is digital," said Colomba as she opened the box. "But your case is still for the most part on paper. We don't have the money to digitize old stuff."

"I'm not 'old stuff,'" he said, sounding offended.

Colomba tossed him a couple of folders. "Just be grateful that Rovere managed to lay his hands on this."

"Where do we start?" asked Dante, leafing through one. It was the report from one of the detectives who had worked on his case.

"With you. You're what I know least about."

"I'll make an espresso."

Colomba and Dante drank a great many espressos as they pored over the documents and discussed them for almost twenty-four hours straight. They ate in the hotel suite and stopped working only to sleep, as Dante's bedroom, strictly off limits to the housekeepers, was gradually buried in a uniform layer of papers and photos. If she wanted to move, Colomba had to slalom between the piles of paper and the empty coffee cups, but most of the time she just lay back on the Le Corbusier chaise longue asking Dante questions about his story. And he told her everything, with great precision, for the first time since he had been liberated.

Dante had been imprisoned in a grain silo in the courtyard of a farmhouse that belonged to Antonio Bodini, a retired army corporal. Bodini had inherited the property from his late parents. The silo in question was one of two that Bodini's father used to store wheat, but before he died he'd sold most of his farmland—now worked by a neighboring commercial farming operation—and since then they had stood empty, at least officially. For the eleven years Dante had been held a prisoner, Bodini had gone on with his life, tending his garden, feeding roosters and hens, and withdrawing his monthly pension at the local post office. In town everyone remembered him as a shy, taciturn man, too rustic to have a family, who might have a brief conversation about the weather if he was buying groceries but who always drank alone at the bar. On summer evenings he could be seen sitting at the table outside his home in tattered pants and a tank top. The discovery of who he really was and what he had done had upset everyone in the town and surrounding areas, and from then on he had been referred to "the nutcase." His grave had been defiled twice, and then he was disinterred and cremated, and his bones had been placed in a common ossuary. The motive for what he had done was accepted by investigators and expert witnesses to be a simple one: the thwarted desire to have a family, metastasized into madness.

"The problem is: he wasn't the Father," said Dante.

Colomba leafed through the documents. "His were the only fingerprints, the property belonged to him, and no one ever saw him with anyone else."

"What kind of accent do I have?" asked Dante.

"Accent?" Colomba concentrated. "Vaguely northern, except when you use expressions in Roman dialect. But a faint one, anyway."

"That's the way it was when I left the silo, aside from the Roman dialect."

"So what?"

"Bodini had finished fifth grade, and he almost always spoke in Cremonese dialect. He can't have been the one who educated me."

Because during his imprisonment, the kidnapper had taught Dante to read, write, and do basic arithmetic with old textbooks. The police had found several of them and had learned that they were editions from the early sixties, most likely purchased at used-book stalls. The education imparted by the Father had been, to say the least, bizarre.

"Sometimes he'd have me learn long passages by heart, passages taken from books I'd never see," Dante recalled. "He'd bring me the pages and leave them for me overnight. If I made a mistake the next day, he'd deny me food and water, or else . . ." He raised his bad hand. The Father forced him to strike it with a wooden club or a knife. That was the part of the body designated to receive punishment. Dante had learned by heart passages from the most respected Italian poets and authors, up to the nineteenth century, and he could still recite them, letter perfect.

For some of them, he'd never read the whole works. The Father had had a fixation with Cremona. Dante had been forced to learn the names of streets on a map like the back of his hand, and one of the Father's favorite mnemonic games involved showing him fragments of pictures of monuments and buildings for him to identify. According to the experts who'd examined Dante after his liberation, the things he had been taught were designed for one purpose only: to exercise dominion over him.

"Maybe Bodini was a self-taught man who concealed his vast culture from the world."

"That's what your colleagues tried to tell me. But it's not credible."

"And then his were the only fingerprints on the books. And also his DNA," said Colomba as she read. "Here I see that they did some tests on samples at the end of the nineties. Did you request them?"

"Yes. When I was rescued, there was no such thing. I had to pay for them myself, and nothing came of them."

"But you're certain that the Father and Bodini weren't the same person."

"Bodini just rented him the fun house. I'm certain of it. Among other things, because I saw his face, and he wasn't Bodini."

Colomba made herself more comfortable on the chaise longue. It was the evening of their second day of research: they hadn't found a thing to support Dante's theory, but she also hadn't been able to poke any evident holes in his account. He was lucid and displayed a steel-trap memory of the details of everything that had happened to him. And that wasn't all; he had an almost perfect recollection of everything.

"Tell me about it," she said.

"It's all written down."

"Not everything. And you know it."

Dante shrugged his shoulders, feigning indifference. "As you wish. There was a crack in the cement wall of the silo. It was small, and it was concealed by the loft where I slept. I peeped out of it when I was certain that the Father couldn't detect anything, and still, even then . . ." He shook his head. "I was always certain that he was watching me."

"What could you see?" asked Colomba.

"A portion of the field and the other silo. It was identical to mine, but I thought it was empty."

"But it wasn't, according to your testimony."

"Which remained uncorroborated, sadly. The silos each had a door, on the opposite sides. They seemed normal, but either the Father or Bodini had soundproofed them. At least, mine had been; from outside no one could hear even if I pounded on it. Which I stopped doing after the first week."

"Which meant you couldn't hear what was going on outside either."

"Not much. The rumbling of the trucks as they went by on the county road, the sirens of ambulances going by, thunderstorms . . . occasionally birds. On the other hand, all the noises inside were amplified. It was as if they rose up to the ceiling and then plummeted down onto my head." Dante shuddered. "You know what seems incredible?"

Colomba shook her head, uncertain she could rely on her voice.

"That I survived it. Fuck, you can get used to anything."

Dante went out onto the balcony to smoke a cigarette. The floor was littered with stubbed-out butts. He came back in after ten minutes, to all appearances calm again.

"I think that the Father entered and exited the other silo, using the little door on the far, hidden side, at least starting from when I started to watch through the crack. And maybe he did it in the dark, because I never managed to see him coming from that side. But the last day I did. He was holding a boy my age by the hand."

Colomba knew this. It had been the most controversial part of Dante's testimony immediately after he was freed. When she'd read it, she'd found it unbelievable, but hearing it in Dante's voice, live, gave her the opposite impression.

"That was the time you saw his face."

"His age was somewhere between thirty and forty, short hair, very light blue eyes. Hollow-cheeked. I tried to work up a composite sketch, but it turned out too generic. It was dark. And I was upset."

Colomba looked at it: the face of the man Dante had seen was barely sketched out. Except for the hard eyes. "The face of God . . . to quote your words."

"Until that moment, he'd always worn a wool ski mask with a military-style cap stitched to it and sunglasses." According to Dante, he'd worn five caps during the time of his imprisonment, all of them identical. "While the boy . . . I saw even less of him . . . it was like . . . looking at a planet against the light of a star . . . He seemed tall and skinny, more than the Father, who was of average height, and my same age. Shoulder-length hair like mine. There's one thing I'm sure of, though. He was laughing or crying. Or both at the same time, because he kept making these strange, high-pitched noises."

Colomba took a look at the identikit of the kid, too, and found it just as elusive. It could have been any kid the age that Dante was at the time. "Couldn't it have been a couple of visitors? Father and son going on a picnic?"

Dante shook his head. "Oh, no."

"Then what happened?"

"The Father led the boy out along the field. He went past my silo. I had a limited line of sight, even when I squeezed my eye against the wall. It was a crack just half an inch wide, for fuck's sake . . . And as they were about to vanish from my field of view, I saw the Father's other hand, the one he was holding behind his back. It held a knife. Now that I know something about these things, I think it was a carving knife."

"You said that you're convinced that the boy was killed. Did you witness the killing in any way? Did you hear screams?"

"No. I know they never found a corpse or any traces of blood, but I have little doubt about what the Father did to him."

"That must have been a shock for you."

"Shock doesn't begin to give the idea. For the first time in eleven years I was seeing the Father's face and another human being. Then, after a few minutes, I saw the Father again. He was alone, and he was coming toward my silo."

"And did he have the knife?" asked Colomba.

"Yes. I heard him opening the door. He didn't expect any reaction from me. I had never reacted in recent years. Instead, I hit him with the bucket of excrement and I ran. I didn't know exactly what to do."

"What pushed you to take action? Were you afraid?"

Dante smiled sadly, a different smile from the usual sarcastic grin. "No," he said softly. "I ran away because he'd betrayed me. I thought I was the only one."

2

Dante went out onto the balcony to smoke a cigarette, and Colomba had an urge to do the same thing, even though she hadn't smoked since her first year of university. She felt as if she were walking into the most intimate, delicate part of Dante wearing her heavy boots, the part that he'd learned over the years to screen off from the rest of the world. With the work she did, she'd interviewed and listened to hundreds of victims, suspects, and criminals, but rarely had it hit so hard. Perhaps because Dante's story was anything but common, or maybe because she was starting to like him.

When Dante came back in, he nonchalantly went on with his story. "I didn't turn around to see how he was, I just ran as fast as I could, and I came very close to breaking my neck climbing down the ladder. I didn't know how to do it, except in very theoretical terms. Like so many other things you can't do in a silo."

"Like riding a bike," said Colomba, trying to lighten the mood.

"Like riding a bike." He smiled. "Or even just running."

Somehow he'd managed to do it, though, and barefoot, too, because he'd made it to the county road, where a car had hit him. Luckily the driver had picked him up off the road and taken him to the hospital without waiting for an ambulance. At the hospital, Dante had managed to tell them who he was and persuaded them to believe him.

By the time the police got to the silo, Bodini had already shot himself in the mouth with a military handgun he'd kept without ever registering it, after soaking the farmhouse and silos with kerosene and setting everything on fire. The masonry silos had survived the flames, though it was difficult for the forensic squad to obtain much usable evidence afterward, but the farmhouse had burned to the ground. They had never found a trace of the other man Dante had described, much less of the boy. No blood, no corpse, no personal effects or clothing. The most broadly accepted theory was that Dante had dreamed it, like a sort of projection of himself, and no matter how much he disputed that version, it had done nothing to make the investigators change their minds.

"If he really existed, how can you be sure he was in the other silo?" asked Colomba. "Maybe he kept him in the farmhouse."

"For two reasons. The first is that he set fire to the other silo, too. If he wasn't using it as a prison, what reason did he have?"

"Maybe he used it for other purposes. He kept things in it, I don't know. Or he simply went around the bend."

"Maybe, but I don't think it was Bodini who did it. It was the Father. He murdered his accomplice, erased all traces of himself, and disappeared."

"Then why didn't he leave the corpse of the second boy?"

"Because it would have led back to him, somehow, I think . . . I don't remember his face, but I remember how he moved. With small steps, astonished and frightened by everything around him. As if he were unaccustomed to being out in the open air. I moved the same way at first, when I was freed from my imprisonment."

"Except for when you ran away."

"I remember only the headlights of the car that hit me."

Colomba reflected for a few moments. "Then the boy had been a prisoner as long as you, or almost."

"I've never been able to identify him, even though they showed me dozens of photographs. Back then, there was no Internet to send out alerts on missing persons, and there was no coordinated database shared by all the attorney generals' offices. Probably more reports than we can guess were simply lost. For a while I continued trying to find out about him; then I just gave up."

"You're not at fault as far as that goes. If anything, the blame's on us," Colomba admitted, looking at the clock. It was 10 p.m. She was starting to get hungry.

"Now you know everything there is to know," said Dante.

"You're wrong about that. All I know is your version. Then there are the investigations and interviews that my colleagues and the magistrates did. I've read through them, but I ought to study them in depth."

"I've already done it. You want to know what I got for my trouble?" Dante stood up and walked over to the plastic whiteboard that they'd hung on the wall and covered with Post-its. He took one off and wrote ZERO with the dry-erase marker. "Everything they found always pointed in the same direction. Just one kidnapper, namely Bodini, no stranger, no other boy."

"Is it possible that there was never any kind of check on the farm-house during the whole time of your imprisonment? Local constables, health office . . ."

"More than once, and Bodini was always there. No one ever thought of searching the silos, even when they thought I'd been kid-napped. The only piece of evidence that sticks out from the rest is the testimony of a guy who lived in another farmhouse, about a half a mile from Bodini's. He said that he would often see the headlights of a car stopping not far from Bodini's farmhouse, but he'd always just assumed that it was young couples using the road as a lover's lane."

"Maybe they were."

"If you believe that, then we're wasting our time."

"Dante, I've already told you. I'm looking for evidence, just a sin-gle shred, proving there is a link between you and the Maugeris' son."

"The whistle."

"Aside from that. We've already talked about it." Colomba opened one of the files she'd fallen asleep reading the night before. It included a list, in some cases with distinguishing features, of the people ques-tioned after Dante's escape or who were suspects in some manner. "The district attorney's office questioned thirty people in the search for a potential accomplice."

"Your colleagues pulled a few sexual offenders and common crimi-nals out of the hat, but they didn't find a thing on any of them."

"And what do you think about it?"

"I dismiss them all. The Father held me prisoner for eleven years, without a break, and I saw him at least once every three days. All of the people they brought to me had served periods of time in prison or in the hospital, which made such a long period of continuity impossible."

"And you are absolutely certain that the Father and Bodini didn't stand in for each other?"

"I was positive then, and I'm even more so now. And none of the suspects they showed me had the right build. He disguised his voice, speaking in a low voice, but he couldn't hide his physique. You've gotten to know me a little . . . do you think I dreamed that man and that boy?"

"I want to be honest with you, Dante. I can't say."

Dante let himself sprawl out. "If you have to choose between kindness and honesty, always go for the latter when you're dealing with me. Above all, no pity."

"That's good, because there are lots of people out there who think I'm not capable of it. Tell me the other points of contact that come to mind for you."

"The age of the Maugeris' son."

"Okay."

"And my father was accused of having done it, exactly like Maugeri."

"But your father wasn't accused of killing your mother. She killed herself."

"He killed with a bladed weapon, just like he did with the boy in the other silo."

"Most family murders are committed with bladed weapons or blunt objects. Not everyone in Italy has a firearm in their home."

"There are no traces of the boy. Not one," said Dante.

"Aside from the blood in Maugeri's trunk."

"The Father put that there."

"In other words, the Father is a ninja. He deflects attention from himself, lands his blows on whoever he aims at, and can never be caught."

"Exactly."

"Then what are the odds we can succeed against someone who doesn't make mistakes?"

"He made at least one. I managed to escape, anyway." Dante yawned and stretched. "I'm hungry, and I'm sick and tired of this. What do you say we have a proper meal for once?"

"Should I put on my evening gown?"

"Do you have one?"

"Do you really want me to answer that?"

They ate dinner at the hotel bar—the restaurant was too confining for Dante—where a table had been set up for them behind a privacy screen.

Colomba was embarrassed by the white-gloved waiters. Not that she'd only ever eaten in diners and grills her whole life, but she'd never risen to the level of a waiter standing right behind her the whole time.

"Enjoy life a little for once, CC," Dante told her. For the occasion, he'd put on a charcoal gray tie and a black Giorgio Armani suit.

"I don't feel comfortable here."

"Pretend you're on vacation."

She smiled. "Then I wouldn't be here with you."

"Thanks. Anyway, it's better than the police cafeteria."

"With the work I did, I was always out and about, and I just grabbed something to eat where I found it. If I ate at all." Dante had nothing on his dish but vegetables. "Are you a vegetarian?"

Dante smiled. "I've spent far too many years in a cage myself not to feel horror at the way livestock is bred."

"Human beings have always eaten meat, and I don't have problems with the fact," said Colomba, spearing another chunk of her tourne-dos Rossini.

"As far as that goes, human beings have always abused their fellow man. Luckily, our intellect allows us to make choices. And I'm protecting myself from colon cancer."

"But not from lung cancer, the way you smoke."

"You have to die of something."

"Why are you so comfortable with luxury?"

"For a while I was reasonably well off," Dante replied. "My father sued everyone and their brother when he was finally able to prove that he hadn't murdered me. He won every case, and he was also reimbursed for wrongful imprisonment by the state, as well as for what happened to him in prison."

"He got sick?"

"He was raped and stabbed."

Colomba suddenly lost interest in her food. "Oh, fuck."

"That's what happens to child molesters. He was in the high secu-rity wing of the prison, but there was a foul-up while he was on his way to a meeting . . . My father is convinced that the whole thing was organized by one of the officers who hated him, but he was never able to prove it. Still, he survived."

"How old is he now?"

"He'll turn seventy this year. We don't talk much. We were never really able to reestablish a relationship after I got back. We were a couple of strangers, and strangers we've remained, though we try to be kind to each other. I think he blames me for having ruined his life. In his way, he has a point." Dante pushed the plate away, and a waiter hurried over to take it away. He hadn't eaten much at all. "When I became an adult, he gave me some money, mostly, I think, to get me out from underfoot. For a while I didn't need to work. I traveled. When I wasn't checked into some clinic, I wanted to enjoy myself."

"Five stars, like this one?"

"Even better, and lots of airy staterooms aboard ocean liners, since the idea of boarding a plane makes me feel like dying." Dante smiled. "I've never been able to hold on to money. And when I was broke, I had to come up with a line of work."

"You didn't pick an easy one."

"I didn't go to college, and I can't work indoors. It was this or become a lifeguard."

The waiter asked if they'd like some coffee. Dante said no for both of them; then they went out into the garden, where smoking was allowed. The trees were illuminated by hidden lights, and the loudspeakers played music at a low volume. The tables were occupied by a clientele that Colomba decided was for the most part non-Italian. They found two armchairs half-hidden behind the bushes and sat down. Dante ordered two Moscow Mules, his favorite cocktail: vodka, ginger ale, lime, and a slice of cucumber. They came in copper mugs full of crushed ice, and with two straws. Colomba took just one sip and found it vaguely acid but refreshing.

"Well, CC?" asked Dante. "Are you throwing in the towel?"

"No. But enough of the past for now. Let's focus on the Maugeri kidnapping. That's a fresh trail, unlike yours, which is ancient history."

"We'll be looking for other points of contact."

"All I need is a snag, Dante. Something that tells me Maugeri didn't murder his wife. At that point . . . whether it's your old kidnapper or some copycat, I'll at least know that we aren't just making it all up. Of course, if they find the child in the meantime, we can all go home."

"That's not going to happen, CC." Dante slurped the last of his glass, then poked his straws into Colomba's. "Since you're not going to finish it . . ."

"Anything that surfaces about the Maugeris will be sent to me in real time by Rovere. We'll line it up with what we already know."

"And what's in it for him that's worth risking his career over? Aside from making De Angelis come off like an ass?"

"I have no idea."

Dante lit yet another cigarette. "I read the transcripts of the first interviews. There's nothing that can be helpful to us. Friends and relatives were asked only whether Maugeri confided in them and whether they know where the child might be."

"Let's just imagine it's neither the Father nor some copycat. That it's a normal kidnapping . . ."

Dante raised an eyebrow. "Normal?"

"One of the kind you've worked on in the past. What would you do at this point?"

"I'd try to find the answer that's been buzzing in my mind ever since I took that walk up at the mountain meadows."

"What question is that?"

"Why did Maugeri's wife go up onto Monte Cavo with the boy? She did it of her own free will; no one forced her to go up there. The kidnapper made an appointment, and she went, leaving her cell phone behind and waiting for her husband to fall asleep. Why? What convinced her?"

"Extortion? Some physical threat?"

"Or else a lover who offered to help her run away from a violent and abusive husband. Or a friend whose shoulder she was crying on. In any case, she must have confided in someone. Even if she did it in a hushed voice."

"You've read the witness list. Who's the most likely candidate?"

Dante stubbed out his cigarette butt and waved to the waiter to bring him another cocktail. "Sisters always know everything."

3

Colomba called Giulia Balestri at breakfast the next day, after getting Rovere's okay. She tried to seem official without making any specific claims, to avoid giving De Angelis any pretexts. "I've been working on your sister's case, and there are a couple of things I'd like to clear up with you," she said.

"Are there any new developments?"

"I'm afraid not. When can we meet?"

"Come before lunch, if you don't mind."

"Thank you."

Colomba hung up, feeling sorry for the woman, who over the phone had sounded like someone who expects only bad news.

Outside the door she found a stack of newspapers, and she read half of them while listening to the radio, until Dante emerged from his bedroom in a coal black dressing gown, with a cadaverous face. "Are you done making a ruckus? It's practically dawn," he said.

"It's ten in the morning. Get moving."

Dante looked with austere disapproval at her cup of caffe latte. "Did you know that milk in coffee produces an indigestible formation of casein?"

"That's exactly what I wanted to hear . . . I called Giulia Balestri."

"Who?"

"The dead woman's sister."

"Ah."

"She's expecting us."

Dante slithered over to the espresso machine before answering. "She's expecting *you*. I don't know how to do cop work. No offense."

"I'll do the cop work. You'll stand by and watch and give me intelligent suggestions."

Dante started two espressos at the same time. "CC . . . that's not my line of work. I'm not good with people."

"You're good at observing them."

"From a distance. Emotional displays make me uncomfortable."

"Poor boy."

"You can't force me."

Colomba smiled and said nothing. Dante went to get dressed.

An hour later, Giulia Balestri opened the door in response to Colomba's ring. "I'm Deputy Captain Caselli. I called you earlier."

Balestri nodded. She was thirty-six, she wore Rasta hair extensions, and she had a rotund body. She was wearing a lounging suit and slippers. "Take a chair."

"If you can come downstairs, a colleague of mine, Signor Torre, would like to meet you."

"Why don't you ask him up?"

"It's a long story. Please."

"All right." Balestri went to put on a pair of shoes.

Colomba peered around at the cheaply furnished apartment, with a small boy's toys scattered everywhere. Outside the bathroom were a pair of men's flip-flops with a tropical pattern. *A happy little family*, she thought.

"We'll have to hurry, because in an hour I need to go pick up the boy at school," said Balestri, as if she'd just read her mind. She'd put on a lemon yellow cardigan.

"How old is your son?" Colomba asked and regretted it instantly; that was none of her business.

"Seven and a half, a year older than Luca." Her face twisted anxiously. "There really is no news?"

"No, I'm sorry."

The other woman tried to read Colomba's expression: unsuccessfully. "He's dead, isn't he?"

"Signora . . . we really don't know. It's better just to hope for the best."

"But how can he still be alive? With no one to feed him . . ."

"Maybe someone's taking care of him, signora."

"A friend of that son of a bitch of a brother-in-law of mine?"

Colomba said nothing. Downstairs, at the front door, they found Dante, who was waiting for them with a grim expression, leaning against the wall and smoking a cigarette.

"This is Signor Torre," said Colomba.

"My condolences," he muttered without looking Giulia in the face.

Giulia saw that Dante's left hand was covered with a heavy black glove. "What do you want to ask me? I've already said everything I know."

"There are details, private ones, we'd like to ask you about."

"About my sister? Like what?"

"Like whether she had a lover," Dante muttered again.

Giulia felt the anger rise. "How dare you?"

"Dante, what the fuck!" Colomba snapped.

"You were the one who insisted on me coming."

Colomba rolled her eyes. "Signora, forgive my partner's lack of tact, but . . . I need you to answer the question."

Giulia crossed her arms. "My sister had nothing to do with anyone who wasn't her husband, though God only knows why. You know he beat her, right?"

"Yes," said Colomba. "That's why we wondered whether she might have—"

"You wondered wrong."

"Why didn't she leave him?"

"Because she was in love with him. With that maniac. She always told me that the day he touched their boy, she'd take off running, but she never did . . . She never got the chance," she corrected herself.

"Were you aware that the boy wasn't well?" asked Dante.

This time Giulia didn't lose her temper. "How do you know that?"

"I looked at the pictures."

"You're right, he'd turned gloomy and he never spoke. When I kept him, he always seemed like he was on another planet."

"Especially in the past year, isn't that right?" asked Dante.

Giulia scrutinized him again, thinking to herself that he was the world's strangest policeman. "Yes."

"And had your sister noticed?" asked Colomba.

"She had." Giulia shook her head in disgust. "But as far as her husband was concerned, the boy was perfectly normal. And he didn't want to hear a word about it."

"Did she ever talk to a specialist?"

"No. Stefano didn't want her to."

But there was a certain lack of conviction, and Dante noticed it. "Did she do it in secret?"

"No, I don't think so. But there was a doctor who wanted to examine him."

"His pediatrician?" asked Dante, whose eyes had turned hard and bright as glass. It seemed to Colomba that the air was crackling around his head, so great was his concentration.

"No. This was a new doctor, who called my sister to make an appointment."

"When did this happen?"

"It must have been two weeks ago."

"And where had they met?"

"During a visit to the local health clinic. Something to do with school."

Dante looked over at Colomba, who spoke up again. "Do you know if they ever met?"

"No. I don't know," she whispered. "I forgot to ask." A tear rolled down her right cheek. She wiped it away with her sleeve. "You think you're going to have all the time in the world . . ." Her lips quivered, and more tears rolled. "Forgive me." She turned and walked a few steps away.

"She's crying," Dante said in a low voice to Colomba.

"Well, her sister was murdered . . . It's a common reaction."

"That's why I usually let my lawyer handle this kind of thing."

Giulia vigorously blew her nose and came back, her eyes red. "You were saying?"

"Do you remember this doctor's name? Or whether your sister might have written down his number?" asked Colomba.

"I only know that he called her on her cell phone. She was just coming by to have an espresso before opening her store back up for the afternoon. Why do you think it's important?"

"We don't know whether or not it is," Colomba said hurriedly.

"Do you think my brother-in-law had an accomplice? Or that it wasn't him?"

"We have to explore all the possibilities. Aside from this doctor, did your sister meet anyone else recently? New acquaintances? Did your nephew have any new friends?" she asked.

"Not as far as I know. And, like I told your colleagues, she hadn't received any threats and she'd never noticed anyone hanging around her apartment. Neither had I." She turned to stare at Colomba again. "The only real dangerous one was already living with her."

"Thanks for your help, signora."

Giulia took a step forward to face off with Colomba with burning eyes. "He won't get away with it, that son of a bitch. Do you understand me?"

"Think about your nephew. He comes before anything else," said Colomba, meeting her glare.

"My nephew is dead," said Giulia. Then she turned and ran back inside.

Colomba sighed and leaned against the wall next to Dante.

"Is it always this tough?" he asked.

"Even worse. What do you think?"

"I think that next time I'm not coming, even if you tie me up."

"Aside from that?"

"She feels guilty about having failed to protect her sister from her brother-in-law when it was still possible. She'd like it if another murderer emerged, because that would relieve her conscience. But she doesn't believe it."

Colomba made a face. "She wouldn't dream up a false story."

"No. The first snag, CC."

"It doesn't even come close."

"So are we just going to ignore it?"

"You have no idea how much I'd like to. Come on, get in."

Colomba had rented a minivan with a sunroof, hoping Dante might feel more comfortable and not force her to drive two miles an hour.

She'd been wrong, but the car did have a modern hands-free calling system, so she could talk while driving.

She used it to call the principal of the Maugeri boy's school. He wasn't surprised to hear from her, seeing that he'd been interviewed repeatedly in the past few days, and Colomba didn't even have to think up an excuse: all she had to do was state her rank.

The principal remembered the child's doctor's appointment. It had formed part of a preventive medicine program being run out of the local health clinic. "Weight, height, chest measurement . . . nothing invasive," he said.

"Did the doctors remain in touch with the families?" asked Colomba.

"I have no idea."

"Was there also a psychological evaluation of the children?" Dante inquired, leaning toward the microphone in the central rear-view mirror.

"Absolutely not. To many families, psychologists are still strictly doctors for lunatics."

"Could you give me the phone number of the local health clinic?" asked Colomba.

"Just a minute, let me go look for it."

He found it, but it didn't do any good. The head physician refused to answer any questions at all, invoking his patients' right to privacy.

Colomba could have forced his hand by identifying herself, but there was a risk that the doctor might demand some official document or complain to the district attorney's office, and that would open a can of worms. So she decided to reach out for a favor from Tirelli, who knew enough cops in Rome to obtain the objective with just a few phone calls.

Tirelli met them at 6 p.m. at the hotel bar.

"You're treating yourself well," he said, sitting down at the table where a silver teapot sat for Colomba and, next to it, a Moscow Mule for Dante.

Colomba pointed at Dante. "He's paying. Dante Torre."

"You're earning more than I do in that case," commented Tirelli as he shook hands.

"I'm a guest. I'm old friends with one of the owners," said Dante.

Colomba bit into a cookie from the three-section tray. "He brought back the man's crazy daughter."

"She wasn't crazy," said Dante in an irritated voice. "And it's not a very accurate term, in any case."

"Bip*o-o-o-o-o*lar," she said, drawing out the *o* mockingly.

"My compliments." Perhaps because of the strangeness of the situation, Tirelli was putting on even more pretentious airs than usual and sat as stiff as a stick. "Can I ask where she was?"

"At the apartment of a junkie friend of hers, with an incipient case of scabies and a strong desire to come home."

"Otherwise you would have left her there?"

Dante shrugged his shoulders: he hated talking about his work with strangers. "I have a deep and abiding respect for the liberty of other people. Whether or not they're bipolar. You can imagine why. Why the interest?"

Tirelli smiled, displaying teeth tinged yellow from licorice. "Because I've heard a lot about you, Signor Torre. And I'm wondering why you got Caselli involved in this idiotic quest."

"It was me who got him involved," Colomba admitted.

"Truer words were never spoken," said Dante.

"But why, by all that's holy? Half the district attorney's office is investigating the Maugeri case, and you're on medical leave. Do you think they're getting it all wrong? That the boy is still alive?"

"Right now, I don't think anything. That's why I'm investigating."

"Does Rovere know?"

"Are you worried about regulations?"

"I'm worried about you. And your career. With everything that's happened to you . . ." His voice trailed off.

"What's happened to me and will happen to me is my business and mine alone. Sorry to have to say it."

"But you're dragging me into it. If I help you, then I'm responsible, too."

"You can tell me no. Just stop preaching the sermon."

A waitress asked Tirelli if he wanted anything, and he ordered a glass of still white wine that came with an enormous bowl of multicolored crackers. He took a sip without a word.

"Well?" asked Colomba, impatiently. "Are you going to help me or not?"

"I'll help you . . . but this will be the last time unless you give me some valid justification."

"If I had one, I'd give it to you. Well? Did you find out who examined the boy?"

Tirelli scrutinized her for a few seconds, then he handed her a scrap of paper folded in four. "Girl, don't make me worry about you, okay?" he said as he got up. He looked at Dante. "And you, try to keep the idiotic pranks to a minimum."

All Dante had to offer in reply was the noisy slurping of his cocktail through a straw.

4

The doctor whose name appeared on the scrap of paper was called Marco de Michele, and he was an internist at the emergency room of the Sant'Andrea Hospital on Via Cassia in the Grottarossa district.

Even from a distance, Dante knew that this couldn't be the Father. Too young, about forty. Could he be an accomplice?

When he stepped out to smoke a cigarette with them, Dante kept an eye on every move he made. Haste, weariness, boredom. There was no sign of guilt in his shoulders, no sign of fear, if not the normal amount anyone feels when meeting with a cop.

De Michele said he couldn't remember any of the children he'd examined for the school program. "Except for the kid who had a bad case of *pectus excavatum*."

"Shoemaker's chest," explained Dante. "It's a deformity, a sunken chest, and they call it that because shoemakers worked that way, clutching the shoe against their chest."

Colomba snorted in annoyance. Sometimes Dante seemed like a walking Wikipedia page. "I'm talking about Luca Maugeri," she said brusquely.

"The name rings a bell . . ." De Michele's eyes suddenly snapped open wide. "You mean the boy murdered by his father?"

Dante decided that his astonishment was believable and exchanged a glance with Colomba, who nodded because she'd been thinking the same thing.

"No, this kid just happens to have the same name," she lied. "Was there more than one doctor for each child?"

"There were three of us, but each one examined a different child at the same time. They took numbers, like at the post office."

"Was there any medical staff, doctors or nurse practitioners, with them while they were waiting?" asked Dante.

"No. Just RNs, and they didn't do anything but open the door to let them in, one at a time." He touched his head, clearly uncomfortable. "Did something happen to the boy? Did someone molest him or . . ."

"The mother received a series of obscene phone calls," Dante hastily put in.

De Michele smiled. "I'm gay. But I didn't call the boy's father either, before you think to ask."

In the car, caught in the monstrous traffic on Rome's ring road, Colomba regretted not having a flashing roof light. "Looks like a dead end," she said.

"He didn't make the call, but someone did, and they knew about the medical exam."

"Any of a hundred thousand people."

"You want to give up?"

"No. Let's look at Lucia Maugeri's phone records and see if we can figure out who it was." Rovere had sent her the phone records along with everything else. "A couple things we can be sure of are that he has no prior convictions and that he wasn't particularly insistent, otherwise the cops would have picked up on it."

"If anyone even bothered to check."

"They must have done the basic minimum amount of work, otherwise the judge would have ripped them a new one at the preliminary hearing." Forgetting she wasn't driving a police car, Colomba hammered her foot down on the accelerator to whip around the car ahead of her, breaking the speed limit and then some.

Dante grabbed onto his seat with both hands. "Isn't De Angelis the judge?"

"He's the prosecuting magistrate. How can you know everything and still know fucking nothing about criminal procedure?"

"Because it's boring and I have a lawyer who takes care of those things. Look out, you're going over the speed limit."

"Are you going to write me a ticket?"

"No, I just don't want to throw up in a rental car. That was my credit card we used."

Colomba passed a truck, brushing it with her rearview mirror.

Dante opened the car window and took a deep breath, filling his lungs. "Has anyone ever told you that you drive like you're drunk?"

"If you prefer, I can let you out and you can catch a cab."

Dante considered the possibility. "We're going in the right direction, CC."

"Only because we're heading in the direction you prefer."

"No. I'm not wrong about this. I couldn't tell you why, but I do know that it scares me."

Dante didn't say another word for the rest of the drive and at dinner practically didn't eat, just stared into the empty air. He even refused to take the elevator, and Colomba followed him up all fifteen flights of stairs, which he climbed slowly, with an apathetic expression. When they reached the hotel suite, he went straight into his room.

Colomba took off her shoes and followed him, sitting down sideways on the chaise longue. "Do you remember if a doctor of any kind called your family before your kidnapping?"

"Now you believe in a connection?"

"No, but I told you I was going to check everything out, and that's what I intend to do."

"No strangers got in touch with my folks in the period prior to my disappearance. At least, that's what they remembered at the time."

"Give me Lucia Maugeri's phone records," said Colomba.

Dante reached under the bed and tossed her a bundle of stapled sheets of paper. To the vast annoyance of Colomba, who only wished she had the same superpower; he always seemed to find everything without hesitation.

Dante went back to sitting in his fakir's position at the center of the bed. "Some witnesses have mentioned seeing a strange car outside our apartment building in the days prior to my disappearance, but nothing was ever pinned down, and it could have been a red herring."

"What about your family doctor?" she asked without looking up.

"He's dead. Back in my day, though, it was normal to be seen by a doctor at the school clinic. They were waging campaigns against rickets and crabs."

"Did you grow up on a pirate ship?"

"I just grew up in the far countryside. Why on earth didn't your colleagues check the numbers?"

"They focused on the day of the murder and any possible repeat phone calls in the preceding days or calls at odd times. They didn't bother to check all the incoming calls. Do you have any idea how long that would take?"

"Especially if you think it's not worth the trouble."

Colomba circled a number on the phone record. "There's a call from a landline in Rome that first appears in the period the sister mentioned, on a Friday."

"What time of day?"

"At two thirty in the afternoon. That would match the closing time of the store."

"See if there are any others."

Colomba scanned ahead. She was reading only the last number in the column, to work fast. The number from the Friday ended with a 9, and every time she encountered a 9, she stopped to check. If she'd had the data in digital format, she could have just searched automatically, but Rovere had been able to get only a paper copy. "That number appears again the following Monday. And she made the call."

"After that, nothing more?"

"No."

"Too few occurrences to catch the eye of your otherwise very astute colleagues."

"Exactly."

Colomba picked up the laptop and checked the number on the white pages site. "It's not listed."

"It's him," said Dante.

"Don't get too worked up; these days most phone numbers are unlisted."

Dante went out onto the terrace and lit a cigarette; Colomba called Rovere and asked him to have the number identified.

The answer came back in minutes, but it was more complicated than she expected. She gestured to Dante, who half-closed the French doors but remained hunched over in the wicker chair with his knees tucked under his chin. "Who is it?"

"Skype," Colomba replied. "If you subscribe, you can get a local number to call from and to receive calls."

"But people who are calling you don't know it." Dante lit another cigarette. "The Father knows that Lucia Maugeri is worried about Luca's symptoms of autism. He gets in touch with her and offers to help her. They meet somewhere, and he persuades her to say nothing to anyone and not to use the phone."

"Or else it's just someone who wants to save on his phone bill."

"A physician calling from the clinic? Quite credible. Just imagine for a moment that someone . . . I'm not saying the Father . . . took the Maugeris' son. Pretending to be a doctor might be a good way to do it."

Colomba agreed in spite of herself. "She was living with a violent man who refused to hear any talk about his son's illness," she said. "It could even have been her idea to meet in some out-of-the-way place. But how did she manage to get away without her husband noticing?"

"How was the husband's toxicology test?"

"Alcohol and psychotropic drugs. But he had a prescription and took them regularly for stress."

"Maybe she added a few extra to his beer."

Colomba was skeptical. "But how would the kidnapper have known all those things about the Maugeris' son?"

"Once he identifies his prey, he starts gathering information. He spies on them. He had two months after the school medical examination."

"For now, all we have is a strange phone number. Maybe we could try calling it."

Dante shook his head. "I just did, five minutes ago. No such number."

"Next time, tell me. That's not standard procedure."

"I was sure that the Father would deactivate the number."

"Don't fixate on him."

"Do you think it's just a coincidence?"

Colomba shrugged. "You know one of the first things they teach you when you start to do investigations? Not to grab hold of any one theory. Because if you believe in it too strongly, you'll start to see things that aren't there."

Dante lit another cigarette off the butt of the one before it. "They told me the same thing when I escaped from the silo."

"You know I wasn't referring to that. While we're talking about hypotheses, do you think the kidnapper would have met the boy at the clinic?"

"Since I don't believe this is just some ordinary kidnapper but the Father, I'd say no."

"A minimal risk in the midst of a crowd. He could pretend to be the loving grampa."

"No," Dante said tersely. "He lived on, undisturbed, for twenty-five years after I got away. He wouldn't have succeeded in doing that if he wasn't cautious to the point of obsession. And believe me, he's nothing if not obsessive."

Colomba shook her head. It was always upsetting to her to hear Dante speaking so confidently about the Father. "I'd still take a look at the surveillance videotapes from the local health clinic."

Dante turned around, his cigarette at half-staff. "What did you say?"

"There must be some kind of surveillance system in that place," Colomba explained. "I can ask Rovere to get the tapes for us."

Dante discarded the cigarette without crushing it out and ran back inside. He grabbed Colomba by her shoulders. "We have to find a way to get into the clinic," he told her.

She shook free, astonished at his intensity. "Tomorrow morning I'll try talking to the director again . . ."

"No. Right now," Dante interrupted her. "Tomorrow morning might be too late."

"It's closed right now."

"Get them to open up, CC. This is important."

"What on earth do you think could happen?"

Dante told her. Colomba got her phone.

5

The health clinic where the Maugeris' son had been examined was in a misshapen rectangle of gray cement on Via Nomentana, at the on-ramp to the eastern bypass road. It looked like a child's play block that had wound up in the oven by mistake, with bubbles and protuberances scattered across the facades in an apparently random fashion. When Dante and Colomba got there around midnight, Alberti's squad car was already parked out front with the roof lights flashing. He came to meet them, accompanied by his older partner, so fat he barely fit into his uniform and reeking of stale sweat: Colomba understood exactly what kind of cop he was even before shaking hands with him. He smiled and nonchalantly stared at her tits.

"And the doctor?" asked Colomba.

Alberti pointed to him. De Michele was standing next to the car, looking annoyed.

She went over to him and shook hands. "Thanks for coming out."

"Your colleague told me this was very important. So I have to guess that the child you asked me about doesn't just happen to have the same name. We're talking about the boy who was murdered by his father."

"We're still not assuming he's dead."

"And what do I have to do with it?"

"You? Nothing."

The night watchman showed up at that moment to open the front entrance, and Colomba went over to the car and tapped on Dante's window. He'd remained in the car, slumped over in the seat like a collapsing bag.

"We're all here but you," she said to him.

"Let's do it some other time."

"Tomorrow morning half the executive staff of the national health service are going to be on the phone to Rovere, and they're going to be hopping mad, so we're not going to have another chance to set foot in there for the next millennium."

"You don't *really* need me to go in with you."

"Get out. Don't make me go all cop on you."

Dante sighed. "Let's make it quick, though," he said. Before leaving the hotel he'd downed a cocktail of pills and drops that would have flattened a horse, but the adrenaline continued to neutralize the effects of the pharmaceuticals. His internal thermometer was at ten, if not above: any higher, and columns of steam would be whistling from his ears. Colomba took his arm, leading him toward the entrance. The watchman opened the door and switched on the lights inside. The fluorescent bulbs in the lobby flicked on in sequence.

De Michele stared at Dante's ashen face. "Are you all right?"

"No, but just show me the way," he said in a strangled voice.

"What way?"

"The way the children went with their families."

De Michele stood there for a moment, baffled, then led them up to the mezzanine lobby. At the far end were the teller windows of the hospital intake office and the information window for the public. They were darkened, and Colomba thought of *The Walking Dead*, where the survivors of the zombie attack took shelter in abandoned public buildings. Her work had often taken her to strange and sometimes dangerous places, but this one had a fascination all its own.

"This is the way in," said De Michele, "and you go up to the second floor, by elevator or else there are stairs."

"Stairs," Dante muttered. The lobby looked to him like a gray, airless cavern. Struggling to control his respiration, he practically ran up the stairs, ahead of everyone else. "What next?" he asked, panting. The hallway was a claustrophobic passageway with just one window. The black night outside pressed in against the glass.

"Your colleague's breathing is quite labored," De Michele said to Colomba.

"That's just because he's happy. Now where to?" she asked.

De Michele pointed to the two doors on opposite sides of the hallway, the walls of which were lined with children's drawings of bugs and flowers. "This is the school medicine ward; in there are the clinics."

He opened one of the doors, revealing a square room with another door and a line of chairs on each wall. "This is where the children and their families wait to be called."

"Which clinic did you use?" Dante asked in a barely audible voice.

"Mmm . . . that one." It was the middle room.

Dante took off at a gallop. He went through the first door, tore through the waiting room, and lunged into the clinic, throwing open the white door. It was a dark box. Dante froze, covered with cold sweat, until the others caught up with him and turned on the light. In the room there was a metal table with two facing chairs, an examination bed, and a screen to undress behind. A door concealed a small bathroom. Dante raised the sash window and took in deep lungfuls of the muggy outside air. The alarm went off immediately.

"Fuck," said Colomba.

Alberti's radio beeped. It was his older partner. "Hey, geniuses, did you know the perimeter alarm is turned on?" he said.

Colomba grabbed the radio out of Alberti's hands. "Tell the night watchman to turn it off."

"He can't do it from here, it's controlled by the Dispatch office."

"Then call Dispatch. And do it now."

"Yes ma'am."

The siren went on howling for another minute. Dante kept both hands pressed to his ears the whole time, miming Edvard Munch's *The Scream*. When the sound ceased, he resumed his probing of the room. Behind the table, he sought a position that would allow him to take in both the patient's chair and the examination bed. *From up high*, he thought. He looked up and saw the air conditioning vent. *So obvious* . . . He pointed it out to Colomba. "Dismantle it."

"Are you sure?"

Dante said nothing and ran out of the room, slamming the door behind him.

"Is he always like this?" asked De Michele.

"Only on his good days," said Colomba. She couldn't reach the AC vent even standing on tiptoes and reaching up. She dragged the desk over and stood on it. Now her face was next to the vent, but all she could see inside was darkness. It was held in place by four Phillips-head screws.

"Do you need a hand, Deputy Captain?" asked Alberti.

"Do you happen to have a screwdriver in your pocket?"

"No."

"I do," said De Michele. "I was a boy scout. *Be prepared.*" He tossed her a Swiss Army knife. "But exactly what do you hope to find?"

Colomba chose a blade with a flat edge. "I just hope I don't find anything at all."

But something was there, and Colomba knew it when she turned the first screw. It moved too easily; someone had opened it recently. She undid the third screw and rotated the vent using the fourth screw as a pivot. And then she saw.

In the HVAC duct, fastened to the wall with duct tape, was a video camera.

6

Dante had smoked the last cigarette in the packet when Colomba came out with two little plastic cups of espresso. "The coffee machine on the ground floor is on," she said, handing him one.

"Are you trying to poison me?"

"Lots of people drink it, and it doesn't kill them."

"Lots of people drink Ganges River water."

"You make things harder than they need to be." Colomba poured the contents of the second cup into the first and gulped it down. "The main thing is that it keeps you awake."

Lieutenant Dino Anzelmo from the Ministry of Justice's postal and communication police came to meet them. He was about thirty and looked for all the world like a college student who'd fallen behind on his exams; he wore glasses with black frames. He'd been sent here by Rovere, and he'd brought along a couple of his men and a search warrant.

"We found some fingerprints," said Anzelmo. "He'd cleaned them off the video camera but not off the cassette, and there's a partial on the wall, as well." He waved the tablet he was holding, a terminal connected to AFIS, the automatic fingerprint identification system. "And we were lucky: We found a match."

"Does he have a record?" asked Colomba.

"He was arrested for assault and battery fifteen years ago," Anzelmo replied. "And there's a criminal complaint for illegal gambling. No sex offenses. But he's a pro at surveillance, the video camera was equipped with a motion detector. If there was no one in the room, it was on standby."

"How old is he?" asked Colomba.

"Fifty," said Anzelmo, reading from the screen, and then he gave her the handheld terminal. Colomba saw a man with a goatee and short salt-and-pepper hair. His name was Sabino Montanari, born and currently residing in Rome. Divorced, no kids.

"He works here, right?" asked Dante.

"As an attendant," Anzelmo replied. "You ought to be a cop."

"I'd only enlist in case of war."

Anzelmo blinked in bafflement and decided to speak to Colomba from now on. "I alerted the magistrate, who issued an order of precautionary detainment. I mentioned an anonymous tip, I'll manage to make it look like one."

"Thanks," said Colomba, who knew what Anzelmo was risking by covering for her. Dante pulled on her arm and walked a short distance away.

"I didn't know you were such a patriot," she observed.

Dante looked at her, uncomprehending. "Patriot?"

"You said you'd sign up if a war broke out."

"Strictly because in wartime more civilians die than soldiers, didn't you know? I need to talk to him."

"To who?" asked Colomba.

"To Montanari."

"Forget about that. The cops are going to pick him up, and he'll be interviewed by the judge."

"The Father went through him to reach Luca Maugeri," Dante insisted.

"Even if there is a connection between the video camera and the kidnapping, Montanari might have done it all on his own."

"If it was him and Luca was who he was looking for, why didn't he take the camera?"

"Maybe he just didn't move fast enough," Colomba replied.

"Was it on or off?"

"On."

"The battery doesn't last four days," Dante noted. "Montanari is a middleman for the kidnapper, whether or not you choose to believe in the Father. And if you let him wind up in the gears of the justice system, we're screwed. I won't get a chance to talk to him until they let him out."

Colomba rolled her eyes and went back to Anzelmo. "What instructions did Rovere give you?"

"He just said to help you out here."

"Then keep helping me out. Let me take part in the arrest."

Anzelmo shook his head. "You're not on active duty." His sidelong stare seemed to imply that he knew why.

Colomba wasn't giving up. "To Montanari I'll just be another cop asking questions. It won't even occur to him to say I was there unless someone asks. And who the fuck is going to ask? Come on, partner, don't make me beg."

Anzelmo pointed at Dante, who stood a short distance away. "What about him?"

"He'll stay in the car."

"And so will you until I've handcuffed him, okay? Because if he has a gun and shoots you, I'd have to find a way to get rid of your corpse."

"Okay," said Colomba. She kept her face impassive, but even from where he stood, Dante could tell she was lying.

7

Montanari lived on Via Salaria, and he wasn't answering the doorbell. Alberti and his older partner forced the lock with a small battering ram and stepped aside to let Anzelmo and Colomba through, guns in hand.

Anzelmo stopped just inside the door, aiming his gun at the center of the room and shouting "Police! Show yourself with your hands in the air!"

Every time he said those words, he sounded to himself as if he were in a bad movie, but he'd never been able to come up with another sentence that was quite as effective. Luckily, given the nature of his job, he didn't have to deal with the issue often, and the only time he'd fired his gun was at the shooting range. Colomba, on the other hand, seemed to be a woman who used her gun for everything, even to open bottles at home. Anzelmo was astonished to see her so determined and active after everything that had happened to her. She might even be a little *too* active. As soon as they'd pulled up in front of the building, she'd hopped out of the car, leaving it in the middle of the street, and had started ringing the neighbors' doorbells to get the front door open.

Anzelmo had run after her. "Have you already forgotten we had a deal?"

Colomba ignored him. A woman's voice burst out of the intercom, and Colomba answered immediately. "I'm locked out without my keys. Could you let me in, please?"

"Caselli . . . are you listening to me?" Anzelmo had said, feeling that she was treating him like a fool.

The front door buzzed open, and Colomba had lunged through it, stopping only to examine the names on the mailboxes. The other two cops had looked at him in bafflement. "She's not supposed to come with us," one said.

"You want to tell her that?" Anzelmo replied.

The other cop took a step back. "No."

Following Colomba into Montanari's apartment were Anzelmo's two partners and, bringing up the rear, Alberti and his partner.

"He's not here," said Colomba, putting her gun back into the holster on her belt.

Anzelmo, who'd checked out the bathroom, too, also holstered his regulation weapon. "I'll have a search warrant issued," he said.

"You think he caught a whiff of something?" asked one of the two partners. "It's two in the morning."

"Maybe he saw us at the clinic," Anzelmo replied.

Colomba started wandering around the apartment, inspecting the place. "I don't think he packed his bags." She glanced over at the one ramshackle armoire in the room, the door shut tight. "Do you have a pair of gloves?"

Anzelmo rolled his eyes. "Caselli, considering you're not even supposed to be here, you're making a hell of a lot of noise."

"Gloves," she said again.

One of Anzelmo's partners tossed her a box of single-use gloves. Colomba put on a pair and opened the armoire, looking around carefully. It seemed to her that there were no significant gaps between the items of clothing. When someone went on the run in a hurry, they always left a considerable mess behind.

"Look here," said one of the two other cops. He'd opened the pantry, revealing a small pull-out desk with a laptop computer. The laptop was hooked up to a MiniDV player, which took the discs used by the video camera they'd confiscated.

"If he's on the run, he didn't come home before leaving," said Colomba. "Otherwise he'd have taken it with him." She stood up and opened the screen of the laptop, which lit up, displaying the Windows start menu.

"Don't waste time on that," said Anzelmo. "I'll take everything to the lab. Then I'll tell you what they found, if you want."

"Can't you do a preliminary on-site examination?" asked Colomba. "We have to wait here anyway, in case Montanari comes home."

"I thought I'd just leave a squad car here," Anzelmo replied. Still, he took a quick look at the contents of the hard drive. "He has a video-editing program but no videos. He must store them online somewhere. Or on some removable storage device. Still, if the content went through the computer at any point, we'd find traces of it."

"Can you do that here?" Colomba inquired.

"No. First we'd have to do an overall backup and make a copy of the content that's on there now. Anyway, I'm no expert. There are some things I leave to the technicians."

Colomba gave him a level look. "Aren't you a hacker or something like that?"

"Should I be?"

"You're from the Special Internet Crimes Division, you spend all your time on computers."

"You're a homicide cop, and you spend lots of time with dead bodies. Does that make you a pathologist?"

"Excellent point." Colomba shut the computer and pulled the plug out of the wall.

"If you're planning to take it away somewhere, I swear that this time I'll handcuff you to a radiator," said Anzelmo.

"Just downstairs."

They got into Colomba's minivan. She and Dante sat in the back, Anzelmo turning to watch them over the seat back.

Dante had one hand on the trackpad and had started opening and closing folders.

"What are you doing?" asked Colomba, who at a certain point was able to keep up with his rapid movements.

"I'm looking for a program run log, so I can find out how they've been used recently."

"I could have done that myself," Anzelmo objected from his vantage point over the seat back, peering down and trying to see something.

"Afterwards I'll let you play with it for all the time you like," Dante said, tolerantly.

"I want him to see what he can figure out," said Colomba.

"Is he a *hacker*?" asked Anzelmo, mockingly.

"No, but he found the video camera."

"But we weren't looking for one," Anzelmo said defensively.

Dante snickered. "Which is exactly the point . . . Okay. Montanari signed on to the Internet using Tor."

"What's that?" Colomba asked. She knew how to use a computer, but when things went over into the realm of the technical, she no longer understood.

"It's a program that renders online connections anonymous," Anzelmo replied.

"That's right," said Dante. "And with it you can find sites you wouldn't be able to otherwise."

"The darknet," she commented.

"Oh, please . . . only journalists use that term."

Anzelmo nodded. "On anonymous sites, once you get access, you can buy things online that are illegal in nearly every country on Earth. Weapons, drugs . . ."

"And child pornography," Colomba summed up.

"True, although most people use Tor only to download pirated movies," Dante pointed out. "We don't know what servers Montanari signed onto, much less where he kept his shit. But . . . let's see . . . he has a PayPal account. And a payment receipt to Leonard McCoy, an American, through a virtual credit card issued from the Cayman Islands. Ten thousand euros. That's something. I can't see any of the other transactions without his password."

"Do you think this McCoy exists?" asked Colomba.

"If you're going to use your real name, you might as well use a normal credit card," Dante replied. "It's the alias of one of his buyers."

"Do you think he was selling the footage?" Colomba probed.

"What do *you* think he was doing with it?"

"Maybe he liked watching them," said Anzelmo.

"Were there pictures of kids in the house, even innocent ones? On the walls, on the fridge?" Dante wanted to know.

"No," Anzelmo replied.

"Toys, children's clothing, kiddie comic books?"

Colomba shook her head.

"But he has four different apps for online casinos. He's a compulsive gambler, he needs money."

"Anything else?" asked Colomba.

"He just has one Skype profile. But he hasn't used it in the past six months. And he doesn't have a subscription for local numbers."

"Why did you think he might?" Anzelmo asked.

Dante and Colomba exchanged a glance but said nothing. "But he did use a chat program," said Dante.

"Can you see what he said?"

"No. He erased that. The last person he chatted with today is named Zardoz. And I have the IP address he connected from."

He showed Colomba a string of numbers that revealed the identity of the server being used by whoever it was that had contacted Montanari; then he punched that string of numbers into the browser on his iPhone to see its provenance. "It's a Tor server," he said after a short while. It seemed to be taking him some effort to speak, as if he'd been distracted by a sudden thought.

Colomba spoke to Anzelmo. "Is there a way to establish Zardoz's identity?"

"No, because the Tor server deletes the connection logs," Anzelmo replied. "But maybe Montanari knows who he is. Let's wait until we catch him, and then he can tell us."

"Can I speak to you privately?" Dante asked Colomba.

She looked at Anzelmo.

"If I go, I'm taking the computer with me," he pointed out, clearly offended.

Dante handed it to him without even glancing in his direction. "Be my guest."

Anzelmo took it and got out.

"What is it?" asked Colomba once they were alone.

"Have you ever seen the movie *Zardoz*?" Dante asked.

"Never even heard of it."

"It's a sci-fi flick from the seventies, with Sean Connery."

"He's a hot guy."

"He's over eighty . . ."

"He's still hot. Well?"

"The film is about a society in the future dominated by a false god who calls himself Zardoz, a character inspired by the Wizard of Oz.

He appears to his subjects as an enormous mask with a thunderous voice, which is a sort of spaceship."

"Does this have anything to do with us?"

"Yes. Zardoz demands a specific tribute from his subjugated people. Wheat. The slaves fill the flying mask with wheat at the beginning of the movie. The mask is nothing less than a flying silo, CC. Zardoz is the Father. And Montanari can take us to him."

8

Sabino Montanari was sitting in his methane-powered Fiat Stilo, parked next to a pylon under the bypass highway, opposite the staircase leading up to the Tiburtina station. Until just two years ago, he'd owned a Mercedes, but he'd gambled it away little by little, same as had happened with the apartment he'd purchased when the cards were still running right for him. Now he lived in a one-room rental so far from the clinic that it took him two hours to get there every day. Two fucking hours of his life wasted every morning and an hour to get home in the evening. He thought about it all the time. Every day. He'd dreamed of quitting his regular job once and for all, once he'd set aside a bit of money, but things had gone the other way.

That's why he'd started up with the videos, even if that shit turned his stomach. The video camera that he'd smuggled into gynecology, sure, every once in a while that yielded some interesting material . . . but pediatrics? Pure shit. It's just that videos of women with their legs spread brought in nothing. If you tried to put them on the market, at the very best you might find someone willing to trade videos. But kids . . .

Kids were pure gold.

For the most part, the children remained fully dressed and the pediatricians just looked at their tonsils. Only occasionally did they take off their T-shirt or, even more rarely, drop their trousers to allow their nether regions to be checked. But he could sell that footage for a hundred euros a minute, and there was always someone willing to buy, even after the free preview. Then Zardoz had shown up. His account was a number assigned by the system, and Montanari had no idea what his real name might be. The system told him only that he'd been on the server for more than a year and that he'd made purchases without problems from vendors who were still operating. That was important information; it gave Montanari a reasonable certainty that the man wasn't a cop from the Ministry of Justice trying to set him up. Zardoz had purchased a couple of minutes; then he'd made an offer that was almost too good to be true: the whole video for a flat fee of ten thousand euros. Montanari knew that there were very rich individuals who frequented the site, but there weren't many clients who wanted to spend it all on a single vendor; they tended to be looking for variety. Instead Zardoz wanted even the dead footage, the parts where the mothers said hello to the doctors and that sort of thing. Montanari had remained skeptical until the money had actually been credited to his PayPal account.

Jack off till you die, he'd mentally wished him as he uploaded the file, but Zardoz had come back for more. And then he'd come back for even more. In the end, Montanari had tapped the guy for thirty thousand euros, half of which he'd basically burned on a green card table in the back room of a butcher's shop in the space of a month. That was the only reason why, when Zardoz had requested a face-to-face meeting, Montanari had even considered the possibility. Which ran contrary to every rule of survival, as anyone who did business on the Internet knew very well. When he sold, Montanari did so through a server in some other part of the world, and he signed on to it via a high-security connection. It was easy once you knew how. He'd learned the technique from a guy who'd skinned him at Texas Hold 'Em and who sold amphetamines on the Internet. He didn't even know who his clients were, the man had told him. He took an order, he waited for the money, and when it came in, he shipped the merchandise by courier, using a nonexistent company on the return address. The secure connection could be rented for just pennies, again online. You passed through a server that made you anonymous. Even if the Ministry of Justice did put you under surveillance, it could follow your trail only that far and no farther. Beyond that point you became invisible.

Meeting clients in person, on the other hand, was like playing roulette. If the wrong number turned up, there could be a cop waiting for you. But the buyer had come up with a request that was typical of people like him: he wanted an exclusive on what he was buying. An exclusive on what Montanari was selling. So he was going to provide Montanari with a sealed video camera along with the money.

Montanari had suggested he drop it off for him somewhere, but the buyer had refused. The device was too expensive, too risky if someone else stumbled on it. They'd have to meet. Montanari had considered rejecting the offer; then the thought of the money that Zardoz had promised him this time—another forty thousand euros, all at once—had won out over his caution. And if he turned out to be a cop . . . he had nothing on him and he kept all his stuff online, on an anonymous virtual disk. Even if they'd arrested him, they wouldn't have found any evidence against him.

Zardoz had made an appointment to meet at one in the morning. Montanari still had ten minutes to wait and was starting to feel sleepy. In the middle of an extended yawn, he noticed someone in the rear-view mirror walking toward his car. From that distance he couldn't make out the face, he could just see someone who looked tall, wearing an expensive-looking raincoat buttoned up to the neck. When he knocked on the window with a gloved hand, Montanari understood that it was him. He lowered the window. "Yes?" he said, keeping it noncommittal. Even the description that he'd given of himself had been intentionally generic. The location was the only thing they had specified.

"I think you're waiting for me," said the man in the raincoat.

"Maybe," Montanari replied.

"Zardoz. Let me in, and we can talk about money."

Montanari hesitated. Zardoz's voice was cold and courteous. He'd expected a slobbering sex fiend.

He clicked the door lock, and once Zardoz got in, he saw that he was an old man. *A rich old pervert*, he thought.

The old man looked him in the eye. By the light of the streetlamp, his eyes glittered electric blue. "It was very kind of you to agree to meet me on such short notice," he said.

"I didn't do it out of kindness. I did it for the money."

"And I imagine you haven't brought anything compromising with you."

"Do you take me for an idiot?"

"No. Of course not."

"Where's the video camera? Is it so small that it fits in your pocket?"

"That was just an excuse so I could meet you, I'm afraid," said the old man. Then he did something with his hand so quickly that Montanari could hardly see it. He felt a sudden flush of cold to his throat. The cold turned into ice in an instant, and then scalding pain.

Montanari opened his mouth to try to say something, but he found it was full of blood and that he couldn't breathe anymore. The old man had something glittering in his hand. He put it into the pocket of his raincoat, which was now dripping with blood. His blood.

The old man leaned over him and unzipped his pants, extracting his member. Montanari tried to push him away, but his hands no longer responded to his will.

The old man looked at him. "Don't worry, I'm not trying to sexually molest you. It's just for whoever finds you, you understand?"

But Montanari no longer understood anything, except that his thoughts seemed to slide away along with the blood from the slice in his throat. The last thought was of the card game he'd miss tomorrow. He imagined the lucky hand he'd be dealt, a royal flush in spades. The black of the cards filled his eyes and his mind.

The old man pulled a plastic bag out of his pocket, and from it he extracted a dirty Kleenex and a hair that he left on the seat. Then he opened a packet containing a condom and placed it, as far as he was able to, on Montanari's member. He immediately removed it and placed it in a bag. After that he hurried away at a brisk pace.

From outside, with his head slumped against the window, it looked as if Montanari were sleeping.

9

The search was over, and now Colomba was starting to feel the lack of sleep. She went up to the apartment and rejoined Anzelmo.

"Has anything else turned up?" she asked.

Anzelmo said no. "Neither has Montanari. We've put out a warrant for his arrest, but for now, no sign of him."

Colomba looked carefully around the ransacked apartment. "From what I can see here, he doesn't have enough money to flee the country."

"Unless he stashed it all away."

"I'm more inclined to believe Dante's theory, that he gambled it all away."

Anzelmo scratched his cheek uneasily. "Excuse me for asking this, Caselli. But exactly who is he?"

"It's a long story, and I don't feel like telling it to you."

"Mighty nice of you," said Anzelmo. "Remind me to keep doing you favors."

Colomba squeezed his arm. "Sorry. When this is over, I'll buy you a drink."

Anzelmo smiled. "I'll count on that."

"But don't start getting any funny ideas."

Just then one of Anzelmo's men came rushing in.

"What's up?" he asked.

"Montanari. He's just been found at the Tiburtina station. Dead as a doornail."

Colomba punched a fist into the wall. "Fuck, no."

"What's going on, Caselli?" Anzelmo asked nervously.

Colomba stuck a finger in his face. "Dante and I were never here, you got that?"

"You don't need to tell me that. I'm already in deep enough shit."

She ran downstairs and forced Dante back into the car before explaining what had happened.

"What do we do now?" asked Dante, his stomach in a knot.

Colomba jammed on the accelerator, and the car took off. "We go there."

"Can't we avoid the sight of the corpse?"

"If you want, I can drop you off."

"No, no. Okay, let's go."

The stretch of roadway running along next to the pylon of the bypass road had already been shut down; two highway patrol officers were rerouting traffic. Colomba slapped her police ID under their noses, barely slowing down, and parked her car just short of the cordoned-off area: she leapt out without bothering to wait for Dante. He went after her with legs as wobbly as Jell-O. In spite of the lateness of the hour, a small crowd of rubberneckers pressed around the pylon, peering past the police barriers. In the midst of the crowd, a couple of news agency photographers were shooting bursts of pictures, waiting to get the authorization to move in closer. Uniformed cops were talking into their radios and cell phones; a couple of ambulance attendants waiting to cart off the corpse were quietly joking around.

Dante knew that this had been Colomba's world until what she referred to as the Disaster and wondered whether she missed it. To him it seemed like a strange dream, with the floodlights flattening the colors and making everything seem unreal. The cone of light was focused on Montanari's car, which glittered and emitted a faint mist of steam. Still a good ten yards away, Dante glimpsed a dark shape behind the driver's side window and realized that it was the dead man's head. His first dead body that wasn't just a picture. He further slowed his pace.

Standing next to Montanari's car were two officers from the Forensic Squad, with Chief Inspector Infanti from the Third Section. Infanti had been Colomba's deputy for three years, and he was also a friend, but like all her other colleagues he hadn't seen her since she'd been released from the hospital. He'd had to settle for Rovere's periodic updates, since Colomba wouldn't answer the phone when anyone other than her old boss called her. That's why when he saw her running toward him, Infanti had assumed it was just a trick of the eyes caused by exhaustion. He only really recognized her when she shoved him bodily aside to peer into the car, stopping just an inch short of the sacred investigative clean zone.

"What can you tell me?" she asked him.

Infanti recovered from his surprise. "Colomba . . . wait, are you back on duty?"

Colomba struggled to take her eyes off the car and turn them to him. "No."

Infanti shook his head, confused. Colomba looked skinnier to him but in good shape. She seemed like the Colomba he'd always known, not the lost, ashen-faced shadow of herself he'd seen lying in the hospital bed. He'd have thrown his arms around her, but she was tense as a violin string, so he kept a respectful distance. "You scared the hell out of me."

"Sorry. Now tell me what you can."

"We just received authorization to take him away. Someone killed him by slicing his carotid artery through with a razor-sharp blade of some kind."

"A scalpel?" asked Colomba, increasingly tense.

"Maybe. His dick was out with traces of something that seems to be spermicide. In the car there was a woman's hair, a condom packet, and a Kleenex smeared with lipstick." He pointed to the street. "He pulled off here with a prostitute, she started giving him a blow job, then they fought over money and she cut his throat. Or maybe she was already planning to kill him, who can say."

"What a funny coincidence, tonight of all nights," said Dante, finally arriving on the scene.

Infanti looked at him, puzzled. "Is he with you?" he asked Colomba.

"Yes. Did you say there was a condom packet?" asked Colomba.

"Yes."

"What about the condom?"

"That we didn't find. The prostitute might have taken it with her. For the DNA."

"So you're saying the hooker left a dirty Kleenex but took the condom with her?" Dante broke in again. "That's an odd one, don't you think?"

"Can I ask just who the fuck you would be?" Infanti burst out.

Dante pointed to Colomba. "A friend of hers."

An unmarked car with a flashing light pulled up, and Rovere got out. "The boss is here," said Infanti.

Colomba chose that moment to have an attack. She'd managed to stave it off the whole distance, struggling with every ounce of will-power she possessed, but at the sight of Rovere she lost the battle.

The world distorted itself around her while a pair of mighty granite arms crushed her chest. She shoved her colleague away and ran, breathless, until she reached the dark little side street. The shadows rose from the asphalt and attacked her; her ears exploded into screams. Colomba hit the wall with her face and fell to the pavement. Her breath came back, along with a surge of sobbing.

"Oh, God," she said between sobs. "Oh, God."

Dante was right. There was a pitiless kidnapper operating in the shadows. There really was. Everything else could be dismissed as mere coincidence, an impression induced by Dante's fixation. But Montanari's death, that couldn't. That couldn't be called a coincidence, not even by the most imbecilic cop ever born. And she was no idiot, even though right then and there she would have preferred to be. They'd come close to the real kidnapper behind the incredible smoke screen he'd succeeded in creating, and he'd reacted by slicing off the only possible living link to him. He was a monster, and they had goaded him into action, to sow blood and death. She still couldn't manage to catch her breath. She bit her lip, and the taste of blood filled her mouth. She spat and started breathing again. *Zardoz*, she thought. *Zardoz*.

A shadow loomed up against the light of the streetlamp, and Colomba almost started suffocating again before she realized that it was Rovere, who was leaning worriedly over her. "Colomba? Are you okay?"

He held out a hand to help her to her feet, but she ignored it and sat up, back to the wall. "Fuck, this is all your fault," she sobbed.

"What are you talking about?"

Colomba tilted her head back to look at him, her face streaked with tears and dust. "You left me to handle the investigation! Not officially, secretly, all the better to screw Santini! And this is the result!"

Rovere leaned over her again. "Are you sure that this murder is connected to the Maugeri kidnapping?"

Colomba dried her eyes. "Yes, goddamn it. But I don't have any way of proving it! If we'd found Montanari alive, we could have used his testimony, brought him to the magistrate's attention. But we don't have a fucking thing!"

"The video camera . . ."

"The video camera filmed several hundred children! And just one of them was kidnapped. If I went in to tell them this story, De Angelis would treat me worse then he treated Dante. And I couldn't take that!" She shouted the last sentence.

"If you've gotten close, you can get closer still," Rovere said in a paternal tone. "You're actually doing this, Colomba! Don't you see?"

"But what if that guy gets scared and kills the kid? Did that occur to you?"

"That's just a risk we're going to have to take . . ."

Colomba slapped away the hand he was holding out to her. "Go fuck yourself, sir."

"Colomba . . ."

"Didn't you hear what she said to you?" asked Dante. He'd appeared at the end of the street, the light from behind him casting a very long shadow. He was clenching his fists to bolster his courage and keep himself from turning to run.

Rovere snapped to a standing position and walked toward him. "Signor Torre, we've never met. I'm Rovere."

Dante took a step back. "I know who you are."

"Colomba doesn't feel well. If you could just give us a few minutes . . ."

Rovere's voice was understanding and reasonable, and once again Dante felt the impulse to leave. But he couldn't do it. "I have a better idea. Why don't you go away."

"Signor Torre . . . maybe you've misinterpreted what's happening here . . ."

"No, I don't think I have." He brushed past him and went over to Colomba, who took his hand and allowed him to help her to her feet. "How are you? All better now?"

Colomba didn't even try to pretend. "Almost."

He handed her a Kleenex. "Your lip is bleeding."

She dabbed at the blood. "It's nothing."

"Breathe slowly, and if you need something, I'm carrying my own personal pharmacy."

"I don't take that crap you use."

Dante turned to address Rovere. "Why did you choose Colomba? Why did you send her to me?"

"Because I trust her."

Dante shook his head. "Fucking liar," he murmured.

"You don't know me, Torre."

"But I know people like you."

"Let's go," said Colomba, heading haltingly toward the car.

Rovere tried to follow her, but Dante shook his head. "You're not included."

"We need to talk about what's happened," Rovere objected.

"Not now," said Dante. "We'll call you." When he got to the car, Colomba was already behind the wheel. "Are you up to driving?" he asked her.

"Do you want to drive instead?"

"I was thinking of a taxi."

"Forget about that."

"Okay, but go slow. I'm not feeling all that good either."

"I don't want to go back right away. I need some fresh air," she said as she pulled away.

"If you open the window in your hotel room, you'll get all the fresh air you want."

"What about Trastevere? It's better. It's my favorite part of Rome."

"Trust me, you need to get some rest."

"No."

Dante looked out the car window until Colomba parked outside the Ministry of Public Education. That late at night, there were hardly any tourists, aside from a group of drunken Englishmen who were laughing loudly.

"I'll wait for you here," said Dante. "Just leave the window down for me."

"Come on, get out. Let's take a walk. Or do you have phobias about walking, too?"

"How sweet," he commented. But he obeyed.

They walked down the boulevard, whose bars and souvenir stands were already closed. Only two Pakistanis selling roses were still at work; the Pakistanis followed them for a short distance. There was also a fake Irish pub still open. The end of summer had even taken with it the street vendor selling *grattachecca*, the sweet slushy drink made with shaved ice from a single huge block, found only in the capital.

Colomba liked being in that familiar corner of the city, far from the stench of blood. She went there with friends and colleagues whenever she could. When there was something important to celebrate, she always went to a restaurant that was popular with theatrical actors, on Via della Gensola, across from Tiber Island.

"I was born near here," Colomba said. "And when I come here, I feel at home."

"Interesting," he muttered.

"Where do you feel at home?"

"At home. In my apartment, where I can no longer go."

"Anywhere else?"

"The Bar Marani, right near where I live. It has tables outside, protected by steel grates."

"I have no more questions." Colomba looked around.

"I'm hungry. Should we go back to the hotel? Everything around here is closed."

"I know a place," said Colomba, her face lighting up. She led him to the rolled-down security blind outside a bakery. "Have you ever been here?" she asked.

"I have bread delivered to my apartment."

"Forno la Renella. One of the best bakeries in Rome."

"I'm from Cremona. Anyway, it's closed."

"Tell me what you want."

"A krapfen pastry with marmalade, made without lard. No, make that two. I've got the pharmaceutical munchies."

"Wait for me here." Colomba went around the corner and knocked on the half-closed frosted-glass door, from behind which came a wonderful aroma of fresh-baked bread. Through the cracked-open door she glimpsed shelves stacked high with overflowing metal trays. A baker Colomba had never seen before opened the door to her, and she ordered Dante's two krapfen and a slice of plain focaccia for herself. The man handed them over, piping hot, and she and Dante ate as they walked back to the car.

Dante burnt his mouth at the first bite. "Ah."

"Don't wolf your food," Colomba replied with her mouth full.

"If you haven't had boiling-hot marmalade slide down your esophagus, you haven't experienced life. Did you come here when you were a little girl?"

"Not when I was a little girl. When I worked the night beat."

"Cops and whores," said Dante.

"And junkies."

Dante swallowed the last bite and started on his second krapfen. "So now are you convinced?"

"That someone kidnapped the Maugeris' son, yes."

"Not *someone*."

Colomba was stuffed. She threw away the last chunk of focaccia, wrapped in the napkin dripping with oil. "If you want me to tell you that I'm positive the Father is behind the identity of Zardoz . . . I'm sorry, but I can't. The story of the wheat in the movie is a beautiful coincidence but . . . it's not enough, just like the whistle wasn't enough."

"Go ahead and keep your doubts. Working with a skeptic helps you to keep an open mind." He threw away the paper bag and washed his hands at a street spigot. "Even if it's a pain in the ass."

Colomba followed suit. The icy water that she splashed on her face wiped the veil of sleep away from her mind for a moment. "That is, if we keep working on this," she said.

"What other choice do we have?"

"Just one: let Rovere take care of it himself. He has a team of investigators. Let him turn them loose to chase down Zardoz, whoever he is. Or let him convince the CIS to get busy."

"Do you think they'd believe you?"

"Rovere needs no more persuading. De Angelis would dismiss

everything as a coincidence; he'd request further investigations, additional evidence . . . And in the meantime Zardoz might decide it wasn't in his best interests to hold onto the boy any longer. And he'd kill him." Colomba locked arms with him and started walking again. Dante was surprised and delighted by the gesture. "If he hasn't already made up his mind to do it."

"So you want to keep working on it."

"The smart thing would be to pull out, but . . ." She shook her head.

"You can't do it."

"No. I can't do it."

"Because of the burden that you're carrying with you."

"Maybe."

He looked at her. "Are you depressed enough to talk to me about it?"

"Five minutes ago, I might have been. But that focaccia made me feel so much better."

"Then I missed my opportunity."

They walked in silence for a few more minutes. "I know that I shouldn't let you be involved in this thing anymore, now that there's been a murder," said Colomba.

"And the most sensible thing for me to do now would be to bow out." Dante flashed his sarcastic grin. "But I've made it a point of honor to live with no regard for common sense."

"How much time do you think we have?"

Dante thought it over for a few more steps. "Every time the Father acts, he increases the likelihood of being caught, especially now that we suspect he's still in operation. He's old. He'll keep the boy to the bitter end."

"All the better for us."

Dante made a face.

"What's wrong?" asked Colomba. "Don't you agree?"

"Yes. But if he, too, thinks that the Maugeris' son is going to be his last victim . . . He's not going to wait patiently until we show up to catch him. And I'm afraid of what he might do."

10

The man who called himself Zardoz went back to the apartment building where no one knew what he really did. On the internal handle of the door to his apartment he had stacked a pile of coins in a very specific order. He barely opened the door and reached his hand around to grab the stack of coins before they could fall. He checked to make sure the order was correct, then swung the door all the way open. The system might be simple, but it worked. It wouldn't have stopped a burglar, but he wasn't afraid of burglars. He was afraid of intruders and spies.

Not that he really thought anyone suspected him. Not after all those months spent forging a gray and unexceptional identity. He took off the raincoat and washed his hands. The scalpel that he had used to kill Montanari was at the bottom of the Tiber, snapped in half. He slipped the gloves and the condom into a bottle of bleach. He made himself a cup of tea, then went into his office.

It was a room ten feet by six, covered with sound-deadening panels, and with lowered wooden roller blinds. At the center stood a small table and a chair, with a computer. No other furniture, except for a chest of drawers. No paintings on the wall, no carpet on the floor. Nothing else. The computer had a microphone and headset and was hooked up to the Internet through an unauthorized connection to a neighbor's Wi-Fi, by means of a password he'd hacked. He pressed his thumb down on the sensor, and the screen unlocked; then he logged on to the remote server where he kept his data and the program he used for his work. The virus that he'd released into the Web had done its work, deleting all compromising content from Montanari's virtual hard drive, and was already doing the same with the site where Montanari carried out his commerce. He had in fact infected them both with a lethal program and could pull the trigger whenever he chose; he had pulled that trigger before going out to kill. Montanari's computer, however, had been taken offline, presumably by the police.

He thought it over for a few seconds. What could they find out? Certainly not who was behind the name Zardoz or what material he'd purchased. That information was gone for good. In any case, he had eliminated every last trace of Zardoz from the Internet. The identity had ceased to exist and to have a history, while entire sites on the so-called darknet were burned to the ground by his attack. But the fact that Montanari's computer had been disconnected so quickly meant that the police were already on his trail. The man who had been Zardoz was too cautious to overlook that signal. There were eyes focused in the right direction, and they were growing from mere problems into a genuine danger.

As dawn brightened the sky, he carefully planned out the next murder.

11

When she got back to the suite, Colomba collapsed in a sprawl on the bed, taking off only her police boots. Dante made himself a green-coffee infusion and waited, watching from the balcony as the windows of Rome doused their lights, smoking one cigarette after the other and jotting down notes. The desk clerk's call came at six in the morning, when day was already dawning; when he got downstairs, he found Santiago stretched out on one of the little sofas in the lobby, his feet clad in gold sneakers propped up on the glass coffee table.

Santiago was a young South American with thug tattoos spouting out from under his shirt onto his neck and wrists, the same images that decorated his jacket. There were symbols of the Cuchillos, one of the Latino gangs fighting for control of the streets of Rome, largely unknown to those in the city who weren't Latinos, with the exception of the police. One arm was wrapped around the waist of a very young girl whose jeans were so tight they, too, looked like tattoos; she wore her hair in dreadlocks: Dante just hoped she wasn't a minor.

"Here I am!" shouted Santiago when he saw him. He got up to hug him and kiss him on both cheeks.

"How are you doing?" asked Dante, sitting across from him on another small sofa.

"Better and better, like always. You know me, right?" Santiago was a second-generation Roman, born and raised in the city, but he put on a Colombian accent because it gave him an exotic air. He caressed the girl. "This is Luna."

Dante sketched a graceful hand-kiss in her direction, and Luna giggled.

"What's your room number?" Santiago asked.

"F," Dante replied after a slight hesitation.

Santiago raised an eyebrow. "F?"

"Hotel suites have letters, not numbers. But I hardly think it's necessary."

Santiago ignored him and caressed Luna again. "You hear that? F. Now go over to the bar." He pointed to the counter at the far end of the lobby, where a sleepy-looking waiter was waiting for his shift to end. "Have something to drink and put it on my friend's tab." Santiago waited for Luna to move off, swinging her hips on her cork wedge pumps; then he turned back to Dante. "Were you afraid I was going to send her up to your room?"

"I'll admit that the thought had crossed my mind."

"She's not working right now: she's with me because she likes me."

Dante nodded. "Of course."

"What can I do for you, *hermano*?"

"A little research on a guy who goes by the name Zardoz on the Web. He buys kiddie stuff."

"Is the name all you have?"

Dante handed him the sheet of paper he'd filled in while he was waiting. "These are the sites he used and the name of a man he's done business with. I wrote down his email address, too."

"And this man?"

"He's dead. I also included a list of sites he might have hacked into. See if he did. Be careful; the police are investigating this case."

Santiago slipped the piece of paper into his jacket pocket. "The way I operate, they won't even see the dust I kick up."

"Be careful anyway."

"It'll cost you, you know that, right?"

"How much?"

"Four grand."

"Two. Then we'll see, depending on what you bring me. How will I pay you?"

Santiago gave him the number of a Peruvian prepaid card. Dante promised he'd wire him the money that day.

Santiago nodded. "But first there's something I want to know, *hermano*."

"Wasn't the rule always *no questions*?"

"If you're sleeping with a lady cop, the rules don't apply."

Dante sighed. He should have guessed that Santiago would be well informed. "I'm not sleeping *with* her. We're staying in the same suite. And she's on administrative leave."

"Yeah, but she's still a cop, though."

"Is that a problem?"

"No. You can do whatever you want. You're my friend, but you're not one of us." Dante nodded. "Still, I have to know why you didn't ask her instead of me."

"You said it yourself, that you're faster."

"Is that the only reason?"

"And because I don't trust her channels."

Santiago laughed. "Right you are. Never trust cops."

"But I trust her, and you might as well know it."

"So you're going to tell her about me?"

"Yes. But don't worry, there won't be any consequences." *Not for you, at least*, he added in his mind.

Santiago stood up, summoning his girlfriend back with a tilt of the head. She set down her umbrella cocktail and hurried over. "I never worry, worrying is for losers," he said.

"Lucky you."

"I'll write you soon."

"How soon?"

"I don't know, *hermano*. A couple of days."

"Santiago . . . I need something fast. Please."

Santiago looked hard at Dante's taut face and nodded. "I'll see what I can do."

After another hug, Santiago left, his arms wrapped around Luna. They looked like a pair of sweethearts.

Dante dragged himself into his room and fell asleep fully clothed, dead to the world. He slept only three hours because Santiago really had gotten straight to work. He'd sent his first results to the server that Dante used for this kind of thing. Once Dante saw them, he lost any desire to sleep.

12

Colomba woke up at two in the afternoon and took a long shower, reviewing in her mind the events of the night before. She thought about Montanari's murder, Zardoż, and even the long stroll with Dante. She'd felt comfortable in Trastevere by night, comfortable in a way that hadn't happened to her with another human being in months. She wondered if she wasn't becoming fond of him. The idea worried her. She wasn't ready for a relationship with anyone, not since the Disaster. And after all, once this case was finished, she'd probably never see him again.

She put on the bright white bathrobe with the hotel's logo and went into the living room, where she found six dirty cups next to the espresso machine. Dante must have been up for quite a while already, and the Hindi music that wafted out of his room told her that he was already at work on something. The Bollywood background music coming from Spotify was his favorite for when he was on the computer, though Colomba couldn't really tell one song from the next.

She made a cappuccino and knocked on Dante's door with the cup in one hand.

When she opened the door, she was assaulted by the stench of cigarettes. Dante was sitting in the middle of the bed, his laptop balanced on his crossed legs, dressed in the same clothes he'd worn yesterday. The smoke was so thick that she had a hard time seeing. He'd put duct tape over the smoke alarm to keep it from going off. When he saw her, he turned off the music.

Colomba threw open the French door, though she cautiously left the curtains drawn. "Do you want to suffocate?"

"You told me that at night I'm supposed to keep the door shut."

"It's not night now." Colomba analyzed the quantity of cigarette butts in a glass on the table, then looked at his exhausted face and decided rightly that he'd gone all night without sleep, or something close to it. "Don't you need sleep?"

"I used to know a guy who never slept," said Dante.

"And what became of him?"

"Someone shot him in the head; now he sleeps all the time." He smiled, but it was clear to Colomba that he was tense.

"What's going on?" she asked, sitting down on the edge of the bed.

Dante rummaged in the pack, pulled out the last cigarette, and lit it, in defiance of Colomba's disapproving look. "I've got some information. And it's useful."

"What information?"

"About Zardoz. I gave everything I knew to an acquaintance and told him to dig around online."

Colomba felt the sudden urge to grab Dante, lock him in a trunk, and let him kick and twist. "Who's this *acquaintance* of yours?"

"His name is Santiago Hurtado."

"Not the guy from the Cuchillos, surely?"

Dante nodded yes.

"Do you have any idea who they are?"

"CC, that doesn't matter right now."

"Like hell it doesn't matter. We arrested Hurtado two years ago, with four of his friends, for stabbing a guy. And the only reason he got off is because three witnesses swore that he was snorting coke at a club at the time."

"Right."

"And now you decide to send *him* confidential information about a murder and kidnapping investigation?"

"In his way, he's a man of his word."

"Honor among thieves," said Colomba sarcastically. "How did you meet him?"

"Can we skip that part?"

"No. We can't."

Dante shrugged his shoulders: he didn't want a fight, and once again Colomba understood that his thoughts were elsewhere. "If you insist. Minutillo was Santiago's lawyer. I gave him a hand tracking down the witnesses you just mentioned."

Colomba seethed with indignation. "Then that means it's your fault."

"Santiago is no longer a Cuchillo in the narrow sense of the word. After what happened, he got out of drug dealing."

Colomba folded her arms. "That's a big consolation . . . No, sorry. I don't want to interrupt anymore. Go on with your story."

"He's always been something of a geek, and he discovered that he was really good at getting into the computers of people who want to keep others out of them. And now that's what he sells."

"From drug dealer to hacker. Just the fact that we're using him could send us both to prison, you know that, right?"

"Luca Maugeri is in the hands of a monster. You do remember *that*, don't you?"

"The Ministry of Justice's Special Internet Crimes Division . . ." said Colomba without much conviction.

"Is that supposed to be a joke?"

"What did he find out about Zardoz?" she asked brusquely.

"That he's burning his bridges. All the sites that Montanari used have been burned to the ground."

"Burned to the ground?"

"The server hard drives have been erased. Santiago doesn't entirely rule out the possibility that he might still find something, but it's going to take time."

"Is that all?"

"No. He found out that about two months ago Zardoz penetrated the server of the local health service. Just a few days after the Maugeris' son was examined at the clinic."

"Is it all so easy?"

Dante shrugged. "With what he used to punch into the health service site, even you could have done it."

"Why? What did he use?"

"A malware spybot, a cute little spy app that installs itself on the server and transmits data remotely back to whoever installed it, allowing them to find the system passwords and so on. According to Santiago, it's identical to what the Chinese hackers used to get into Apple's servers."

"I doubt that Zardoz is Chinese."

"You can download that kind of software from the Web, no problem. All you have to know is where to find it. It's just that he's very well informed. He's a professional. Or else he has a professional working for him, the way Santiago works for me. And he used a similar kind of software."

Colomba thought it over for a while. "So Zardoz didn't trust Montanari enough to ask him for information about the boy. He took care of that himself."

"But the boy's file didn't provide enough information to identify him."

"How do you know?"

"I called the director of the local health clinic. After what happened, he was much more cooperative. I got him to give me the lists."

"Did you pass yourself off as a cop?"

"Not directly."

Colomba shut her eyes. "We're getting deeper and deeper into the shit."

"From the lists that the medical director sent me, it was possible to identify the names of the children who had taken part in the school medical examination program, but there are no pictures, physical descriptions, or indications of date or time. And there were over three hundred children."

"So how did Zardoz manage to find the right one?"

"The same way I did. I discarded the little girls and the boys on whose files there was a father's signature."

"Because Luca was taken in by his mother. You can see that in the video," said Colomba.

"Exactly. That left twenty names. I discarded the ones with a female doctor."

"Because you can see the doctor in the video, too . . ."

"Which left fourteen. I called those fourteen people this morning before you woke up."

"And?"

"Four of them got a phone call from Zardoz."

Colomba's heart skipped a beat. "Holy Christ," she whispered.

Dante put out his cigarette and set the glass back on the nightstand.

"Two conversations were very brief because the misunderstanding emerged immediately. One conversation was a little longer because the mother got worried."

"Zardoz was looking for a very particular child. He wasn't interested in any other."

"Yes. The autistic son of a lonely woman. Who would do anything for him."

"How did he introduce himself?"

"As Dr. Zedda of the National Health Service." Dante shook his head. "I checked, there's no such person. But I needn't have bothered. Zed is a character in the movie, the man behind the flying mask."

"Zed, *Zedda*," said Colomba.

"Exactly. Dr. Zedda said that the doctor at the clinic had talked to him and had reported the child's worrisome symptoms. Then he started asking questions, trying to determine whether the child was distracted, absent, sad, and so on. When the mother started to seem puzzled, he inquired about the child's appearance and then apologized for having mixed up the files. The fourth mother, however, was so worried that she said yes to everything. Zedda made an appointment to meet at the Termini train station. He pretended to be passing through Rome for a conference. She waited for him, but he didn't show up. He had figured out that she wasn't the right person."

"Fuck, that was a close call," said Colomba, but the tense expression on Dante's face told her there was something else. "Or was it?" she whispered.

"She says that while she was leaving, she had the feeling someone was watching her and . . . maybe she was mistaken, but maybe . . ." He snickered, though he'd never seemed so tense. "Maybe she saw him."

13

The wrong mother was named Chiara Pacifici. She was drinking a hot chocolate at Castroni, one of the favorite cafés of upper-class Rome, with a St. Bernard dog that was dying from the heat. Another hundred or so people were packed in among the refrigerators and shelves piled high with *gourmandises* at jewelry store prices. Colomba showed her police ID and asked her to sit down at one of the outdoor tables outside the bar next door to avoid the crowd.

"I had no idea it was such a serious matter," said the woman, nervously.

"Oh, it isn't, signora, it's just a normal administrative check," Colomba lied.

"But if you came all the way here to talk to me . . . Tell me the truth, who was the man who called me?"

Dante ineptly tried to block the question. "A stalker, signora," he replied. "He pretends to be a doctor so he can lure women to meet him, and then he molests them."

"Oh, Lord . . . but what if he comes back? If he wants to hurt me . . ."

Colomba grabbed Dante's arm to make him shut up. "You misunderstood, signora," she said. "The man we're looking for isn't dangerous, and he isn't violent. He's—"

"—an exhibitionist," Dante concluded.

"Someone who goes around exposing his *thing*?" the woman asked.

"Exactly, he goes around exposing his *thing*."

"Disgusting," the woman commented, more relaxed now. "It's a good thing he didn't try it with me."

"But he has tried it with many other women, and we're trying to track him down," Colomba explained. "He's sick in the head, he's not a criminal."

"How can I help you?"

"You said you might have seen him."

"I can't be sure it was him. He was near where I was waiting, and that's where I would have been if I had been waiting for someone myself. I don't know if that makes sense to you. But . . . maybe he was just someone who . . . who was looking at me. I mean, some people think I'm not horrible to look at."

Dante didn't pick up the cue until Colomba kicked him in the ankle. Then he put on the fakest smile she'd ever seen in her life. "I'd certainly say you're not, signora."

"But if it actually was him, it would help us a great deal if you could describe him for us," said Colomba.

"I'm not sure how well I remember him."

"Still, he made an impression on you," Dante insisted, his patience stretched to the limit. "Otherwise you wouldn't have told me about him." He pulled a notebook and a pencil with a silver clip out of his pocket and held the pencil in his good hand. "If you describe his appearance . . . I can try to do a sketch of him."

"Like one of those police sketches you see on TV?"

"Exactly. Creating identikits is sort of my specialty. But to do it, I'll have to take off this," he said, holding up his bad hand covered with the black glove. "It's awkward to hold the edge of the paper with my glove on. I had an accident, and it's not a pretty sight."

"Don't worry, I'm not easily frightened," the woman said, but after Dante bared his hand, her expression changed. "You poor thing. Does it hurt?"

"Only when I play the piano . . . Shall we give it a try? Let's start with his physique."

"Big."

"Big?"

"Not so tall, but built like a truck driver."

"Broad shoulders?" asked Colomba.

"And a bit of a gut."

"Age?" asked Dante.

"About sixty, I'd say. Maybe a little older. He was wearing a suit and tie, and he was carrying a valise. A briefcase."

"Eyes?"

"Blue. A very light blue."

Dante's good hand twitched so violently that he dropped the pencil. He froze in place, his eyes fixed in the middle distance.

Without letting the woman see, Colomba squeezed his leg. "We've been rude, Dante. We haven't even asked if the lady would care for something to drink. Why don't we go get her whatever she'd like?"

"I'd love a Coke," she said.

"We'll be right back," Colomba replied, clenching her fingers around Dante's thigh again, but harder this time. He snapped to, and they stood up together, with Colomba supporting him by the arm, all the while doing her best to seem kind and considerate and nothing more.

"Not inside," she murmured to him as soon as they'd walked a short way. "Too many people."

She pushed him around the corner. Dante leaned back against the wall, trembling uncontrollably. Colomba took his good hand in hers. "Everything's okay. Dante . . ."

Colomba's voice came to him from an infinite distance, as her face vanished and a gray wall appeared between them. The wall of the silo. The crack in the wall. The Father who looked at him from the meadow with a knife in his hand.

"It's him, CC," he said so softly that even he couldn't hear it.

Colomba delicately held his face, forcing him to look at her. "Stay with me, Dante."

Dante closed his eyes for a moment; then he opened them again and was back. "I'm here," he announced, with a rasp in his throat.

"Good boy. Do you want me to clear the café so you can go in and wash your face?"

He smiled weakly. "It's the kind of thing you could do."

"That's nothing."

Dante curled up, holding his belly and breathing slowly. "Thank you. Go back and talk to her while I get myself calmed down, and then I'll go find a waiter. Okay?"

"Can I rely on you?"

"Don't think twice."

Colomba went back to the café table while Dante continued to control his breathing and started feeling better. The Father was no longer an abstract entity, he was no longer a phantom fluttering invisibly in the air around him. He was a human being, flesh and blood, who breathed and talked on the phone, who wore a tie. He was a person.

He was fallible.

He stood away from the wall, found a waiter, and asked him to bring the drinks. Then he went back to their table and sketched for the next half hour, following the instructions of the woman who had seen him. Colomba was astonished at how precise his hand was, like the lines of the old sketch artists the police used to use before graphics software. And how he managed to stay out of the process: he didn't add any details, he didn't embellish, and he made no suggestions. When the sketch was complete, the man looking out at her from the sheet of paper had the concrete quality of reality: a man over sixty with a large neck and flesh sagging beneath his chin, haggard cheeks, a protuberant nose, and a brutal expression. The gray hair was trimmed short and receded from the forehead, which was furrowed by three deep creases, like scars. Dante had also sketched his hands, which the woman remembered well: veins stood out on the backs of his powerful hands, broad thumbs with squared-off nails. A farmer's or a factory worker's hands, certainly not the hands of the refined intellectual that Dante believed him to be. The hands of someone capable of cutting off heads and slitting throats.

Once Dante had finished, Colomba thanked the woman and said good-bye, reassuring her and promising to keep her apprised of any developments. She asked her not to mention the investigation to anyone, and she reiterated the point more than once. The wrong mother seemed to take the point, though Colomba felt certain that the woman would get on the phone and tell all her friends every detail as soon as she got home.

She waited until the woman had left; then she ordered a granita al caffè for herself and a straight vodka for Dante, who didn't trust the quality of the cocktails.

"You know why that foolish woman is still alive?" asked Dante. "Because the Father doesn't know he was seen. Otherwise we'd have three corpses; that is, assuming there aren't other corpses out there we don't even know about."

Colomba couldn't seem to take her eyes off the identikit. "She's not that big of a fool if she recognized him," she said. "But maybe he was some average Joe on his way to catch a train and we're building a complicated plot based on a chance encounter."

Dante pulled a folded sheet of paper out of his pocket. It was the identikit of the man he'd seen through the crack in the silo wall, the one drawn up by the Cremona police. He lay it down next to the other one, and the resemblance was so striking that it took Colomba's breath away. The same shape of the face, the same small ears, and especially the same eyes. Even if the rest was incomplete, the sketched-out lines of the old identikit overlaid the new lines perfectly, despite the marks of time. It was the same man, twenty-five years older. Dante had been right from day one.

14

An hour later Colomba parked the van in Largo Martin Luther King, across from one of the entrances to Villa Pamphili, and turned off the engine.

"Do you think you can be left alone for ten minutes?" she asked Dante. He was practically stretched out, with the back rest of his seat tilted all the way back. He'd wrapped his tie over his eyes to keep out the light, and the effect was more comical than pathetic.

"Go on," he said.

"Don't start popping those crap pills of yours."

He stuck out his tongue, and poised on the tip was a two-tone capsule. "Already have."

She slammed the door and walked into the park, filling her lungs with the smell of freshly cut grass. She reached the Ponte Nanni, the bridge stretching across one of the ponds, just as a team of runners crossed it, iPod earbuds in their ears. She saw Rovere standing motionless at the middle of the bridge, leaning on the railing and smoking with his head bowed. He seemed even older and wearier than he had when she'd last seen him in the mountain meadows. He noticed her and waved hello, with a tense smile. Colomba went over and stood next to him, careful to stay upwind of his cigarette.

"Thanks for calling me," said Rovere. "After yesterday, I thought you were angry with me."

"Oh, I'm angry with you, all right, for having gotten me into this mess. But I certainly can't go forward all alone. Especially not now." She handed him the identikit, and Rovere's eyes opened wide. For an instant, he looked scared to Colomba. "Do you know him?" she asked.

"No . . . it just caught me off guard. Who is it?" he asked, without taking his eyes off the sheet of paper.

"The man who kidnapped the Maugeris' son. And held Dante Torre prisoner."

Rovere stared at her feverishly. "Are you sure?"

"Yes. He used Montanari to find his prey; then he killed him. Online, he uses the name Zardoz. He's good at disappearing, and he's been on the loose for thirty-five years committing all kinds of foul crimes. Dante saw him kill a boy before escaping."

"I remember," Rovere murmured. "But it was never proven that the boy even existed."

"Either the cops who investigated were bumbling idiots, or else he, Zardoz, the Father, or whatever you want to call him, really is a genius at making corpses disappear."

Rovere had recovered from his astonishment. "Someone who kidnaps children isn't a genius. He's mentally ill."

"If so, he's the healthiest mentally ill person I've ever heard of. He knows what he wants, and he takes it."

"A well-organized serial killer," said Rovere. "He wouldn't be the first."

"Yes, but *this* organized is something well beyond the levels described in any textbook case. He uses accomplices, he palms himself off as a doctor, he surfs the Web like a pro, he confidently manipulates crime scenes . . . And he does all this so he can play sadistic games with children and then murder them as soon as they get too old." Colomba shook her head. "It doesn't hang together, but I can't come up with a better explanation."

"Who saw him?" asked Rovere.

"One of the mothers he contacted when he was trying to find the Maugeris' son."

"And does he know that he was seen?"

"Luckily, no. Now what do we do?"

Rovere folded the sheet of paper and put it into his jacket pocket. "I'll put the identikit into the system and see what comes out. In the meantime, you and Signor Torre stay put."

"Excuse me?" asked Colomba.

"Until just a short while ago, we were operating in the field of hypothesis, but now we're certain that we have a murderer at large. I don't want to put you in danger."

"Dealing with murderers is my job."

"It used to be."

Colomba couldn't believe her ears. "Are you sure you're the same person who wanted me to keep going while I was lying on the sidewalk, practically dying? What the fuck has happened to you?"

"Nothing. I'm just worried about you. Let me do my research."

"We need to talk to the other mothers, to Maugeri, to the neighbors, to the people who were up at the mountain meadows," Colomba insisted.

"I'll take care of that. But in the meantime, you be a good girl. Okay?"

Colomba, in an outburst of exasperation, slammed a hand down on the railing. "I can't believe it. You drag me into this case, and when it finally starts to make sense, you want to take me off it."

"Colomba, the problem isn't just your personal safety. Today the chief of police asked me about you. De Angelis busted his chops, and he wanted to know what you and I were up to together. And the Ministry of Justice also wants to find out what you know that they don't."

"Who the fuck cares about the Ministry of Justice and the chief of police? We have a chance of catching him!"

"Not if we act impulsively, we don't. Rest up for a couple of days. I'm not asking you, I'm telling you."

Colomba stood looking at him for a few seconds without a word; then she turned on her heel and walked away, taking long strides, shoving aside a long-distance runner coming from the opposite direction.

When she got back, she found Dante stretched out on his back on the hood of the car.

"If that's where you want to ride, be my guest," she growled.

"I just wanted to look at the sky." He leapt to the ground and seemed to be the usual Dante again. "What does that genius of a boss of yours have to say?"

"Nothing helpful."

"Did I already tell you that I don't like him?"

"You made it clear. Let's go back to the hotel."

"Not yet. Santiago called me; apparently he's found something big online. I don't know what, because we don't feel safe talking on the phone. Are you ready to take a walk on the wild side?"

Colomba thought back to her conversation with Rovere and his advice to drop all further activity. "I can't wait," she said.

15

Still feeling tense, Colomba drove to the outlying neighborhood of Tor Bella Monaca, where Santiago lived. It was one of the neighborhoods with the highest crime rates in Rome, where fifteen-story apartment houses were connected by internal labyrinths of alleys and tunnels, subsidized housing inhabited by poverty-stricken families, and mafiosi doing business in new and greener fields. The roundups and arrests that Colomba had been involved in there had always culminated in hails of rocks and bottles out of high windows, burning car tires, and screaming crowds. When a policeman entered Torbella— as its inhabitants liked to call it—he was entering enemy territory. Colomba knew that many of the people who lived around there were good folks who just couldn't afford to move anyplace else, old people and the unemployed held in subjugation by the face-slapping arrogance of their criminal neighbors. But that did nothing to lessen the hatred she felt for that Roman quarter, knowing as she did that out of any doorway a gun barrel might poke, ready to fire the bullet that would punch a hole in her forehead.

Dante directed her toward a group of four public housing projects six stories tall, arranged like a stretched-out C, with outside walls a smoky gray and ramshackle window fixtures. The mailboxes were blackened by the blasts of firecrackers or spray-painted various colors, while the intercom panels had been yanked out of the walls. Out front, there was an expanse of lawn that was mostly stumps and scrub, and heaps of rubble, where a group of even dirtier and dustier children was playing war, hurling clumps of dirt at one another.

All the apartment buildings were connected to the same interior courtyard, and Colomba drove toward one of the entrances. Immediately, the way was blocked by three boys on scooters. They were driving without helmets, and the oldest of the three, a Maghrebi, couldn't have been even fourteen.

He was the one who knocked on the window, right next to Colomba's head. "Who are you going to see?" he asked.

"None of your fucking business, kid," Colomba replied.

Dante leaned out almost simultaneously. "Santiago's expecting us."

"What's your name?" the boy inquired.

"Dante."

The Maghrebi signaled to one of the other boys, so tiny that he could barely put his feet on the ground with the moped stopped. "Go call him."

The littlest boy revved up the moped and vanished into the inner courtyard. The two others moved a couple of yards away from the car but still blocked its way. They lit cigarettes.

"That's the way it is here," Dante said to Colomba.

"I'd take the parents of these boys and send them directly to jail without passing Go."

"That's probably where they already are," said Dante.

After a few minutes Santiago emerged from the basement with two boys, who might have been eighteen at the most. They were South Americans, and unlike Santiago, who dressed in a nondescript manner aside from his leather jacket and colorful track shoes, they wore sagging trousers, backward baseball caps, and T-shirts with thuggish slogans. Colomba, to her surprise, actually recognized one of them. His name was Jorge Pérez, and she had arrested him for assault two years ago, when he was still a minor.

Santiago slapped the Maghrebi amiably on the back and sent him away with the other sentinels, while Jorge started cursing in Spanish. "That lady's a cop," he told Santiago while making a rapid gesture in Colomba's direction that in the language of the street was a mute death threat.

She raised her middle finger in return, but with her other hand, unseen, she pulled her pistol out of its holster and propped it between her legs.

"Did you see what she just did?" Jorge asked Santiago.

Santiago ignored him. "Why did you have to bring her with you?" he asked Dante. "I told you to come alone."

"Because he doesn't go anywhere alone," Colomba replied.

"I wasn't asking you," said Santiago.

Dante got out, and Colomba felt her lungs tightening up. If any one of the three were armed, he might take Dante's action as aggressive and shoot him. But Santiago remained calm, and none of the others made a move.

"I told you I trust her. And we're in this together."

Santiago looked at Jorge and then asked how he knew her. "*¿Cómo es que la conoces?*"

"*Me ha enviado a la cárcel,*" Jorge replied, repeating the menacing gesture. She had sent him to prison.

Santiago spoke to Dante again. "No."

"You've already done the job. Do you really want to give up the money?"

"This is how I make money," said Santiago, snapping his fingers in front of his face.

"You want to give up a friend like me? I've been useful to you in the past. I might be useful again someday."

Santiago looked down at the toes of his shoes, uncertainly. "Do you vouch for her?"

"Certainly."

"If she's going in, we have to search her," said Jorge.

Colomba stuck her handgun back in her belt and got out. "Just try it, you dickhead."

"If she has a gun, she can't come in," Santiago stated. "That's a point I can't meet you halfway on, Dante."

"Your people are armed."

"My people aren't cops."

Dante looked at Colomba. "I'm going to have to ask you to trust them, then."

"No gun because I'm a cop?"

"Exactly."

Moving slowly and holding it out by the tips of her fingers, Colomba pulled the gun out of her belt and slid it into Dante's. "He's not a cop, is he?"

Santiago laughed. "No, Dante's not a cop."

Jorge tried to object, but Santiago shut him up with a kick to the seat of his pants, and warned him not to make him lose his temper. "*Cállate antes de que yo me enojo, ¿OK?*"

Dante looked at the dark, narrow tunnel running beneath the building and felt his breath fail him. "Can't we talk here? It looks a little tight in there."

"Don't worry. I know your tastes," said Santiago. "We'll go up."

"Up?"

Santiago pointed to the roof. "That's where I have my office."

They started off toward the entrance. Dante let Colomba walk by his side. "I don't feel particularly comfortable with this," he said, pointing to the butt of the pistol.

"Shut up. And stick close to me. Right now you're my walking holster."

The elevators in the building were out of use, the cables long ago snapped. They climbed up a long metal fire escape that rose up, attached to the interior facade of the main building.

For Dante, even climbing that staircase was no laughing matter, because he froze with every creak and groan of the structure, and they were frequent. In the end, he closed his eyes and Colomba was forced to act as his seeing-eye dog during the ascent. Taking care not to be noticed, she studied the place. It was structured like a full-fledged fortress, with lookouts standing sentinel, almost all of them young men, boys, or even little kids, keeping an eye on every access point, either straddling the saddle of their moped or else standing at windows. There were also watchmen at each floor, on the landings of the fire escape. On one of those landings, she even noticed a junkie shooting up. The others ignored him, and Colomba did the same, though the urge to call for uniformed reinforcements was almost overpowering.

"Are we here?" Dante asked in a faint voice.

"Yes, you can open your eyes," said Colomba. "And you have no idea what a lovely spectacle you missed on the way up."

They'd reached the rooftop, the area that had once been designated as a shared common space where residents could sunbathe or hang out laundry to dry. Santiago and his gang had transformed it into an open-air rec room, dragging up there a half-dozen or so swaybacked sofas, as many plastic tables, and a refrigerator pirating electric power through a cable that disappeared down the interior stairwell. Next to one of the sofas stood a hookah that was more than a yard tall, with four mouthpieces made of corrugated rubber. The cement surface was littered with cigarette butts, empty bottles, and bird shit—all except for one perfectly clean corner. There, under a plastic canopy with a drape down the sides to keep off the rain, was a little electronic workshop, with two brand-new desktop computers, a thirty-inch screen, and a digital disc burner, all of them hooked up to a satellite dish antenna.

Noticing that Colomba was looking at it, Santiago patted the dish. "For our connection, we go directly via satellite. The ping is high, but no one can sniff the network."

Colomba nodded, baffled by the contrast between Santiago's general attitude and his unmistakable technical prowess.

Dante had recovered from the ascent. "What did you find that's so interesting?" he asked Santiago.

Santiago pointed to his two fellow thugs. "Your friend Zardoz did good work. I've never seen so many sites burned down in a single night. But even he made a couple of mistakes. He used another site for his business. He burned that one down, too, but not all the way to the ground."

"I found it," said Jorge, lighting himself a joint. "He used it five months ago."

"Are you talking about another darknet site?" asked Colomba, making everyone present shudder in horror.

"You watch too much TV, cop lady," said the second gangster, who up until that moment had remained silent. On the back of his hands he had the word "MIRRORSHADES" tattooed, "MIRROR" on the one hand, "SHADES" on the other.

"Anyway, it was another e-commerce site. No PayPal or any of that shit, strictly Bitcoin," Santiago added.

"Electronic cash," said Colomba.

Everyone smirked again. "All right. What you said," Jorge conceded.

"And what did he buy with Bitcoin five months ago?" Colomba asked in alarm. "More videos?"

"That's the weird thing; he didn't buy, he sold," Jorge replied.

"And he sold it for *un montón de dinero*. Twenty thousand euros," said Santiago. "He might have sold other stuff, but we can't find out. And if he did . . . *puff* . . . it all disappeared."

"What did he sell?" asked Dante.

"We can't tell from the burned site. But we tracked back to the buyer. He's a French *maricón*. I found his virtual hard drive. Just *full* of shit. Kids and animals, *¿lo entiendes?*"

"You can't leave him at large," said Dante, his eyes hard as glass.

"That's not my problem. It's not our job."

"I'll pay you extra," Dante said. "Screw him."

Santiago looked over at his laconic fellow gangster. "We can do it. We can just send an anonymous email to the police in his country, with a link to his hard drive. After all, I removed the one he bought from Zardoz."

"Do you have it here?" asked Colomba.

"That's why we asked you to come," said Santiago.

Dante ran his tongue over his dry lips. "How bad is it?"

"Not very. It's just . . . *extraño.*"

"I can look at it if you don't feel up to it," Colomba suggested to Dante.

Dante shook his head. "No, it's okay. We'll watch it."

Santiago sat down at the console while the other two stretched out on a sofa. When he moved from one machine to the other, even his physical demeanor changed. His motions became almost delicate. *"Con mucho gusto."*

He typed rapidly, and the moving progress bar of the video appeared on the screen. At first he only saw a black screen seething with other, darker patches, then the image was tinged green: whoever was shooting the video had made use of a night-vision video camera. The lens focused from above on a boy, little more than a child, who was washing himself with a rag. The boy dipped the rag into a bucket brimming over with water that stood on a wooden bench; then he scrubbed his body. He scrubbed meticulously, running it over his genitals and between his butt cheeks, and perhaps that was the part that most excited the buyer. Hard to say. When he ran the rag over his neck, Colomba saw that he was keeping his eyes closed. He had an oval face without much of a chin and wavy black hair.

"The details of the room have been blanked out. We tried to clean it up, but there was no way," said Santiago. "Zardoz did an excellent job."

Colomba nodded, understanding now why it was possible only to see the area around the boy, like a faded circle.

"Every centimeter twice. Every centimeter," murmured Dante. "Every centimeter twice."

Colomba took her eyes off the screen and realized that Dante was imitating the boy's every action as if in a trance, rubbing his good hand over his neck and face. "Every centimeter twice," he said again. His eyes were glued to the screen.

"Turn that gadget off," Colomba ordered Santiago, then dragged Dante over to the sofa and forced him to sit down. "Don't you have anything here to drink?"

Dante was now immobile, but he was still staring into the void.

Santiago brought a bottle of whiskey and placed it against Dante's lips. "Get this down."

He gulped, coughed, then took another, more substantial gulp.

"Take it easy, with all the pharmaceuticals you've downed," said Colomba. "How are you?"

Dante's internal thermometer dropped a couple of notches, so he could speak. "It caught me off guard," he murmured.

"The boy in the video? You've seen worse."

"But this is the first time I've seen someone who was just like me." He wiped away the tears brimming over in his eyes. "A prisoner."

16

Santiago made a copy of the video and a number of color printouts. In exchange, Dante used his computer to transfer what struck Colomba as an outrageous sum of money to a foreign bank account. The sheer number of criminal offenses she was committing in order to investigate this case was proliferating from one day to the next, but she realized that by this point she didn't much care. She'd never been much of a stickler about rules, but unlike many of her fellow cops, she'd never crossed the line between the unorthodox and the criminally actionable, however fine that line might be. Not out of fear of the consequences but rather out of respect for what the uniform that still hung in her armoire represented, a barrier between all the good that existed in the world and the chaos that threatened it and undermined it around the edges. As she gradually sank into the morass of this case, though, she realized that she cared less and less about the violations. She only wanted to lay her hands on the Father, while all the rest sank into the background. At that moment, after having watched the video, she felt herself filled with a white-hot rage that was only waiting for the chance to burst forth.

On the way back down, they retraced their steps without an escort; Santiago and his men had stayed behind to snort coke on the roof terrace. Before getting back in the car, Dante made her take a stroll into the field of brush. Even if no one came near them, much less tried to bother them in any way, Colomba felt she was being watched from every lit window in the facade behind them.

Dante smoked a couple of cigarettes without speaking.

"You can't be sure he's a prisoner," Colomba said once she thought he was capable of replying.

"The way he washed himself . . . It was the same way he taught me. The same movements. I still repeat them sometimes when I'm in the shower. Only water was a scarce commodity in the silo."

"If the Father already has a prisoner, why would he kidnap the Maugeris' son?"

"One is not enough. Nobody believed me when I told them, but there was another boy along with me. And now there's another one with Luca."

"Don't call him by his name."

Dante dismissed the objection with a luminous wave of the glowing cigarette ember. "Cut it out. For what he does, the Father needs money. Selling videos to dirty old men is the best way to get it. They won't talk, and if they do, there's no way to track back from them to him or the victim. The boy in the video could have been filmed anywhere in the world. We're the only ones who even know he's Italian."

"We just think we know. But maybe the Father took a little trip overseas."

"I already told you: he's too old to change his ways. If we need proof, we have Luca's kidnapping. If he wanted to go to Thailand, he'd have gone by now. And he'd have saved money by doing it."

Colomba stopped to think. "He sold the video five months ago, just before he started looking into the Maugeris' son."

"Funds for the new operation," Dante pointed out sadly.

Colomba sat down on a piece of cement the size of a bollard, waving away a buzzing insect. "It could be anyone."

"Santiago's video is five months old. How old do you think the boy in it could be?"

Colomba took another look at one of the pictures by the light of her cell phone. "Seven, maybe. But considering the conditions he's living in, he could certainly be older."

Colomba saw a red dot bobbing up and down in the darkness: Dante was nodding with the cigarette in his mouth. "I would agree with you. Somewhere around seven or eight. No older. If he was taken when he was six or so, he'd have been a prisoner for one or two years before this video was shot."

"So he was kidnapped sometime between 2011 and 2013, unless we're completely off track. We can check the missing-children reports."

"There's no point," said Dante.

"How do you know that?"

Dante heaved a sigh. "This is my area of expertise, don't you remember? There were roughly one hundred fifty minors reported missing in those three years, but there were very few actual children among them, and everyone remembers their names. In most of the cases, moreover, it was one of the parents who took their child out of the country."

"Well, couldn't it be one of those cases?"

"The age and the face don't match up. No matter how much they might have changed."

"Have you seen all the pictures?"

"Of course I have."

From the apartment house behind them came the sound of breaking glass and two male voices arguing in Arabic. *I'll read all about that in the newspaper tomorrow*, Colomba thought bitterly to herself. "So you're suggesting it would be a kid that nobody thinks of as having been kidnapped?" she asked, after a minute. "And how could that be?"

"Consider my case."

"They assumed you were dead."

"Bingo."

"And you're saying he did the same thing with the boy we saw in the video?"

"Why not? They'll think that Luca's dead, too, sooner or later, unless we find something. That his father murdered him and buried him in the woods."

Just a few days ago Colomba would have dismissed that hypothesis as implausible. Now she would have laid odds on it as the likely explanation. And why not, after all? If someone was crazy enough to be a serial kidnapper of children, he was certainly likely to have an equally deranged plan for making ends meet. "A child that everyone assumes is dead but whose corpse has never been found . . . I can't think of such a case anytime recently."

"Not necessarily a murder. It could have been a car crash. A car that wound up at the bottom of a river would work just as well."

"There must be quite a list," said Colomba.

"Up until 1994, at least a hundred children died in car crashes every year in Italy; the number might be a little lower nowadays, with seat belts and car seats required by law, but we don't have any reliable statistics."

"Because if we did, you'd know about them, right?"

"Sorry if I'm good at my job . . . Then there are the cases of children drowning at sea or falling into some fucking crevice or ravine in the mountains. But in most cases, the body is found."

"We'd need to get records from the highway patrol, the national park rangers . . . It's a hell of a lot of work."

"Don't you have a central database?"

"We only just got one recently for murders."

Dante blew out his cheeks in exasperation. "I'm amazed you still occasionally arrest people. Can you ask Rovere?"

"No. He's decided that he no longer requires our assistance."

Dante stopped short, just as he was about to light another cigarette. "When were you planning on telling me that?"

"Why, what's it change for you?" Colomba barked, angry at being caught in the wrong.

"I never trusted him. And I trust him even less now that he's cut us out of the investigation."

"He says that he's worried about me."

"Bullshit. He cares about you, but that's not what's driving him. He has other motives, it's just that I can't seem to figure them out. That's why I'm worried."

I'm starting to see things the same way, Colomba thought, but she kept it to herself. Instead, she shrugged her shoulders; even Dante couldn't see her. "But he's not the only person I can ask. Let's head back to the city. Tonight I'm planning to drink so many of those cocktails of yours that I won't know my own name."

17

Colomba had one other source of information, and that was Lieutenant Carmine Infanti, who seemed even unhappier to receive a phone call from her than he had been to see her anywhere near the car containing Montanari's corpse. He could certainly have refused to help her, but he was accustomed to taking orders from her and he still respected her, and those factors pushed him in the opposite direction. After ending the conversation with her, he started reaching out to contacts, asking for favors and promising others in exchange. An unexpected source of assistance came from the Italian National Clearinghouse on Traffic Safety, which had recently completed a detailed study on the deaths of minors over the previous five years, and also from an old carabiniere friend who'd climbed the ranks and was now a senior officer.

He took a whole day to gather a sufficient quantity of data, and during that day Colomba actually drank very little, while Dante smoked constantly, staring up at the ceiling of his room where he'd taped up the photos taken of the video of the child. He listened to music at such high volume that for the first time, the hotel management complained.

They talked little, as if each of them were processing what they'd discovered in their own way, and the only news for Colomba was a phone call from the police personnel office, asking her to come in as soon as possible. The person on the phone was polite, but Colomba had no doubt that this was just the first step toward a definitive dismissal from the force. It might have been the fact that she'd kicked Santini in the face, or else maybe Anzelmo had reported her presence at the search of the local health clinic, but it was inevitable in any case that sooner or later her extracurricular activities would start to come out. She wondered whether it had been a direct action on the part of the chief of police, as Rovere had feared. To ward off her nervousness, after making Dante promise not to leave the suite, she went home to

get a change of clothes and sort through her mail. The book lying abandoned on the armrest of her chair threw her into a terrible depression.
She didn't know whether she missed her old life or was just regretting
the time she'd spent living like a hermit while a monster was at large,
harvesting children. To drive the sadness away, she got into her tracksuit and gym shoes and went for a run along the Tiber embankment,
at sunset for once, sweating out bad dreams and stress. When she got
back, she saw that she'd missed Infanti's call to her cell phone. She
called him back, and they agreed to meet at the end of the second shift.

At eight that evening she swung by to get Dante and dragged him
off with her, ignoring his protests, to the Momart Restaurant Café in
the Nomentana district, which had a nice outdoor patio for smokers.
That meant Dante wouldn't be forced to wait in the car.

Infanti was already there with a beer on the table in front of him,
and he stood up to greet them. "We've already met," he said to Dante.

"Did you find the condom in the end?" Dante asked him, sarcastically.

"Have you heard of pretrial secrecy, by any chance?"

Dante smirked. "So you didn't find it."

They sat down at the outdoor table, and Dante ordered his usual
Moscow Mule, while Colomba asked for a mineral water. She'd felt
out of shape on her run, and she decided it was time to lead a healthier
life than she had been lately. It was a pleasant evening; Dante decided
for the millionth time that the weather in Rome was one of the few
good reasons he stubbornly continued to live there.

Colomba and Infanti exchanged a few conversational gambits
about nothing at all while Dante explained in maniacal detail to the
waitress exactly how the cocktail ought to be made. Then Colomba
nonchalantly asked about Rovere.

"I haven't seen much of him lately," Infanti said cautiously. "But he
seems sort of down."

"Down how?"

"Unshaven, rumpled clothes. Do you remember what he was like
after his wife died?"

"Not really; most of the time I was in the hospital. But I get what
you're talking about."

"Yesterday he didn't come out of his office, and he didn't answer the phone either. Today he skipped the meeting with the chief of police . . . the chief went off on him because he said Rovere had been avoiding him for the past week. Maybe he needs a vacation."

Colomba mulled over the information. If what Infanti was saying was true, Rovere and the police chief hadn't met in the past few days. The decision to cut her out of the investigation had been Rovere's alone and once again reinforced Dante's view and his suspicions.

"Rovere is a widower?" asked Dante.

Infanti nodded. "It's been a year. His wife, Elena, had a grim struggle before dying."

"Any children?" Dante inquired.

"No." Infanti opened his bag and pulled out a laptop to change the topic. He didn't like talking about his boss in front of a stranger, especially one who seemed morbidly interested. "I have what you asked for, Colomba."

"You found everything?"

"All the fatal car crashes and all the murders involving minors. As far as the murders are concerned, I'm sure I have them all. It's forty or so."

"Forty-three," Dante corrected him.

Infanti nodded. "Yes, that's right. Well done." He opened the computer, which started up with a whoosh. "When it comes to the crashes, I doubt I have absolutely *everything*. But I did the best I could."

"Do the reports include the state of the corpse?"

"Not always, but once again . . ."

"You did the best you could," Colomba finished his sentence for him. "I know you did, thanks."

Infanti inserted a flash drive that was so beat up it was basically held together with Scotch tape. "I transferred everything into Excel. There are 312 files," he said, pointing to the screen. "I'll make a copy for you."

Dante peeked over his shoulder. "There are no pictures," he mumbled with the cocktail straw between his teeth.

"No pictures of the corpses?" asked Infanti, clearly irritated. He was doing his best to put up with Dante, but it was obviously a struggle.

"Pictures of the victims before they became corpses."

"We don't have them in our systems, and you won't find them in the systems of the police agencies. At most, I could find pictures of the accidents, through the highway patrol."

"We'll just have to ask the families for them," said Dante.

Infanti was stunned. "You *are* joking, aren't you?"

"Yes, it's just my twisted sense of humor."

Infanti turned to Colomba. "Could you explain why you want pictures of dead children?"

She shrugged her shoulders uneasily. "We're doing some research."

"What kind of research?"

"Don't ask."

"No, I'm going to ask, and I want an answer. All I need is for any one of those people you call to complain, and it'll come out that I helped you. Why don't you tell me what I'm getting into here."

Colomba sighed. "I can't."

Infanti grimaced unhappily. He'd assumed he was helping his old superior officer, who had always displayed uncommon competence and confidence during the three years they'd worked together. But the woman he was looking at now was just a shadow of the one he remembered. Depressed, off balance, with something eating at her from within. He realized he'd made a mistake. "I'm sorry, Colomba, I've changed my mind."

Dante lunged forward and plucked the flash drive out of the slot. The computer emitted a discontented *pling*. "Too late."

Infanti grabbed his arm and jerked him closer; he snarled at him: "How dare you, piece of shit?"

Dante said nothing but kept his fist clenched, with his treasure firmly grasped in it. Violence was such an alien experience to him that his customary reaction to the aggressivity of alpha males or domineering individuals was to retreat into himself. Except for the two or three times in the past when he had simply lost control and gotten into trouble with the law.

"Give it," said Infanti, applying pressure.

Dante continued to oppose passive resistance, without looking the other man in the eyes. He felt extremely uncomfortable.

"Let him go, Carmine," said Colomba. "Don't be a fool."

"Tell him to give me back my flash drive."

"Let go of him, Lieutenant."

The tone of voice belonged to the old Colomba, and suddenly Infanti released Dante, dropping his eyes as he did. "This is about the child up at the mountain meadows, isn't it? You're fixated on that kid."

"None of your fucking business."

Dante unbuttoned his shirt sleeves to examine the red marks on his skin. "That's going to leave a bruise," he muttered, displaying his usual sense of humor. No one paid him any mind.

Infanti pointed at him. "Was he the one who got you into this fucked-up case? What kind of ideas did he put into your head?"

"Nobody put any ideas into my head."

"Then why are you investigating where you shouldn't be? And without the magistrate's authorization?"

"Lower your voice, everyone's looking at us," said Colomba.

It was true. The adjoining tables were occupied mostly by college students, and many of them had turned to stare at them. They all assumed it was a family quarrel or some fight over a cheating spouse. Him, her, and the other man. In the informed opinion of all the onlookers, neither of the two men was worthy of dating Colomba. One of them was skeletal and foppishly bizarre in appearance; the other one was a diminutive fireplug with a pug nose. The athletic woman sitting across from them could certainly aspire to better, and many of the male onlookers would have been more than happy to volunteer.

"Tell me what you're hoping to discover all by yourself, working with this halfwit?" Infanti continued in a slightly lower voice.

"Hey," Dante protested.

"You're turning nasty, Carmine. Let me get the check."

"No, no, I wouldn't dream of it," he said angrily, tossing a ten-euro note on the table and getting to his feet. "I couldn't wait for you to come back from leave. I never believed what everyone else was saying."

Colomba narrowed her eyes, and once again Infanti realized he couldn't withstand that green gaze that had darkened in response to his angry reaction and was now pure emerald. "Why, what were they saying?"

"Forget about it."

"What were they saying, Lieutenant?"

Infanti hesitated for a fraction of a second. "That you left your mind in Paris. And now I have to admit that it's true."

Paris? wondered Dante. *Is that where whatever happened to her happened?* He started reviewing in his mind the things that had happened north of the Alps in the recent past.

"You can go now," Colomba retorted in an icy voice.

"I'm really sorry for you," said Infanti, slipping his computer into his bag and turning to leave. "But maybe it really would be better for you to find another line of work."

"What an asshole," Dante commented once Infanti was gone. But he kept thinking: *Paris . . . Paris . . .*

Colomba shook her head. "No. If I were in his shoes, I'd have behaved the same way. Before long, someone is going to ask me to explain just what I think I'm doing. We don't have much time."

"I'd figured that part out," said Dante absentmindedly.

Colomba made a face as she realized the direction Dante's thoughts were going in. "Well, have you got it?"

Dante blinked. "Got what?"

"I see the gears turning in there."

Dante tried to crack his sarcastic grin, but it failed him because at that moment an idea had surfaced in his mind. "How long have you been on leave?"

"Including time in hospital, convalescence, and leave? Almost nine months as of this date." Colomba gestured to the waiter and, when he came over, asked for a beer.

Dante froze. The images of devastation that had been reprised obsessively on all the news broadcasts a year ago spun through his mind. "I didn't know that there were Italian policemen there, too," he murmured.

"Just one. Me." Now her eyes had turned even darker, like an open sea. "The inquiry cleared me, but I know: those deaths, those people who were injured, it was all my fault."

18

Even though Dante had understood just what burden Colomba was carrying with her, he was desperate to hear her version. But he'd have to wait till they got back to the hotel, because she wasn't about to tell her story in the middle of a crowd.

They took seats on the balcony outside the room, where Dante could smoke, with the lights turned off and the awnings drawn for added security. In the dim light left by the lamps down in the courtyard that filtered though the bars of the railing, Colomba felt sufficiently certain that Dante wouldn't be able to read her face and detect emotions she didn't particularly want to share.

"A year ago we got a tip," she began, "that a multiple killer was hiding out in France. His name was Emilio Bellomo."

"I know. People talked about it."

"Just let me tell the story my own way, because it's hard enough as it is."

"Sorry."

"Bellomo had been convicted of two murders, a number of robberies, and attempted murders for pay."

"Versatile."

"He did it all for the money. He'd been on the run for three years, and the last tip that had come in on him dated back about seven months, when he'd jumped out of his car at a carabinieri checkpoint and escaped on foot. The carabinieri *cousins*, as they were known, had opened fire, but he'd managed to get away. They thought he'd been wounded, but he hadn't gone to any local hospital, which meant he must have administered his own medical care, or else he'd found a willing physician. Because he'd committed his first murder in Rome, our district attorney's office had first shot at the investigation. We found out where he was because one of his old accomplices, Fabrizio Pinna, ratted him out. Bellomo had stayed with Pinna to recuperate after the firefight with the carabinieri and clearly trusted him enough to tell him that he was planning to go to Paris to stay with his girl-friend."

"What was her name? I can't come up with it right now."

"Caroline Wong, half French, half Chinese. Pinna only knew her first name, but we found her, even though we had to move cautiously because the minute Bellomo figured out we were onto him, he'd take off. He was clever, and he'd given proof of that already."

"Why on earth did Pinna talk?"

"Because immediately after Bellomo's departure, he found out that he had terminal cancer and didn't have long to live. Rovere and I figured he just wanted to get it off his conscience. Even though later . . ." Colomba shook her head. "Let me take things in order. Well, then, Rovere assigned me to supervise the operation with the French authorities. And I had the added benefit of knowing one of the cops over there, someone I'd met at one of the many Schengen liaison meetings we had to attend, plus I speak a little French. So we put Wong's apartment under surveillance, along with the place she worked as a coat check attendant, a deluxe Japanese restaurant atop a boutique."

"*That* restaurant."

"Exactly, that one. The operation was being left to the local cops, I was strictly an observer. They let me keep my sidearm as a courtesy, and I was supposed to do nothing but take custody of Bellomo once they caught him, but after two days of unsuccessful stakeouts, since one member of the team was always supposed to be at the restaurant, I went in instead, pretending to be a client. My bad luck. I was there pretending to eat when Bellomo came in. He spotted me and recognized me." Colomba shook her head, stricken. "You know the rest."

"Bellomo set off the bomb."

Colomba had gone back for a moment into the midst of the smoke and the flames. "Yes," she said softly. "And it was a massacre. He had it in the coat check room. His girlfriend was doing him a favor. I don't know if I should be mad at her or feel sorry for her."

"Sorry for her, I'd guess, seeing that she's dead. How did Bellomo manage to recognize you? Had the two of you ever met?"

"Never. There are two possibilities. Either he had an exceptional nose for cops, and from a guy like him I wouldn't have been a bit surprised, or else Pinna had described what I looked like. I know for certain that he recognized me. And Pinna had put him on the alert, from what we found out later."

"So Pinna betrayed you?"

"He hanged himself the day of the explosion, begging forgiveness for all the mayhem. In his suicide note he explained that he'd changed his mind and had warned Bellomo 'out of friendship.' I'd imagine via Wong."

"Why didn't Bellomo try to escape?"

"Maybe he was just tired of running. Maybe he just wanted to be remembered as the piece of shit that he was. And he'd prepared a welcome for us." Colomba took a deep breath; her lungs had started to hurt. "I saw him trigger the detonator, you know. He was looking me right in the eye, and he put a hand in his pocket. I tried to pull my gun, but . . . I wasn't fast enough. The sky came down on our heads."

After the explosion, Colomba had awakened with her ears ringing and her head pounding. She couldn't remember anything from the last minute . . . What had she done? What had happened?

The power had failed, and Colomba's eyes had had to become accustomed to almost total darkness before she was able to make out through the drifting smoke the shapes of the yawning gaps that had once been windows. Flames were licking at one end of the dining room, and in that surreal phosphorescent grayness she had glimpsed one of the models who had been sitting at the central table. She was now sprawled on her back just a few feet away, her outfit ripped to tatters. The blood streaming from her mouth formed a black puddle. All around was scattered rubble, dust, flames, and more smoke. *A bomb*, Colomba had decided. *It was a bomb*.

She'd lost her earpiece, but even if she'd still had it, she couldn't have used it because the explosion had compromised her hearing. Slithering out from under the table top that had protected her, Colomba had made her way over to the model and shaken her lightly. Her head had moved like a doll's. Under normal conditions, Colomba would have understood immediately just what had happened, but she was anything but lucid. She was in shock, with severe traumatic brain injury, two broken ribs, a knee out of commission, and a sprained shoulder. But right then and there, she didn't feel all that bad, just very, very tired, and she was having a hard time focusing on anything near at hand. She thought in a muddled way that the girl was injured and needed immediate medical attention. She'd gotten up without her shoes and had cut and injured the soles of her feet, clad only in socks, by walking on red-hot rubble and broken glass. But she hadn't felt the cuts or burns, either. She'd taken the model in her arms, as delicately as she knew how, and had made her way through the smoke. She'd staggered, unable to see where she was going. She was heading for the windows, which she could just glimpse, but she'd kept stumbling over wreckage and fragments of furniture, coming dangerously close to falling or dropping her burden. At a certain point she had stepped on something soft and felt it move. She'd leaned down and seen that it was a hand sticking out from under an overturned rack of shelves loaded with bottles.

Even now, Colomba didn't know who that hand had belonged to. It seemed like a man's hand, but in the dim lighting she couldn't be sure. Whoever it was, he might have died because she didn't stop to help him, but of all the wrongs she blamed on herself, she'd absolved herself of this one. In those fleeting moments her only thoughts were for the girl she carried in her arms, and most of the time she didn't think at all. She'd continued her trek, which seemed to stretch out endlessly as she stumbled around in circles. One at a time, her ears had started to work again, and through the ferocious buzzing she'd been able to make out the sound of the fire devouring the curtains and the flakes of plaster falling from the ceiling. And the cries, weak and desperate, of those who had been left buried under rubble or too gravely injured to be able to move.

"I'll come back soon to get you all!" she had shouted, or had thought she'd shouted, her throat burning with the dust and smoke. "I swear I'll come back!" But in the meantime she had managed to make out the shape of the door that led to the restaurant's front entrance. She'd headed straight for it, and as she got closer, the air had cleared up while the draft swept away the fumes; out on the landing, which had once contained a small reception desk, an emergency light that had somehow been left intact pointed her toward salvation with its green eye. It was the staircase, and on the first steps lay sprawled the dead body of a legless waiter. In her delirium, Colomba had thought: *God, how lucky we are, me and this girl. It came so close. Really close.* With her load, she wouldn't have been able to make it down the stairs, but just then a small crowd emerged from the darkness. Waiters, black-clad salesclerks from the boutique downstairs, passersby who, instead of taking to their heels, were trying to help. They'd rushed toward her, all shouting and sobbing, all of them trying to take the girl out of her arms, saying "Sit down, stay calm, come here." She'd pushed them away. She'd shouted, or imagined she was shouting, "Take care of the others, the others!"

She'd regained consciousness at Paris's Sainte-Anne Hospital, and through the dull daze of the sedatives, a sad-faced doctor had told her that the girl she'd carried, the Albanian fashion model stuffed with cocaine, had died instantly when a table—the same table that had saved Colomba's life—had shattered her skull. But Colomba had learned the news with almost total indifference. She no longer had guts and organs, she no longer had anything. She was a void held together by a thin layer of skin. And the fact that that void should go on breathing and maintain the appearance of a human being would have seemed incredible to her if she'd still had the capacity to be amazed at anything. She'd hardly uttered a word for the first week. She hadn't spoken to her fellow cops or to her mother, who came to embrace her, to the representatives of the major institution, who "stood with her, deeply moved, in solidarity and fellowship," to that piece of shit who had once been her boyfriend but who now fled from her side in the months that followed, unable to put up with her in this new incarnation of a sick and suffering creature.

Interacting with them would have forced her to feel like a human being again, and Colomba had neither the ability nor the desire. She wanted to be a section of wall, a bedsheet, one of the flowers in a vase that the chief of police had sent her, "with deep affection and immense sympathy." An ordinary everyday object that could feel nothing, a thing among things. She couldn't actually do it, but she'd still whiled away the time making the attempt, while they were operating on her to adjust her tendon and shoulder, while they were trying to force her to eat, finally talking her into it, but only moments before resorting to force-feeding. And not even Rovere's visit had been able to shake her out of it; when he had sat down beside her and had understood and had told her that it wasn't her fault and had gone on saying it in the days that had followed, while the panic attacks started coming, along with the nightmares and the hearings of the internal affairs panel. Rovere, who was every bit as tested by the ordeal as she was, perhaps even more because he was fresh from the loss of his wife—one sorrow piled atop the other—and weighed down by the sense of guilt for having sent Colomba to what could so easily have been her death.

"In the end, the internal affairs panel acquitted me. But I'd have willingly accepted a guilty verdict. I felt and I still feel that I made a terrible mistake," Colomba concluded her story.

In the dense darkness that surrounded him, and in the darkness evoked in that account, Dante almost hesitated to breathe. "CC . . . But why should it have been your fault? What could you have done differently?"

"Stop him before he got into the restaurant."

"But you didn't spot him until the last minute."

"I didn't. But my colleagues down in the street did. They'd seen him come in through the front entrance of the boutique. But I told them to wait. That we had him now, that he was certainly coming upstairs to see his girlfriend. That I'd keep an eye on him and wouldn't let him shake me. The exits were all under surveillance, he had no escape route, we could do things on our own schedule. Technically, I wasn't in charge of the operation, but my French colleagues took my advice. And they wrote in the report that they'd done so, 'relying on my experience and knowledge of the subject,' their exact words. We're talking about the worst foul-up committed by the French police in the past half century, and possibly in all of Europe. No one wanted to take responsibility for it. The city prefect resigned, the French chief of police was looking wobbly for a while, things got vicious among the embassies. And ever since, relations between us and them haven't been good."

"I'm sure you had your reasons. I know the way you think."

"I knew Bellomo's priors. I was afraid he might be armed and could start shooting in a crowded place. That someone might be hurt. But I let something even worse happen."

"He'd have set off the bomb in any case the instant he sensed you were about to capture him."

"That was the finding of the internal affairs panel, and they made sure my name was kept out of the newspapers and I wasn't kicked off the police force. And that's what I keep telling myself. But the fact remains that I made the wrong decision. That's why I can't do my job anymore. Not because of the panic attacks. You can get over those. But because I no longer trust myself and my judgment."

Dante slid down on the chaise longue to get closer to her. Now he was just inches away, and he felt the sorrowful and almost irrepressible desire to hold her. God, how he missed wrapping his arms around a woman, and in that moment of fragility Colomba appeared, a simple silhouette against the light, as the very essence of what he wished he could feel pressed against his body. As he formulated that thought, Dante surprised himself and caught himself in the midst of reaching out to take her hand. That wasn't a good idea, decidedly not. He leaned back against the chair. "CC, I'm not much when it comes to comforting other people. I've wallowed in self-pity for so long that my strategy when other people are in pain is just to wait for them to get over it. But I can tell you something. I feel sure that if you had been working on my case when I was locked in the silo, you'd have found me."

Colomba snorted. "That came out nicely."

"Really? It just popped into my head. Do you want to get some sleep?"

"No." Colomba stood up and stretched, making the vertebrae in her neck crack. She felt a pleasant numbness in her leg muscles from the run that afternoon and once again told herself that she needed to amp up her training. "I don't know if I would have found you, but I do want to free that child in the video before he turns into someone like you. The world only needs one Dante Torre."

19

When the sun rose, the list of cases that Infanti had put together had been winnowed down to thirty or so, and by ten that morning to just six. The others had been discarded because of confident identification of corpses or because of the age or sex of the minors. The first to be eliminated were the murder victims. Most of them were newborns or infants. The six they'd kept were a sampling of the cruelty of fate. A child swept away by the current during a flood and never found, another burned to death in his parents' home, a third buried in an avalanche, the fourth and fifth killed in car crashes caused by high speeds and the idiocy of the motorists, their bodies so enormously damaged that even their surviving relatives were unable to identify them. The sixth was the cruelest and most grotesque of them all. A minivan carrying six people on a pilgrimage to a religious sanctuary in the province of Macerata had plummeted into a ravine, exploding upon impact. All the occupants of the vehicle had been killed, rendered unrecognizable because they'd been crushed in the impact, as well as by the explosion of the gas tank, an event as common in movies as it is rare in real life. That parish-owned minivan was old and had none of the modern safety devices, and perhaps it shouldn't even have been on the road.

With the six names written down on a pad of paper in front of her, after downing a pitcher of single-origin arabica coffee from Santo Domingo, Colomba prepared to complete the most painful task, contacting the families. Dante had stepped aside. As much as he enjoyed lying and fabricating on the phone, he was completely incapable of dealing with other people's sorrow, especially the scalding pain of losing a son or daughter or a grandson or granddaughter. In personal contacts, his capacity for observing facial expressions and body language made him more detached, but when the interaction with his interlocutors was strictly verbal, he was unable to avoid recognizing in their voices the thousand nuances of suffering and at the same time feeling those emotions inside himself. And although most people have an array of conventional phrases and gestures to offer in situations of mourning, Dante was a complete social idiot and always did more harm than anything else.

She had expected the task to be painful, and so it proved, even more than expected. Colomba's phone call awakened nightmares and caused weeping, cursing, and, in at least one case, screams of pain and sorrow. Nonetheless, she had no choice but to insist. "Could you send us a picture, please? By email would be best, but we can work with a fax as well." She talked about police statistical research projects, the assembly of databases that would help save lives, and she was only partly lying. To add discomfort to the moment, there was the additional inconvenient detail that only two of those contacted had an Internet connection or a computer, and so Colomba had to persuade the others to go to a local tobacconist or an Internet café and arrange to do it at their earliest convenience. Miraculously, no one refused to do it, and in just a few hours she managed to obtain them all.

Meanwhile, Dante was sleeping fitfully, with a black sleep mask covering his eyes, nodding off and jerking awake in continuation because his brain wouldn't stop churning. It was as if in his restless state he was trying to assemble a jigsaw puzzle with pieces that refused to fit together. And among the pieces was certainly the Father, but also the mysterious boy and Rovere's still more mysterious motives. Just how they linked up with the rest, he couldn't say, but he sensed that his sorrow and his motives were an important thread in the weft he was trying to untangle. His thoughts were feverish, typical of serious sleep deprivation. But still he reiterated the well-known points, the way you do in those Griddler crossword puzzles that require you to black in squares in order to reveal the hidden features of everyday objects.

Suddenly a flood of light brought him back to consciousness. Colomba had yanked the mask off his eyelids, and now she was staring at him with a weary expression. "I've got them. And I've come up with an idea."

"The pictures of the kids?" he muttered with a parched throat, reaching around in search of his cigarette pack.

"Yes. They're on the computer. Are you ready, or do you want to stall a little longer?" she asked sarcastically.

"Just a minute, let me wash my face."

He'd thrown himself onto the bed fully clothed. He took off his shirt and splashed cold water on his face at the bathroom sink, then took a complex assortment of drops and pills designed to take away a little of the anxiety that had been tormenting him. Then he returned to the living room with his towel over his shoulders.

It was the first time that Colomba was seeing him bare-chested, and once again she was reminded of David Bowie in that old sci-fi movie, skinny as a twig. Still, in spite of his undoubtedly bad habits, he wasn't skinny in an unhealthy way. In fact, it seemed somewhat like the thinness of a teenager who'd just been through a growth spurt. If it hadn't been for the hint of white whiskers that had sprouted in the past two days, when he'd stopped shaving, you would have thought he was younger than his years.

"All done?" she asked.

"Not quite. Sorry, I just need some caffeine."

"Take your time, eh . . ."

"It'll just be a minute, don't be nasty. Do you want an espresso?"

Colomba would have liked one, but she didn't want to give him the satisfaction, so she refused the offer. Dante made himself one of his coffee blends with the touch of a fine herbalist, then downed two demitasses in a row without giving them time to cool down. "Ready," he said. "Where are they?"

"Here." Colomba turned the computer screen toward him. While she was waiting for him, she had put the six pictures together into a single screen shot; down at the reception desk, she'd scanned the ones that had come in to the hotel fax. They'd stood out because they were black and white. Six pictures of children between the ages of five and six, all of them with identical smiles on their faces. As she looked at them again, Colomba realized for the first time that the one they were looking for, if he was among them, was the lucky one. Kidnapped and held prisoner by a madman but still alive, unlike the others.

Dante looked at the composition for ten seconds, arms crossed, then pointed decisively at a photo. "Him," he said.

Colomba let out her breath in a hiss. "He seems the most likely one to me, too, but I can't be a hundred percent certain. And neither can you. Children grow up fast, and they change."

"A hundred percent, for sure," he insisted. "Who is it?"

"The one from the minivan in Macerata. Ruggero Palladino."

"Fuck." And the echo of the dream-not-dream came back into Dante's mind for a moment, muddling one massacre with another. But he said nothing to Colomba, in part because there was nothing reasonable he could tell her. "Six dead just to get him."

"Tell me why you're so certain?"

"Don't you notice anything? Something that differentiates him from the other children."

Colomba thought back to the pictures of the Maugeris' son and the precise analysis that Dante had done of his condition. But here there was just one photograph, and it was posed, to boot. Then she noticed his eyes. "He looks kind of Asian."

"Narrow eyes, close together, right. And what about the chin, what do you see?"

Colomba sighed. When Dante started talking like a professor on a podium, he truly was insufferable. But she played along. "Receding, not prominent. Like the chin of the boy in the video, but he was in another position and I couldn't swear to it."

"A receding chin, as it's known. But he doesn't look that way because he resembled his father or his mother. It's a facial dysmorphology, due to a developmental problem with the inferior maxillary bone. It's a typical warning sign of FAS."

"Of what, excuse me?"

"Fetal alcohol syndrome," he said, as if it were the most obvious thing. "That idiot mother of his got drunk while she was pregnant. A fetus isn't capable of disposing of the metabolic residue of the alcohol that comes to it through the placenta—"

"Yes, I know that. I'm a woman of childbearing age."

Dante treated the interruption like the buzz of a fly. "—and malformations ensue."

"How bad off is he?"

"There are various degrees of severity of FAS, depending on the quantity of alcohol consumed by the mother and the timing, whether it's in the first three months or even later. It's called ARND, or alcohol-related neurodevelopmental disorder, when there are disabilities in neurodevelopment, and ARBD, or alcohol-related birth defects, when there are serious physical problems. The boy in the video was moving easily, so I'd say ARND. God only knows how he's doing in captivity." He looked at Colomba. "That's why I'm sure that Ruggero is the right boy. He had learning and cognitive developmental delays, just like Luca, though of a different nature. Apparently the Father is drawing his cards from the deck of the least fortunate."

20

Under normal driving conditions, it takes a little more than two hours to get from Rome to Fano. Traveling with Dante, however, was anything but normal, given his fixation with speed limits and his frequent impulsive demands for fresh air, so Colomba resigned herself to the idea that it would take twice the time and they'd get there late at night. She secretly vowed that next time she'd slip the entire contents of one of his illicit bottles of pharmaceuticals into his coffee. But whenever her frustration reached the boiling point, exacerbated by her lack of sleep, Colomba had only to mutter the three magic words—"the least fortunate"—that were guaranteed to immediately silence her troublesome passenger.

"It's a decision he made recently," he said once he was heartily sick of the reference. They'd just left the highway and the tollbooth behind them, and were driving along the county road. It was already dark, and the traffic consisted almost entirely of heavy trucks.

"But you're the one who said he never changes his method. That it's always the same."

"His *methods* are always the same, okay? Not his choice of victims."

"They're always children, about six years old."

"That aside, he did *not* use to seek out the least fortunate."

She gave him a sidelong glance. "Are you sure?"

"I was a very good student in nursery school. And I already knew how to read, a little, when I was taken. And I could write all the letters in the alphabet. No cognitive deficits of any kind."

"If you say so."

Dante threw his head back. "Why don't you phone my father and ask him about it? And I was also very sociable with kids my age."

"Well, then, you've changed considerably."

"Oh go to hell," he said, tipping his seat back and pretending to go to sleep.

She tapped him on the shoulder. "Don't get too comfortable, because we're here."

Topped by a sign reading MILITARY ZONE and by strings of barbed wire, before them stood the barracks of the local carabinieri; Colomba had called them during the drive, in search of the warrant officer whose name appeared at the bottom of the accident report. If they'd arrived early, he was going to wait for them in a café in town, but seeing the time he must have gone back on duty by now. He was working the night shift. Colomba pulled in to the first available parking space, and Dante sprawled out, getting even more horizontal, if such a thing were possible.

"I'm not going in there."

"Don't worry. I've already had problems of my own justifying my interest. With you along, I'd just raise eyebrows. Speaking of which . . ." She unclipped the holster from her belt and slid it under Dante's seat. "Keep an eye on this for me."

He sat up straight. "Are you done leaving that thing around like it was a toy? One of these days you're going to shoot me by accident."

"It won't be an accident," she said with a credible imitation of Dante's sarcastic grin. Then she got out. Actually, though, her mood was by no means one of unconcern. If the warrant officer happened to sniff out some flaw in her story, he'd retreat into the characteristic vagueness that the *cousins* were so good at emanating when they chose to erect a wall against outsiders. That was just one more reason she chose to leave her sidearm in the car. It wasn't a regulation-issue weapon, and a carabiniere would notice that immediately.

Colomba rang the bell and identified herself to the officer standing sentinel at the front entrance; he saluted and buzzed her in through the high-security door. It was a small barracks, its walls in need of a coat of paint and four plastic chairs at the disposal of those waiting their turn to file complaints. At that time of the evening, no one was there, just a lance corporal with a plastic cup of coffee who eyed her for a moment curiously, until he saw the golden badge that Colomba had hung on her belt, with her police ID turned inward. *Spataccare*, that was the verb in Italian slang, and it meant showing off tinhorn trinkets. But it was something that came to her instinctively every time she had to visit police stations or carabinieri barracks where she wasn't a known quantity. It was faster than having to introduce herself each time, and it warded off wolves. Not always, but most of the time at least.

Warrant Officer Colantuono, about sixty years old, boasted whiskers worthy of being featured on a calendar and a Sicilian accent, from Palermo, to be exact. He turned out to be anything but suspicious and was happy to tell her everything he knew about the minivan crash. Colomba always underestimated the effect she had on men, whether or not they were in uniform, and she tended to forget the times that leaving the top button of her blouse undone had been far more effective than waving her police ID and badge.

So the warrant officer swallowed her story of a vague additional investigation triggered by an independent plaintiff filing a new criminal complaint. After treating her to an espresso that Dante would have heartily disapproved of, he told her what he knew. It was the Macerata highway patrol that had sent the first responders to the scene of the crash, but it had fallen to his barracks, and to him in person, to inform the families and arrange for the bodies to be identified. The minivan was registered in the name of the parish priest of Sant'Ilario, and it had gone off the road at a hairpin curve on county road 362.

"At that point on the road, there's a steep embankment several dozen yards in extent, and the vehicle hurtled over it subsequent to the motorist losing control. I swear to you, Deputy Captain, that I've never seen a bigger puddle of mayhem in all my born days."

"Was the driver speeding?" asked Colomba.

"From what the mechanical examination was able to determine, there had been a problem with the brake assembly. And I should add that I knew the parish priest very well, and he was a slow driver even on his bicycle, let alone on those dangerous curves."

"What was the condition of the bodies?"

"Listen, Deputy Captain, I'm not trying to gross you out, but you know what it looks like when you leave a sausage too long on the grill? That's what they looked like. If you hadn't known that they were human beings, anyone could have made that mistake."

"Did their relatives identify them, though?"

"Yes, and it wasn't hard. I might have been exaggerating a little." The warrant officer opened the window and pulled out a cigarette. "Do you mind if I smoke?"

"No, go right ahead."

"Nasty habit. I just can't seem to stop. When I try, I put on five pounds and then I start smoking again. And I keep the five pounds. What was it I was telling you?"

"You were explaining how they identified the bodies."

"Yes, as I was saying, they all had parts that were still intact. You could still clearly see the facial features of *u parrinu*—excuse me, the parish priest, my Sicilian still comes out now and then—and the same was true of the schoolteacher. They recognized the other priest from his clothing. One of the children—and when I think back on it, it still breaks my heart—was all hunched over with his arms wrapped around him, trying to protect himself." He pointed vaguely with his lit cigarette to an area between head and belly.

"You remember very clearly."

"Well, like I told you, I'd never seen anything like it. And believe me, I've witnessed a substantial number of bad crashes."

"There were two children in the van."

"Yes. The schoolteacher's son, the one who was curled up in a ball. The other one, the Palladinos' son, was a piece of charcoal, though. They identified him by a chain he wore. And by his wallet."

"He was the most badly burned."

"Now that you mention it, I'd have to agree. He was already born unlucky. With the problems with his mother . . . Just think, she'd committed herself to a clinic to stop drinking when she learned she was pregnant. Then her baby was born the way he was. Her husband, Signor Palladino, told me all about it. He works for the city, and he still looks like a ghost."

"So was a DNA test done on the bodies?"

"No. Why should we have? There was no mistaking them."

Colomba stood up and extended her hand. "Thanks. You've been very helpful."

"Are you already going?" The warrant officer smiled. "What a pity."

"Maybe I'll come back and see you some time if I think of any other questions to ask."

"I hope you do. If I may, we don't see women as lovely as you very often, and I'm pretty sure that's true where you come from, too."

"Thank you."

As he was walking her to the exit, Warrant Officer Colantuono added, "A nasty crash, and an ironic one, too. They'd just gone to pray at the sanctuary, and look at the gift the Good Lord gave them. Who can ever say what He's thinking?"

"Yeah, who can say," said Colomba, who'd stopped asking that question back in Sunday school.

"Still, it could have been worse. There could have been one more dead."

Colomba froze. "One more?"

Colomba went back to the car. Dante had stepped out to smoke a cigarette, and he'd bought himself a Toblerone nougat bar at the smoke shop nearby. He offered her a piece.

"No, thanks," Colomba said. "I know how they did it."

"How they staged the accident?" asked Dante, getting the point immediately.

"Yes." They got back in the car, so they could talk far from prying ears. "A motorist who went past the minivan before the crash said that he'd seen it pulled over on the side of the road and a man was talking to the driver through the window. He remembered it because he recognized the parish priest at the wheel."

"Did he see the man who was talking to him?" Dante asked.

"Not his face, and he didn't provide a description. He said that he just assumed it was a hitchhiker. It was dark out, and he just lit him up for a second with his headlights."

"The Father. He killed them there and took the boy."

"Or maybe he just drugged them and then pushed the van off the road. But it still doesn't add up, Dante. It's almost impossible for one person to have done it all."

"The driver didn't see anyone else."

"Back in your day, he had a helper, Bodini. Maybe he has one now. Someone hiding by the side of the road. Or, more likely, in a car nearby. And that's where they had the corpse they switched out."

"Where'd they get the body?"

"I'm hoping they stole it from a morgue somewhere, or maybe they paid off a doctor. But I'm afraid that it was—"

"—another one of his victims. A prisoner who wouldn't obey, for instance . . . so young." Dante seemed to be about to explode. "We need to have the child's body exhumed," he said frantically. "We have to find out who he is."

"That would take an order from the magistrate. And we don't have anything to justify it but our theories. If we can find the Father, we'll get all the different pieces of the puzzle to slide into place. That child's in no hurry. And neither are his parents. If what we think is true, they already assume he's dead."

"Christ," muttered Dante. Then, just to drive home the point, he stuck a pill in his mouth, taking it without a glance and swallowing it without water. "In all these years he's just gone on kidnapping and murdering."

"We can't be sure of that. He might have just started up again recently."

"I *am* sure of it. He never stopped. And he's not going to stop until you put a bullet in his head. By the way, take your gun back."

She did. "I'm not a vigilante with a death wish, Dante. I'm a cop. I want him in prison."

"Not me. I want him dead. He needs to stop breathing the same air as the rest of us."

She could see he was trembling. "He'll never lay a finger on you again, I swear it," she told him.

"I still can't—" he started to say, then stopped and started again with a firmer voice. "I still can't control myself when I sense his presence nearby. I thought I'd be able to, sooner or later."

"You're doing fine. I'd be afraid if I were in your shoes. After everything he did to you."

"Doesn't he scare you?"

"No, he just makes me angry. And I don't know . . . maybe aghast is the right term. It seems inconceivable to me that a monster like him could really still exist. He's like an ogre out of a fairy tale, like Freddy Krueger. But I'm not going to go on pretending I don't believe in him. He exists, he's out there somewhere, and we have to find a way of convincing everyone else that he exists." Colomba put the car into gear. "Now we have to go see the Palladino family. Don't even dream of trying to stay in the car. I need your opinion."

"Even if I'm rude to the mother?"

"Just try it, and I'll lock you in the trunk."

"You wouldn't dare."

"Try me."

But it turned out that there was no need. Dante's bellicose impulses subsided in the presence of the sorrow they found in the home of the couple, surprised by their arrival just as they were finishing their frugal dinner. It was as if the two of them had been hollowed out from within by some disease, the kind that takes you apart bit by bit without ever finishing you off entirely. From what Colomba and Dante had learned, the father was forty and the mother thirty-five, but to look at them you'd say they were closer to retirement age: he had deep creases, thinning hair, and haggard cheeks; she had prematurely gray hair that dangled in long messy shocks over her eyes. Colomba realized that the woman had never ceased to blame herself for her son's death, denying herself even the minimum of grooming that would have dictated the occasional visit to the beautician and a touch of makeup when needed. And her husband's eyes seemed to be sinking away into their sockets. Though Colomba had never before encountered Fathers or serial kidnappers, she was thoroughly accustomed to couples like this one, with all the murders she'd investigated. Victim's relatives, murderer's relatives, or the murderers themselves. The latter, brought face-to-face with their guilt, had begun to understand that they'd ruined two lives: their victim's and their own, which could now be measured out by the yardstick of prison. And the Palladinos' single-family detached house showed the effects of the loss they'd suffered, with pictures of their son displayed everywhere, even in a sort of altar that occupied an entire living room wall, with crucifixes and images of the Madonna.

Under the onslaught of their grief, Dante as always took shelter behind a clinical analysis of their gestures as they spoke. From his position of safety, next to the large bay window in the living room that looked out onto a sickle moon, he understood that they had no doubts whatever about their son's fate and that they blamed themselves every day for having let him go without them on that excursion organized by the parish priest, whom they considered responsible for all that had happened.

"He was too old to be driving," said the man. "And he went every-where in a van that was a rolling wreck. I should have taken my son there in my own car, if he really was that keen on seeing that fucking sanctuary."

"Carlo . . ." the woman admonished him under her breath.

Her husband looked at her with pity and not even a flicker of love. "She still believes in God," he told Colomba and Dante. "I don't. Would you go on believing after what happened? Now, exactly why are you here?"

Colomba gave them a slightly modified version of the story she'd told the warrant officer. That there was an investigation under way into the circumstances of the accident, under a Good Samaritan law, for failure to provide assistance, and she implied that she'd let them know in case of any further official developments. She had presented Dante as an expert on cases of this kind.

"Even if they'd stopped to help, what good would it have done?" the husband asked. "My son was killed instantly."

"Was that the finding of the autopsy?" asked Dante, opening his mouth for the first time.

"We didn't have an autopsy done," the mother replied. "He'd already been torn apart. They autopsied Don Paolo, who was driving. They wanted to see if he'd had an attack or a seizure."

"And had he?" asked Colomba.

The mother shrugged. "He was fine."

Colomba thought to herself that events always seemed to conspire to ensure that the Father's plans turned out successfully, while Dante, who didn't believe in coincidences, saw in this new development an added wrinkle of complexity, something he couldn't seem to decipher.

How had the Father succeeded in covering his tracks so successfully? How had he erased the evidence?

Now that they'd broken the ice, Colomba went on to questions that had little to do with the details of the accident. Dante had assured her that they wouldn't be suspicious but that they might get angry at being forced to relive what had happened. Nonetheless, whatever anger might have been in them seemed extinguished now. Even when the husband cursed, there seemed to be no force or conviction behind it. "Was it the parish church that organized the trip?"

"No." The wife replied this time. "It was a personal project of Don Paolo's. He went there to pray whenever he could. He asked if we wanted to take part, too, or whether we'd prefer to let Ruggero go with him. We said yes and that we were glad to let him go . . ."

"How far ahead had he told you about the trip?" Dante asked.

"What does that matter?" the husband asked.

"I'm afraid my commanding officers might ask me questions I don't know the answer to. And I wouldn't want to have to bother you again," said Dante.

"A week in advance. He called me and asked," the mother explained.

This time, Colomba and Dante both thought the same thing, namely that a week wasn't much time to organize a kidnapping, unless you were already prepared to take advantage of the occasion. The Father had put their home under surveillance. But how had he selected his prey?

"And was anyone else involved in organizing the trip, aside from the victims?" asked Colomba.

"I don't think so," said the man.

"Didn't anyone get in touch with you in the days before the trip? Like a doctor? A new doctor?" Dante enquired.

This time the question was so bizarre that the boy's parents were astonished. "Why a doctor?"

"I was thinking of one of the doctors caring for him. For his special needs," Dante added, giving the mother a level look.

The woman lowered her head and blushed bright red, as if she'd just been slapped in the face. "Ah, so you know," she murmured.

"Yes," said Dante, continuing to stare at her even though she'd turned her eyes away.

"I stopped right away, the minute I found out I was pregnant," the mother tried to justify herself.

"These people don't care about that," said the husband, letting his anger show. "And anyway, it wasn't exactly right away."

"But almost right away. Almost," the mother said, looking around for understanding.

Dante sat impassive, while Colomba smiled at her, feeling a bottomless pity. "Tell us about the doctor, please," she said, trying to change the topic.

"There was his pediatrician. And then there was Silver Compass."

"What's that?" asked Colomba.

"It was a support center for children with problems."

"Why are you talking about it in the past tense?" asked Dante, antennae quivering.

They learned that the foundation had had offices all over Italy but that soon after the child's death it had closed because of serious financial problems.

Colomba and Dante asked a few more questions that led nowhere and then headed for the door.

On the patio, Colomba whispered, "Do you think he chose the child through Silver Compass?"

"Maybe he wasn't the only one. We need to acquire lists of the patients," Dante replied. But he said it distractedly, not only because he was focused on the pleasure of the fresh, open air—he'd suffered greatly indoors, though his internal thermometer had always remained under the "danger" notch—but also because his mind was occupied with grim thoughts that he couldn't dispel. The threads linking the various events he was investigating were now inextricably intertwined, but at the same time full of gaps and tatters. Gradually, as the investigation moved forward, instead of finding answers to his questions, he kept finding new questions that were increasingly difficult to answer. When he imagined the Father lurking in the dark, ready to pounce on him, he wasn't surprised in the slightest that no one had yet managed to track him down. First of all, no one aside

from him even believed in the Father's existence, and—after all—
Dante's respect for his kidnapper's intelligence was every bit as great
as his contempt for the intelligence of the authorities. Now that he'd
learned, however, that the Father had continued to operate, murdering without pity, he wondered just how he'd managed to cover his trail
so thoroughly. How could it be that with all the things that could have
gone wrong—for instance, a despairing parent demanding a DNA
test on a child's remains—everything had worked out instead? Even if
that hadn't resulted in his capture, such a wrinkle might have created
a hint of suspicion, a tangle of interference that would have made the
Father's "work" just a bit harder. Dante, who'd never had much good
luck himself, didn't believe in it, and he certainly didn't think that the
Father relied on it. Therefore, the Father must have developed a complex and sophisticated plan for survival that Dante was not yet capable
of even glimpsing. And there was another thing that tormented him:
Why had the police, the minute they'd glimpsed a snag in the Father's
overarching strategy, turned to him of all people, to Dante, who had
been one of the Father's victims? It was an enormous coincidence,
too big for him to believe that that was all it was. But once again, now
that he'd identified the problem, he'd been unable to find a solution
to it. Or at least he'd been unable until the moment—as he was saying
good-bye to the boy's mother, who had walked him to the door—his
glance chanced to fall on a sort of small-scale monument adorning the
house's front entrance. It consisted of a marble pedestal about a yard
tall, atop which sat a bronzed pair of child's shoes. The click in his
brain as several pieces of the puzzle finally slid into place was so loud
that he assumed the others could hear it. He pointed to the statue
with a trembling hand and asked the woman what it was, even though
he was quite certain he already knew the answer.

"After Ruggero had his accident, someone left his shoes in front of
our home. Maybe they found them on the road and brought them to
us. My husband had them bronzed. At first, we thought about putting
them on his grave but . . . they stayed here."

Dante seemed to be in the throes of some kind of delirium. As pale
as he'd been before, that's how red-faced he was now. He was panting,
and his breathing was labored.

"Are you all right, Dante?" Colomba asked him in a worried voice.

He gestured in a way that could have meant anything or nothing and then hurried after the boy's mother, even as she was waving good-bye and closing the door.

Colomba heard him say "Sorry. Just one more thing," as with his good hand he pulled his cell phone out of his pocket and showed the woman, and then her husband, something on the screen. Colomba couldn't see what it was, nor did she hear what they said, but she saw the husband and wife nod their heads, and Dante become even more agitated, like a jack-in-the-box.

When he came out he was transfigured. The first solution to the enigma that had been tormenting him had torn through him like an orgasm.

"Dante, what is it?" Colomba asked. "I'm getting upset, and that's not a good thing, because I need to drive. And you don't like when I drive all upset."

Dante's mouth opened into the sarcastic grin, and then spread out from there into a thousand-watt smile. "Have you ever had a satori?"

"A what?"

"An illumination."

"About the Father?"

"Only marginally. I just figured out why you and I are actually working on this case. I don't know where it's going to lead, but it cleared some of the cobwebs off of my brain." He looked at Colomba, and then his smile faded. "You're not going to like what I figured out, I'm afraid."

"There's no part of this story that I like. Well?"

"Rovere," said Dante. "I know what he's hiding."

21

What are you willing to lose? The words of that song had been stuck in Rovere's ears all day. They'd made their way into his head that morning when his clock radio had gone off, playing that song. He didn't know who the singer was, and he'd forgotten the rest of the lyrics, but he knew the answer to the question.

Everything. That was the answer. He was willing to lose everything, as long as it would put an end to his obsession.

The patrol car dropped him off in front of his apartment building, depositing him into nighttime darkness, and Rovere waved good-bye to the officer distractedly before trudging toward the front door.

Even though his parents had been fervent Catholics, Rovere had grown up with a lingering doubt, the same constant doubt and the same determination to understand that had helped him in his police career. God probably existed, but he was so distant from the world and from mankind that it didn't make much difference whether or not he believed in him. But when Elena had fallen sick, he'd started praying again, the way he had when he was a child. If there was even the remotest possibility it might help, he couldn't neglect it. He'd applied himself to prayer methodically, the way he did everything, splitting the day up into novenas and the short prayers called aspirations. And he'd kept it up even after Elena had died, taking comfort in it at times of torment, when loneliness was a lead weight dragging him down.

In the last week, though, he'd stopped, and he knew he'd never start again. If God had ever turned his gaze down upon him, there could be no doubt that he'd turned his back on him now, contemptuous of his error and his stupidity.

He lit a cigarette at the front door. The light from the atrium filtered through the tiny flowered pattern on the frosted glass, picking out his silhouette on the facade of the building across the street. He was astonished at the sight. He felt disembodied, devoid of substance.

What are you willing to lose?

He took the last drag and opened the door. That was when two hands emerged from the darkness, grabbed him, and hurled him against the wall. Rovere wasn't accustomed to violence. His career as a desk officer had always kept him clear of the street fights, the ugly arrests, the kicks, and the punches. He reacted all the same, trying to throw a weak elbow at whoever was behind him, aiming at his attacker's face. In the meantime, he cursed himself for the idiot that he was. He should have known it would happen, that the monstrosity acting under the name of the Father would understand sooner or later just how dangerous he was. His attacker seized his elbow in a painful grip and slammed him with even greater force against the cement.

"Hold still, goddamn it," said a woman's voice.

The instant he recognized it, Rovere stopped struggling. "Colomba!" he shouted.

It was she, furious and exhausted after the drive from Fano, with the accelerator pressed to the floor and Dante complaining much of the way, shouting and vomiting out the window until he collapsed, weak as a kitten. A horrible trip, with her fury building mile by mile, her thirst for blood, literally. She had never felt herself so betrayed, so used. "Try raising your voice again, and I'll shatter your teeth!" she roared. "Put your hands against the wall!"

"Colomba, I don't understand what's happening," said Rovere in a calmer tone.

Colomba kicked his left ankle to force open his legs. "Up against the wall, and don't move." She started searching him.

"You know I'm not armed."

"There are lots of things I thought I knew."

Out of the corner of his eye, Rovere saw Dante arrive. He seemed even paler than usual, but perhaps that was just the light from the landing. Dante lingered in the doorway, as if the building concealed who knew what dangers.

"Signor Torre, would you at least be so good as to explain to me . . ."

Colomba lost it. She grabbed Rovere by the collar of his raincoat and shook him violently, banging his chest against the wall over and over again.

"That's enough! Enough lies, enough trickery. Tell us the truth, you fucker!"

"You knew about the Father. From the very beginning," said Dante.

Rovere sighed, feeling a mix of pride for someone he considered his protégée and fear because of how she might react. "No, I didn't know!"

"Goddamn it, I told you to cut it out!" Colomba bellowed.

"I'm telling the truth. I only had"—here he broke off—"certain misgivings. Suspicions. I thought I was crazy just for thinking it."

"So then you used us to dispel your doubts," said Colomba. She was doing her best to stay under control, but she knew she was on the verge of exploding.

"How did you figure it out?" asked Rovere.

"I was trying to make it make sense," said Dante. "Trying to make sense of why I was dragged into this investigation. Unless it was pure coincidence, it meant that you, who had involved me through the person of CC, necessarily knew more than you were telling us." Dante paused, inwardly reviewing all the reasons he ought to feel like a fool. "But I didn't understand how that could possibly be. You called CC immediately after the discovery of the corpse up at the mountain meadows. How could you have figured it all out so fast? Were you involved with the Father? Impossible, he'd never have kicked up so much dust. Had you known the victim? I ruled that out. The Father's modus operandi couldn't be identified in this kidnapping, unless you were the only one aware of a detail that would mean nothing to the others. Then I understood: the shoes. The Father leaves his victims' shoes in plain sight. It's a message. Am I right?"

"Yes."

"Do you know what it means?"

"No."

"But you already knew it before going up to the mountain meadows. Through the Palladino family?" asked Dante.

"Yes," Rovere admitted, as if talking to himself.

Colomba felt the strength drain out of her and released him, falling back a step. So. It. Was. All. True.

Feeling the pressure ease up, Rovere turned around, smoothing his jacket. "I'm sorry, Colomba. I'd have told you about it when the time was right."

Colomba said nothing, incapable of even looking at him.

"How did you get to the Palladinos?" Dante asked him.

"I can't tell you that. Not now. I can only tell you that the two of you together have performed a miracle."

"A miracle," Colomba echoed him, broken-hearted.

"This is the most important investigation of your life, Colomba. And you were the only person I trusted," said Rovere in a tone of voice that he was clearly doing his best to make convincing. "And he"—he pointed to Dante—"was the only one who could steer you in the right direction."

"You're just lucky that I detest violence," said Dante. "*And* that I left my baseball bat at home."

"I want to know everything," Colomba drove in with determination.

"This isn't the time. Trust me, I'm begging you. Just for a little longer. I'll try to keep you out of everything that's going to happen." And with those words, he headed off toward the stairs.

It took Colomba who was caught off guard, a few seconds before she set off after him. "Where the fuck do you think you're going?"

"Home. A patrol car goes down this street every half hour. I'd prefer they not see us together."

He tried to go upstairs again, but this time Colomba's hand shot out and grabbed him by the arm, overcoming the powerful sense of estrangement that was forcing her into immobility, like a pillar of salt. "Either you tell me what you know, or I'll call De Angelis and he can clear this up with you." She pulled out her cell phone and showed it to him, with the magistrate's number already queued up on the display.

"He'll whitewash the whole thing," said Rovere. "I still can't tell if he's merely an opportunist or a full-fledged enemy, but you shouldn't trust him."

Colomba put her finger on the call button. "Last chance."

Rovere realized that Colomba would never yield. What remained of the relationship of respect and affection that had bound them together was evaporating second by second, one word after the other. Rovere understood, to his sorrow, that it would never be restored, however hard he might try. "You have to promise me that you won't tell a soul what I'm about to tell you, unless I give you permission to do it."

"No promises. I'll decide for myself afterward."

Once again, Rovere realized he'd have to give in. "All right." He gestured for her to follow him, and together they walked up to the mezzanine. "Let's talk in my apartment."

Colomba turned to look at Dante, who stood grimly leaning against the glass street door. "What are you going to do?"

He stared at the atrium, chewing on the glove covering his bad hand. Now that the timer had turned off the overhead lights, the place looked less inviting to him. But he was interested, and how, in what Rovere had to say. "Just give me a minute to catch my breath. But don't start without me."

"In that case, get moving," Colomba replied, then caught up with Rovere, who was just turning the key in the lock.

"I'd prefer that Signor Torre not take part," said Rovere.

"What you prefer is no longer any concern of mine. Come on, get moving," Colomba ordered.

Rovere pushed open the door. In the darkness of the apartment, an electric spark glared. It was practically white, so luminous it left a ghost image on her retina. It was the last thing Colomba saw before the explosion.

22

The explosion hurled Dante onto the sidewalk. He was momentarily stunned, but when he recovered he found he was covered with shattered glass, but without a scratch on him. The apartment building was shrouded in complete darkness. All the panes of glass up to the fourth floor were completely gone. Dense, greasy smoke came billowing out of some of the windows. *A bomb*, he thought groggily, as he struggled to his feet. *That was a bomb*. Car alarms up and down the street were wailing and beeping. A man shouted something he couldn't understand from a window in the building next door.

"Are you all right?" the man asked him.

Dante ignored him. Around him a dozen or so people had gathered, dialing calls or taking pictures with their cell phones. He shoved through to the front entrance, doing his best to peer through the smoke. He couldn't see a thing. *CC's in there*, he thought, still in shock.

An elderly couple in pajamas emerged through the cloud of smoke, coughing.

Dante squared off in front of them. "There was a woman on the stairs. Tall, black hair. Did you see her?" he asked, slurring the words in his urgency.

The man cleared his throat. "It's too dark!" he said. "And the smoke . . ."

A woman in a bathrobe and a man in a suit and tie who looked as if he'd just come home from the office also emerged. The man was talking calmly on his cell phone. But no Colomba. Dante thought of her dying amid the flames and falling plaster while he stood there on the sidewalk like an idiot. He needed to go to her aid, and right now, if it wasn't too late already. The little voice that whispered bad news to him said it was pointless, that to judge from the blown-out windows, the center of the blast had been on one of the lower floors, probably exactly where she was now. That little voice, rendered even more shrill by stress and fear, pointed out that there were probably tattered shreds of her body in the dust and smoke swirling through the air. He was never going to see her alive again.

Dante silenced the voice and shut his eyes. He thought of sun-kissed beaches, blue skies. He thought of flying like a glider, running in a meadow at night. He tried to project himself back to when he lay in his bed and looked up through the glass ceiling of his balcony bed-room at a night sky filled with stars, and felt he was about to drop off into slumber. A solid minute went by, and two old people emerged, helping each other along. No Colomba.

His thermometer dropped, as did his heart rate. *I can do this*, he told himself, doing his level best to hush the little voice that kept insisting no, no, he couldn't, that this was sheer madness. He loosened his tie, removed it, and grabbed a bottle of water from the backpack of a high school student intent on snapping pictures with his smart-phone. The student objected loudly, and the crowd murmured angrily in disapproval. *They can fuck themselves*, he thought. He poured the water over the tie and wrapped the wet strip of cloth around his nose and mouth, turned on his cell phone flashlight, and went in.

For a second he saw nothing. Then the smoke cleared and the LED light illuminated the foot of the staircase, which appeared to be intact. The explosion didn't seem to have damaged the building's load-bearing structure, but blackened chunks of plaster kept falling from above, along with drops of plastic from the melted electrical wiring.

"Come back!" someone shouted to him from outside.

Dante was about to do it, too, because the feverish determina-tion that had driven him initially was starting to subside. Then he saw something light-colored moving feebly on the landing at the top of the first flight of stairs, right next to the huge, jagged gap in the wall that had once been Rovere's apartment, out of which purplish flames and toxic fumes now spewed. That was enough to push him upward, dart-ing the beam of light from his phone to sidestep obstacles as he met them. The staircase held all the way up to the second floor. Just before the landing, a step was missing and Dante was forced to leap over it, landing clumsily on a heap of rubble. When he regained his balance, he realized that the white thing he'd seen was a plastic ceiling light panel tossing in the gusts of heat and smoke. *Fuck*, he thought. *I can't do this anymore. It's too much.* But, just as he was turning around to head back downstairs, he spotted a dark mass huddled against the wall of the hallway. By the light of the phone he made out Colomba's face, half-buried in shattered plaster. She was covered in a white powder that glittered in the glow of the flames.

Dante called her name and bent over her. Her face was covered with blood, and at first he thought the worst, but then he realized that the blood was flowing from an injury on her forehead. A surface wound, thank God.

"CC!" Dante shouted. Colomba's eyelids flickered. "Can you hear me? CC!"

A blast of smoke enveloped them, and Dante coughed until it felt like his lungs were splitting, in spite of his drenched tie. When the cloud thinned, another light had appeared in the hallway. It was a camping lantern, in the hand of a tall, powerfully built young man in shorts who had a wet handkerchief pressed to his face. The young man kept his distance. "Are you all right?" the young man shouted, to make himself heard over the crackling of the flames.

"Help me carry her out of here," Dante replied from under the tie.

"We need to wait for the ambulance before moving her. That's what they always say," the young man replied.

"We can't leave her here," Dante insisted. "We don't know whether the building's going to come down."

"Then maybe we ought to get out of here, don't you think?" the young man pointed out.

"Not without her," said Dante.

A father, a mother, and three children came running down the stairs, all in pajamas. The man was seeing his way by the light of a torch made of flaming newspapers. *What an idiotic thing to do*, Dante thought, *right after an explosion.* As they went past, a large chunk of plaster fell between Dante and the young man, who took a step backward in fright.

"Wait! Don't go." Dante bent over Colomba again. She'd opened her eyes. "Can you hear me?" he asked her.

"Yes . . ." she replied weakly.

"Move your legs. Move them!"

"What?"

"Your legs! I have to see if you have spinal damage."

She weakly twisted first one foot around, then the other, clenched her hands into fists.

"How is she?" the young man asked.

"She can walk if you give me a hand," said Dante, hoping with all his heart he wasn't making a mistake. But he wanted to get Colomba out of there as quickly as he could. And himself with her.

A new cloud of smoke billowing out of the apartment enveloped them. This time it reeked of burning paper and wood: the fire had reached the bookshelves in the living room.

The young man finally came closer and helped Dante get Colomba to her feet.

As soon as she was standing erect, she vomited dust and blood. "Rovere," she stammered. She was standing on her own, but she was still confused and weak.

Dante thought: *Let him burn*. A second later, though, he realized that he wanted what Rovere knew, and he wanted it more than he wanted fresh air. "Can you get her out of here on your own?" he asked the young man, amazed that he was still able to speak at all.

"Yes. I think so."

"Take her down and wait for the ambulance. Don't let her out of your sight until it gets here, or I swear I'll track you down."

Dante's glare was sufficiently fierce that the young man nodded. "Don't worry."

"Careful of that top step."

Dante reluctantly turned away from the young man and Colomba and moved toward the entrance to the burning apartment. The explosion had demolished the apartment's central wall, blasting rubble in all directions and twisting rebar out of the perimeter wall its entire length. It had also shattered the ceiling, so that the living room of the apartment upstairs had collapsed down into this one. It was through that hole that most of the smoke was being channeled, sucked upward and out the blown-out third-floor windows. That was the only reason

Colomba hadn't died of suffocation, why Dante was still there to play explorer. The adrenaline was pumping in such quantity that his heart was bursting in his ears. He stuck his head through the enormous ravaged gap. The flames were crackling violently at the end of the front hall, and the heat made it impossible to venture any farther forward. A marble table from the upstairs apartment had plunged down into the floor, and it was pure chance that it hadn't made it collapse like the floor above. The rest of the furniture had been splintered and was starting to catch fire.

There wasn't a trace of Rovere. Dante played the beam of light around the apartment again, then decided he couldn't go on, because the nightmare was slamming down on him like a slaughterhouse sledgehammer. He imagined himself trapped under a section of wall, struggling, with his face covered in plaster and dust, unable to breathe. Actually, rather than imagining it, he was perceiving it. He needed to get out of there now, while he was still able to put one thought in front of another, before the mercury in his internal thermometer rose to the top and triggered alarm bells. As he was taking a last look around, he thought he saw the apartment's front door, blown off its hinges, move slightly. It was an armored door, the only thing that had saved Colomba's life. Almost completely intact, it now lay on one side of the hallway, atop what seemed to be a heap of rubble, but that Dante now realized was a human head. Rovere's smoke-blackened head. The door had landed atop him and was pinning him down, flat on his back, from the waist down. With his free arm, Rovere was trying to touch his face.

Dante kneeled down beside him, cleaning the rubble and dust away from his eyes and mouth. "It's me, Torre. Hang tough."

Rovere opened his mouth, unable to speak, and Dante saw that he no longer had teeth. His mouth was filled with a clotted clump of blood, dust, and bone fragments. Stifling his revulsion, he stuck in a finger and extracted the bolus, allowing Rovere to breathe a little more freely. The blood oozed out so dark it looked black, but Rovere opened his eyes. He grabbed Dante's bad hand with a spasmodic grip.

"It won't be long," said Dante. "I think I can already hear the sirens. They're coming to get you." Suddenly he didn't give a damn anymore about the man's secrets. All he wanted was to get out of there.

The grip grew stronger still. Rovere was afraid, a fear that was stronger than his. A fear of being abandoned in that inferno of heat and death.

Dante closed his eyes for a moment. *Blue skies, seas, meadows, cosmic space.* "All right, I'll stay here with you. Let me see if I can get this thing off you." He set his phone down on the floor so it could illuminate his movements. "Let go of me for a second. I swear I won't go anywhere," he said, short of breath, gently sliding his hand out of Rovere's clasp. Using both hands, he grabbed one side of the door and tried to lift it, but he couldn't budge it a quarter inch. Maybe he could slide the door off him if he could find something to use as a lever, but first he needed to check on Rovere's condition.

He knelt down to look underneath and let his breath out in a long sigh of horror. A section of the door's armored metal had been twisted into a rough triangular blade and had pierced Rovere through, right below the sternum, penetrating the spinal cord and nailing him to the floor. The blood had formed a broad puddle that dripped into a crack between the slabs of marble floor tile, falling to the floor below as a red drizzle.

Dante got back on his knees and looked into Rovere's desperate eyes, trying to come up with a reassuring lie to tell him. Then he realized he couldn't do it. No one deserved a lie as their last farewell from the world.

He stroked his forehead. "You're a goner," he said quietly. Understanding flickered in Rovere's feverish eyes. "I'm sorry. Whatever fucked-up thing you've done, to me and to Colomba, consider yourself forgiven. Okay?"

Rovere murmured something else, which Dante heard but didn't fully register. By now he was living in a dream state, and everything seemed so surreal that it made him feel strangely calm. Maybe he himself was dead and didn't know it yet.

He sat down and gently touched Rovere's forehead. "Does it hurt?" Rovere moved his eyes to say no.

"Then that'll make it easier. You're about to make the journey, you know? The most important journey of them all. The only one that really counts. Trust me, it will be beautiful. Soon you'll know everything there is to know about everything. There will be no more mysteries, no more shadows, no more fears."

Rovere's breathing started to slow.

"Now the journey is about to start. Just pretend you're boarding an enormous airplane, as transparent as the air around us," Dante went on. "You see it? It's already on the runway. It's tossing in the wind, it can't wait to get up off the ground and into the sky. There are lots of people sitting on board, just waiting for you. Because where it's going, time doesn't exist and you can meet anyone you want. All your friends, anyone who's loved you, people you thought you'd lost forever. Just look how many there are . . . You never knew there were so many, eh?" Rovere smiled faintly and closed his eyes. "Wait, wait, don't just sit down in the first seat you find. There are lots of people who want to say hello to you. There are your parents. You see them? Look how good they look, in their best outfits, dressed for a special occasion." Dante gulped down a bitter taste. "And there's your wife. Look how lovely she is, how happy she is to see you! She's been waiting for you so long! You feel her arms around you?"

Rovere's breathing grew ragged.

"Now you can go. And the wonderful thing is that everything you always thought was important is actually worth less than a minute of this journey . . ."

Dante fell silent because Rovere had stopped breathing. Meanwhile, outside, the first responders had arrived.

Before they could start up the stairs, Dante started searching the corpse. As he did, he thought back to the last words Rovere's bloody lips had managed to utter: *He's not alone*.

He's not alone.

- VII -

BEFORE

He bites the hand that shakes him. It's an instinctive reaction, he's still half-asleep. He even tries to grab it before he remembers where he is. Then he remembers, curses, and opens his eyes. Next to his cot is Limpwrist in his underwear, shaking his hand and whining in pain. He says he just wanted to do him a favor. He says he wanted to keep him from taking a punishment. Fabrizio is happy it was him. If it had been any of the others—Redneck or Stankfoot, for instance—they'd have fought back. Fabrizio would have been forced to defend himself, and his fists might not have been enough. Fabrizio has a knife, which he keeps tucked in his mattress, and a gym sock full of coins. He's already used the gym sock before, the second night he was in there. He's only displayed the knife, so the others would know they'd better leave him alone. In there, nearly everyone has a knife. Stankfoot even has a pair of brass knuckles. He says he made them at the place he used to be, where they'd put him to work in the metal shop. Fabrizio doesn't believe him: Stankfoot doesn't know how to do a fucking thing. He must have taken it off some other poor bastard, or else he bought it.

Limpwrist, on the other hand, isn't the kind who's going to fight back. He just tries to be friends with everyone, or else he whines and screams. The way he did when two guys got into his bed at night. He yelled until they put a pillow over his face. What they did to him, Fabrizio doesn't know and doesn't want to know. But the next day, the two guys were wearing big fat smiles, while Limpwrist had a sick day. They ought to send Limpwrist home, he's just not suited. But he must have gotten on someone's nerves, and now he's paying for it.

Fabrizio turns to look out into the barracks room. The others are already all up and in the middle of the room, standing at attention, doing their level best to look military. He must have missed a surprise second roll call.

He gives Limpwrist a shove and gets into line with the others.

*It's fucking freezing, and his feet turn to ice immediately. What god-
damned time of the night is it, anyway? He sees from the clock on the
wall that it's 3 a.m. No wonder he didn't wake up. This isn't a second
roll call, it must be some other kind of bullshit, like a night drill, a
cross-country run through the mud.*

But that's not it either, and the sergeant tells him so, short little
Calabrian that he is, standing a yard and pocket change tall at most,
with eyes that look like a pair of dead flies. In his fractured, ungram-
matical Italian, half dialect actually, he says there's a delivery to be
made and they need only six men. And that, seeing as it's a miserable piece-of-shit job, he's going to pick the ones who've gotten on his
nerves the most in the past few days. The ones he picks are the guy
who hasn't been there even a week and might have opened his mouth
twice in all; Stankfoot; the ones they call the Twin Brothers because
they're always together; Pharmacist, who's always half-stoned; and,
of course, him.

When he picks him, the sergeant looks him in the eyes and flashes
him a bastard little grin. Fabrizio is immediately tempted to go for
his throat. But he holds himself back, because it was exactly that kind
of dumb move that got him sent to the military prison of Peschiera in
the first place. Another sergeant, another bastard little grin. That first
sergeant had reported him for having dirty boots. And they weren't
even dirty. It was just that he'd forgotten to put polish on the stitching
with a toothbrush, which was such a stupid thing to expect anyone
to do that Fabrizio always forgot. So that other sergeant with that
other bastard little grin had given him a serious dressing-down. Told
him that he could forget about going out that night, and the whole
weekend, too. And that he was getting off easy, because the sergeant
had been keeping his eye on him, he'd spotted him for the slacker that
he was. And that's when Fabrizio took off his right boot and pounded
the sergeant's face with it until the sergeant hit the floor. And when
the sergeant was sprawled out on the floor, he'd told him that he was
getting off easy, too, because Fabrizio had had his eye on him for a
while, too.

Of course they had come for him. And of course he'd spent the
year and a half since then cursing his fucked-up personality, while

doing his best to keep from being beaten to death by the guards or eaten alive by the insects. Because what they all said was true, that a military brig was a filthier shithole than a regular prison and that the worst bunk in the worst barracks was far preferable to the nicest cell.

So this time Fabrizio doesn't react. In fact, he remains standing to attention and snaps out something that sounds more or less like "Sir, yes sir," which, coming from him, is practically a joke. And in fact the sergeant doesn't bother to listen.

The lucky ones get back into their cots, while the six men pulled out of the deck of cards are given ten minutes to get dressed. When they get out into the yard, there's already a canvas-top truck waiting for them. And when they get in, ready to be carted off who knows where in the middle of the night, they have the happy surprise of find-ing a carton full of mini-liqueurs in a bag. Someone must have left it behind by mistake, *Fabrizio thinks, even if* Pharmacist *says that they left the box there on purpose. They polish off half the box as the truck jerks and jolts along the country roads leading away from Mezzanone di Zerbio. Mezzanone, near Caorso, is the place they'd built the "pow-der keg" military prison. There are just fifty prisoners, with an officer and two NCOs; it's a place built especially to contain troops of their kind, the soldiers they don't want anywhere else.*

The trips lasts maybe half an hour, what with the jolting and the drinking. Everyone's cheerful from the alcohol, except for Stankfoot, who complains as always about his boots and his blisters. He says that by the time he gets out, he won't be able to walk anymore and he'll find a lawyer and he'll sue until he's reimbursed for every penny, as if there were lawyers out there willing to listen to losers like him. As if he didn't know that when you do your military service you take what you get, if you're not smart or skillful enough to get out of it entirely. Especially if you snap and wind up in a punishment barracks, as all of them had.

The truck comes to a halt, and the sergeant yells for them to dis-mount. They're parked in front of a hangar made of cement and sheet metal, about sixty feet long. The hangar is in the middle of a fenced-in area, and the fenced-in area is in the middle of a nowhere made up of trees and darkness. Fabrizio guesses it must be a military storage area, even though there are no indications, aside from the sign, that it belongs to any specific barracks or unit. There's a dump truck parked next to the industrial shed, with civilian plates, and standing next to the truck are four soldiers in camo, who aren't members of their unit. Fabrizio tries to figure out what company they might belong to, but they don't have insignia of any kind. Aside from one of them, that is, who's wearing the bars of a corporal and is ordering the others around with brusque gestures. He has an average physique, but Fabrizio understands immediately that he needs to steer clear of that corporal. It's as if he has an aura around him like saints are supposed to have. Except that his aura is black as pitch.

The sergeant climbs back aboard the canvas-top truck and drives away without a single fucking word. The six of them exchange astonished glances: What the fuck is happening? One of the soldiers in camo explains it to him in a few words, without a smile. They have to go in and empty out the warehouse. There will be trucks coming and going; they just need to load them and be done before dawn.

The soldiers without insignia are just finishing loading an assortment of metal drums onto the dump truck; they look like diesel fuel drums. They're full and they're heavy, but the men do it all by hand, without a forklift. Fabrizio hopes that the things they'll be loading aren't all that heavy; otherwise he'll just run away, and the corporal with the face of a murderer can go fuck himself. He's in luck: inside the shed, there are several hundred trash bags sealed with packing tape and a lot of old furniture; it looks like office furniture. It looks like the stuff was shoved into the shed in a hurry and piled up at random.

The soldier without insignia explains to them where they can find more packing tape to seal up the torn bags and tells them that they can smoke if they want, and also to go on drinking, because he's noticed that the Twin Brothers are passing the liqueur back and forth furtively. The main thing is that the work can't stop. While he's speaking, no one even thinks of contradicting him; everyone just nods his head. And Fabrizio, who has been tormented by a vague memory from the very start, suddenly remembers where he's seen him before. The soldier without insignia is from his town. He didn't recognize him right away because the last time he saw him they were still going to the local parish recreational club to play soccer and trade dirty comic books. Emilio, that's his name, Emilio. While the others start loading, Fabrizio goes over and introduces himself. They slap each other on the back, but Emilio doesn't answer his questions about that place and about what company he belongs to. He just tells him to get moving, that this corporal isn't fooling around. Emilio, too, seems to be afraid of this corporal with the vicious eyes, so much so that when he sees him come into the shed, he immediately stops talking.

Fabrizio, too, acts as if nothing had happened and bends over one of the first sacks. It's soft and light; maybe it's full of rags.

Then one of the sacks splits open, and Fabrizio sees what's inside.

He'll have nightmares about it for the rest of his life.

- VIII -

FOLLOW
THE COMPASS

1

Everyone responded. Firemen and ambulances, the bomb squad and the military corps of engineers. Patrol cars and armored cars, cranes, hook-and-ladder trucks. The mayor showed up, and so did the prefect; the chief of police came, accompanied by the deputy chief; the president of the Chamber of Deputies, along with a handful of parliamentarians. Reporters and photographers showed up, as did an onslaught of rubberneckers, news vans from the leading national TV networks, correspondents from the ANSA wire service, a crew from a Japanese television network, and the Rome correspondent for CNN. Chief Inspector Infanti showed up, as did Lieutenant Anzelmo from the Ministry of Justice, commanding officers of the Mobile Squad not currently engaged on calls, and all of Colomba's former colleagues.

She didn't see any of them, just as she didn't see the arrival of Santini and De Angelis, because she'd already been rushed to the emergency room with a concussion and a series of bruises and abrasions. For many hours, she let herself be moved like a doll, aware only in stretches of where she was. She frequently got mixed up and thought she was back on the day of the Disaster. The same white noise in the ears, the same taste of ash and plaster in her mouth, the same burnt stench.

Meanwhile, Dante was being picked up by detectives from the CIS and transported to police headquarters. In spite of his loud objections, he was locked up in an office, handcuffed to a chair, and left alone with just one guard, who ignored his requests to be moved to an open area. He immediately started feeling sick, and his condition was made even worse by the effort he'd made in the burning building just a couple of hours earlier. He yelled until he was blue in the face, he stamped his feet. When his guard hauled off and smacked him in the face, he tumbled to the floor and broke his chair. He leapt quickly to his feet and held the guard at bay, in spite of his attempts to grab him, by whirling the broken armrest handcuffed to his wrist through the air. Three more officers rushed in and crushed him to the floor. Short of breath, he passed out.

When he came to, he was handcuffed to a balcony railing, while Santini was berating the uniformed officers for having kept him in a confined space. Dante's mouth was dry and he was having a hard time focusing, and only the pain in his stomach brought him back to the present. Down below, Via San Vitale was blocked by police barriers and squad cars.

"They're holding me prisoner against my will and torturing me!" he shouted loud enough to be heard from the street. "Someone alert my lawyer! His name is Roberto Minutillo, you can find him online."

Santini came running. "Shut that trap, or I'll have you dragged back inside. And I'll make sure that wherever they put you, there'll be no windows."

"And if it kills me? Will you dispose of my dead body?"

Santini leaned over him. "A ranking police official has been murdered. How worried do you think I'm likely to be about what might happen to you?"

"I was there, or have you forgotten?"

"Which is why we brought you in." Santini pulled a wheeled stool over to him. Half a dozen officers, uniformed and in plain clothes, crowded into the French doors and watched the scene on the balcony. "Let me make the situation clear to you. There's been a bombing. There are people calling for martial law, there are others talking about the resurgence of the Red Brigades. It's the duty of people like me to figure out what happened. And we have very little patience with people who refuse to cooperate."

"No one has asked me a single question yet."

"But I'm about to start. On behalf of the investigating magistrate."

"Let me guess, De Angelis?"

"That's no concern of yours. You'll meet him afterward for the formal drafting of the deposition."

"That is, if I'm a good boy; otherwise you'll throw me off this balcony."

Santini clenched his jaw. "Why are you trying to make me lose my temper?"

Dante decided that Santini really was in an uncontrollable rage. Was he about to beat him? He didn't think so. As much as he might want to, the eyes of the nation were trained on police headquarters right now. If Santini thought that Dante had had something to do with it, he might have thrown caution to the winds. But just then, Santini was confused. Dante could see it clearly in the line of his shoulders, the way they bore the weight of all that had happened; the way he constantly touched his face and imperceptibly licked his lips, betraying confusion and fear. Santini was raising his voice, but he didn't understand what was happening. Or else—another hypothesis—Santini knew exactly what was going on but still didn't know what move to make. That was more worrisome.

Until that moment, Dante had thought of Santini as a brainless brute, a dime-store cop who was capable of stamping all over the evidence with his size 12 flat feet and creating nothing but confusion. But Rovere's last words meant that the Father wasn't working alone, and Dante very much doubted that he had been referring to some henchman pressed into service when needed, which was all Bodini had been. Rovere feared that there were other accomplices. Who could they be? A CIS officer, by any chance? The same one Colomba was supposed to look out for?

Dante sensed that the truth was almost within reach but still just out of his grasp. He needed to get out of there, and if Santini really was involved, the only way he could do so was to pass himself off as a fool. He thought all this in just a couple of seconds, while Santini scrutinized him suspiciously. *Remember that he's a cop, that he's used to people telling him lies*, Dante said to himself. And if he was involved, then he wasn't half the fool he seemed.

"Ask me what you want to know," he said, dropping his eyes in a plausible imitation of humility. "But first, sir, please tell me how Deputy Captain Caselli is doing."

"I don't have any news from the hospital, but she didn't seem to be in serious condition," Santini replied, still studying him. "Are you very close?"

"No."

"You certainly seemed close."

"Is that what you wanted to know, whether we're close?" said Dante, forgetting the part he was supposed to play.

"It's one thing."

"No, we're not. We just spent some time together in the past week."

"Is that why you've been living together in a hotel?"

Fuck, so they knew. "We don't live together. I live there," Dante replied. "She came to see me a few times. Ask the desk clerk if you don't believe me."

"Right now, I don't care. What were you doing in Captain Rovere's apartment house during the explosion?"

"I came in after the explosion."

Santini moved even closer. "After? Are you trying to tell me that you went into the building *after* the explosion? You, who can't even sit in an ordinary room, went in like a firefighter?"

Dante pulled his legs up, pretending to be more frightened than he was. He needed to make Santini think that *he* was in control of the situation. "I was in shock," he murmured.

"I didn't hear you," Santini barked.

"I was in shock. I don't really know what I did."

Santini nodded with satisfaction, like a dog owner after his pet has rolled over on command. "So why were you there?"

"I'd accompanied Deputy Captain Caselli to meet Captain Rovere," said Dante in a louder tone, faking a slight quaver in his voice.

"And just why were they meeting?"

Santini had plenty of experience and had conducted thousands of interrogations. Dante couldn't lie openly. He had to limit himself to twisting the truth, conceding what little Santini had already guessed. "The Luca Maugeri kidnapping."

Santini nodded. "So Deputy Captain Caselli was still looking into it?"

"Yes."

"For what reason?"

Here, too, it did no good to lie. "At Captain Rovere's request. He had his doubts about how you were conducting the investigation."

"We, meaning the CIS?"

"Yes. And he didn't think much of the magistrate either. He said he was a cretin." The last thing he'd said was a complete lie, but he figured it would pass. Someone like Rovere *might* have said it, even if only to reassure Dante about his objectives. Concealing his real purpose.

He's not alone.

Santini made a face. "Maybe we shouldn't make that a part of the deposition transcript, eh? Let's not make the dead look bad."

"That's up to you."

"Was it Captain Rovere who asked for you to consult on the investigation?" He said "consult" as if it were a dirty word.

"Yes."

"And what were you going to see Rovere about last night?"

"We were going to tell him we needed more time."

"Was it Rovere's idea to have you check the lists of children who'd been killed in the last several years?"

Infanti had sung like a canary, and immediately. Colomba needed to get herself some better friends. "No, that was one of my ideas. I was looking for details that might fit with what happened up at the Vivaro mountain meadows."

Santini narrowed his eyes. Genuine interest or fear? And if it was fear, was it fear of being made to look like a fool or for some other reason?

He's not alone.

"And did you find any?"

Dante needed to play this next move as well as he knew how. And he did it by protesting. "I need more time, damn it!" he said. "There are thousands of cases that might be connected." He intentionally exaggerated the number.

Santini couldn't repress a smile. Derision or relief? Dante hated being left in doubt. "Thousands?"

Dante lunged again, aggressively. "The Father has been lurking in the shadows, spinning his webs for more than thirty years! Do you know how many kids he might have grabbed?" He'd basically just spoken the truth, but anyone else would have assumed he was crazy as a loon.

"So the Father is your kidnapper, is that right? Come back from the afterlife."

Dante ventured a faint retort. If he acted completely submissive, Santini would start to become suspicious. "You're making fun of me."

"Absolutely not," said Santini with a slightly broader smile. "And the proof is the whistle that you found nearly a mile away. Right?"

"If that's how you want to put it."

"Right?"

"Yes," said Dante, humbly.

Someone in the background murmured in disbelief, and to Dante it was like the first round of applause for his performance.

"And Caselli believes you?"

Careful. "She was starting to come around," he replied, clearly conveying the opposite.

"'She was *starting*.' I understand. And did you give her any other *proof*"—he leaned on the word—"aside from the whistle?"

"I was trying to find it. I told you, I need more time!"

Santini scrutinized him. Dante knew that Santini's instincts were telling him not to believe him, but, whether or not he was involved, what Dante was telling him was exactly what someone like him would most want to hear.

"Had you ever been to Captain Rovere's home before?" asked Santini.

"No."

"We have ways of knowing if you're lying to us, Torre."

"Why should I lie to you? Do you think I planted the bomb?"

"Well, then, who did plant it, in your opinion?"

Dante held his breath. This was it. "The Father. The man who kidnapped me."

This time there was a burst of murmuring. Santini whirled around to shut them up, but Dante understood that he was just hogging the spotlight. Santini liked having an audience. "Have you found another whistle, Torre?" Santini asked.

"There was only one."

"Right. I was forgetting. Yours was the only one. And why would the man who kidnapped you want to kill Captain Rovere?"

Dante felt the way he had when he was twenty and he had bet all the money he had to pay his hotel bill at the roulette wheel on the terrace of a casino in Bad Gastein. It had been a bold bet: everything on red. And now he was doing the same thing. "Because he's afraid of me. Because he knew that sooner or later Rovere was going to believe me."

Back at the casino in Austria, Dante had been forced to run for it in the middle of the night without paying his hotel bill, leaving his suitcase full of clothes behind him. This time his luck was better. Santini's shoulders sagged a quarter of an inch, and Dante knew he'd won. "I see."

Santini asked him a few other routine questions—if he'd seen anyone, if he'd heard anything—then got to his feet. Dante put the cherry on top of the cake: he extended his bad hand and pulled on the hem of Santini's jacket. The lieutenant pulled free with a disgusted yank, but he pretended not to notice.

"You do believe me, don't you?" he asked pathetically. "You'll investigate the Father?"

Santini turned his back on him and addressed one of the uniformed officers. When the officer stuck his head in, Dante saw that it was Alberti. He forced himself not to give him a wink.

"Bring him some water and something to eat," said Santini. "Let's show him we're not animals." Then he left.

Alberti came over, acting solicitous. "What can I get you, Signor Torre? Would you like an espresso?"

Dante's expression changed. "Don't you dare. A tea is all I need. And cigarettes, for Christ's sake. I've been going through nicotine cold turkey, and I feel like I'm dying."

Astonished at the sudden transformation—Dante had seemed crushed and exhausted to him—Alberti brought him a lukewarm cup of tea, a packet of cookies from the vending machines, and an unfiltered cigarette.

An hour later, after Dante's handcuffs had been removed, Minutillo arrived.

The lawyer demanded to be allowed to speak to his client without witnesses and shut the French doors in the policemen's faces.

"How are you?" he asked once they were alone.

"You can imagine." Dante, who couldn't be sure no one was eavesdropping, spoke in a low voice. "Santini convinced himself that I'm not a danger to him. For now."

"Why would you be a danger to him?"

"Maybe he's involved."

"With the Father?"

"Rovere was convinced that someone was helping the Father. And he explicitly said not to trust De Angelis." He lit the cigarette that Minutillo had brought him.

"Why should he or Santini want to help a murderer?"

"I don't have any idea." Dante puffed out a smoke ring. "If you'd asked me that question six hours ago, I would have said that it was nonsense. But after the bomb . . ."

"The two things might not be connected."

"And I kidnapped myself, I suppose."

"Don't dismiss the possibility out of hand, Dante."

Dante shook his head. "Did you get rid of the stuff in my hotel room?"

"Of course. That's why I took so long to get here. As soon as I heard that they'd picked you up, I hurried over to the hotel. And just in the nick of time, I'd say. While I was on my way out, I saw what looked like a group of plainclothes detectives on their way in."

"Probably from the CIS. Who alerted you?"

"I have friends on the inside there. And so do you. More friends than Santini does."

Dante put on his sarcastic grin. "That doesn't take much. I'm about to do something disgusting, Roberto. Let me apologize in advance, but keep up your end in this." Then, in a loud voice, he added: "I don't feel too good. I'm . . ." He bugged out his eyes, lurched forward, and vomited tea and cookies onto Minutillo's shoes. And with the tea and cookies came up the thing that had been caused him stomach cramps until that moment. A little blue plastic rectangle. A USB flash drive.

"Oh, my God," yelled Minutillo, jumping theatrically to his feet.

"I'm so sorry! Hold on, let me help you!" Dante exclaimed, clumsily pretending to try to clean off the lawyer's shoes with a paper napkin. He skillfully grabbed the flash drive with the napkin and balled it up.

"Hold on, let me do it," said Minutillo, taking the napkin from him and using it to wipe himself off. While he was bent over, he whispered into his ear, "What's in it?"

"It was in Rovere's jacket. I hope it's something useful. Otherwise he would have left it in the office with his computer."

"Understood," murmured Minutillo, anything but pleased. Then, in a loud voice, he said, "I'm going to rinse off in the bathroom."

Dante looked hard at him. "Good idea."

Minutillo headed off with the dirty napkin in one hand, held out in plain view. As Dante had guessed, no one even thought of examining it to see what it held.

2

While Dante waited to be allowed to leave police headquarters, if possible before anyone could notice that his testimony didn't entirely add up, and as Minutillo headed toward his law office feeling as though he were carrying a hand grenade in his pocket instead of a flash drive, Colomba was spending the day in the third-floor room in the general hospital under the effects of tranquilizers and painkillers. The mix kept the crisis at bay, muffled the memories, and made time pass quickly. At 4 p.m. the nurse removed the IV, and immediately afterward a familiar figure strode through the door with a bouquet of flowers in his hand. It was De Angelis. A short while earlier, he'd been interviewed and photographed with the flowers. He'd explained to the press that he was paying a courtesy call to a courageous police-woman. Colomba turned her face to look out the window. She could see the trees on the hospital grounds. Without drugs, her head was beginning to throb.

De Angelis dropped the flowers on the table. He dragged a chair over next to the bed and sat down. "How are you feeling, Deputy Captain?" he asked.

"That's none of your business," Colomba replied in a low voice. Her throat was scarred by the scalding smoke. "And I don't think you care anyway."

"I know that you were very fond of Captain Rovere, Deputy Captain Caselli," the judge said calmly. "And I can imagine just how upset you are now. I want to tell you that I'm sorry about what happened, too. I've had opportunities to appreciate his skills. He was a great cop." Colomba didn't move and said nothing. De Angelis went on, unruffled. "And I'm sorry to be here bothering you now. But it's essential that the two of us come to an understanding immediately."

Colomba didn't say a thing.

"The last time we met, it didn't go all that well, Deputy Captain,"

De Angelis continued. "But that doesn't mean that things can't change. That we can't help each other out."

"What do you want?"

"We just want to catch whoever killed Captain Rovere."

Colomba snapped around and saw stars. "And do you think I don't?"

"That's why I'm here. We already know that you've worked in a, shall we say"—he flashed a brief smile—"*clandestine* fashion on Luca Maugeri's kidnapping. In search of a theory that is somewhat different from the one being pursued by my office."

"So what if I did?"

"It's a certainty, it's not a question," said the judge, displaying a hint of toughness. "And while previously it was just a venial sin, one you could get away with, with just a slap on the wrist, things have changed now, Deputy Captain. I have to know whether you think Captain Rovere's death is connected to your investigation."

De Angelis's words sounded eminently reasonable, and Colomba felt them pressing against her will, more fragile than ever at that moment. But Rovere hadn't trusted De Angelis, and that mistrust had been his last will and testament. "I don't know," she replied. "How could I possibly know?"

"Don't trifle with me, Deputy Captain. If you happen to have stumbled upon some evidence that points to a, shall we say, *alternative* theory concerning the kidnapping of Luca Maugeri, that might be a sufficient reason for an unbalanced kidnapper and murderer to try to stop the investigation. Especially if Captain Rovere was encouraging you in the investigations. Or was actually the original cause of them."

"Are you talking about the Father?"

"I'm talking about anything that can help me to identify those responsible for the bombing. There are six dead besides Captain Rovere, you know? And two people seriously injured."

"I doubt you'd believe me."

"Try me. And as for your own personal culpability, however irregular it may have been, I'll be glad to declare that your investigation was undertaken with the authorization of my office."

He's already throwing Santini under the bus, Colomba thought to herself. *Maugeri has been in jail for a week, and he still hasn't confessed. De Angelis hasn't come up with any further evidence against him. He's starting to get scared he might have arrested the wrong man.* Had she been certain that that was the case, she would have told him everything, but once again she took Rovere's suspicions as her own.

"I haven't found anything."

"I see. And what did you do with the information you asked Lieutenant Infanti to get for you?"

Colomba decided she needed to get some new friends. And, without knowing it, she clung to the same version as Dante. "Signor Torre wanted to examine similar cases, hoping to find some matches. Unfortunately, he didn't find any."

"If he hadn't found anything, why were you meeting with Rovere?"

"Just a courtesy call."

De Angelis took off his heavy black-framed eyeglasses, cleaned the lenses with his tie, and put them back on. "So you have no suspicions, however vague? Not just about the kidnapper known as the Father. Anything Captain Rovere might have mentioned to you."

"He wasn't expecting to be killed. That much I can guarantee." To conceal her tears, Colomba once again turned her head to look out the window.

De Angelis grabbed her chin and turned her face toward him. "I came here to offer you my friendship. I'm asking you to accept it."

Colomba leveled her eyes into the judge's. Her eyes seemed those of an alien, with the green of the iris standing out against the reddened corneas. De Angelis's eyes were two opaque mirrors behind his tinted lenses, from which it was impossible to gather the slightest trace of what he was thinking. "Don't you ever touch me again," she said to him. "Or I won't be able to answer for what happens next."

The magistrate withdrew his hand. "And . . ."

"I have nothing else to say to you."

De Angelis stood up. "You've made your choice, Caselli."

On his way out, he pretended to bump into the table. The flowers tumbled off and hit the floor.

3

It was as if De Angelis's visit had unblocked the logjam. In the two hours that followed, Colomba didn't have a minute alone. First her mother showed up, anxious to be consoled; then came the couple of friends whose dinner party she'd missed the night she'd gone up to the mountain meadows to see Lucia Maugeri's corpse and whom she hadn't spoken to since. When they asked her if she needed anything, she asked them to go to her apartment and pick up a change of clothes, since her mother had already said she was too upset to do it.

Another visitor to the hospital was Alberti, clearly ill at ease in this unaccustomed role. He was in plain clothes, and his Abercrombie sweatshirt and jeans made him look even more like an overgrown high school student. Colomba was happy to see him, even if the press of activity was exhausting her.

Alberti handed her a small package. She opened it and found it contained an MP3 player. Not exactly a brand-new model, but still in working order. "You're crazy, I can't accept this," she told him. "I know how much you make."

He blushed. "Actually, it's contraband, and to start with it's just a cheap Chinese gadget. The gift is what's inside."

Colomba looked at the MP3 player, in surprise. She was having a hard time focusing, what with the medicine and the blow to her head. "So what's in it?"

"Music. That I composed. Emotional electronica. I don't know if you've ever heard of Nicolas Jaar . . . I take my inspiration from him."

Colomba didn't have the faintest idea of what Alberti was talking about. "I think I stopped back at the Red Hot Chili Peppers, but thanks anyway. I didn't know you were a composer."

"For now it's just a hobby. If you don't like my pieces, just delete them and put in whatever you prefer." He hesitated. "I saw Signor Torre today."

Colomba lost the smile and grabbed Alberti by his arm. "How is he?"

He lowered his voice. "He says that it was his kidnapper who did it. That he's taken thousands of children. If you don't mind my saying so, he seemed kind of out of his mind."

"Who was questioning him?"

"Santini. But he didn't believe him. And frankly, it wouldn't have been easy."

"How did Dante justify his statements?"

"He didn't. That's why Santini laughed in his face. I felt sorry for him."

Colomba shut her eyes for a second, overwhelmed. They'd grilled Dante and he had kept quiet, even at the cost of looking like a fool. He didn't trust them any more than she did. "Where is he now?"

"Still at police headquarters, though his lawyer is raising holy hell. I think the magistrates are going to release him soon. They don't have any justification for holding on to him, do they?"

Alberti's gaze was practically imploring. "He has nothing to hide," said Colomba.

"I never doubted it for a second, Deputy Captain. I like him, even if he is a real bear. He's had a lot of bad luck in his life."

"What's known about the explosion?"

"The Forensic Squad is still investigating the site."

"Was anyone seen going in? Have they found anything?"

"Deputy Captain . . . if anything's come out, I'm the last person they're likely to tell. I'm just a penguin in a patrol car."

Colomba realized that he had a point. "If you do find anything out, please let me know."

"Sure. Well, I'll be going. You should get some rest now."

"Thanks."

But Colomba's head was too full of thoughts for her to get to sleep. Every time she tried, she instantly started to see the flickering flame being lit in the darkness of Rovere's apartment, she heard the crackling of fire that was so similar to the flames that had consumed the restaurant in Paris. And she was suddenly transported back nine months in time, and the whispering shadows whirled through her head again. She woke up and went back to sleep at least three times, until she finally gave up and convinced the doctor not to give her any more tranquilizers. In the IV they gave her before dinner, there were only antibiotics and painkillers to relieve her headaches, at least enough so she could think straight. Her grief over Rovere's death continued to surface in her consciousness, however hard she struggled to keep it at bay. She still found it difficult to believe that she had lost him. She remembered him from the early years in Palermo, one of the few ranking officials to go out onto the street with his officers when something happened. As a deputy captain, she had asked if she could go over to the marshals service, but Rovere had insisted on taking her with him to the Drug Enforcement Division. He believed that a woman could work better undercover, and he had been right. For two years, Colomba had been variously drug buyer, junkie, and dealer, and no had ever suspected that she was actually a cop. Then her face had become too well known, and she had been moved over to street crime—the first woman to work regularly with the Hawks—the whole time with Rovere following her progress from a distance and supporting her against the sexist officials who had tried to minimize her achievements.

Colomba had lost her father when she was just a girl; it had been a heart attack. She'd always been attracted to powerful men, and to some extent they were clearly father figures to her. Frequently they'd disappointed her, the way her boyfriends had when they'd been unable to keep up with her in the many sudden changes in her career. Rovere had never failed her; he'd always been there. At a discreet distance—there had never been any expressions of emotional attachment in their relationship, no socializing except for a few dinners together before Elena had fallen sick—but unswervingly. Then he'd betrayed her in that way. Or had she actually started it?

With the lucidity made possible to her by her worsening fever, it occurred to Colomba that perhaps she had been the first to break their bond, when she had decided to quit, and she had done so without revealing the truth about her condition to him. Her panic attacks, her fears. But had that been enough to justify what Rovere had done next, the way he had used her as a pawn in his chess match against the Father?

She told herself no. There had to be another reason, something more powerful than the fondness that, Colomba felt sure, Rovere felt toward her, stronger than the loyalty he had always shown toward his direct and indirect reports, much more than toward his superior officers. And it certainly had nothing to do with any power struggle to take Santini's job at the CIS. Now Colomba could clearly see that that had been a lie, a way to get her to stop wondering about the real reasons that were driving him. Rovere had been willing to have her think he was an envious, despicable careerist, as long as it got her involved. If he hadn't been killed, Colomba would have quit the game, but now she knew she had to take up his legacy, however heavy the burden.

And while she was thinking about how to carry on, the shadow of a man in a lab coat loomed up between her and the window, through which came pouring the last rays of the setting sun. It was Tirelli, and he was looking at her tenderly.

"Mario, what are you doing wearing a lab coat?"

Tirelli smiled, putting his stick of licorice back into his chest pocket. "Have you forgotten that I'm a doctor?" He stepped closer to take a good look at her. "Let me see how you're doing. Your pupils look fine . . . Raise your eyes toward the ceiling . . . Now to the right . . ."

Colomba moved uncomfortably. "You're not thinking of giving me an examination . . ."

"Is there some problem?"

"Just the fact that your patients are usually dead."

"I have other specialties, little lady. But I'll admit that I'm at my best working with cold bodies." His expression turned sad. "They asked me to perform the autopsy on Rovere, but . . . I preferred to leave the job to my assistants."

The tears that Colomba had successfully choked back over the past several hours welled up again. "How did he die?"

"From massive hemorrhaging due to a lesion to the superior mesenteric artery. A metal fragment ran him through."

Colomba blew her nose on a Kleenex. "Did he suffer?"

"Not much. And I'm not saying it just to comfort you. He had a serious lesion to his spinal cord; he was numb from the sternum down. And he didn't die alone."

"Who was with him?"

"Your friend. Signor Torre. He stayed with him. When the first responders got upstairs, he was sitting there holding Rovere's head."

Colomba was stunned. "Dante went in?"

"Yes. Don't you remember?"

"Nothing. But Dante is afraid of closed places, so you can imagine how he'd feel about going into an apartment house in flames . . . How did he bring himself to do it?"

Tirelli caressed her face. "Maybe he had a good reason. He made sure someone carried you out of there."

"God . . ." Everything seemed even more surreal to her. "Mario, you have to give me a hand."

Tirelli sat down in the chair from which De Angelis had delivered his little speech just a few hours ago. "With what?"

"Dante was right. The Father was behind the kidnapping of the Maugeris' son. And I think it was he who planted the bomb in Rovere's apartment."

"You need to rest, Colomba . . ."

"No, no. I haven't gone around the bend." Colomba pulled herself up into a sitting position and did her best to put an expression on her face that wouldn't make her look like a pathetic nutcase in the throes of delirium. "We investigated. We found definite points of contact. And Rovere knew that the Father was still active. That's why he had me bring Dante in on it."

Tirelli studied her. "Are you sure of what you're saying?"

"Rovere confirmed it before dying. He knew something he didn't have time to tell us, which is why he was killed."

Tirelli pulled out the licorice and bit it. "I'll admit it, you've caught me off guard. Have you talked about this with De Angelis?"

"No. Rovere didn't trust him. And neither do I. If I had any solid evidence, I'd slap it in front of somebody. But I don't. All I have are guesses. I know that they're right, but still . . . I have to prove them." She took a gulp of water from the bottle to soothe the pain in her throat. "Can you imagine what would happen if I went to the chief of police and told him about my suspicions? He already thought that the Disaster in Paris was my fault. But if I can just bring him something . . ."

"What do you want me to do, Colomba?"

"Have you ever heard of Silver Compass?"

"No."

"It was an association that looked after children with problems."
She told him about the Palladinos and what she and Dante had figured out.

"And you think that the Father found the child through the association?" Tirelli asked at last.

"It's a possibility. And it might not be the only one."

"But the child from the mountain meadows wasn't going to this
Silver Compass . . ."

"The association went out of business, and the Father was forced
to find another way of selecting his victims."

"That is, if there really is any connection."

"That's why I'm talking to you about it. You know lots of people:
doctors, volunteers . . . Can you find out who ran it? All I need is for
you to find me someone I can grill."

Tirelli got laboriously back to his feet, with his knees creaking. "Do
you remember that old TV show *Quincy, M.E.*?" he asked. Colomba
shook her head no. "It was about a medical examiner who hunted
murderers. I always thought it was ridiculous. I investigate the insides
of bodies, not out in the streets."

"You're the only one I can ask."

He nodded. "I know, that's why I'm not telling you no. I'll make a
few phone calls."

"Thanks." Tirelli turned to go. She called him back. "Mario . . . talk
only to people you trust, and tell them as little as you can. Be careful."

Tirelli smiled. "Of course I'll be careful. I plan to hold on to this
old carcass of mine," he said, pointing to his chest.

Colomba followed him out the door with her eyes. Thinking
about what the Father had proved himself capable of, she couldn't
help but worry.

4

The man Colomba and Dante called the Father had based his way of life on systematically keeping a low profile. He shopped only at department stores, changing the ones he frequented to avoid becoming a familiar face to the cashiers. He wore only nondescript suits, but always clean and neat to keep from attracting attention. He eschewed bright colors, flashy patterns. He preferred gray and brown, never black, which was too extreme. His car was a station wagon that he'd bought used, he lived in a one-bedroom apartment, his gymnasium was a set of exercise equipment he kept in a closet and pulled out every morning. He had no bank account in his name, he never ate out, he never went to the movies or the theater. Once every fifteen days he'd indulge in a prostitute, chosen off the street from among the foreigners who didn't speak Italian. He paid what was asked, then never saw her again. His only other distractions were watching TV and reading military history. He didn't drink, he didn't smoke. He was sufficient unto himself, and all he required was his work to fill his life. He had no friends, and of the few human beings who knew him at all, only a tiny number knew his real name and what he really did.

One of that tiny number was sitting next to him at that very moment, at the gas station at kilometer marker 8 on the Rome beltway, off in a corner of the asphalt apron far from the security cameras. The man had aged poorly, he thought to himself. The belt of fat around his waist and his sagging pectoral muscles clearly bespoke an absence of physical exercise, while the broken blood vessels on his nose meant he drank. And then there was the fact that he smiled and chatted like a fool, trying to remind him of episodes he had prudently long ago forgotten. Eyeing him, the man whom Dante and Colomba referred to as the Father or Zardoz thought about giving up the idea entirely. Act nonchalant, say good-bye, then follow him home and kill him. Someone like this man, incapable of self-discipline or sobriety, who didn't know how to keep his mouth shut, was nothing but a danger. But an even greater danger now hovered over his work, and he realized he couldn't do the easy thing, the obvious thing. That he'd have to get rid of him eventually was obvious—but later, when he could no longer be useful to him. Right now he needed a partner, to minimize the risks. A *temporary* partner.

The man he hadn't seen in more than twenty years nodded contentedly when he offered him the job, and the contentment turned into eagerness as soon as he heard the sum he would never live to enjoy. After lots of pointless chitchat, after wisecracks and laughter and slaps on the back, he asked the only question that mattered: When and where?

"Tonight," the Father answered. "At the hospital." And he handed him the syringe.

5

It was seven in the evening by the time Minutillo managed to spring Dante out of police custody, and the lawyer was forced to support his client as they made their way down the stairway of police headquarters. Dante hadn't slept in more than twenty-four hours, he'd eaten only cookies from the vending machines, and he was in withdrawal from pharmaceuticals and caffeine. What little lucidity remained to him after the first interview had been consumed by his encounter with the magistrate from De Angelis's team who had taken his testimony. After that experience his memory was patchy at best, up to the moment that his lawyer's friendly face had appeared on the balcony where he'd been confined, luckily by this point without handcuffs.

Just as he'd done after the meeting at the autogrill with De Angelis, Minutillo took Dante home and waited until he had finished showering and downed a dose of assorted psychotropic drugs that would stun an elephant, along with a tub of coffee. Unseen by his friend, Dante tossed a couple of tablets of Ritalin into the mix, the medicine that was prescribed in the United States to sedate hyperactive children but that had the opposite effect on grown-ups. What with the caffeine and the various pills and capsules, before long Dante was capable of thinking straight again. Minutillo even managed to persuade him to choke down a soy protein burger and a package of crackers. At that point, though, Dante noticed that something wasn't right: the things in the apartment were far messier than he had left them. The stacks of books had been knocked over, the boxes of food were no longer arranged according to color, the various envelopes had been torn open. All that was left of his computer was the screen; the dresser drawers all hung open so their contents could be seen. As he focused on details, he realized that his clothing, too, had been tossed into random heaps and that when he had changed, he'd had to rummage through a tangled pile at the bottom of the armoire. If he hadn't been moving like a robot, he would have noticed immediately. "What happened here?" he asked, already fearing the answer.

"They searched the apartment," the lawyer replied.

Dante dropped his utensils. "Oh, fuck."

"Don't worry, I'll make sure you get everything back."

"What do you mean, everything? What did they take?"

Minutillo hesitated, embarrassed. "Dante . . ."

But he wasn't listening anymore; he'd already rushed into the guest room. The "time capsules" that had once filled the room to the ceiling were gone. All that lay on the floor was the case from the *Supercar* videocassette and a small heap of phone cards. Dante leaned over to pick them up: they were of various vintages. The police had probably opened the boxes and tossed everything around indiscriminately.

"I'm sorry," Minutillo said from behind him.

Dante grabbed the phone cards and twisted them in his fist, cutting himself on the stiff plastic. "Fuck! Fuck!" he shouted. "Two years of work up in smoke! Two years of research, of cataloguing!"

"It'll all come back home."

"Dirty, mixed up! Fuck!" Dante hurled the phone cards against the wall, then grabbed the metal bed frame that for the past few years had served as the platform for his collection and shook it, banging it against the floor, kicking up a cloud of dust while cursing in three different languages.

Minutillo let him vent until he ran out of steam; given his friend's state of physical weakness, that didn't take long. Dante let himself drop onto the sprung bed frame, feeling miserable and violated, his eyes glistening. He felt like crying.

"I was here the whole time," said Minutillo, doing his best to comfort him. "I limited the damage the best I could."

"Now I understand why the coffee tasted so foul. They mixed up the beans. I'll have to separate them one by one. Or just throw them all away."

Minutillo tried to lighten the mood. "You can call it the 'Judge De Angelis blend.'"

"It was his order, wasn't it?" Dante raised one hand. "No, don't answer. I already feel like enough of an idiot for having even asked the question. It's obvious. Am I officially a suspect?"

"Not yet. But the fact that you were on the scene of the explosion is reason enough for the district attorney's office to turn you inside out like a sock."

"Have they searched CC's place, too?"

"Yes. And they also suspended her from active duty on a cautionary basis. Which makes no sense since she's already on medical leave. They told me that they confiscated her gun and police ID while she was sedated."

"De Angelis is making her pay for sticking her nose into the Luca Maugeri investigation," said Dante grimly.

"If I know anything about the way these things work, this is only the start. If he has anything he can use against you, he'll use it. And—"

Dante threw his arms wide in a gesture of malaise. "And what? Come on, spit it out. Worse than this . . ."

"The rumor will get started from the district attorney's office, one way or another. About the fact that you're a 'person with information about the crimes' or else a suspect. You'll wind up in the papers."

"The whole old story will come out."

"Yes."

Dante cradled his head in his hands. "Fuck."

"I'll find a place for you to stay."

"Do you know how much it's cost me to design this apartment to my specifications?" asked Dante, still incredulous.

"Yes, I know." Minutillo smiled. "Remember, you sued the architect."

"Because he was a charlatan. And now I'm going to have to sell it. And who would buy an apartment in this condition? An exhibitionist? A pornstar who wants people to see her naked from the street?"

"Once things calm down . . ." Minutillo started to say.

Dante interrupted him. "Things aren't going to calm down. Even if the Father were to magically disappear along with De Angelis and all his little friends, that would just mark the beginning of the procession through here of people in search of vanished relatives. 'Please, we need you to save us,'" he said, mockingly imitating a despairing voice. "I've been through that."

Minutillo didn't reply, knowing full well that Dante had a point. It had happened once before, exactly as he'd said. "Okay, but still, let's just not make things worse. The important thing is not to give De Angelis any excuses. Otherwise, he could definitely make things much, much worse."

Dante looked down at the tips of his shoes. "What was on Rovere's flash drive?"

"I couldn't open it. It wanted a password, and I preferred not to type in random attempts."

"Do you have it with you? Give it to me, please."

Minutillo ran a hand over his hair, so short it was practically a crew cut. "Did you hear what I told you earlier? About what you could be risking?"

"Maybe De Angelis will leave me in peace if I bury my head in the sand, but what about the Father?"

"Till now, he's never gone after you directly."

"True. He's only killed . . . how many people? . . . and all because we were investigating him. Do you think he's just going to drop it now?" Dante shook his head. "I'm getting closer, Roberto. It's too late to give up."

Minutillo sighed and handed him the small plastic drive. "What do *you* think's on the flash drive?"

"Who do you know that takes the trouble to put a password on a flash drive?"

"No one."

"In that case, whatever it is, it must be important."

Minutillo stared at his friend for a few seconds without speaking. "I'm worried about you, Dante," he finally said. "More than I've ever been before."

Dante smiled and pretended to yawn. "Well, stop. I'm too tired to get myself into trouble. In fact, I think I'm going to take a good long nap right now."

Minutillo left, and when Dante heard the sound of his car going away down the street, he slipped the flash drive into an envelope, put the envelope into his pocket, and went out wearing a gunmetal gray parka that practically swallowed him up. The stairs were a walk in the park compared with what he'd been through lately, or maybe he'd just hit the exact blend of pharmaceuticals. He got downstairs in only ten minutes. Once out in the street, he looked around alertly. He'd never been tailed in his life, but he was sure that he'd know if someone was following him. After countless twists and turns through the streets of San Lorenzo, which were just starting to fill up with kids, he was pretty sure no one was.

He made his first stop at the Bar Marani, at the beginning of Via dei Volsci. The owners knew him well; he was the only client who'd sit outside in the rear patio even in the winter rain, and they were fond of him. He left the envelope with them and told them someone would come by to pick it up before they closed the bar that evening. From there he walked to the pay phone on Via Boccanegra. It took him about twenty minutes, and the walk did him good, sweeping the last few cobwebs from his brain. He called Santiago, told him where to pick up the envelope, explained what he wanted done, and pleaded with him to work as quickly as possible. Yes, there was money in it for him, he reassured him, but only once the job was completed.

When he hung up, he realized that he didn't feel like going home and going to bed. The Ritalin, which at first had simply eliminated any traces of sleepiness, now burned inside him like gasoline. His brain kept spinning, elaborating hypotheses and scenarios, and once again, at the center of each of them was Rovere. Now that Dante had solved the mystery of why he'd been drawn into the Luca Maugeri investigation, he was starting to ask other questions: When had Rovere started working on this matter? And, most important of all, why?

What little he'd been able to find out from Colomba about him, and about his previous investigations, in no way suggested a connection with the Father. The impression he'd gotten of Rovere was that he was a solid, cautious cop, careful of every step he took both in and out of the line of duty. He certainly wasn't reckless to the point of sticking his nose into someone else's case just for the fun of it.

Dante hoped that at least a partial answer might come from the flash drive, which would soon be safe in Santiago's skillful hands. But he was eager to find out immediately, and there was only one person he could reach out to. He waited for a Maghrebi to finish his phone call to his faraway girlfriend, and then Dante made a second phone call. This time he called a woman who had been trying to track down her sister for years, until Dante had found what was left of her under her father-in-law's basement floor. She felt a debt of gratitude toward Dante, and she worked at the hospital where Colomba was being treated. She told him the room number but apologized and said she wasn't working a shift right now. Dante asked her to explain the layout of the ward and understood that he could make it in without her help. It didn't even occur to him that he might wait until the next morning, so uncontrollably was his brain seething with activity. He called a cab and rode over with all the windows wide open. He asked the driver to drop him off just a few yards away from the hospital; then he climbed over the fence and made his way into the grounds. As he walked, he looked up at the third-story windows, counting. The map of the building rotated in his mind: if he closed his eyes, he could see it as if it were a three-dimensional rendering. He stopped at the foot of a cypress: the room was straight overhead, on the third floor. He climbed the tree as if it were a ladder. That was child's play for him; he'd always been a good climber. He scrambled through the branches like a monkey even though he had only one fully functional hand; his light frame was a help. One of the highest branches with enough structural integrity to bear his weight was just at the level of the window in question. He clambered out onto the limb on all fours but realized that the windowsill was still too far away for him to leap across. From where he was, though, he could see the bed, dimly lit by the night light that Colomba had left on, and her face among the pillows.

As he was considering whether to climb down and get some pebbles to throw at the glass, he noticed that someone was moving in the hospital room. From Dante's vantage point, he could barely make out the unknown visitor, who was right at the edge of the band of light cast by the streetlamp outside, but he was immediately positive that he was up to no good. The man was wearing a lab coat, but he wasn't moving the way doctors or nurses do in a hospital, with spare, almost brusque gestures, typical of people accustomed to dealing with the suffering of others. Whoever this was, he was clearly quite tense, as if he knew he was somewhere he wasn't supposed to be.

The man took a step toward the bed, and now Dante could see his hands. He held them so they gripped the hem of the lab coat right at chest height, in a universal gesture of anxiety and self-defense. He moved farther into the light. Dante saw a face he would not soon forget. The man's furtive movements were those of someone about to embark on a difficult or dangerous task. Dante didn't want to wait for him to act; he had to sound the alarm, wake up Colomba and the entire hospital, if that proved necessary. But before he could even try to take action, a whispering arose from the darkness among the trees and slashed him like a cracking whip. Dante immediately began trembling uncontrollably. That whispering stirred terrible nightmares deep inside him that had never entirely subsided, nightmares that gnawed at his bowels and made his blood run cold.

He clutched the branch, as if some irresistible force were dragging him down to earth. *Don't look*, he told himself. *Don't look down.* But the whispering was doing its work inside him, destroying his will. Slowly he turned his gaze toward the origin of the sound, the strip of darkness between two lampposts. A man was standing with his back to the hospital wall, arms hanging at his sides, eyes glowing almost white, as if blank. Eyes that Dante had seen only once in his life but could never forget.

The man was telling him to come down. He was telling him he was a stupid Beast and that he was going to punish him.

6

In Colomba's hospital room, the man in the lab coat took another step toward the bed, cursing himself for what he was about to do. Not that his conscience was giving him problems of any kind; it was just that he'd thought he'd left the days of blood and risk behind him. But no one could say no to the German, especially when he eyed you as if he were taking your measurements, the better to cut your throat. He'd made a terrible mistake by not slamming the phone down the instant he'd heard that unmistakable voice out of his distant past.

But who would ever have imagined that the German was still tangled up in the same old business? Truth be told, the man had just assumed he must have died years ago. Instead, there he'd been, and even if his hair was white now and his neck was wrinkly, he was still the same old dangerous son of a bitch. The worst one of all.

The German . . . The man in the lab coat turned the word over in his mind, stalling for time with himself. He'd never actually known his real name. *No names. No notes. No chitchat.* Those were the rules that the German had set back in the golden years, though they had never applied to him. He'd always known everything about everyone.

He wiped the sweat off his forehead with one sleeve and once again considered giving it all up and leaving. But even if he managed to get away and ditch all pursuit for a while, he still knew what would catch up with him eventually: hunger. No more monthly check, no more easy living. And the idea of looking for work again after all the years he'd spent doing nothing but scratching his ass really didn't tickle his fancy. Not at all. Better to obey the German's orders, get this job done, and forget about it, and then it was back to the easy life.

The man in the lab coat took another step toward Colomba. He could see her clearly now that his eyes were accustomed to the darkness: she was breathing gently, with the sputtering hiss of someone whose nose is stopped up. *I wonder what she did to piss off the German*, he wondered. He hadn't asked. He hadn't even asked why she had to die.

He pulled the syringe out of his pocket, after rummaging around a little on account of the latex gloves that interfered with his sense of touch. The syringe was just two inches long and terminated in a stout needle, the kind veterinarians use, tougher and less likely to snap off. The German had told him to insert the needle into the IV plug so that he'd leave no marks on the body. An easy job, and one he could have done on his own. It was just that she knew the German's face and would be alarmed if she saw him in her hospital room. Peace and quiet were an essential requirement for that job, as was anonymity.

He'd entered the hospital under the pretext of visiting a relative, and he'd hidden in the toilet of the café on the ground floor, where he'd waited for night to fall. He knew they wouldn't clean the toilets until the next morning, just as he knew that there were only two night nurses in the ward where his target was located, while the physician on duty was normally down in the emergency room. He'd waited till well past midnight; then he'd donned the lab coat and climbed the stairs, sticking to his preestablished route and ducking out of sight if anyone went past. It had been easy, and it would be easier still to get out. And then if anyone did spot him . . . well, his instructions didn't include getting caught.

The man in the lab coat studied Colomba's face again, making sure she was still asleep; then he reached his arm out over her to grab the flexible IV cannula hanging on the far side of the bed.

It was just at that moment that he heard the crash of breaking glass behind him. He whirled around, his heart in his mouth, and saw that someone had shattered the window by throwing a shoe through it, a shoe that was now slowly tumbling across the floor.

"What . . . what's happening?" Colomba murmured, almost completely voiceless.

Shit, now she's awake, thought the man in the lab coat. "I just need to change your medication," he said with a smile, doing his best to seem professional. "Why don't you go back to sleep."

Colomba wrinkled her nose. The man reeked of alcohol and looked nothing like any of the male nurses who had told her good night. Then she spotted the broken window and propped herself up on her elbow in confusion. "Wait a minute . . ."

"Please stay still." The man in the lab coat placed a hand on her shoulder to push her down, while he reached out the other hand toward the IV again.

Colomba, wide awake by now, felt in every fiber of her being that something was very wrong. She pushed him away. "Don't touch me."

The man's only response was to grab her by the throat with his free hand, and he did it so suddenly and violently that Colomba felt her lungs shut down all at once. The shadows in the room immediately rose up and began to flail and her ears filled with shrieks and yells. The man shoved her down onto the bed, pinning her with one knee while he continued to choke her with his right hand and reached out for the cannula with his left. On the verge of passing out, Colomba aimed at her attacker's face with the stiffened fingers of her right hand. She was lucky: she hit an eye and felt the nail of her index finger drive into the eyelid. The man grunted and grabbed at his face with his right hand, momentarily freeing Colomba's neck. She immediately tried to yell, but not even the faintest thread of a voice came out.

Now the man punched her in the face, and she rolled over onto her side and then slid to the floor, dragging the IV with her in her fall. She hit her head hard, and the sharp stab of welcome pain chased the shadows back. She took a large gulp of air and again tried to shout, but her throat clamped closed like a trap snapping shut. Her attacker, his left eye streaming blood, kicked her in the ribs, slamming her against the wall, then tried to stab her in the neck with the syringe. By this point he didn't care about doing things according to instructions. He just wanted to finish her off.

With her last remaining strength, Colomba lifted her leg and smashed her instep into the man's testicles. The man dropped to the other empty bed in the hospital room, panting and moaning, and she scampered on all fours toward the door, incapable of getting to her feet. She reached her hand up to the door handle and turned it, but the door remained in place. Only then did she realize that her attacker had jammed the door shut with a wooden wedge. The man grabbed her from behind and spun her against the wall. For a second Colomba saw nothing but darkness spangled with silver stars. The pain in her head was overwhelming.

The man in the lab coat, half-blinded by blood, once again tried to jab her with the needle. Colomba desperately blocked the blow with both hands, just inches from her chest. Crouching over her, the man sweated and puffed like a bellows, his face red with effort, mouth wide open as he exhaled the foul stench of his breath. "You goddamned slut," he muttered. "I'll fix you, bitch."

Colomba suddenly modified her grip, yanking the arm downward. The syringe followed an arching trajectory and planted itself in the flesh just below the attacker's kneecap. She jammed the plunger down with a flat-handed slap. The man opened his mouth to shout, but no sound emerged. The veins on his neck and face bulged and turned scarlet; then he tumbled over onto his side, his unbloodied eye suddenly glassy, foaming at the mouth. Whatever that was in the syringe, it took effect immediately. Colomba heard him gurgle and watched him writhe for a few seconds like a worm on a griddle, until he stopped moving. She put her fingers on his neck, feeling for a pulse, but there was nothing. He was dead.

Just then, someone knocked at the door.

7

From the hallway a nurse was shouting Colomba's name and trying to open the door. She didn't answer, just lay there staring at the corpse, trying to catch her breath.

I killed him, she thought. The scathing sensation of having put an end to another life overwhelmed her for an instant, and a tremor shook her from within, threatening to shatter her. Whoever that man might have been, she'd just taken everything away from him. Future and past, dreams and fears. With a single act, she'd transformed him from living being to thing. In a flash, she again saw the dead of the Disaster, then the armed robber she'd shot her first year in Palermo, remembering how she'd watched him die there on the sidewalk, and then her first corpse, a junkie she'd found in an apartment where he'd been lying dead for a week, sprawled on a filthy mattress, his face covered with flies. She felt the burden of all those deaths, like a layer of cement, and she felt herself suffocating again. She dug her nails into her palms. *Not this time*, she told herself. *Not for this son of a bitch who wanted to kill you.*

The pounding at the door continued. The female nurse's voice was joined by the voice of a man.

"I think the policewoman must have fallen out of bed," the nurse said.

"It's not the door handle," the man replied. "There's something blocking the door itself."

Colomba got to her feet as quietly as she could. What should she do now? The logical thing would have been to open the door and have them call her colleagues, but she knew that no one would believe her when she told them that the man had been sent by the Father to kill her. And in the meantime precious minutes and even hours would be lost. While the Father erased any traces he might have left, if indeed he had left any.

"Let me go get something I can use to pry it open," said the man outside.

Colomba ran a hand over her face. If she decided to act on her own, the risks she would be running were enormous. She could be investigated for murder, first of all, because the innocent victim of an unprovoked attack doesn't just flee the scene, leaving a corpse on the floor. Or if she does, she opens herself up to suspicion. She shook her head, irritated with herself. This wasn't the time to worry about the consequences. She owed something to Rovere and to the children that the Father had carried off.

She looked around for a way out. She saw the broken glass and remembered the shoe that had flown in through the window, waking her up just in the nick of time. A shoe that she now recognized, because when it came to people who wore Doc Martens Clippers with two-inch soles, only one name came to mind.

She leaned out the broken window. She'd expected to see Dante down on the grass below and was stunned to find him clutching the branch right in front of her. The light from the lamp cast a glow on his haunted face and staring eyes. "Dante!" she called, forcing her hoarse voice into action.

Dante crouched motionless, his gaze fixed. He was clutching the branch with his arms and legs and seemed completely oblivious to where he was.

Meanwhile, the male voice outside the door had returned. "Let me try with this," he said, and there was immediately the sound of something metal being pressed against the door frame. "Did the lady inside answer you?"

"No. She wasn't in serious condition. I just hope she didn't hit her head."

"I'll work as fast as I can."

"Oh, shit," Colomba murmured. She grabbed her dead assailant by the collar and dragged him into the bathroom. He was shorter than her and scrawny, but still the effort almost made her pass out. She shut the door and ran over to the bed to stand the IV back up again, sticking the tube back onto her arm with the bandage on it. Then she pulled the curtain shut over the broken window and kicked the Clipper under the bed, where it couldn't be seen. The floor was still covered with broken glass, but there wasn't much she could do about that. She just moved the side table to the middle of the room and placed the chair in front of the door; then she yanked the wooden wedge out from under the door.

The door swung wide open with a metallic tremor. The nurse and the maintenance man found Colomba sitting in front of the door, blocking their way in.

"Did you jam this door shut?" asked the man in surprise, a large screwdriver in one hand.

"No," Colomba murmured. "It was stuck. I tried to tell you that, but my voice is shot."

"Are you all right?" asked the nurse.

"Yes."

The maintenance man gathered his tools and walked off, clearly baffled.

The nurse stood there, studying Colomba. She wasn't sure what she ought to do now. If this had been any ordinary patient, she'd have just made her go back to bed, but the lady cop was a specimen unlike any other. Everyone in the hospital knew who she was, and unsettling rumors were circulating about her. First and foremost, that she was out of her mind. And that even her fellow cops had suspicions about her. All you had to do was look at their faces when they came to her room or left it. The nurse wondered why they hadn't put a guard on the door, the way they do in the movies. "You need to get back in bed," she said, doing her best to sound authoritative. "Let me help you."

"I'd rather remain seated," Colomba whispered, staring at her.

In those eyes the nurse glimpsed a dark menace, even though what Colomba was actually telegraphing was a mute plea: *Please, go away.*

"Are you sure you're all right?"

"Considering the shape I'm in, yes," said Colomba. "Please, just leave me alone."

The nurse took a step back. She'd never been attacked by a patient, but some of her coworkers had, and one of them had even caught hepatitis after being bitten by a wino with the DTs: none of that for her, thanks. "I'll send the doctor up to take a look at you," she said.

"There's no need," Colomba replied.

"We'll see about that," muttered the nurse, turning away and feeling a shiver go down her back as she did so.

Colomba waited for a few seconds, then leapt to her feet and came dangerously close to tipping over. She felt as if she had a pumpkin in place of her head. She shut the door again, reinserted the wooden wedge, and went back to the bathroom. Her attacker's body was where she'd left it. A large puddle of urine had spread across the floor beneath him. *Now this*, thought Colomba as she leaned over to go through his pockets. She found a wallet, a bunch of keys, the remote control for an Opel automobile, and a magnetic ID card. No cell phone. She turned the ID over in her hands. She knew that in many hospitals, the staff used badges like this one to get into certain wards, but they were supposed to have the name and a picture of the bearer. This one didn't.

It was a fake ID card, cloned to allow her assailant to enter her room and kill her. There was some money in the wallet, along with a credit card and a driver's license. The license looked authentic and had been issued to Luciano Ferrari, born in 1958, residing at Via Pompeo Magno no. 1 in Rome. Colomba put the license back into the wallet, then slipped the wallet back into the man's pocket. She hid the card, the keys, and the remote in her pajama sleeve. She went over to the small metal locker in the corner of the room. Her clothes weren't there anymore. She cursed herself as she remembered giving them to the friends who had come to see her.

She grabbed her cell phone and put on her boots. When she leaned over to lace them, she felt the blood surge to her head and the lights went out. She was on the verge of fainting. Once again she dug her nails into the palms of her hands and retained consciousness. She took a look out the window—Dante was still out there, gripping the branch—kicked the wedge out from under the door, and gently opened it just a crack: the corridor was deserted. She remembered the shoe and went back to get it, then left the room and headed for the stairs, making it there without being seen. Walking down the stairs was a challenge and made her headache worse, until she began to feel nauseous. On the ground floor she found herself looking down the hallway that led to the front desk, her way blocked by two automatic glass doors that had been deactivated and, in the other direction, an emergency exit. She was about to go out that way when it dawned on her that doing so would sound the alarm throughout the hospital.

She walked down another flight of stairs and came to a metal door on which was written ENTRY FORBIDDEN—MEDICAL PERSONNEL only. It was locked, but on the wall next to the door she saw a magnetic card reader. She tried the badge. The door clicked open, and she walked into a utility hallway lit only by dim orange bulbs. Several colorful plastic arrows pointed in different directions: locker rooms, storerooms, laundry. She followed the hallway, hoping to find a door to the outside. She did find the door to the covered parking structure, and from there a door out to the hospital grounds; the floor around it was littered with cigarette butts.

Shivering from the cold in her flannel pajamas, she followed the outside perimeter of the building, trying to find the location of her room. It seemed to take forever, but at last she recognized her window, with a section of curtain fluttering out through the broken glass. She looked up at Dante, who was still gripping the branch. In vain she tried to catch his attention, and finally, seeing that she couldn't do it, she threw the shoe instead, aiming for his arm.

Instead she hit him in the temple, and Dante came close to falling headfirst, startled and in pain. The shoe weighed nearly a pound, and the impact hadn't been a love tap. Still, it helped to bring him out of his trance. "CC?" he murmured, as if waking from a dream.

"Come down, get moving," she whispered.

For a few seconds Dante didn't budge; then he slid to the ground with a blank expression. "You're alive," he said.

Colomba retrieved his shoe and handed it to him. "Yes, partly thanks to you. But let's talk about that later. Give me your jacket."

Dante took off his parka, doing so as if he were sleepwalking, and stood there in just a black mock turtleneck sweater. She put it on. It was a little narrow in the shoulders, but it hung down below her knees. If it weren't for the pajama pants dotted with piglets, she would have been quite presentable.

"I saw him, CC," said Dante in a dreamy voice.

"The man in my hospital room?"

"No. The Father."

"You always see him at the least convenient times," she said. "Come on, let's go."

Dante grabbed her by the arm, stopping her. "You don't understand, CC. The Father was here. He spoke to me."

"So what did he look like?"

Dante blinked rapidly. "I can't exactly remember."

"Okay, you can tell me all about it later. Right now, we need to get out of here."

To leave the grounds, they went out through the emergency room. They went in through the rear entrance, making use of the magnetic ID card, walking past busy doctors and paramedics who barely noticed them, blended in with twenty or so people waiting to be seen, and then left through the front door. They moved quickly, though, because as Colomba dragged Dante away from the grounds, she noticed the light in what had been her room being turned on, and before ten minutes were up, she felt sure that the place would be full of cops on the alert. As they were leaving, Dante told her about his vision of the Father.

"Is that why you threw a shoe?"

"I couldn't move," he said. "Or shout."

"Are you certain that the Father was really there?" Colomba asked, dragging him into the first cross street, far from the surveillance cameras on the main thoroughfare.

"Yes."

"Because if it had been a hallucination, you would have known it, right?" she asked again, skeptically.

"I always know when I'm going around the bend." Dante was starting to think clearly again, and his gait was more fluid. The immediate past was a mix of gaps and disjointed images.

"And he would have left before us?"

"He might still be inside." Dante stopped. "We have to look for him, CC."

"They'd stop us at the front entrance."

"Why? What happened to the guy in your room?" he asked suspiciously.

"Wait." Colomba pulled him into a patch of darkness because she'd spotted the lights of an approaching patrol car. The car went past without spotting them.

"Did you kill him?" Dante insisted.

Colomba sighed and said nothing.

"Oh, fuck. I was hoping for a less definitive solution. But it was legitimate self-defense. I'll testify on your behalf."

"I can just imagine how much weight that will carry . . . We need to find a car. We can't cross the city on foot."

"Let's use his car. You took his keys, didn't you? Let me see them."

"How do you know I took them?"

"If we're running away in such a hurry, it's because you want to investigate him. Otherwise you'd be back there answering questions."

"You can be annoying sometimes." She threw the key at him.

"It's an Opel Agila, judging from the remote," said Dante. He looked around. "He didn't park by the entrance, but he can't have left it that far away. He might have needed to get away in a hurry, too, and he knew it." On the map on his smartphone, he studied the main road, which curved around the emergency room entrance, and then the various streets leading off from it. He dismissed the ones that were too close, the one next to the traffic light, and the one-way streets. That left two. He pointed to them. "Let's split up, and the first one who finds it can let out a whistle."

"Like hell I'm letting you out of my sight. We'll go together."

It took them just five minutes to find the dark red Opel Agila; meanwhile, the sound of a police siren drew closer. Colomba got behind the wheel, and Dante lay down on the backseat.

"Doesn't it worry you to drive around in a stolen car? Because it probably is."

"If he was using it, it's probably pretty safe." Colomba started the car and pulled out. Via Pompeo Magno was in the Prati district: it would take them twenty minutes or so if they didn't run into trouble. But she wanted to be sure she wasn't going to the wrong apartment. She called Alberti, who was surprised to hear from her. Maybe surprised was an understatement, seeing the time of night. Luckily he'd set his phone to vibrate, because he had a pair of headphones on and was composing music.

"Deputy Captain . . . did you listen to the pieces?" he asked immediately.

Colomba didn't have the heart to tell him that she'd left his two-bit MP3 player behind in the room with the corpse. "Not yet. Listen, sorry, I need a favor. I need you to check out a name for me."

"I'm not on duty, Deputy Captain."

"You must have a friend who's on duty, though, don't you? Call him and ask."

"All right. Go ahead."

"Luciano Ferrari, as far as I know born in 1958 in Rome. See if he has any priors, and get his current address and call me back. And if they ask why you're interested in him, just say the two of you had a fender bender."

"Deputy Captain, actually I shouldn't . . ."

But Colomba had already ended the call because she had an incoming call from Infanti. Dante shut his eyes so he didn't have to watch her drive with one hand, and he would have jumped out the window if he'd had any idea of her actual condition. Her headache and nausea were now compounded by luminous sparks that burst into her field of vision like streamers, and she was having difficulty focusing on the road ahead of her.

Infanti's voice exploded in her ear. "Where the fuck are you?" he shouted.

"They've already told you?" asked Colomba.

"Of course they've already told me. Half the office is at the hospital, and you've disappeared!"

"I couldn't stay."

"You couldn't stay? What the fuck are you talking about? Who's the guy in the toilet?"

"I don't know," she lied. "But he wanted to kill me."

"And then what happened?"

"There was an accident."

"There was a murder, there wasn't an accident! You have to come back."

"The hospital isn't safe. I'll come straight to police headquarters."

"Right away, Colomba, or there'll be trouble."

"Practically right away."

"Colomba!"

She hung up and powered down her phone.

"You should pull the battery out of your cell phone," Dante muttered. "To keep them from tracking you."

"They're not going to start hunting me right away. We have a few hours."

"And then?"

Colomba blew through a red light. "Then I'll turn myself in."

"And what will you tell them?"

"That I ran away because I panicked."

"They're not going to believe you."

"But they won't have any grounds to detain me."

"But what if they do? You can't trust De Angelis."

"Then you'll just have to go on digging. Until you can find something bombproof that connects your case and the Maugeri case. Until you do, I'll keep my lips zipped, even if they give me life without parole."

"I can't do it all by myself, CC," Dante whined. "You can't put that responsibility on me."

"You walked into a burning building to save me. You'll do better than you think. Thanks for that, by the way. And thanks for the shoe."

Dante sat up straight and spoke into her ear. "CC, the Father knows we're getting closer. Otherwise he wouldn't have exposed himself to get rid of you. It's not like him to operate out in the open like this."

Colomba saw Ferrari's face again for an instant, twisting with fury just inches from hers. She felt her lungs tighten. "So?"

"So we don't have much time before he disappears, eliminating any traces that he's ever existed. And by traces, I mean Luca and the other children. If I have to work alone, it might take too long."

"What alternatives do we have?"

"Don't turn yourself in. Go on working with me on this thing."

"They'd come looking for me, and it wouldn't last long." Colomba parked next to a florist's stand, closed now, at the foot of a rose-colored building.

Dante saw the street number 1. They'd arrived. "It could last long enough. There are places where I can hide you. And I know people who can provide you with fake IDs . . ."

Colomba took a deep breath. "Dante, I can't. I've done a lot of stupid things since you and I started working together, but I'm still a cop. I can't and I won't go past a certain point." She opened the car door. "Come on, let's go."

Dante looked up at the facade of the apartment building and shook his head. "Sorry. I'm afraid I can't."

"Now of all times?"

"I have my moments, CC. You know that. But I can help you from here."

"How?"

He pulled out his smartphone. "Video call. Via Skype."

Colomba understood that there was no point in insisting and got gingerly out of the car. "Don't stay in the car. If there's a bulletin out on this car, they'd better not find you sitting in it. But before you get out, wipe it for fingerprints."

Dante nodded. "Okay."

Colomba started walking toward the building. But she stopped short almost immediately. There was a question she hadn't dared to ask until that moment, a question she couldn't put off any longer. "Did he suffer?"

Dante understood that Colomba was talking about Rovere. "Like a dog. At least from the waist up, because from there down . . ."

Colomba raised a hand, regretting she'd asked. Dante was incapable of sugarcoating things. She replied, "That's enough, thanks. And turn on that fucking phone." Then she opened the downstairs door with the dead man's keys.

8

Ferrari's apartment house was an elegant, aristocratic building with an old-fashioned concierge's booth with a bow window, mailboxes made of dark hardwood, a variegated marble floor, and a vague scent of lemon air freshener. A setting where you'd expect a tax adviser's office, not the home of a murderer. Because Colomba had not the slightest doubt that Ferrari *was* a murderer, prior convictions or no prior convictions. He'd been too determined to be a first-time killer, too precise in his movements, at least until she'd fought back. What's more, if the Father had sent him, he certainly wouldn't have chosen the first person he met in the street. But what connection did they have? Why would Ferrari work with a deranged serial kidnapper? She thought back to Rovere's words, to the fact that the Father wasn't working alone. Here was proof of the fact.

She powered her cell phone back up, and it immediately vibrated with a series of missed calls and texts. Half the police force was looking for her, and that, more than anything else, gave her an appreciation of the situation. She was now being hunted by her own colleagues, something she never would have thought could have happened to her, not even in her darkest hours. But here she was, breaking and entering after committing a murder, albeit one she'd committed involuntarily (But had it *really* been unintentional? Hadn't she *intentionally* jammed down that plunger on the syringe?), turning her back on her old life in a way far more radical and violent than if she had simply handed in her resignation.

One text from Alberti contained details about Ferrari from his public records, including the fact that he was unmarried. Then she saw Dante's face on the screen, bathed in a sinister faint blue light. "Are you in?" he asked.

"Not yet," Colomba whispered. "I'm still looking for the door." None of the doors was marked with anything but a number, so she had to examine all the keyholes to find the one that matched her key, by the light of her cell phone. She cursed the mania for anonymity and privacy as she climbed one flight of stairs after the other, feeling weaker with each one. Her legs were wobbly, and more than once she was forced to lean against the wall.

"Ask the doorman," Dante suggested.

"Congratulations, that was a funny joke."

She finally found the right door on the fourth floor. On the door-bell only the number 9 appeared, but the key matched the lock. "This is it," she said and turned the phone around to show it to him.

Dante stared into the lens. "What are you going to do if there's someone home?"

"According to his ID he's a bachelor."

"Maybe his girlfriend is waiting for him in his bed."

"A guy like him doesn't have a girlfriend. If it turns out I'm wrong, though, I'll just tell her that Ferrari gave me the keys so I could bring him a change of clothes." She stuck the key into the lock. "I'm more worried about a burglar alarm."

"Don't worry. You don't put in a burglar alarm if you have some-thing to hide," Dante pointed out. "You'd run the risk of finding the cops in your home if it went off when you were out."

"Right," said Colomba and turned the key. She slipped in quickly and shut the heavy door behind her.

The dark apartment reeked of cigars and a sickly sweet smell that was familiar but that she just couldn't place. Something organic, that smacked of an animal . . . The answer came to her in a flash.

Dog!

At that very moment she heard the skittering of claws against mar-ble come out of the darkness in front of her, along with a deep, gut-tural growl. She was able to dodge just in time for a dark mass to go hurtling past and thud into the heavy burglar-proof door, scratching furiously as it went. Colomba reached around for the light switch, found it and switched it on, and found herself face-to-face with the taut muscled body of a Doberman that stared at her, snarling.

"What's going on, CC?" Dante shouted into her ear.

Colomba didn't answer; she was too busy sizing up the distances.

At the superior police academy at Ostia she and the other officers in leadership training had worked with an instructor from the K9 unit. The man had shown them a video of a German shepherd savaging a mannequin, and he'd followed that with some basic tips—never look the animal in the eyes, don't turn and run, don't show fear—and then he'd explained how to attack the dog in case it became necessary. But none of the simulations called for her to be in a hallway, unarmed, with the added problem of having to remain absolutely silent.

The dog laid its ears flat and barked twice; then it lunged at Colomba, aiming directly at her throat. She instinctively raised her left arm, and the Doberman locked onto it: she felt the teeth pierce the fabric and sink into her flesh. Instead of trying to break her arm free, she shoved it in deeper, bracing the dog's jaws open and preventing it from clamping down with all of its strength. She fell to her knees and found herself eye to eye with the beast for an instant: eyes that stared at her viciously. Eyes that seemed to be saying to her *I know what you did*, transforming the dog into the incarnation of revenge. Colomba was terrified, but still she went on pushing, and the teeth sank deeper. A clamp was ravaging her arm and her blood was dripping to the floor, mixed with drool. To keep the dog from breaking free and biting another vulnerable part of her body, she wrapped her other arm around its head and pulled him close to her. The dog tried to get away, but its paws scratched on the marble, unable to get purchase. She pressed harder. It was like trying to maneuver a rubber tube under high pressure, a coiled steel spring, but she could sense the dog losing impetus, being partially suffocated by the flesh it was trying to gulp down.

With an effort that seemed to make her head explode, Colomba turned the dog on its side and started pounding its ribs with her elbow, where she guessed its heart must be. The dog tried to twist free, but she grabbed it tighter and continued pounding. With her fifth, desperate blow, something broke, though Colomba couldn't say whether it was her elbow or one of the animal's ribs. The Doberman's eyes had grown larger, and its fury had given way to fear and suffering. Colomba went on pounding it with her elbow until she felt it sinking in, no longer encountering resistance. "Die, die!" she moaned. "Please, just die!"

The dog regurgitated and defecated, and Colomba held it tight until its paws stopped trembling; then she fell back on her ass, cradling her wounded arm. The animal's eyes were glassy, and a pool of blood was spreading under its body where the shattered ribs had perforated its internal organs.

Colomba slipped twice in the morass of blood and shit before she could get to her feet. Her arm was bleeding and throbbing, in time with the ache in her head, and her ribs burned where Ferrari had kicked her. She went into the bathroom and used a towel to stop the bleeding. In spite of Dante's jacket, the teeth had sunk all the way to the bone, and Colomba wept from the pain when she poured hydrogen peroxide onto the wound. Half-blinded by tears, she cleaned the wound as best she could, then wrapped a clean towel around her arm to stop the hemorrhaging. She was leaving blood and prints everywhere, she thought sadly. *What a mess. What kind of mess am I making?*

When they questioned her, she'd have a hard time justifying any of what she was doing, but right now it didn't seem to matter. That was a development that still lay too far in the future; right now, just making it through, from one hour to the next, struck her as a titanic undertaking. She staggered back into the hallway and picked up her phone from the edge of a puddle of blood, though whether it was her blood or the dog's she couldn't say. She looked down at the carcass, afraid it might leap to its feet snarling again and plunge its fangs back into her. This time she'd be incapable of defending herself; this time she'd just be eaten alive.

On the screen, above the worried face of Dante silently moving his lips, was a list of texts and missed calls. Another dozen. She deleted them, too, and put in her earbud. "I was just about to come upstairs," said Dante in relief.

"There *was* a burglar alarm," Colomba informed him in a faint voice. "One with four legs and a tail."

"I saw. Poor creature."

"Poor creature, my ass, if you don't mind. Instead of going all PETA on me, help me out, because I'm having a hard time thinking straight."

"Turn on all the lights, and let me take a look."

Colomba did as he told her, moving through the apartment with her cell phone held out in front of her the way an exorcist holds a cross. Ferrari's apartment measured some 2,200 square feet, with marble and parquet floors; the furniture was classic, all mahogany and glass. Three bedrooms, though only one seemed to be in use, a large living room with a silver-framed giant-screen television set, leather sofas, and a small workout room that had been turned into a storeroom.

Colomba rummaged through the closets and dresser drawers, her head and arm throbbing with pain that got worse by the minute. Her vision blurred a number of times, and each time it did she had to stop and splash her face with cold water. The face that gazed back at her from the mirror looked like a ghost's.

She found nothing compromising, nothing that could be even distantly connected to children or violence, with the exception of the military photographs hanging just about everywhere and a collection of old muskets and sabers from the times of Garibaldi and the First World War, on prominent display in the living room.

"What do you think?" asked Colomba.

"That this apartment was already furnished when he bought or rented it. The old furniture clashes sharply with his taste in clothing and the rest of the furniture. The red refrigerator, the television set straight out of *Star Trek* . . . Plenty of money but not so much taste. And then . . . let me see the bookshelf . . ."

Colomba took him over to the one piece of furniture that contained printed paper of any kind, a console table right outside the kitchen. They were all history books, many of them about fascism.

"Now the bed, if you don't mind."

Accustomed by now to Dante's brusque manners, Colomba obeyed promptly. The king-sized bed was beautifully made and tucked in.

"Did you notice? Bed made. How many men do you know who'd make a bed so neatly?" asked Dante.

"Not even many women, actually, but maybe the maid came."

"No. His breakfast coffee mug is still in the sink. He made his own bed. And you know which men instinctively make the bed every morning, perfectly?"

"Obsessive-compulsives like you," Colomba retorted.

"And anyone who's spent years in an institution where you're punished if you leave things a mess."

"Like a prison?"

"No, either boarding school or the army. Did you see the photo at the entrance, where Ferrari is making a parachute jump?" Dante asked.

"Yes. A civilian flight."

"But that suggests retired military to me."

"It's a possibility," Colomba replied.

Rummaging around, Colomba found Ferrari's cell phone, which she pocketed, a handful of bills, and an official-looking letter, still unopened, from the Blackmountain Fund of Italy. In it was an account statement; she showed it to Dante. "Does this mean anything to you?"

"A little. Your friend owned an annuity fund with Blackmountain that made monthly payouts," Dante explained.

"Which means . . ."

". . . that every month he received something like six thousand euros, after taxes. That means a substantial chunk of cash invested in stock. My father set up something of the sort for me, but I burned through the principal almost immediately."

"So Ferrari lived on a fixed income, some kind of trust?" Colomba asked.

"Apparently. Have you found any other pictures of him besides the one by the front door?"

"A couple in the kitchen. Of him with the dog."

"Nothing old? Nothing that might refer to his past?" Dante queried.

Colomba sat down on the king-sized bed, ruining its impeccable crease. Its yielding softness lured her like a siren's song, and for a few seconds she sat there, fast asleep with her eyes wide open.

Dante's voice brought her back. "Colomba, are you still there?"

"Yes, sorry . . . what were you saying?"

"That if he really was nostalgic for his time in the army, he ought to have something to remind him of it."

"Maybe he wasn't in the army; maybe he's just an obsessive who never served a day. Like those survivalist maniacs."

"Survivalists stay fit. His home gym looks neglected," Dante pointed out.

"Or else he kept his most cherished memorabilia somewhere else."

"Can you go through the drawers again?"

"Dante, in a little while they'll be here looking for me. I took his cell phone, and that might prove useful, but I don't want them to find me here."

"Please, just try once more."

Colomba got up with some effort as a voice inside her screamed for her to stop and let herself fall onto that irresistibly inviting bed. A voice that didn't care that it was a dead man's bed. She started the routine all over again, checking the bottoms of the drawers and underneath the armoires, turning all the picture frames and examining the backs. "Nothing. And now I really need to go. I'm just about out of time, and that's not all I'm running out of."

"Okay," said Dante in disappointment.

Colomba went back into the bedroom to get bills and receipts, but as she was leaving Dante cried out.

"Go back . . . what a fool I am . . ."

"What did you see?" asked Colomba, who was losing her voice again.

"The photograph on the wall, the one in the silver frame . . ."

"So?"

"It's an old picture that seems to have been cut out of a military magazine, not a high-quality print like the others. But he hung it across from the bed, where he could always see it."

"The picture could have a special meaning for him . . ."

"Maybe it does, but check it anyway."

"I already did," Colomba objected.

"This is the last thing I'm going to ask you."

Colomba went back and grabbed the frame. She'd turned it around once already and found it sealed shut in the back. Looking at it against the light, she'd seen that it contained only a photograph of a tank from the Second World War. Despite her state of extreme exhaustion, Colomba had to agree with Dante: that magazine clipping, raggedly cut, moreover, was out of place with everything else. The voice inside her that wanted to go to sleep went on berating her, but Colomba told it: *Soon*, and then removed the picture frame from the wall and once again held it up against the light. "There's nothing else," she confirmed, but even as she said it, she realized she was wrong: the center of the picture was opaque because there was something blocking the passage of light. She discovered that a thin piece of cardboard had been glued to the back of the page from the magazine; between the piece of thin cardboard and the photo there was a thin square about four inches on a side. *You're slipping, sweetheart*, whispered the voice that wanted her to get some sleep. *I told you you needed some rest.*

Colomba wrapped the frame in a corner of the bedcover and smashed it against the edge of the nightstand. The glass shattered; she extracted the print and scratched the cardboard backing away: an old Polaroid slid onto the bedside rug.

Colomba picked it up. It depicted five men in camouflage military uniforms, three of them sitting on the deck of a flatbed truck and two standing. One of the seated men was unquestionably Ferrari, thirty years younger, and next to him was a guy who looked remarkably like the identikit of the Father that Dante had helped produce. All of them had combat boots laced together and hanging around their necks, as if that were some inside joke for them, and they were flashing victory signs.

"You were right, Dante," Colomba whispered. "You won't believe what I'm about to . . ."

She suddenly broke off, breathless. She'd just recognized one of the standing men. She'd recognized his smile, though much younger, and his glance. A sinkhole gaped open in her mind.

"What did you find?" asked Dante, who stood leaning against the florist's stand and scrutinizing the screen of his iPhone, trying to decipher the shadows. Colomba said nothing, and Dante realized that she was walking with the phone pointing at her feet. He saw strips of the floor, an alternating pattern of light and dark as she walked down the stairs muttering prayers and curses. He saw her emerge from the front door of the building, uncertain of her footing, looking as if she'd seen a ghost, and he ran toward her, shuddering at the sight of her ravaged arm dripping with blood. She was panting, avoiding his eyes.

"CC . . . what is it? What did you see?" he asked, in a worried voice.

Colomba, without speaking, handed him the picture and sat down at the edge of the sidewalk, as if she had no idea where she was. Dante took the picture from her and saw the face of the man he called the Father. For a few seconds he was incapable of tearing his eyes away from the eyes of the man in the picture, eyes that seemed to see him, penetrating the acetate coating. Camouflage uniform aside, he was identical to the man he'd seen that night in 1989, walking toward him with a knife in his hand. For a moment Dante went back in time, and once again he was a boy who'd grown up in an environment ill suited to human life. Then Colomba's hand weakly seized his and brought him to.

"Not him," she murmured. "Not him." And she shut her eyes.

Dante reviewed the other faces. He recognized Ferrari from having watched him through the window of the hospital room. In this picture the man was practically a kid, but still identifiable. All the others, though, were unknown faces . . . or were they?

He realized that the man standing next to Ferrari looked somehow familiar, and maybe it was him that Colomba was referring to. He imagined that face older, with a receding hairline, fatter, and when he put a graying beard on the chin, he felt a shiver, and a number of missing puzzle pieces suddenly slotted into place. The man smiling lazily into the camera lens was Emilio Bellomo, the murderer whose picture had been all over the newspapers after he'd blown up the restaurant in Paris.

9

A little girl, three or four years old, dressed in nothing but a pair of panties, was staring at her while sucking on an enormous spiral lollipop. "*¿Estás despierta?*" she asked.

"What did you say?" Colomba asked, bewildered.

The little girl said nothing and ran out of the room shouting "*¡Mamá! ¡La policía está despierta!*"

La policía? Colomba wondered, still unable to think straight. She was in an unfamiliar bed in an unfamiliar room that reeked of fried food; through the walls she could hear voices shouting in Spanish and Italian and the very loud audio of a shoot 'em up video game.

Colomba felt rested but weak. Her headache was gone, but the bite on her left arm still hurt, though not as much as before. The wound had been dressed with a clean gauze bandage held in place by adhesive tape; it itched a little, while her right elbow had a purplish bruise that extended all the way to her forearm. As she moved, she felt a stab of pain where Ferrari had kicked her, but nothing seemed to be broken. She vaguely remembered collapsing onto the sidewalk, and even more vaguely tossing and turning in a fevered sleep, waking up for short intervals in darkness and light, as someone gave her something to drink and helped her piss into a plastic jar. A dark-skinned woman, that much she knew, but the image was as blurry as a forgotten dream.

She tried to stand up, but as soon as she put her feet on the floor, she felt the bed spin under her; she remained seated, staring around her. The room was small and cluttered with large clothing boxes still covered with cellophane, poorly lit by a window with a broken blind, looking out onto a sunset sky. On the wall across from her were an enormous crucifix and a plastic bust of the Madonna, covered with artificial flowers. Dazed though she was, Colomba was quite certain she'd never seen the place before in her life.

Through the door the little girl had run out of came a woman Colomba judged to be about forty, with thick curly hair and a pair of enormous earrings that jangled at every step. She, too, was Hispanic, and she wore a T-shirt that left her belly button uncovered and a pair of skin-tight jeans. The woman sat down next to her and took her hand. "*¿A dónde vas?*" she asked. "You're not supposed to get up!"

From up close, Colomba realized that forty was about fifteen years too old: the heavy makeup and the creased, weary face had deceived her. She gently pulled her hand away. "Where am I?" she asked.

"You're in my home. My name is Ayelén."

"Did you take care of me?" Colomba pointed to the hospital gown dotted with tiny hearts that she was wearing. "Did you give me this?"

"Me and my mother. And my sisters. You slept a long time."

"How long?"

"Three days."

Colomba shut her eyes. "Fuck," she murmured under her breath. Her colleagues must already have written her off as a missing person. "Where are my things?"

Intimidated by Colomba's curt tone, Ayelén lost her smile and recoiled. "*No sé,*" she replied.

"Do you at least know where Dante is? He's the one who brought me here."

"*¿El gringo loco?*"

"That's the one."

"He's with my brother. *En el techo.*"

"Sorry, didn't get that last part."

"On the roof."

Colomba connected the Spanish word for roof—*techo*—with the Italian word—*tetto*—and understood. "Is your brother called Santiago, by any chance?" she asked grimly.

"Yes, ma'am."

Propelled by her fury, Colomba got to her feet, overriding all objections, and strode quickly out of the room. She found herself first in a hallway dominated by a large poster of Che Guevara, and then in a small living room where Jorge Pérez was playing with a PlayStation 4 hooked up to a television set that Colomba thought she must have seen somewhere before. A couple of kids in shorts and tank tops were watching, enthralled, and rooting eagerly.

Jorge smiled mockingly as she walked through the door: "Well here she is, *la puta*."

The children laughed and repeated the word: "*Puta, puta.*"

"I'll show you who *la puta* is around here," roared Colomba, grabbing Pérez by the throat with her good hand. "And quit fucking talking in Spanish, seeing that you were born in Rebibbia, right here in Rome."

"What the fuck do you want?"

"Santiago. And my boots."

Five minutes later Colomba emerged onto the roof, police boots on her feet and a blanket draped over her shoulders. Dante, who was sitting on the swaybacked sofa talking to Santiago, ran joyfully to meet her. "*Ciao*, CC! So good to see you!" he shouted. He was wearing his parka, which had a tear on the left sleeve that was impossible to miss and light spots on the fabric where Colomba's blood had been washed off.

She shoved him away. "*So good*, my ass. What am I doing here?"

Dante seemed embarrassed. "Let me explain."

"There's nothing to fucking explain. You should have just called an ambulance and had me picked up. Or called Carmine at police headquarters! Not hidden me in this pigsty!"

"They would have arrested you."

"It was legitimate self-defense!"

"Tell her, Dante!" Santiago shouted from the couch. "*Si no rompe las bolas todo el día.*"

"You think I'm busting your balls *now*?" Colomba shouted back, happy to find that her voice had returned. "Let me show what I can do with my boots, I'll bust your *bolas*, all right." Santiago flashed her his middle finger.

"CC . . . things have kind of gone south . . ." said Dante.

"Of course they've gone south! I left the scene of the crime and went missing! Find me a phone or get me a ride to police headquarters."

"I'm not talking about Ferrari," Dante broke in. "Or not only about him."

Colomba felt a shiver run down her back, and she pulled the blanket tighter. "Then what's this about?"

Dante sighed. "Sit down, CC."

"What the fuck do you have to tell me?"

"Please. Just sit down. Otherwise I won't tell you anything."

Colomba thought about grabbing him by the neck, as she had Jorge, but Dante's sincerely worried expression dissuaded her: something really wasn't right. She sat down on a Naugahyde armchair next to the computer workstation. "Well?"

"You're wanted for the murder of Rovere."

Colomba's heart skipped a beat. "What did you say?" she said in a whisper.

"When they searched your apartment, they found traces of C-4."

Another thud to the heart, this one stronger. Colomba had to gulp twice before she was able to speak. "Who told you that?"

"Roberto."

"Minutillo? Your lawyer?"

"That's right. When you passed out I didn't know what to do, and I called him. He told me the rumors he was hearing from the district attorney's office. Luckily, he has friends there."

Colomba couldn't seem to think clearly. "They can't actually believe such a thing . . ." she stammered, and it was the first time she'd stammered in her life.

"De Angelis can't wait to throw you in prison and throw away the key, with me in the cell next to you. To say nothing of the fact that it could easily have been him or Santini who planted the evidence."

Colomba let herself slump back in the armchair. "And this"—she waved her hand to take in the roof terrace—"this was the solution you came up with?"

"I couldn't think of anything better. While I was at it, I got rid of anything that could point to you. Ferrari's car wound up in a scrap metal compactor, and now it's no bigger than this." He held his hands out in front of him. "And Santiago's boys cleaned the apartment with plenty of bleach."

"Is that why Ferrari's television set's here now?"

Dante made an embarrassed face. "I knew you wouldn't miss that detail. But we could have spared ourselves the trouble. No one seems to know how it happened, but the apartment caught fire two hours later. Someone was even more worried than we were."

"The Father."

"That's right. Like I told you, he's sensing that time is tight. And I'm afraid of what he might do next."

Colomba's mind continued to slide. She was outside her environment, outside her world. She couldn't understand. "Why did Santiago agree to help you?" she asked.

"Because he hopes that I'll owe him a debt of gratitude, and for the money." Dante made a face. "I've run through my supplies. If we ever get out of this situation alive, I'll have to find a way to make some cash in a hurry."

"Are they accusing you, too?" Colomba asked.

Dante pulled a folded page from a newspaper out of his pocket with his bad hand. He wasn't wearing a glove, a sign that he felt more at his ease there than Colomba did. It was the front page of *La Repubblica*, and at the bottom right was an old photograph of Colomba and a more recent one of Dante. The headline read: "MYSTERY COUPLE STILL ON THE RUN—From the slaughter bombing of Paris to the suspicious death in the Rome hospital: what links the ex-policewoman to the boy in the silo?"

"They dragged out everything. Paris, the multiple deaths . . . your part in it. And my life, with loads of hearsay. What they have to say about me is that I'm crazy, and about you that you've probably gone crazy. And that you were holding a grudge against Rovere for having sidelined you after Paris."

"He didn't sideline me. It was me who—"

"I know. But they don't. So if you go and tell them what you do know, it will just seem like more craziness. Roberto says that the only reason I'm wanted, officially, is as a person with knowledge of events, but that if I do turn myself in, it's unlikely they'll let me go, so I'm staying clear of them and keeping you company." Dante pulled up a stool and sat down.

"I can just imagine my mother . . ." Colomba murmured.

"She went on a TV news show and appealed to you to turn yourself in. She seemed a little, how should I put this . . . a little melodramatic."

Colomba closed her eyes. This was worse than anything she could have imagined. She felt herself sink into the armchair and did her best not to move, for fear she'd plunge downward, floor by floor, to the center of the earth, into the midst of the damned souls. And the damned soul who was laughing loudest had Bellomo's face.

She opened her eyes wide. "The picture! Where is it?"

Dante pulled the photograph out of his parka and handed it to her.

Colomba waved it in the air. "Bellomo and Ferrari are connected! They'll have to investigate that."

"And what could they discover, if they discovered anything at all? Bellomo's life has already been investigated from top to bottom without finding anything linking him to the Father, and it's not going to go any differently with Ferrari. As far as your colleagues are concerned, the Father doesn't exist. And they'll probably say that the man in the picture isn't Bellomo, just someone who looks like him. If you didn't know what you do know, would you believe it?"

Colomba's lips took on a bitter curve. "Easier to think that you and I are the latter-day Bonnie and Clyde."

"Bonnie and Clyde didn't plant bombs, and their reputation has been blown out of proportion to what they actually did." Dante lit a cigarette using his bad hand, something just short of an act of prestidigitation. "In any case, at least we now know why Rovere got us into this. He started investigating the Father immediately after the bombing in Paris and the death of his wife. He wouldn't have done it if he hadn't known about a connection."

"His sense of duty would still have made him dig into it, if he'd had any actionable information."

"Alone? In secret?" Dante shook his head again. "His sense of duty alone isn't enough to justify his actions, but a sense of guilt would."

"That's a good theory, but you can never be certain," said Colomba.

"You're wrong there." Dante cracked his sarcastic grin, and Colomba realized just how much she'd missed it. "Because our man Santiago was able to break into Rovere's flash drive."

10

To the attention of the Illustrious and most Honorable Minister
of the Interior,
and to the Esteemed Chief of Police of Rome,
and to the Esteemed Prefect of Rome,

Let me begin by apologizing for the unorthodox nature of
this communiqué of mine, which I have composed in the past
few days after careful consideration and much personal torment, but I have come into the possession of information such
that it demands recourse to extraordinary measures to ensure
that public safety and the welfare of the citizenry be secured,
measures that only the highest authorities of our nation can
hope to implement. I am writing with the full awareness that
my actions over the past several months may merit, and indeed
may receive, disciplinary action, but I have been compelled by
the uncommon circumstances in which I found myself. Allow
me in this missive to be as clear and concise as possible, even
though the facts I am about to set forth present, through no
fault of my own, numerous gaps and murky details.

The affair to which I draw your attention was brought to
my attention at the end of last year during the investigation
that led to the capture of the fugitive and murderer EMILIO
BELLOMO, grimly known to our office, first, for the homicide
of his cohabiting girlfriend ROSSELLA CALABRO, and
subsequently for a series of criminal acts covered in the reports
attached. During the course of this investigation, my office came
into contact with a friend and confederate in wrongdoing of
Bellomo's, a certain FABRIZIO PINNA, with prior convictions
for embezzlement, breaking and entering and burglary, and
armed robbery, at the time terminally ill with lung cancer.

Pinna, when interviewed by the investigating magistrate and by my office, denied having any information that might be useful to the investigation but subsequently entered into direct contact with me at the medical institute where he was undergoing chemotherapy and where I was accompanying my wife to receive the same treatment. Perhaps feeling a certain kinship to me given the circumstances, Pinna, apologizing for the intrusion, explained to me that he wished to get a burdensome weight off his chest before his illness came to its unfortunate but undoubted conclusion, provided and agreed that it was I who took the weight of this knowledge from him and spoke not a word about it to anyone else. He stated, and I have no reason to doubt his word, that he had chosen to make his confession to me because he was certain that he was speaking to an "honest policeman," as well as one who could understand the state of health that afflicted him.

Having willingly agreed to the oath of secrecy, a promise that, let me assure you, I never had the slightest intention of keeping, and after obtaining authorization from the investigating magistrate, I promptly proceeded to have a series of meetings with Pinna, who gradually opened up to me, telling me in great detail about his relationship with Bellomo, a relationship that began, according to his account, in December of the year 1989.

In that period Pinna was performing his military service in a so-called punishment unit for having seriously assaulted a superior officer during his compulsory term of military service. That assault earned him a two-year sentence in military prison, after which he was transferred to an armory barracks in the vicinity of the nuclear power plant of Caorso.

In the dark of a December night—he was uncertain as to the exact date—Pinna and five other fellow soldiers, all of whom had also been assigned to the same punishment battalion, were awakened and loaded without advance warning onto a canvas-top transport truck and taken out into the countryside, at the boundary with the neighboring province of Cremona. Pinna and the others, including one soldier whom Pinna had nicknamed "Stankfoot," were thereupon assigned the task of completely emptying a military storehouse that stood "in the middle of nowhere," to quote Pinna's own words. This storehouse contained, aside from furniture of military description, cartons of clothing and medical equipment, as well as books and victuals. All of it was to be burned by them in the adjacent field, and whatever proved not to be combustible was to be reduced to its smallest possible component parts and buried. No explanation was furnished to them, but Pinna had noticed that all activities were overseen and supervised by soldiers from another unit, who wore camouflage jumpsuits devoid of insignia and who were apparently accustomed to what was happening. Among the members of this unit without insignia was Emilio Bellomo, who was an acquaintance from Pinna's childhood in the province of Latina. Bellomo and Pinna exchanged only a few brief words, but Pinna gathered from their short conversation that Bellomo was not unused to similar assignments. The conversation had been brief, especially because Bellomo had told Pinna that he was afraid of his superior officer, nicknamed "the German," according to Bellomo a dangerous and violent person. This German was present at the scene of the operations in question and, according to Pinna, did not seemed pleased at the sight of the two men talking. Pinna described the German as a man of average height and powerful physique, with a bull neck, blond hair, and eyes of a distinctive light blue.

According to Pinna's account, he and Bellomo lost track of each other during the rest of his mandatory military service but saw each other again the following year, in their home town, where Bellomo was living a life of comfort and ease, on the verge of downright luxury. Bellomo had shown himself to be friendly and generous to Pinna on more than one occasion, but he was unwilling to talk about the period of obligatory military service. Pinna told me that it had been his impression that Bellomo was worried and felt uncomfortable about something that had happened during that period.

The sole indiscretion that Pinna was able to pry out of Bellomo was that the cause of his discomfort had to do with "a little boy," whereupon at first glance Pinna had suspected that Bellomo had a history of child molestation, even though his sexual conduct in that period had seemed to be normal and he was in a stable sexual relationship with Rossella Calabro, the woman who would later become his first victim. After going on the run in the aftermath of Calabro's homicide and without any other means of support, Bellomo subsequently joined up with Pinna and began a criminal conspiracy, committing a series of burglaries and armed robberies, a chain of crimes that ended with Pinna's arrest and subsequent imprisonment in 1999. During this period, Pinna declared that he had broken off all contact with Bellomo. Pinna knew only that Bellomo's flight from the law was ongoing and that, according to several mutual acquaintances, he might be outside of Italy.

Pinna, already sick, had been released from prison in 2010. He'd found work as a manual laborer for a construction company; according to him, he had ceased all interactions with the criminal world. He had been greatly surprised when, at the beginning of 2013, he was paid a visit in the middle of the night by Bellomo, in Pinna's home. Bellomo, wounded in an exchange of gunfire not far from Latina during a routine traffic check, was seeking shelter in the justifiable belief that he was the object of a manhunt. On that occasion, he told Pinna that he intended to cross the French border on foot in order to take refuge with his lover, a certain Caroline Wong, of Franco-Chinese descent. Wong worked as a coat check attendant in a fashionable Paris restaurant. Bellomo moreover revealed, according to what Pinna quoted him as saying, that he had made a grave error when he had accepted, in his desperation, a "job" offered him by his former superior officer, the previously mentioned German. In the days required for his complete recuperation from his wound, while being cared for by Pinna, Bellomo had gradually added various details. That the job in question, which remained otherwise vague, had taken place near the city of Fano, in Marche, and that Bellomo had accepted in payment enough money to start a new life. He had also stated that what he had done weighed heavy on his conscience, because once again a young boy had, in his exact words, "paid the price." After staying at Pinna's place of residence for a week, once his wound had healed Bellomo left for France, informing Pinna of how to get in touch with him in case it became necessary. Since Pinna had never betrayed his trust, even during his incarceration, Bellomo considered him to be a safe and trustworthy individual.

I feel obliged to inform you that Pinna's testimony, which I have here reported in a concise and chronological fashion, actually took place at various junctures, in some cases at my home, at other times at Pinna's, on occasion at the hospital, and that it took an often muddled form, interspersed with outbursts of anger, weeping, or complete blank silence. During one of the moments of greatest turbulence, Pinna revealed to me that the reason behind his decision to collaborate with the law but to speak only with me had to do with the fact that he trusted neither the corps of magistrates nor my colleagues. Over the years, in fact, he had come to the belief that the mission he had been sent out on in December 1989 as a member of a military detail operating in support of the unit to which Bellomo belonged had actually been meant to cover up a critical nuclear accident that had occurred in the Caorso area, an accident that the authorities had concealed from public knowledge.

Pinna believed that the individuals who had been contaminated were secretly treated in the warehouse he had helped to dismantle and that the boy mentioned by Bellomo on the occasion of their first meeting had not been a victim of Bellomo's pathological lust, as he'd originally believed, but had instead been killed by radiation. As proof of the truthfulness of his statements, he gave me a tin whistle left behind by Bellomo when he fled to Paris. Pinna believed that the whistle had belonged to the little boy in question and that Bellomo had jealously kept it with him over the years as a sort of sorrowful memento, a reminder of the guilt he carried with him. Pinna added that he was certain his own disease had come about as a result of his exposure to that radiation, due to the mission performed that night in 1989 without any protective garb or equipment.

As you can easily gather from my account, Pinna's story appeared to be nothing more nor less than the ravings of a madman. In spite of that fact, while awaiting the information needed to capture Bellomo, I felt it my duty to perform further investigations. I discovered, as I had already supposed, that no incident of any major importance had ever taken place at the Caorso nuclear power plant, with the exception of a leak of only slightly radioactive dust that occurred in 1985, contaminating several plant workers though without any negative consequences for any of them. If there had been other accidents in the years that followed, they would surely have been brought to the public's attention, since the monitoring activity of the self-proclaimed antinuclearists at that time was very intense, as demonstrated by the fact that the previously mentioned leak was given extensive coverage in the press and was even the subject of a parliamentary inquiry.

As far as Bellomo's military service is concerned, the information in my possession also fails to match up with Pinna's report. I requested information from the Ministry of Defense, and I received in return a brief note informing me that Bellomo had been discharged as unfit for duty. For that reason, and in fear that Pinna might be considered a wholly unreliable source, I wrongly reported to the investigating magistrate only the last part of my conversation with him, the part regarding Bellomo's new location in Paris, considering it to be reasonably solid. I then proceeded, in concert with the French authorities, to move forward with the operation that was meant to lead to his arrest. Given the sensitivity of this case, I assigned it to my most trusted collaborator, Deputy Captain Caselli, in part to protect my office in the eventuality that Pinna's account concerning Bellomo proved to be the fruit of pure fantasy.

But two grim events undermined my confidence about how much might be fantasy and how much reality in the story Pinna told me. The first of those two events was the horrible outcome *of the operation designed to culminate in Bellomo's arrest, a massacre of which I hardly need remind you. The second was Pinna's death as a result of suicide by hanging in his home on the same day as the unsuccessful outcome of our attempted arrest.*

In those terrible days, made even grimmer for me by the death of my wife, while I was performing with great sadness the duties of my office, a doubt was, however, worming its way into my mind. However hard I might try to dispel that doubt, it insisted on returning to torment me with ever greater insistence. I wondered whether, setting aside the fanciful hypothesis of nuclear contamination, Bellomo's unit without insignia might actually have existed. Pinna's account of his meeting with Bellomo was vivid and rich in details that, in contrast to other accounts, appeared completely rational and sequentially linked. And if that were true, it meant that the ministry was concealing the truth out of national interest, that same national interest that, it is sad but necessary to point out, still covers part of the activity of the state agencies responsible for the fight against terrorism. I wondered whether the responsibility for what had happened was mine because I had, as the saying goes, opened the proverbial Pandora's box of a military secret that had been successfully concealed over the years, perhaps concerning intelligence operations into the last lingering offshoots of the subversive activities of the seventies, which were focused on the area surrounding the controversial nuclear power plant.

The nighttime mission to the warehouse that Pinna and Bellomo took part in might perfectly well have involved the dismantling of an eavesdropping and surveillance center, kept secret and properly so, even though nothing could justify the repeated reference to a little boy who was a victim of that activity, with the possible exception of the cover-up of an accident that had taken place during the unit's service and that might even have been kept secret from their own superior officers.

If such was the case, however unlikely it might appear, it could mean that the bomb set off in the Paris restaurant and Pinna's death were not unconnected events, due simply to the mental instability of isolated individuals, but rather actions taken in order to deflect duly appointed investigators by what remained of the platoon without insignia, in order to prevent the authorities from learning the truth about what had happened in the past. I know, it may seem from this text that I have contracted the same madness as Pinna, but I felt the responsibility for those deaths weighing upon me, and I needed, for my own peace of mind and conscience, to find out how much truth there was in his words.

In the weeks that followed I therefore burst into a frantic round of research in an attempt to find any confirmation of what Pinna had told me, a story I had at first dismissed. I started with the most recent events, that is, the "job" that, according to Pinna, Bellomo had done in early 2013, a job in which another boy had been a victim.

My attention had been attracted by the sad story of a terrible accident that had occurred during an excursion to the sanctuary of the Blessed Rizzerio in the township of Coda di Muccia, in the province of Macerata. In January 2013, during the festivities of Epiphany, a minivan traveling to the sanctuary in question plunged into a ravine, as a result of the driver's having lost control of the vehicle due to a mechanical fault believed to have resulted from normal wear and tear, compounded by the failure to perform proper maintenance. Riding in the minivan were several adults—two priests and a female elementary school teacher—and two children, ages six and eight, from the parish church of Sant'Ilario in Fano; they all died on impact. That impact was so devastating, and was further complicated by the rare event of the resulting combustion of the gas tank, that the recovery and reassembly of the bodies had presented a significant challenge. What struck me was the extraordinary coincidence in terms of place and date, according to Pinna's account, with the "job" performed by Bellomo, a job that had triggered in him the crisis of conscience described above. What if that job had involved sabotaging the vehicle in order to cause another senseless massacre? But why? Should this too be filed *under the category of cover-ups of past activities? Was there someone in that minivan who needed to be silenced once and for all? It was sheer madness, I realize and I repeat, even to think it, but the idea never left my mind.*

Utilizing my own free time and the time off that I had accumulated in considerable quantity, I therefore went to the site of the accident and consulted with the local police in order to learn more about the previous investigations. I found that during the expert examinations, nothing had emerged that might point to any tampering with the vehicle—tampering that someone like Bellomo, an experienced mechanic, could certainly have undertaken—but that nonetheless all the investigators were unwilling to accept the virtually uncanny coincidence that had resulted in the deaths of all the passengers. The minibus, in fact, had gone off the road at precisely the most dangerous spot on the route, where the steepest drop yawned, and where a powerful and swollen river scattered and further lacerated those unfortunate remains. Far from satisfied with what I'd discovered, and in fact even more deeply tormented by the thought that the "coincidence" could instead have been the product of a specific strategy, I went to meet with the relatives of the dead, in search of any potential link between them and the elusive platoon without insignia. I will spare the reader any account of the immense pity I felt for those families, deprived of their loved ones. Their irreparable sense of loss and guilt only further reinforced my determination to find out whether there was some other truth cloaked behind the facts.

The only odd detail, if I may say so, obtained during this personal investigation of mine, was related to me by the parents of one of the children killed; they declared that they had found their child's shoes left on their doorstep, a detail that was never explained. A few months later, this detail would prove crucial in showing me that my suspicions might actually have a basis in fact, but upon departing the city of Fano I was left with nothing but doubts and coincidences . . . and a sense of uneasiness that I couldn't stifle. While the investigations attributed the responsibility of the massacre of Paris to an act of insanity on Bellomo's part, I continued to search for anything that could refute or confirm my theories. I therefore began to delve into both Bellomo's and Pinna's pasts, in search of any evidence confirming that anything in particular had actually happened on a December night in 1989. And as I researched what had happened at that time, I stumbled upon the case, notorious though shrouded in the mists of time, of the so-called boy in the silo. It was then that

That was how Rovere's file ended, with a brusque white space. The flash drive contained a few other files on individuals implicated in the case, but nothing more. Still, what Colomba had read was enough to bring back the Rovere that she knew, the boss who had always helped and supported her, the honest man incapable of looking the other way. He had kept his secret in order to defend the institutions he believed in, and as the secret had begun to spill out someone had put an end to his life.

11

Dante grinned when Colomba looked up from the sheets of paper, though he looked much less cheerful than his usual self. By now the sun had set and the rooftop terrace was lit only by a few solar-powered Ikea lamps and the embers of Dante's and Santiago's cigarettes; Santiago was sitting in front of the computer with Jorge and the guy with the tattooed hands, talking in low voices and typing.

Colomba ran her hands through her hair and sighed. "So that means Rovere planted the whistle; it wasn't the Father at all."

"Yes, he did it to rope me in to the investigation."

"He was clever, that one."

"Chi per la patria muor vissuto è assai," said Dante, quoting an Italian opera, as if sensing Colomba's thoughts. "He who dies for his country has lived well and truly."

"Hush," she snapped.

"Take as long as you need to process the information. It took me three days, and I'm still not done. Too bad he didn't tell us everything right away, your boss," he added sarcastically. "Maybe we'd be a little further ahead right now."

"He didn't want to—" Colomba began, but she cut herself off immediately.

"Yes, I know," Dante went on with some irritation. "He thought he'd just stumbled onto one more of the ten thousand Italian secrets, and he was afraid of unleashing a scandal. Too bad that the child Bellomo was talking about was me. Or the kid I saw murdered."

"You can't be sure of that."

"Of course I can. Look at the dates. December 1989. That was when I ran away. And the Father's little squadron eliminated all the traces. But Rovere was afraid of the scandal. Muddying the reputation of the institutions." Dante got to his feet and leaned back against the rooftop railing, a black shadow against the city's white light reflected off the clouds. "But he was wrong. It's been twenty-five years. Who do you think gives a damn about a couple of kids who got caught up in some military maneuver? They'd have just covered it all up, anyway."

"*I* give a damn about them. And a *lot* of people give a damn, people who do their jobs, without fear or favor," she said bitterly. What she'd read was still churning angrily inside her. "Or do you think that we're all corrupt or compromised?"

"No, just outclassed by an organization far more powerful than yours."

"Which organization?" asked Colomba.

"I don't know that. But clearly someone in the army is involved. The photograph, Pinna's account . . . And then Bodini, the man they accused of being the Father and who killed himself. He was from the army, too."

"Do you seriously think that we're up against the army?" asked Colomba, aghast.

"Not now. The Father turned to an old friend to have you killed. If he'd been able to turn to the army or the intelligence agencies, he'd have used someone younger and much more efficient: there's always plenty of cannon fodder lying around ready to leap into the breach. Not to mention the fact that they could have just had you removed from the hospital with a few official stamped documents, and now you'd be in Guantánamo." He paused briefly. "But in the eighties . . . what do you think?"

"I don't know what to think."

"Neither do I. Whether it was for their own ends or on behalf of some organization, why did they kidnap me? Why did they kidnap the other boy and then the Palladinos' boy and Luca? And you want to know the thing that I find most upsetting?" Dante turned to look down into the courtyard, his shoulders bent. "I've spent my whole life believing I was the victim of a maniac, a brilliant one but still crazy. But now I realize there was a whole battalion and that they might actually have had a motive. A *motive*, do you understand that? To keep me aging like a piece of beef in a butcher's freezer."

Colomba stood up and went over to him. Then, a little surprised at herself even as she did it, she put her arm around his neck. The contact gave her an expected feeling of comfort. How long had it been since she'd hugged anyone? "Pinna thought there was some kind of an atomic plot," she said, trying to lighten the mood. "Maybe they wanted to use you as a guinea pig."

"I'm not radioactive. And they didn't test lethal weapons or bacteria on me," Dante retorted with a forced smile. "Aside from my hand and the malnutrition, the doctors found nothing out of the ordinary. And after all, the Father wouldn't have wasted time teaching me to read and write."

"Could it have been a vendetta?"

"But for what reason? My birth father has a terrible personality, but they turned his life inside out like a sock when I disappeared. He didn't have any links to crime or the army, and if he had, they would have found them. He didn't even do his military service because he had a heart murmur."

"Whatever motive the Father might have had, when we catch up with him we'll make him spit it out if we have to kick it out of him. I promise you that," said Colomba, trying to seem more confident than she was.

Dante shrugged his shoulders, taking care to move as little as possible. He didn't want Colomba to move away. "What are the odds that we catch him?"

"What do you think?"

"I don't know. But we still have some ammunition we haven't used yet. Let me tell you what I did while you were sleeping."

To Dante's disappointment, Colomba moved away and went back to sit in her armchair. "I'm listening."

Dante leaned against the railing again, assuming a pose of sorts. "Well, then, if we dismiss the nuclear issue, I figure that the five men in the picture were working in the Caorso area because it's the most tightly controlled place in Italy, on account of the feared terrorist attacks that never materialized. No foreigners, all access roads watched, video cameras along the roads. Anyone in uniform, on the other hand, could move freely."

"And the Father was the chief of the little group in uniform—that is, if he really is the German," said Colomba.

"He didn't have a German accent, that much I can swear to you, but it's certainly him. And he was the one who made Rovere realize that it hadn't all been a dream. Do you remember when he asked you to stop investigating?"

"I'd just shown him the identikit done by the wrong mother," said Colomba, remembering how strange Rovere's attitude had seemed to her and how sudden his change in mood.

"The identikit probably matched the description Pinna had given him, even if years later. He could no longer doubt that it was all connected. You'd brought him the proof he needed, and now he could tell you to go back to your kennel. He'd understood that Bellomo and the Father were connected. Which meant that the bombing in Paris might have another explanation." He paused. "And now that the Father has killed Rovere with a bomb, it's reasonable to imagine it might have been *his* handiwork in Paris, too, not Bellomo's. He just wanted to shut Rovere's mouth; he didn't trust him."

"Are you sure about this, Dante?"

"Yes. You've been tormenting yourself pointlessly for all these months, CC. It wouldn't have changed a thing if you'd shot Bellomo the minute you saw him. The Father was somewhere around there. And it was the Father who pressed the detonator."

"But they found fragments of it on Bellomo's body." Colomba was short of breath.

"He doesn't work alone, that's something we know now. Maybe he has friends there, too."

"God," Colomba murmured, covering her face with both hands. Dante stood there looking at her, but he lacked the nerve to get any closer. He cursed himself for a coward, then undid the parka and put it around her shoulders. She smiled. "You'll have to just give me this jacket, sooner or later."

"As long as you stop letting dogs chew on it."

Colomba wrapped herself tighter in the parka. "The Father must have considered Ferrari even less reliable than Bellomo, if he brought him in later."

"Seeing how he acquitted himself in hand-to-hand combat, I'd have to say you were right," Dante sneered. "I checked the cell phone you took from his apartment. Many of the numbers are of no importance, others need to be checked out, but there's one that we can definitely trace back to the Father. A Skype number, like the one he used to call Luca's mother, though not the same one."

"Not that we need any other evidence to show that they were working together," Colomba pointed out.

"No, I'd say not." Pulling the picture out of his pants pocket, he pointed to the faces of the two nameless ones. "Coming back to the group of uniformed men, I'd say that these two we don't know are even less reliable or out of play entirely. Dead, or else they emigrated with a nice pile of cash."

"Like Ferrari with his regular income," said Colomba.

"Or Bellomo, who burned through his. Pinna said that before he killed his girlfriend he led a comfortable life. Then he lost it all. They stopped paying him once he murdered her. There must have been a good-behavior clause in the agreement."

"Established by whom?"

"Maybe by the Father himself." Dante twisted his mouth. "I don't like the idea that he isn't the boss. Still, even the Father must have run out of money at a certain point."

"The video," said Colomba.

"Exactly. He wouldn't have had to sell the video of the Palladino boy if someone was still financing him. Which means he's operating on his own resources now. He has cover, collaborators, and accomplices; plus maybe someone who helped him back then, or even someone who gave him orders, is still in a position of power and can give him some help. Especially when they see a pair of shoes hung up at the scene of a crime. I think it's a signal of some sort: 'This was our work, stay out of it.' And his friends cover up for him. They *forget* to have an autopsy done on the Palladino boy, they hasten to arrest Luca's father . . ."

"A signal more or less like what we assumed the whistle was for you," said Colomba.

"Even though we now know that it was Rovere who put the whistle there to draw me in. Just like he did with you. What a remarkable coincidence that he happened to have the *exact* newspaper clipping to show you that would make you believe. Truly a cunning son of a bitch, if I may. It must have been interesting to work with him."

"Like playing in the major leagues. Always," Colomba replied, battling against the memories that came crowding into her mind. "Did you ask your friend Santiago to dig into Blackmountain? To see if we can find the names of any other beneficiaries?"

"Yes, but it's impossible. It's an international holding company based in Portland, and its servers are too well protected. Plus it has millions of shareholders around the world, and it sits on the board of directors of I don't know how many banks and major corporations. Name a company, and it's part of the inside power structure, from armaments to tobacco, by way of pharmaceuticals and aerospace. And plenty of nonprofits and charities, too, including Save the People." Dante tried to extract a cigarette from his pack, only to discover that it was empty. He made a gesture of disappointment and hurried over to Santiago, coming back with one cigarette, lit, in his mouth and another tucked behind his ear. "We don't know whether other members of the Father's little group might have received money from the same holding company. Even if they did, it's more or less like using a bank. There's only one detail that might be of some significance, though it also might not."

"Which detail?"

"Save the People was one of the international financers of Silver Compass, the support center where the Palladino boy went. Two years ago, they cut off the funding."

"That could be pure chance," Colomba began. "We don't even know whether Silver Compass was really connected."

"But if it was, then it means that the Father had international financers."

"To kidnap children?"

"This is something big, CC," Dante said in a whisper. "So big that we have trouble seeing the outlines of it. That's why we have to work back to the origins. The eighties. What Pinna was talking about."

Colomba grimaced in distaste. "If I were still on duty, I'd ask the Ministry of Defense for information."

"Luckily, Rovere already did. The ministry didn't give him any-thing about Bellomo, but they told him where Pinna had been. The General Annoni Barracks, which was actually a reconverted ammuni-tion dump. It was open only as long as the Caorso power plant was in operation, from 1981 to 1990. They mostly sent men there who had criminal records or were disciplinary problems. In those nine years, roughly a thousand conscripts passed through there, about eighty in the same period Pinna was there."

"Do we have all the names?"

"There were about eighty of them, and seventy or so are still alive, scattered the length of the peninsula. But before going through them one by one I'd like to test a hypothesis."

"Namely?"

"Pinna said that when he dismantled the warehouse, Stankfoot was there too, right? If he mentioned him but not the others, I'd have to imagine that they were pretty close friends."

"Maybe."

"In the documentation on Pinna that Rovere put on the flash drive there was also a criminal complaint for a brawl while he was still doing his military service. He got into a fight in a bar not very far from where he grew up. According to the police report, he was with a certain Augusto Stanchetti, twenty. Stanchetti, *stanky, stankfoot* . . ."

"Now you're just taking wild guesses," Colomba observed.

"Maybe so, but since we have to start with *someone*, he might just turn out to be the ideal candidate. Let's go see him. He lives in Cre-mona," said Dante with a dark flash in his eyes. "A chance for a home-coming visit."

Colomba shook her head. "We're wanted, Dante. We can't go around as if everything were all right."

"Santiago will put us in touch with someone who can get us a car."

"And maybe even fake IDs," she said, feeling a wave of irritation rise inside her.

"That would take too long. But my birth father will find us a place to stay."

"They're going to keep him under surveillance if they're looking for you."

"But I know how he spends his days and where to find him. And he's the only person I trust, aside from you and Roberto."

"I don't know, Dante . . ."

"What alternatives do we have? Stay here and wait for them to come get us, or turn ourselves in and hope that they believe us?"

Colomba thought it over for a solid minute, while her mind teemed with disastrous scenarios and her heart filled with suffering. She'd started out by breaking the rules, then she'd turned into a fugitive from the law, and now she was going to scrape bottom, piling deceit upon subterfuge.

She sighed. "I'll have to dye my hair. Find some clothing . . ."

"Santiago's sisters have everything you'll need. If you want, you could even add fake nails. I'll think of something."

"When do you want to leave?"

"Tomorrow morning. Tonight we'll make our preparations, and then we'll get moving at dawn."

"Rush hour would be better. Harder to spot us."

"Right." Dante put out his last cigarette. "If you go downstairs, would you bring me up a pack of cigarettes when you come back? There are a few cartons lying around."

"You're not coming?"

He shook his head. "Too many people down there. Up here I have a sleeping bag and a sofa. And there's a bathroom in the garret, so I can use it."

"A full life."

"I really miss my balcony," said Dante sadly. "I really, really do."

Colomba went back down into the chaos of Santiago's apartment, where there were now three more girls between the ages of thirteen and sixteen and the mother, a fat bleached blonde who eyed her suspiciously.

Ayelén understood what Colomba needed, supplied her with a bottle of hydrogen peroxide, and told her to choose between a

bottle of mahogany red hair dye and a light blue one. Colomba concealed her disgust and chose the mahogany red; she refused Ayelén's
offer of help, though. As a girl she'd dyed her hair more than once
and thought she remembered how it was done. Ayelén went away,
promising to get her some clothing and make her something to eat.
Colomba suddenly realized that she was hungry as a wolf. She shut
herself up in the bathroom, at least as much as the ramshackle door
would allow, and took off her hospital gown. She was covered with
bruises, and the bags under her eyes made her look like a junkie: she
pitied herself. She took an enormous hamper of dirty clothing out of
the tub and ran the water, getting ready to wash her hair. Outside the
bathroom, in the meantime, the hubbub had grown more intense,
punctuated by bursts of laughter, shouts, and the ringing of phones.
One of the cell phone ringtones caught her attention because it was
identical to her own, a ringtone she'd very carefully chosen out of
the less overused and abused ones, and she instinctively turned her
head toward the door: in the gap between door and door frame, she
spotted one of the thirteen-year-old girls answering a cell phone.
When their eyes met, the girl suddenly looked guilty and slipped
away. Colomba also noticed that the cell phone the girl was using
looked exactly like hers.

That can't be, she told herself, struck by an alarming thought. She
was convinced that Dante had gotten rid of her cell phone, along with
Ferrari's car. But she'd never asked him.

She slipped the hospital gown back on and went in search of the
girl, whom she found sitting on the bed in the master bedroom. She
was talking into the cell phone in a low voice, and even seen from up
close, it looked like her phone. When the girl noticed that Colomba
was staring at her, she hid the phone behind her back. "What is it?"
she asked.

"Where did you get that?" asked Colomba.

"It's mine."

Colomba held out her hand. "Let me see it."

The girl shrank into herself. "I'd used up my own phone card . . . I
swear, I only used it twice."

"Give it to me now!" she roared.

The girl left the phone on the bed and took off. Colomba grabbed it and removed the battery.

She ran out of the room and almost crashed into Santiago, who was sprinting down from the roof. "Dante and I have to get out of here," she told him.

Santiago grimaced. "It's too late." And that was when Colomba heard, above the ruckus that surrounded her, the distinct sound of sirens.

12

Dante had stayed up on the roof, alone, stretched out on the sofa, wrapped in the parka that Colomba had given back to him before heading downstairs. He was going off coffee cold turkey, refusing to drink the foul swill Santiago's mother made, so his head hurt. He lit a cigarette, trying to assuage his anxiety.

Cremona.

Cre-mo-na.

He turned the word over and over again in his head: the city where he had been born was a clump of nostalgia and regrets, but the thought of going back there summoned up the worst memories. He'd believed for years that the Father might still be there, hidden in one of the ancient, dusty streets, though now he knew that that city had been just one of many stops in his career as a kidnapper and murderer. But even if Cremona was no longer any more dangerous for him than any other city on Earth, he still trembled at the thought of going back. With a sigh, he selected a tablet from his now sadly depleted supply and gulped it down with a mouthful of vodka from the pint bottle he kept under the sofa, hoping that the combined effect would lower his internal thermometer, now dangerously close to sounding alarm bells. He almost thought he heard that alarm bell ringing, until it dawned on him that the sound was coming from outside and below him.

Police sirens.

His eyes opened wide and he saw Colomba emerge from the fire escape, followed in short order by Santiago and Jorge. She was wearing only the hospital gown and her police boots, but she carried what looked like a bag of clothing. "They've found us," she said. She didn't say who, and there was no need.

Dante leapt to his feet. "How did they do it?"

"Santiago's sister used my cell phone. High intelligence must be a family trait."

"Watch your mouth, *puta*," Santiago snarled.

Colomba ground her teeth. "What'll you do to me if I don't?"

Dante grabbed Santiago and Colomba each by an arm to separate them, the way you do with children when they fight. "How are we going to get out of here?"

"You can't," Santiago replied, continuing to stare at Colomba. "My boys downstairs say that the cops have surrounded the building."

"And no doubt they've set up roadblocks on all the roads leading to the area," said Colomba. "At least, that's what I would have done. Or better yet. I'd have put the apartment building under surveillance and waited for the suspect to emerge. Or at least I'd have waited for the light of day. They certainly must be in a tremendous hurry to catch me," she added bitterly.

Santiago slapped Dante on the back. "Sorry, *compadre*. I hope that you'll respect our agreement and tell them that I had nothing to do with it."

"Yes, of course I will," Dante replied mechanically.

Jorge had started dismantling the computer workstation, and Santiago went over to give him a hand.

"How much time do we have before they arrive?" asked Dante.

"All the way up here? Maybe half an hour if no one helps them. They found me by tracing my cell phone, but they don't know anything about Santiago, otherwise they'd have made a targeted raid instead of coming en masse. They're going to have to go through all the apartments."

"Then add a few more minutes: it's not going to be that simple," said Dante.

He was right, because at that very moment, six floors below, a group of officers from the Mobile Squad, dressed in riot gear, were facing off with a compact mob of screaming, furious tenants filling the lobby and the stairway. Between the two formations Chief Inspector Infanti was yelling himself hoarse, trying to make himself heard.

"People, please! Don't interfere with the work we're here to carry out. We're looking for a person who doesn't live here! This has nothing to do with you!" he shouted. As he did, he pondered the fact that until just a few months ago the woman they were looking for had been his direct superior and that he still couldn't believe that she was guilty of the things they accused her of. A bit of a nut, no doubt, but capable of planting a bomb in Rovere's apartment? That wasn't possible. As for the evidence, someone on the Forensic Squad must have screwed up. It would hardly be the first time. Still, no one had asked for his opinion on the matter, and most of his colleagues were less disposed to defend her innocence.

A stout woman stepped forward, banging on a saucepan with a spoon to silence all the others. She was wearing a heavily teased-out wig and a dress with vertical stripes that made her look like a barrel. "Who is it you're looking for?" she asked in a strong southern Italian accent.

"Signora, that's not any of your business. You just need to let us do our jobs."

"You're looking for him in our homes, so it's definitely our business now. Do you think we're just going to let you in like this?"

"We're trying to find him, that's all. None of you are going to have any problems."

An old woman stuck her head down the stairs. "Liar!" she shouted. "That's what you always say! And when you took my son away, you said it was just for a routine check."

"Signora, I swear it's true," said Infanti, increasingly worried about the turn the situation was taking. He wondered why he hadn't just called in sick that evening. Especially once he found out that the judge who had issued the arrest warrant was De Angelis. That college-educated donkey.

At that very moment, the educated donkey in question was leaning against an unmarked police car parked across the street from the front entrance of the building. He was uneasily watching the kids in the glare of the floodlights as they stared back at him from behind the line of armored cars. They couldn't have been any older than twelve, and they already seemed eager to grab handguns and start shooting, he thought with a faint sense of disquiet. Santini, a couple of yards away, was talking in a low voice into the radio.

"What the fuck is going on?" De Angelis asked him. From what he could see, the officers who should already be searching apartments were just standing, half in and half out of the apartment building entrance, while from inside bursts of shouting and cursing could be heard rolling out at intervals.

Santini held the radio away from his ear. "There's a problem with the tenants," he said. "This isn't an easy neighborhood."

"We aren't easy either. Let's give them a wake-up call."

"Caselli can't go anywhere. Let's wait until things calm down."

"Let's wait, my ass."

"Are you sure, Judge?"

"Stop asking questions and get going," said De Angelis, irritated.

"Yes, sir."

Making his way through the officers, Santini emerged alongside Infanti, who was still trying to negotiate. "Why aren't we moving?" he asked.

"You can see for yourself, Deputy Chief," said Infanti, sweaty-faced. "They're afraid we want to take away one of their people."

"Just one of them? They don't understand a thing. Let me explain something to them." Santini signaled a member of the squad to hand him a small megaphone and took a couple of steps forward. He switched on the device, and it emitted a piercing electronic shriek. "Now, then," he bellowed into the microphone, and his voice, transformed into the voice of a robot, echoed all the way up to the top floors. "Either you get IMMEDIATELY out of our way, or else we'll cart you all off for resisting the orders of public authorities and interfering with the duties of law enforcement officers. Is that clear? You all need to DISPERSE THIS UNLAWFUL ASSEMBLY RIGHT NOW." He lowered the megaphone for a second, and the place was silent as a graveyard. Then a bedside lamp flew down the stairwell and shattered half an inch from his feet. "Who threw that?" he shouted, red in the face, forgetting he was holding a megaphone. "Who the fuck threw that?"

"Your mother did," someone shouted back from two stories up. There was a round of laughter.

Santini tried to figure whose voice that had been, unsuccessfully. He went back and stood next to Infanti. "Charge them," he ordered.

"We'll wind up in the newspapers, sir," he replied.

"So much the better. Maybe they'll think twice about it next time."

Infanti took his helmet off his utility belt and put it on. He hadn't worn a riot helmet since the G8 summit in Genoa, and things hadn't gone well for anyone back then. He gave the signal.

The sounds of distant shouting reached the roof of the building. Colomba was still standing next to Dante by the sofa. "You need to hide, they don't know you're with me. And if you're lucky, once they've caught me they're not going to waste a lot more time around here."

"What then?"

"Then you continue."

Dante shook his head. "That won't work, CC."

"We've already talked about that, I think."

"But I wasn't comfortable with it then, and I'm much less okay with it now." He broke away from Colomba's side and went over to Santiago and Jorge, who had now been joined by Tattoo-Hands. They'd almost finished breaking down all their equipment, and they were stuffing it into two large backpacks. He leaned close to Santiago and whispered into his ear. "You need to get her out of here."

Santiago angrily threw the Phillips-head screwdriver he'd used to dismantle the dish antenna to the ground. "How dare you come ask me such a thing? *¿No es suficiente el caos que has causado?*" He pointed at the dismantled computer. "*¡Mira!* My office has been destroyed. It's how I made my living! And now I have *la policía en mi casa!*"

"You always knew this could happen, Santiago. But try to understand that it's going to be better for everyone if they don't catch her. Better for you, too."

Santiago turned his attention back to the equipment. "There's no way."

"If there's no way, then why are you putting your computers into backpacks? Where are you planning to take them?"

"That has nothing to do with you."

Dante forced Santiago to turn and look at him. "You can't let them catch her."

"Dante. If I show her how to get out of here, she'll tell all her cop buddies! And I'll have to find another place. ¿*Entiendes?*"

"I promise you she won't tell anyone anything," said Dante, knowing it was a lie. Colomba was intractable when it came to certain things.

Santiago was about to retort when Colomba shouted, "The helicopter! Get under cover!"

Dante looked up over the roofs. A shaft of light was dropping out of the sky toward the street and moving toward the apartment building, accompanied by a swelling noise of rotors. In the give-and-take of the discussion, he hadn't even noticed.

Colomba came sprinting over.

"Is it going to land up here?" Santiago asked her, clearly worried.

"No, it's going to continue to circle overhead, mainly to make sure no one gets away in the dark. But if they see us they'll tell the cops to come straight up here."

Tattoo-Hands pointed to the lower shed roof, on the far side of the roof from where they were. "Over there!"

The shed roof, about ten feet long, sheltered in its overhang a dozen or so rectangular planters full of dirt, from which not so much as a green sprout was growing. It had been an experimental home-grown marijuana plantation, which Jorge had undertaken a few months earlier. The reason for the dismal results might have had something to do with the fact that the canopy was made of corrugated metal, instead of translucent plastic like most others. Tattoo-Hands and Santiago hastily grabbed their backpacks and made for it at a dead run, with the others hard on their heels. They crouched down around the planters as the shaft of light raked over the roof and the sound of chopper blades grew deafening.

Dante couldn't believe that this was actually happening, and to judge from Colomba's expression she was thinking the same thing.

"Santiago!" Dante shouted to make himself heard above the racket. "You have to make up your mind! Tell us how to get out of here!"

"Is there a way?" Colomba asked. "How?"

Santiago said nothing, and Dante, at the risk of being spotted by the helicopter, scooted over and crouched down in front of him. "Santiago. You understand what CC and I are doing."

"I don't care."

"If you really didn't care, you wouldn't have helped us. I haven't paid you enough for the risks you've been taking. You know who we're hunting, you know what he does to children. And I know you. We may not be in agreement on a lot of things, but we are on one: you don't touch kids."

"*Los niños son bendecidos por Dios*," said Santiago, against his will.

"If they catch CC, no one will free the children who've been taken. The way they took me. You know my story. Children the age of your littlest sister. And they'll grow up like animals in a cage."

"And the lady cop can find them?" Santiago replied mistrustfully.

"Yes. I know she can do it. And I'll help her."

"And the *chico* in the video, too?"

"Yes, him, too. And if we can do it, it's going to be in part thanks to you."

"Don't waste your time listening to them," said Jorge. "They'd say anything to get their asses out of here."

Santiago glared at him. "I know this man," he said, pointing at Dante. "He's not a liar."

"What about the lady cop?" asked Tattoo-Hands.

"The lady cop isn't a cop anymore. She's someone who's on the run. *Y no me gusta enviar a la gente a la cárcel.*"

"Well, how do you get out of here?" asked Dante.

"Through the basements," said Santiago. "They're all connected. Our building, the next one over, and the one after that."

"The police have surrounded the whole neighborhood," Dante objected.

"But not the park," Santiago pointed out, gesturing in the direction of the Giardini dei Tre Laghi, a public if somewhat decrepit park not far away. "There's a way to get there from the third building."

"If we reach the park, will we be far enough away from your colleagues?" Dante asked Colomba.

"If we move fast, maybe," she replied. "But once we get there, we're going to need a car."

"Can you take care of it, Santiago?" asked Dante.

"*¿No crees que estás exagerando?*" Jorge broke in. "Now you want us to get a car for your girlfriend?"

"I didn't ask anyone for anything," said Colomba.

"I did," said Dante. "It doesn't do us any good to make it to the park and then get caught. And they'd figure out how we got there in a second."

Santiago heaved a deep sigh, then looked over at Tattoo-Hands. "Call Enrico and tell him to leave a clean car at the bend in the road, keys in the ignition."

"You're certainly giving her the full service, this whore," said Jorge, infuriated. "I don't understand."

"Which is why I'm the boss," Santiago shot back. "*¿Tiene usted algun problema conmigo?*" he asked ferociously. "Do we have a problem?"

"No," Jorge hastened to reply.

"But we can't get down into the basement," said Dante. "There are cops all up and down the stairs."

"We'll get in through the building across the way. I know how to do it." Santiago nodded in Jorge and Tattoo-Hands's direction. "I'll lead the way for Dante and the lady cop. You two grab *las mochilas* and bring up the rear."

While Tattoo-Hands was calling Enrico, Colomba studied the movements of the helicopter. It was describing a large figure eight over the three connected buildings and the adjacent streets. If they took off when it was at the far end of the loop, they could get down off the roof without being seen, but it would probably spot them entering the second building. At that point, their only chance was to run as fast as they could.

"Tell us when to go," said Santiago, who understood that Colomba was calculating the timing.

The roar of the helicopter subsided, and the roof fell into shadow. "Just another couple of seconds." Colomba counted in her head. "Now!"

The five of them took off at a dead run, following Santiago's lead. The first stretch was fairly straightforward. An exterior access ladder led down from the roof to the top of the covered walkway joining the two adjacent buildings. They got down it without mishap; among other things it had round rungs, which were easy to grip. Colomba kept Dante right above her the whole way, so that she knew where he was, and she watched him clamber down the rungs with great agility, while she could use only one hand because of her bag of clothing. Jorge and Tattoo-Hands had the hardest time of it, because they had to take off their backpacks and carry them balanced on their heads to keep from getting caught in the safety cage.

Once they were down on the roof of the walkway, they pressed against the wall until the helicopter had gone overhead; then they ran the length of the walkway to the far end, where a rusty door awaited them; it was a little over a yard high and was covered with obscene graffiti. They could hear the twittering of the cops' radios and their voices coming from below. The faraway shouts, on the other hand, had ceased, which meant that the officers had managed to clear the front entrance to the building.

The door was fastened with a massive padlock. Santiago unlocked it with a key, then threw open the door. "Here we go."

Colomba stuck her head in. The darkness was absolute. She asked Dante for his lighter so she could see the interior of the shaft: the guide rails down which the elevator ran were fastened to the walls; fifteen or twenty feet down was the roof of the elevator car. To reach it, she'd have to climb down a ladder much narrower than the one before, and with no safety cage around it. "Does the elevator work?" she asked in low voice to keep from being heard from below. "I don't want to be turned into a pancake."

"It's never worked," Tattoo-Hands replied. "You climb down to the roof of the elevator car, and you're already in the basements."

"I'll go first," said Santiago.

He went in, turning as he found the rungs of the ladder, and his head dropped instantly out of sight.

"You're next, Dante," said Colomba.

Dante seemed hypnotized by the low door. He stared into the darkness beyond it, his eyes open and his breathing labored: it was a giant ravenous mouth, a dark abyss that wanted to slurp him down.

He felt himself being pulled toward it and had to flex every muscle in his body to keep from tumbling into it and being lost.

"Dante, it's the only way."

He shook his head, then with effort lifted his eyes to hers. "CC . . . I just can't do it. I'm sorry. You go."

"I need you."

Dante was sweating furiously. "You said that if we're separated . . ."

"That if they separate us, *you* can keep going on your own. But I can't. Without you, there's no way I can find the Father."

"To your colleagues, CC, I'm nothing but a witness. They'll let me go . . . and I'll join you wherever you are." He was swallowing his words, he was so upset. "We can invent a code to communicate."

"That's not possible."

"I'm begging you . . . Colomba . . ."

Colomba looked at Jorge. "Give me your backpacks."

"Why?"

"Because I'll carry them. Come on."

It could have been her tone of voice, or else it was the situation, but the two men promptly obeyed. Colomba tossed her bag of clothes into the hole after calling for Santiago to catch it; then she put one backpack on each shoulder. They must have weighed at least thirty pounds each, and she felt tremendously overbalanced and in danger of tipping backward. It would have been a problem if she had been about to go down a flight of stairs.

"What now?" asked Tattoo-Hands.

"Keep an eye on him," she said, tilting her head in Dante's direction. "I'll take the backpacks down and then I'll come back up, and together we'll get him down."

"CC . . . you'd never do such a thing to me," Dante stammered.

"Sorry," said Colomba without meeting his eyes. "Come on, or do you want them to catch us up here? Here comes the helicopter!"

Dante tried to bolt, but Tattoo-Hands was behind him immediately, clapping his hand over his mouth before he could scream. Jorge, after glaring furiously at Colomba, hastily grabbed him by the arms. Dante was writhing and jerking uncontrollably, and Colomba felt a pang in her heart. *It's the only way*, she kept telling herself. She went down the shaft as fast as she could, praying that she wouldn't fall and crack her head open. Midway down she did lose her grip, and the only reason she didn't fall was that she managed to grab one of the grease-smeared elevator rails.

From atop the elevator a yellowish light shone up. It was Santiago with a flashlight. "Where are the others?" he asked her when she'd climbed the whole way down and stood next to him.

"They're holding Dante. I'm going up to get him now."

"This isn't the place for him."

"You don't have to tell me that."

Without the backpacks weighing her down, Colomba climbed back up easily. When she got to the door, she tapped lightly to attract their attention. Dante's head was pushed into the elevator shaft, followed by the upper part of his body. He opened his mouth, as if he were about to yell, but Colomba promptly clapped a hand over it. "Please. Don't yell. I'll help you," she whispered into his ear.

Dante snorted and shook his head.

Colomba continued to hold her hand over his mouth. "You brought me here, and now I'm taking you away from here," she said. *Or at least I'm going to try*, she added mentally. She told the two Cuchillos to push and suddenly found Dante's full weight on her, as he clutched at her spasmodically. She was forced to use both hands, one to hold onto the ladder and the other to hold him, but Dante never shouted. He just panted loudly and refused to look at her. She thought they could make it, unless all four of them fell. Just then the reflection from the helicopter's spotlight hit them.

They'd been spotted.

13

Reports of the strange activity on the roof of the walkway immediately made their way back to Dispatch, which then forwarded them to the radio of Siena One, as Santini's squad car was known. The S in Siena stood for CIS. Or "shithead," as the cops in the Mobile Squad liked to say about the deputy chief of the CIS: they hadn't much appreciated his interference. When word came in, the revolt had just been put down, and a fair percentage of the district's inhabitants were under guard in the courtyard or else handcuffed in the armored cars, with cuts and abrasions on their scalps and, here and there, a skull fracture or broken arm. The search parties had made it up to the fourth-floor apartments, but the minute Santini received the message, he deployed his officers to the building next door, leaving only a few to keep an eye on the prisoners and stand sentinel. He now realized that Colomba was escaping from over their heads.

Actually, the fugitives had already reached ground level, and below. Their descent into the elevator shaft had been precipitous, as had their race to the cellars. Colomba kept one arm around Dante's shoulder to support him and comfort him.

Santiago led the group through an enormous basement room filled with junked equipment, then down an underground corridor that joined the two apartment buildings, and after that through another vast cellar room. They jogged along fast and silent, attentive to every noise. From time to time, the beep and crackle of police radios penetrated the darkness from the street above, and on one occasion they almost ran straight under a grate while a small group of officers went running overhead in the opposite direction: they would certainly have been spotted, but they managed to avoid contact. Over the years, in fact, the basements had turned into a formless agglomeration of rooms where the law of the jungle held sway. Some were piled high with garbage and rubble; others had been enlarged by demolishing partition walls and the annexation of adjoining spaces, transformed variously into dining areas, well-stocked pantries, guest bedrooms, and fortified rooms in which who could say what kinds of merchandise lay concealed.

Colomba even saw a barbecue area set up where two corridors met, with a Peruvian family grilling a chicken under the grating that gave onto the parking area, indifferent to the damp and the din and confusion overhead. At certain points the corridor was blocked by heavy doors or jury-rigged barricades, but Santiago had keys to all the locks, or else he knew how to get around them.

Their flight ended when they reached the door to a storage area, locked with another heavy padlock like the one on the door to the elevator shaft. Santiago unlocked it: the storage area contained a dozen or so beat-up toilets.

"Is this the way to the park?" Colomba asked, baffled.

"*Exactamente*," Santiago replied. "But you've still got a way to go. And this is going to be the hard part." He turned his flashlight toward a rack of shelves piled high with paint cans. "Move it," he ordered.

Jorge and Tattoo-Hands obeyed, revealing a hole in the wall about a yard across. Then they went back to stand guard.

Colomba studied Dante's reaction, but he had none; he didn't seem to understand what was going on around him. *Better that way*, she decided. Otherwise, all alone with him, she wouldn't be able to control him. "Did you guys dig the hole?" she asked.

"Two months of hard labor," Santiago said proudly. He explained that just a few yards away was a drainage tunnel that channeled the rainwater from the park into the sewer main that ran under the apartment building. The Cuchillos had dug a homemade connection tunnel that they used as an emergency exit when the building was searched. When it rained, it sometimes became impassible, as the drainage tunnel filled completely with water. Lately, though, the weather had been dry.

"This is how you got away two years ago when I was chasing you, isn't it?" asked Colomba.

He laughed. "I was innocent, just like you are."

Tattoo-Hands came running back in. "Cops on their way. I heard footsteps and walkie-talkies."

"It's time to go." Santiago handed her the flashlight and slapped Dante on the back; once again, Dante didn't react and remained calm even when Colomba pushed him ahead of her and then climbed in behind him. The tunnel was narrow and tight and reeked of sewage.

Colomba turned around and looked at Santiago. "Thanks," she said reluctantly.

"Oh, what nice manners the lady cop has." He laughed as he sealed the hole back up.

The three Cuchillos hurried out and padlocked the door behind them, then split up and fanned out into the basements to hide their backpacks. Midway to the exit, Santiago came face-to-face with Santini and a group of officers and realized he was screwed. They slammed him against the wall and handcuffed him, skipping the usual legal niceties, same as they'd done for everyone else they'd run into underground.

"Where is she?" asked Santini, slapping a photograph of Colomba in front of his nose.

"Never seen her," replied Santiago with a smart-ass grin.

Santini gave the order to scour the cellars and knock down all the walls if necessary, while Santiago sagged, dead weight, in the hands of the officers who were dragging him away. Before being shoved into the packed armored car that awaited, he spared a thought for that *gringo loco* who wanted to save the children and the cop lady with the eyes that could drill holes in your flesh. *"Mucha suerte y adelante, compinches,"* he whispered. For what felt like the first time in his life, he was rooting for someone other than himself.

Meanwhile, Colomba and Dante were slithering through the tunnel. Actually, Colomba was slithering and pushing Dante, who moved jerkily, his eyes closed, often slipping and sprawling face-first into the mud. After ten minutes or so, the dirt walls gave way to cement, and Colomba realized that they'd entered the sewer main. From there they were able to begin crawling on all fours, as the air grew steadily cleaner and cooler. After a curve, however, they found themselves face-to-face with a high cement curb that almost entirely shut off the tunnel. In the space that remained open between the curb and the roof there was a piece of sheet metal that seemed solid.

A surge of terror swept over Colomba as she wondered whether Santiago had intentionally deceived her. Sealed off ahead and behind, they'd be trapped like rats. An anxiety attack clenched at her lungs, and she saw the shadows shudder in the flashlight's beam. "Fucking hell, not now," she muttered and pushed on the metal plate as hard as she could, bracing against the wall. The metal plate tumbled out with a tremendous crash, and the tunnel was dimly illuminated by a pale light that poured in from above. Colomba helped Dante into the opening she had created, then she pushed the bag of clothes through, and finally she wriggled through herself. She fell into the drainage ditch, a wide dry V-shaped cement culvert, its top open to the sky, partly concealed by roots and branches.

She switched off the flashlight to keep from being seen, and once her eyes got used to the darkness, she saw beyond the treetops the outlines of the buildings they'd just escaped: the helicopter was turning in the sky overhead like an angry horsefly.

She leaned over Dante, sprawled facedown on a pile of leaves; he was breathing loudly through his mouth. He was covered in dust and dirt, and the elevator grease had left long black smears along his face and arms. She shook him and saw that his eyes were regaining a little life.

"We're out," she told him. "We did it."

For an instant Dante remained inert; then the fresh air and the difference in the light began to have an effect on him. "Out where?" he asked weakly.

"I'll explain later. Do you feel strong enough to stand up?"

Dante didn't move, so she grabbed him by the shoulders and pulled him to his feet, then pushed him along the ditch, which continued through the trees, blocked here and there by branches and rocks or else badly cracked, with shallow puddles to wade through. The park was deserted at that hour, and Colomba saw what looked like a man-made lake cordoned off with barriers for maintenance work under way.

They approached the hurricane fence that separated the park from the road. There were no squad cars awaiting them, and Colomba heaved a sigh of relief, even as she marveled at how quickly she had come to consider enemies those who had once been her boon companions.

"Stay here," she told Dante; then she hid behind a bush and changed clothes, taking off the hospital gown that by now had turned into a tattered rag and putting on the clothing that Santiago's sister had given her: a pair of jeans, a T-shirt with a patently counterfeit Giorgio Armani logo, and a sweater. She felt better, though she'd have given a quart of blood for a shower; she was caked with filth to the very tips of her hair.

When she got back to Dante, he was in the same position she'd left him in, his eyes following the helicopter, which was now moving in widening circles.

Someone knows we left, thought Colomba, and before long they'd be setting up roadblocks, if they had enough squad cars to do so. "Can you climb over the fence, do you think?" she asked Dante.

He nodded, but as it turned out there was no need, because the hurricane fence was cut at more than one point and they got through it without difficulty.

A few yards farther on, at the bend in the road next to the park entrance, they found a gray Opel Corsa with the keys in the ignition. There was no gift ribbon on the hood, no handwritten note, but still Colomba understood that this was a token of Santiago's generosity. *The last one for a good long time*, she told herself. Given his priors, he could expect to spend some time in prison, at least until she'd proven her innocence.

She helped Dante lie down on the backseat and then got behind the wheel herself. As she sat there, the gravity of her situation began to collapse atop her like a leaden avalanche, crushing her very bones. She was fooling herself, she thought; she'd never be able to prove her innocence. The children would remain in the Father's hands, and he'd continue torturing them until he was too old to go on. She felt like sobbing, and her hands clenched into fists on the steering wheel until she regained some semblance of self-control. She couldn't allow herself to be weak. No one would help her to her feet if she fell.

As if he could hear her thoughts, Dante muttered from the back-seat, "When do we leave?"

She quickly wiped away the tears with her sleeve, concealing the fact to keep him from realizing she'd been crying. "Right now," she answered in a broken voice and started the engine.

By the time Santini and Infanti found the tunnel entrance behind the rack of shelves, Dante and Colomba were long gone.

14

Dante and Colomba's trip was long and full of obstacles. They couldn't take the superhighway or the high-speed bypasses because they were monitored by video cameras and patrol cars, so Colomba took the slower state road to Via Aurelia, which led north from Rome, frequently and unhesitatingly pulling off it to even slower county roads the minute she caught so much as a whiff of a road-block or a checkpoint. At two in the morning, when the traffic was too thin to offer even the slightest cover, they parked on a dirt road behind a line of trees and waited for sunrise, dozing off for brief intervals, both too tense to really get any sleep. When they talked, it was about the Father or the children he had taken in those years, what he might have done to them and why, constantly rehearsing the same hypotheses.

Dante had recovered somewhat, but he was still grim-faced and locked in his thoughts, tense in his condition of hunted fugitive, in a car that reeked of sweat and sewer. He needed a shower and a hot espresso, a bed and someplace safe. And he still couldn't manage to remain in solid touch with reality. From time to time it eluded him, like sand slipping through his fingers.

They set off again at dawn, sorely tested by exhaustion and the cold, taking a road where they'd encounter less traffic and fewer watchful eyes and where it would be harder to identify them. But they knew that in any case it was a crapshoot: all that was required was a local constable with an eye for faces to put an end to their time on the run; for that matter, a nosy pedestrian might do the trick.

They filled the tank at a gas station too old to have video cameras, and in the bathroom Colomba dyed her hair, emerging with her head wrapped in a plastic bag. She rinsed off at another equally antiquated gas station about sixty miles down the road, and by that time her scalp itched so furiously she would gladly have cut her own head off just to make it stop. But at least the dye had taken, and now her hair really was mahogany red: with the zebra-stripe sunglasses she bought at a cigarette shop and her garishly colorful clothing, she didn't look much like the photograph that the CIS had distributed widely. Dante, on the other hand, shaved his head bald with an electric razor and bought a suit of clothing too big for him at a market stand in a small town they drove through. In those clothes he looked like a refugee, even skinnier and more miserable than before, but as long as he kept his bad hand in his pocket—in their rush to escape he'd lost his special glove—no one could ever have associated him with the onetime boy in the silo whose face was pictured on the front page of all the newspapers. They bought some food at an out-of-the-way bar, chosen because its owner carried himself in a way that indicated he had no taste for sticking his nose into others' business. She counted up their money and tried to reckon just how much farther they could go without having to raise more cash.

Before leaving Rome, they'd used Dante's card to withdraw all the money they could, but now they couldn't use the card again without leading their pursuers straight to them. Unless they found the help they were hoping for when they got to Cremona, they'd be facing serious problems just getting food to eat. Colomba would, at least, because Dante's appetite had diminished even more than usual. Since the start of the trip, he'd eaten only a couple of apples and a stalk of celery, and Colomba looked on with concern at the pale shadow of starvation that had crept over his face.

At eleven in the morning they finally crossed the line into Emilia-Romagna. As they drew closer to their destination, Dante became even more nervous and insecure, talking at breakneck speed about trivial topics and chewing his nails, something that Colomba had never before seen him do. She tried to soothe him by asking him about the good memories he had of his native city; she was surprised to discover that Dante didn't have any. He remembered little or nothing of his life before the kidnapping, and when he'd tried to reconstruct it, he'd found that his early childhood had gone up in smoke.

"When my mother killed herself," Dante said, lying with the seat back fully reclined and the wind from the car window buffeting his face, "my father got tremendously drunk and set fire to the house, though it's still unclear whether it was on purpose or by accident. He wound up in prison for the first time, and the house was saved, but almost nothing was left of the family possessions. And in particular, nothing of mine. The only surviving photographs are the ones in the case file in the district attorney's office, the ones you've already seen."

Even after the silo, there wasn't much that Dante could tell her about Cremona, for better or worse. He'd stayed there for only two years, taking his tests and graduating from middle school, as his state of mind grew steadily worse. In the end, his father had sent him to a psychiatric clinic.

"In Switzerland, too: how unoriginal." Dante straightened his seat and lit a cigarette. "Don't think it was a prison camp; it cost too much for that, and my father blew through a sizable chunk of his settlement to send me there. More than anything else, it was a controlled environment, with a constant drizzle of pharmaceuticals and mandatory psychotherapy sessions of every description, I don't know how many times a day. I guess these days we'd call it rehab."

"How long were you there?"

"Four years."

"Fuck."

"After the first year or so, they let me travel. At first with a chaperone; after that alone, on organized tours. If I acted crazy or got sick, my permission was revoked. I was always under supervision, you see, so I was let out and sent back on a constant, rotating basis. But after four years I finally succeeded in getting the family court to recognize that I was in full possession of my faculties, and after that, it was so long, suckers."

"And that's when you did all the luxury travel you've told me about?"

"Exactly. Though not as much as I would have liked. Airplanes are off limits for me, and there are places you just can't get to overland or by sea. But since I returned to Italy, I've never once set foot in Cremona."

"Not even once?"

"The thought alone was enough to trigger a crisis. The same is true now, though after what I've been through in the past few days, I doubt I could get any worse."

"How long has it been since you've seen your father?"

"We ate dinner together last year. On neutral territory, in Florence. He complained the whole time about his kidney stones. An unforgettable evening out."

"Maybe we should try to come up with an alternative solution."

"There is none. It's hard to hide in Cremona unless someone's helping you. And he's the only person I know around there who's willing to help me."

They arrived at four in the afternoon, crossing the steel bridge over the Po River, leaving Emilia-Romagna and entering Lombardy. Beneath them rushed the waters of the river, almost in flood, and two scullers pulling their craft upstream. At the first roundabout, where they were greeted by an abstract metal depiction of a violin, Dante asked Colomba to take a road that ran down toward the river and then pointed the way along the riverbank. On their right flowed the river Po; on the left were the gates of the various bathing facilities and swim clubs. It was a clear day but cold and damp; there were very few strollers and bicyclists about, and nearly all of them were elderly.

They stopped in front of a low red building with palm trees in the courtyard and a large open patio with a light blue kiosk. The sign read: FRIENDS OF THE RIVER. The patio was deserted, but behind the glass there were signs of life.

"Here we are," said Dante. "This is the club where my birth father plays checkers every afternoon."

Colomba turned off the engine. Dante crammed the Mickey Mouse baseball cap he'd bought down on his head and stuck his bad hand into his pocket.

"Are you sure you're going to be able to go in?" asked Colomba.

Dante stopped with his good hand on the car door. "I've been bracing myself spiritually for the past two hours. And just look, it's got plenty of windows." But his tone of voice wasn't relaxed.

"You go in on your own. I'll keep a low profile out here—the last thing we need is for someone to recognize me. If you start having problems, get outside quick and we'll try again some other time."

Dante nodded sadly. "All right," he said and then stepped out of the car and slowly headed over to the building, breathing calmly and pretending it was nothing but a fake facade that opened onto an open space, like on a Hollywood film set. *Come on*, he told himself, *you've been through a basement. You've been down an elevator shaft. After those things, this ought to be a breeze.* But he couldn't talk himself into it; he felt weighed down and fragile. When he reached the steps, he stopped and lit a cigarette.

Colomba watched Dante's movements with her heart in her mouth. Seeing him walk very slowly down the middle of the street made her fear for his safety. She practically expected to see the Father jump out from behind a wall at any moment and take him away for good. But that of course didn't happen. Dante finished the cigarette and then dodged into the club.

Colomba waited patiently for a few minutes, then less patiently for two more. From where she was, she couldn't see the inside of the room. If Dante was in trouble or if someone had called 911, the only way she'd know would be when the flashing lights appeared in the distance. Getting out and taking a look, on the other hand, would expose her to the risk of being recognized. The two alternatives battled it out in her head until she impulsively threw the car door open and strode, head down, to the club's plate-glass window.

She shielded her eyes with both hands and peered in. It was an unpretentious place, decorated in a maritime theme with fake fish and netting hanging on the walls, with the inevitable photographs of second-rank VIPs. A dozen or so people were scattered around the room playing cards or checkers, and not one was under sixty. Tilting her head, Colomba finally spotted Dante, seated at a card table talking with a wiry old man with a woolen cap on his head and glasses that clumsily concealed his hearing aid. Colomba guessed that the old man was Dante's birth father and wondered why Dante was staying inside with him instead of bringing him out immediately and introducing her.

Behind Dante's shoulders, a card player looked up and waved hello when he saw her peering through the glass. Colomba moved away immediately, leaning against a pole on the patio. Beyond the railing, the waters of the Po ran swirling. The river looked treacherous, full of whirlpools and hidden currents, capable of sucking you under and never spitting you out again. *Just like the mess we've wound up in*, she thought bitterly. A pickup truck stopped right in front of her, blocking her view of the river. An enormous old man got out; Colomba guessed he must weigh about four hundred fifty pounds. He was dragging himself on two canes, moving slowly. Colomba lowered her head to keep him from seeing her face, but she thought she'd detected a glint of interest in the fat man's porcine eyes, and instead of climbing the stairs he made his laborious way over to her.

He squared off in front of her, leaning his whole weight on his canes, which looked as if they were about to snap. From up close, he looked even bigger, his nose disfigured by a purplish birthmark. "Haven't I seen your face somewhere before?" he asked in a rheumy baritone.

Colomba forced herself to smile. "No. I doubt it. I'm not from here."

"I didn't say you were from here, I just said I'd seen your face before."

This time Colomba looked him hard in the eyes. "Could you leave me alone, please?"

The man seemed unfazed. Instead he smiled fiercely and stuck a forefinger in her face the size of a salami. "You're the policewoman!" he exclaimed. "The one from the bombing. They ran your picture on TV."

"You're wrong."

"I'm never wrong. What are you doing here?"

Colomba considered punching him and taking to her heels. But Dante was still inside, and she couldn't leave him here. She decided to do the only thing possible: she dodged around the fat man and hurried into the club.

Dante spotted her and immediately leapt to his feet. "What's happening?" he asked.

"Some guy recognized me. We've got to get out of here right away." Then she leaned closer to the old man, who was staring at her, wide-eyed. "I'm very sorry. Dante will get in touch with you later. Please don't tell anyone we were here."

The old man stared at her in astonishment. "I don't understand," he stammered.

Colomba dragged Dante toward the door. "You should have just brought him outside first thing."

"But why? He's not my father."

"So who is?"

They'd reached the door, but clearly the fat man could move fast when he needed to, because he was there on the threshold, monumentally blocking the way. He aimed one of his canes at Colomba's face. "Madame, you're quite rude!" he roared. "I wasn't done talking to you!"

Colomba got ready to knock him to the ground with a shoulder butt, but Dante, guessing her intentions, reached his bad hand out to restrain her. "*He* is," he said, pointing at the man filling the door. "But I see you two have already met."

15

Dante's birth father was named Annibale Valle, he was seventy years old, and he had emphysema and a bum heart. He got into his pickup, and Dante and Colomba followed him in Santiago's car, keeping an eye peeled in case anyone was following them. Apparently no one was; traffic was light, and they would have noticed.

During the drive, Colomba tried to recover from her shock. She hadn't expected Valle to look like his son, but she hadn't expected an ogre three times Dante's size either. The only thing they had in common was the color of their eyes and the conviction that they knew more than anyone else about everything.

Valle took them through Cremona until they reached a small single-family house in the Boschetto quarter, on a street with twenty other identical houses that could be told apart only by the color of their garage doors. The small enclosed garden boasted magnificent cyclamen bushes and numerous garden gnomes. Colomba pulled the car into the garage and covered it with a tarp. Valle parked behind them.

Valle asked the two of them to give him a couple of minutes to talk to the lady of the house; then they were welcomed by a woman in her sixties with dyed hair, bedecked with bracelets and dainty necklaces. She ushered them into a living room that was furnished like a Swiss chalet in a TV commercial. Over the fireplace with a gas log was an oil painting of her, a few years younger, standing next to a man dressed as a hunter. Wanda immediately hugged Dante, who had prudently stayed close to the window, concealing his discomfort at being in that strange place. He sensed it was a friendly place, though, and that had made it possible for him to enter; still, his thermometer was rising.

"Here he is, Annibale's son," said the woman in an accent and dialect so thick that Colomba barely understood a thing. "Let me take a look at you."

"Pleased to meet you, signora," Dante replied, embarrassed and stiff.

"You don't have to be formal with me. You can't imagine how I've been longing to meet you." Then she caressed his face, which Dante accepted, tilting his head to one side like a cat being petted. It occurred to Colomba that Dante hadn't had a lot of petting in his lifetime.

"Signora . . ." Colomba began.

The woman turned to look at her. Her eyeshadow was the same light blue as her pendant earrings. "Call me Wanda."

"Wanda, did Signor Valle explain the situation to you?"

"Yes. That I can't tell anyone that you're here."

"We'll try to be out of here as quick as we can," Colomba went on. "But you ought to be aware that, if they find us, you'll be in serious trouble for having helped us."

"But you haven't done anything, have you?" asked Wanda.

"No. We haven't done anything wrong. But that doesn't change the way things stand. You'll be the accomplice of a woman on the run, facing a murder charge."

A forced smile appeared on Wanda's face. "Are you trying to scare me?"

"No. I just wanted you to know the risks you're facing."

Wanda turned to look at Valle, who was slumped in an armchair with a glass of whisky in his hand. "Annibale vouches for you."

"Only for my son!" he muttered. "I've never met the policewoman. But for the moment it seems impossible to separate them."

Wanda sighed. "Then I'll just have to take them both."

"Thank you, Wanda," said Colomba, sincerely appreciative. In the not-too-distant past, she'd have merely considered the woman a criminal for sheltering fugitives from the law.

"I'll show you where the bathroom is, so you can get freshened up if you like."

Colomba was the first in, and she stayed in the shower until her fingertips were thoroughly pruned up, with a shower cap on her head to protect her newly dyed hair. Wanda had given her fresh underwear and a T-shirt that fit her nicely, and when she walked out of the bathroom she felt almost human.

She found Dante in the living room with his father, with a discontented look on his face. It didn't take a sleuthing genius to deduce that the two of them had fought; maybe that was why Wanda had retreated to the kitchen.

"Did you leave me any hot water?" asked Dante.

"Sure, go right ahead."

He slipped away, moving as if every corner of the house might conceal some unwelcome surprise. Colomba and Valle sat staring at each other in silence for several seconds.

"Are you the one who put those things into his head?" Valle asked suddenly, from the armchair he was sprawled out in.

"What things?"

"That he needs to hunt down the one who kidnapped him. That he needs to turn into a vigilante."

Colomba pulled up a chair, placed it across from Valle's armchair, and sat down with the back rest in front. "He doesn't need to turn into a vigilante; I'm just asking him to help me keep children from being harmed. As for which of us talked the other one into this, I don't even know anymore. It was a team effort."

"If Dante just reported you to the police, all his problems would go away," said Valle.

"Have you tried to talk him into doing that?"

"What do you think?"

"I think that Dante might not have any more problems with the police if he did listen to you. But that *only* takes care of his problems with the police."

"And who else would he have problems with?"

Colomba narrowed her eyes, which now glittered cobalt green. "You know exactly who."

Valle took a gulp of whisky. "Are you two sleeping together?"

Colomba felt herself blushing, and her irritation sharpened. "It wouldn't be any of your business if we were."

"So that's a yes."

"So that's a *you can mind your own business*."

"He's my son. This *is* my business."

"He's old enough to take care of himself."

"Really?" Valle snorted. "I bet you're the only person on Earth who thinks that. And what you're doing is only going to make his condition worse. That is, if he doesn't wind up going to prison with you."

Colomba studied the man, but the expression on his fat face was inscrutable. He looked like a large mangy cat or a ragtag Buddha. "Do you truly not care that whoever tortured your son is still out there, at large, and free?"

"Even if that were true . . ."

"It *is* true," said Colomba tersely.

"I don't think that hunting for him is the best thing for my son. Maybe he should just try to forget and go far away. And you could go with him."

"From the way you're saying it, it sounds more like a suggestion than a theory."

Valle drained his glass and poured himself more liquor from a bottle he picked up off a glass side table. "I'm a rich man, Signora Caselli. The money I was paid by the Italian state—what I didn't give to my son, anyway—I invested very well, when that was still possible, and I've been lucky. I'm willing to offer you everything I have, except for a small sum I'll need to live on for the few years still left to me. Buy yourselves tickets for wherever you want to go, buy yourselves a fucking island for all I care. You're a policewoman, you can surely figure out a way to leave the country."

"Is that what you want for your son? To spend the rest of his life on the run?"

Valle drained the second glass as well. He poured himself a third. "I wept over his death for a long, long time. I don't want to do it again."

"Right now there are other parents weeping over children they think are dead."

"They're not my children. They don't matter to me."

"I'm guessing you made the same proposal to him. What did he say to you?"

"He told me to go hang myself. And you know what I said to him? That I'd do it if I thought it would give him a happy life."

"And I'd suggest the same thing. Only I doubt there's a rope thick enough to hold you."

Unexpectedly, Valle burst into laughter that soon turned into a racking cough. "Think it over," he said as soon as he'd recovered, mopping his face with a handkerchief. "By the time they arrest you, it'll be too late for you to accept."

Wanda emerged from the kitchen. "Annibale told me that Dante doesn't eat meat. But you do, don't you, Colomba?"

Colomba stood up. "I'm sorry, but we don't have time to stay. We have to see a person, and the sooner we do it the better. Do you have Internet access or a city map? I just need to get my bearings."

"I have a map, anyway," Wanda replied. "I'll go get it for you."

Just then Dante emerged from the bathroom. He was barefoot, and he was wearing a clean T-shirt with the logo of a local hunting club; it hung on him like a circus tent.

"Get dressed, we have to go," said Colomba.

"So I imagined." He looked at his father, who sat motionless with his chin on his chest. "We need your pickup truck," he told him.

"Well, what if I refuse to give it to you? Would you take the keys from me by force?"

"Papà . . ."

Valle tossed him the keys, then turned to Wanda. "Give him your cell phone."

"I couldn't possibly . . ." Dante replied.

"Oh, yes, you could. Wanda never uses it, and I've certainly never called her on that phone. If they're tapping it, it means the cops have suddenly turned into geniuses. And I don't believe that's happened."

Colomba nodded, and Dante put the cell phone into his pocket.

"This thing's going to end badly, Dante," Valle said again.

"The question is, badly for whom?" said Colomba.

16

De Angelis had subjected Santiago to the regulation first interview the night of his arrest and then grilled him again the following evening. The suspect had refused to answer all questions, and the magistrate had had a hard time maintaining control of his temper. Now, as he returned to his office in the district attorney's office, he threw a full-blown tantrum for a good solid five minutes, until Santini knocked at the door and walked in, accompanied by a man De Angelis had never met.

"Here he is, the genius," De Angelis said sarcastically. "Any news?"

"None, Judge," Santini replied.

"If you'd conducted the operation the way you should've, we wouldn't be here playing hide-and-seek right now." Then he suddenly seemed to remember the man who had entered with Santini and who was waiting patiently. He was in his early sixties, with a thick reddish mustache speckled with gray and hair the same color. The judge held out his hand. "De Angelis."

"Maurizio Curcio," said the other man.

"I'm sorry, I thought you'd already met," Santini broke in. "Maurizio Curcio is the new chief of the Mobile Squad. He was the chief of the marshals service, in Reggio Calabria."

"Congratulations on your promotion," said De Angelis. "Though it certainly came about in unfortunate circumstances."

Curcio sat down. He was a calm man who chose his words carefully. "That's why I've ventured to bother you, to ask for some updates on the investigation now under way."

De Angelis looked at Santini; then he cleared his throat.

"Torre made an ATM withdrawal two hours after Caselli's flight from the building in Via del Redentore, in the Tor Bella Monaca quarter, where we believe that both she and Torre were being harbored by the ex-convict Santiago Hurtado," said Santini. "We believe the cash withdrawal was used to finance their illegal flight from the law."

"Hurtado is a member of some sort of South American gang, if I'm not mistaken?" asked Curcio.

"Yes," Santini replied. "He used to belong to the Cuchillos, but now he's gone out on his own."

"And just why would this person help Caselli? It's hard to imagine they have any shared interests."

"That we can't say," De Angelis said brusquely, cutting off that line of inquiry. "But maybe Caselli can tell us that when we catch her."

"Her relationship with Torre is a mystery, too. At least according to what I've read."

Santini and De Angelis exchanged a glance. "As far as we know, Caselli has involved Torre in some kind of unauthorized investigation of the kidnapping of Luca Maugeri."

"Is the boy's father still under arrest?" Curcio asked.

"Yes," De Angelis replied. "Because we think he's the guilty party."

"But Caselli doesn't agree."

"Frankly, it's hard to figure out what Caselli thinks."

Curcio stroked his mustache; a gesture that for some reason grated on De Angelis's nerves.

"Unless there's something else . . ." said the judge. "I've had a grueling day, and it's time for dinner."

"I was just wondering why you're so sure that Deputy Captain Caselli is guilty."

"Have you forgotten about the traces of explosive in her apartment?" De Angelis asked.

"I haven't forgotten and I don't have any explanation, but I remain puzzled. She was a good cop until the bombing in Paris. Did she suddenly turn into a terrorist?"

De Angelis slid back in his chair and stared at him hard, eyes narrowed. "Have you read the psychiatric report on her hospital stay?"

Curcio nodded. "Yes. PTSD, pretty normal after what happened to her."

"Did you know that she stopped her psychotherapy sessions after she was released from the hospital?"

"That happens."

"A person in her condition, with no medical attention . . . Who can say what goes on inside her head?" De Angelis tapped his temple.

"I had two encounters with her after her stay in the hospital," said Santini. "The first time she attacked me verbally for trivial reasons. The second time she hit me, without the slightest provocation. I filed a report on the incident."

"In my opinion," De Angelis continued, "she should have been dismissed from the service, not just given extended leave. I'm sorry to say this, but Rovere is partly responsible for what's happened. He was protecting her."

"Undoubtedly," said Curcio, but De Angelis understood that he meant the exact opposite. "And how does the man who tried to kill Caselli fit into the picture? Ferrari."

De Angelis arched an eyebrow. "That he tried to kill her is what she told a colleague over the phone. We don't know what actually happened."

"It's hard to imagine that it was Caselli who lured Ferrari to the hospital so she could kill him by injecting him with poison."

"According to the forensic squad, it wasn't ordinary poison," explained Santini, "but rather a mix of pancuronium bromide and potassium chloride. Substances that cause immediate paralysis and cardiac arrest. And that are very easy to get your hands on in a hospital."

"And just how do you think Caselli was planning to dispose of the corpse?" asked Curcio in an exaggeratedly courteous tone. "Or do you think that going on the run was part of her plan?"

De Angelis concealed his annoyance by fiddling with his cuff links. "We still don't have all the answers," he said. "But she might have been forced to act in order to keep Ferrari from reporting what he knew to the police."

"We believe that Ferrari was her accomplice in the bombing," Santini broke in. "Ferrari had no prior convictions, but no one seems to know how he made his living. Especially given that he had no visible means of support, no job, and his parents were dirt poor. We are therefore looking for any connections he might have had in the criminal underworld."

"Did you know about Ferrari's links to Bellomo?" Curcio asked.

De Angelis and Santini both stared at him.

"There's a report from the carabinieri dated October 1998," Curcio went on. "From what we know, Bellomo seems to have used a car registered under Ferrari's ownership to make his escape. Ferrari was questioned, but he stated that the car had been stolen, and all charges were subsequently dismissed."

"Did you happen to know anything about that?" De Angelis asked Santini, glaring daggers at him.

"It's the first I've heard of it," Santini replied.

"I've only just received the report from the *cousins*," said Curcio with an apologetic smile. "I haven't had time to pass it on to the Central Investigative Service. Certainly, it might just be a coincidence, but there's a good chance that Bellomo and Ferrari were in contact."

"For what purpose?" De Angelis asked.

"I don't know," Curcio candidly admitted. "It's as if this whole case has too many pieces that don't fit together. It doesn't add up to me."

De Angelis gave him a hard look. "I don't like having to remind you, but it doesn't have to add up to *you*. I hope I've made myself clear."

"Why of course, Judge, your honor," Curcio replied, standing up and shaking De Angelis's hand. "Thanks for the time you've taken."

Curcio turned to shake Santini's hand and then left.

"This one's going to turn out to be a pain in the ass, I can just tell," De Angelis told Santini. "He's going to be a royal pain in the ass."

"He's just trying to prove he's the first in the class. Do you have any instructions for me?"

De Angelis nodded. "Let's investigate Torre's friends and relatives, too. If Colomba's with him, he might be helping her to hide. Nut jobs tend to get along."

Santini nodded. "What about Hurtado? Did he let anything slip during the interview?"

De Angelis shook his head. "He clammed up. In part thanks to that dickhead lawyer of his, who gives him such excellent legal counsel. And who also just happens to be Torre's lawyer, by amazing coincidence."

"Minutillo," Santini said. "What about Hurtado's other friends?"

"Unfortunately the preliminary investigating judge refused to confirm the arrests, due to a lack of solid evidence of a crime," De Angelis
repeated.

"Are we still arguing about solid evidence?" Santini asked. "With
people like this?"

"That's right," said De Angelis. "I had to order their release."

One of Hurtado's other friends was Jorge, who at that moment was
walking down the streets of Rome with a song in his heart and wings
on his feet. He wouldn't have bet a bent penny on his chances of getting out of jail this easily, not with the mess that had gone down in
Torbella, even though he hadn't resisted arrest when they'd finally run
him down in the cellars. Instead, he'd spent just a single night behind
bars, enough time to say so long to Santiago, who was resigned to the
fact that he was going to spend a good long stretch in there. When
he'd called Anita with his last remaining ounce of battery, she'd burst
into tears of joy. She'd already been making up the package to send
him behind bars, with several changes of underwear.

"I told you I always land on my feet, didn't I?" he'd pointed out to
her, boasting of his unfailing good luck.

"You're coming home, aren't you?" she'd asked. "I want to see you."

And he'd sworn he would. He loved her, after all, plus where was
he going to find another sweet setup like this one, with a girlfriend
who never busted his balls even if he stayed out all night or brought
a bunch of friends home, the guys from his posse? And she never
objected, though every time they left the apartment was littered with
garbage. She wasn't even jealous; all she cared about was not having
to actually watch him fooling around with other girls.

Jorge and his girlfriend lived in the San Basilio quarter, in one of
the nearly three hundred apartments of a public housing project that
looked from overhead like a gigantic and horrible letter U, with a dirty
pink facade. The complex was a filthy mess: the stairs always stank,
and there were little kids crying first thing in the morning—you could
hear everything because the walls were made of tissue paper—but the
rent was nothing. The original tenant had been Jorge's grandmother,

but when she'd died he'd moved in. In spite of the fact that the housing authority sent him letters every now and then warning of an impending eviction, Jorge knew they'd never actually take action. He couldn't even begin to count how many others there were just like him, with no right to live there, in that building, and even more in the neighboring buildings. What was the city going to do, toss them all out to live in the streets?

When he got out his keys and opened the apartment door, he expected Anita to come running to hug him, but nothing happened. "We-e-endy, I'm home!" he said, imitating Jack Nicholson's cavernous voice in *The Shining*, the way he did when he was kidding around. But still, nothing happened. "Anita?" he called. Could she have gone out to buy him something to eat? Or maybe she was just in the shower. As he was opening the bathroom door to see, he noticed a drop of red on the hallway floor, almost perfectly circular. He brushed his finger over it; it was sticky.

Blood. A drop of blood that had splattered onto the floor but still hadn't congealed. Jorge noticed another drop not far away, and then another and another. Anita must have cut her finger or something like that, but it was strange that she hadn't run into the bathroom to medicate the cut, because the line of drops led straight into the bedroom. There was one drop in the middle of the hallway where he was standing, as if Anita had cut herself in front of the door.

Somewhat apprehensively, Jorge called her name again, then stepped into the room.

Anita lay sprawled on the floor like a bundle of rags, and beneath her spread a puddle of blood so big that Jorge understood immediately that there couldn't be a drop left inside her. On the bed, cleaning the blade of a knife with a piece of paper, was an old man with eyes so pale and blue they seemed transparent.

"You and I have a little talking to do," said the man whom Dante called the Father.

Jorge tried to yell, but nothing came out.

17

Augusto Stanchetti, Pinna's old brother in arms, lived not far from the cathedral. Colomba parked Valle's pickup close to the pedestrian area surrounding the baptistry, across from the stone lions that stood guarding the portal. Dante looked at the lions, trying to place them in his childhood, but he came up empty. No matter what he laid eyes on, his mind drew a blank, with the exception of brief flashes from the period following his liberation. Had he ever climbed on those lions as a child? Had he ever attended Mass in the cathedral? He had no idea. Cremona was insubstantial to him, though he liked what little of it he had seen, especially in the center of town, which still preserved its ancient Roman grid.

Colomba shook him out of his thoughts. "Who's going to make the call?"

"A woman has a better chance of getting him to listen than a man does," said Dante. "Especially a woman with a pretty voice."

"Do I have a pretty voice?"

"When you're not giving orders."

"But you're a better liar. You do it."

"Any suggestions?"

"Don't make him run. Don't scare him. Try to find some excuse to meet in person."

"Okay."

Dante picked up Wanda's cell phone and punched in Stanchetti's number, putting him on speaker. "Stankfoot?" he said when the man answered.

Colomba started: she hadn't expected such a brutal opening.

Stanchetti hesitated for a moment. "Yes. Who's this?" he asked cautiously.

"My name is Dante Pinna. My dad was Fabrizio Pinna."

She jerked again in shock; Colomba reached out to try to grab the phone out of Dante's hand, but he turned his back on her to prevent that.

"Ah. I'm so sorry about your dad. My condolences. How can I . . ."

"I'd like to see you," Dante interrupted him. "I urgently need to talk to you. Can I come by your place in ten minutes? I'm with a friend; she'll come, too."

"Excuse me, but I'm eating dinner with my family. I can't just—"

"You'd better try to make up some excuse."

"Why, exactly, would I do that?"

"Otherwise I'll call the police and you'll have to explain why you told them nothing about my father contacting you before committing suicide."

Colomba shut her eyes, and Dante waited while Stanchetti panted into the phone for about ten seconds.

"And all you want is to *see* me?" Stanchetti asked.

Dante flashed a V for victory. "And talk to you. I'd say an hour of your time. So shall I come by?"

"No, I'll come to you. Tell me where."

"The front entrance to the baptistry, not fifty feet from where you live. I'm in a pickup truck."

"All right. See you soon."

Dante ended the call with a triumphant grin and lit a cigarette to celebrate.

Colomba opened her window; now that she'd been able to clean up, the smoke had started bothering her again. "How did you know that Pinna had contacted him?"

"If you haven't heard from a person in twenty-five years, when someone says their name you don't react so promptly. Instead, he clearly had Pinna in the front of his mind, and from his tone of voice, Pinna worried him, too. That means he'd heard from him before the Father hanged him, and he was afraid that sooner or later he was going to be called to account."

"He might have read about him in the newspaper."

"He reacted too promptly to the nickname, too. That was just a lucky guess, but if he hadn't recognized it, we could have saved our time. Ah, here he is now," he said, pointing to a man in his mid-forties wearing a quilted tweed jacket and crossing the street. It was definitely colder in Cremona than in Rome, especially at night, when the air turned humid and dank.

"Do you know what he looks like?" Colomba asked.

"No, but just look at his shoes. They're the kind with perforated uppers, just perfect for people who suffer from hyperhydrosis. And if they called him Stankfoot, there must have been a reason."

The man pointed at the pickup truck, and Colomba realized that Dante had nailed it. She got out and extended her hand. "Signor Stanchetti? Nice to meet you. Have a seat," she said, opening the rear door.

"Couldn't we go talk in that café over there?" he asked, pointing to the gelateria at the corner. "It's practically empty."

"We'll be more comfortable here. Have a seat."

Stanchetti shrugged and got in. Colomba got in next to him. Dante stayed in the front but turned around so he could watch.

"And you must be Pinna," said Stanchetti.

"Remarkable hunch. But feel free to talk to my friend," Dante replied.

"I swear I have no idea what's going on."

Dante grinned. "It's called conversation."

"Why did Pinna contact you, Signor Stanchetti?" Colomba asked.

Stanchetti turned to look at her. "If I can be perfectly frank, because he wasn't right in the head."

"Go on," Colomba encouraged him.

"Fabrizio was obsessed with the idea of radiation. He said that his cancer was caused by his military service. He asked me to contact the others from the Annoni Barracks and find out who else was sick, but I'd lost touch with everyone. Like I'd lost touch with him, for that matter. When he called me, it came as a surprise." He paused. "And even more of a surprise when I read in the papers that he'd been in prison and that he was a friend of the guy who planted the bomb in Paris."

"Bellomo."

Stanchetti nodded. "Yes. Fabrizio was a brawler back in the day, just like me. We were all a little pissed off, otherwise they wouldn't have sent us to the Annoni Barracks. But then I changed. I started a family, I got my feet on the ground. He didn't."

"Definitely not," Colomba said, with a glance at Dante, who nodded almost imperceptibly: Stanchetti was telling the truth.

"What else did he tell you?" Colomba insisted.

"He asked me if I remembered a special mission we were sent out on one night. He was convinced that that was when we'd been contaminated."

"And you remembered it," said Dante. There was no question mark.

Stanchetti nodded again. "Yes. It was one of those odd things you do when you're in the army and that stay with you later. But the idea that there was radiation is pure bullshit. I work for the city, and I'm in charge of the public green spaces. There's never been a radioactive leak in Caorso. The nuclear waste remains dangerous for several million years, but now it's all in France. Then there's the nuclear core, which actually—"

"So tell us about this special mission," Colomba interrupted him.

"Excuse me, but are you a cop?" Stanchetti asked. "Because I have the distinct impression I'm being questioned."

"Do I seem like a cop to you, too?" Dante asked.

"No, I'd say you don't."

"That's a relief."

Stanchetti smiled. "Well, then, I don't remember the exact date, but it was in December, before the holidays. The sergeant yanks us out of our cots, then he chooses six of us for a special job. They load us onto a truck and take us out a few miles. Middle of the countryside, blistering cold. There's a military warehouse, and they tell us to dispose of everything that's inside."

"And what was it you disposed of?"

"Furniture, medical supplies, books, but especially bags of clothing."

Dante stiffened. "Clothing?"

"Yes. Used. Civilian clothing, not military. It disgusted me to touch it, because the clothing s'ank and it was filthy. But it was nearly all wrapped up in plastic bags. We burned it all. I remember that Pinna was especially horrified to see the clothing."

"Why?" Dante asked, his eyes drilling into him.

Stanchetti hesitated. "It's been so many years."

"Give it a try anyway," said Dante, his eyes unwavering. He looked like a snake face-to-face with a mouse.

"He said the clothing was too small for an adult. Something little children would wear. Or kids, anyway."

Colomba and Dante sat in silence.

Embarrassed, Stanchetti went on. "But probably he was wrong. We burned most of the bags without opening them. And after all, what can a bunch of kids have to do with the army?" Dante and Colomba continued to say nothing, and Stanchetti started to worry he'd said something wrong. "On the phone, Fabrizio told me he thought it was clothing that had belonged to children killed by the radiation. That that place was some kind of a secret hospital, to keep the contamination under cover. But like I said, he was clearly raving . . ."

Colomba snapped to and pulled the Polaroid out of her pocket. "Pinna said that there was a group of soldiers that came from another barracks. That they wore camouflage, without insignia. Is this them?"

Stanchetti looked at the photograph. "I'm not much when it comes to remembering faces . . . I remember that the guys from the other barracks scared me, but now these guys look like ordinary kids to me. Aside from *this* one," he said, pointing to the German. "He scares me even now. Maybe he was the one who was in command, but I can't be certain. I'm sorry." He handed back the photograph.

"What else do you remember?"

"What I told Fabrizio. That I saw the guys from the other company load drums of diesel fuel onto a truck. Fabrizio asked me if I was certain it was diesel in the drums, and I told him I wasn't sure at all." First he looked at Colomba, then at Dante. "On account of the nuclear theory."

"He thought they might have contained nuclear waste?" Colomba asked.

"Exactly. But I told him that we'd all have been contaminated in that case, and that doesn't seem to have been the case."

"Why?" asked Dante.

"Because I know where they dumped them."

"How do you know that, Signor Stanchetti?" Colomba enquired.

Stanchetti leaned against the truck door. His neck was starting to hurt from turning to look the woman in the face for so long. Though she was worth looking at, in spite of the ridiculous hair color. "Like I told you, I work for the city. I've surveyed the gravel quarries in the area, and I'd know if there was any radioactive contamination. Gravel quarrying is one of the mining activities that's pretty prominent in the province of Cremona. Gravel and topsoil. Though most of the quarries have been shut down for years now. Some of them have been turned into dumps for asbestos processing, or else they've just been abandoned."

"Thanks for the explanation," said Colomba with some impatience. "Let's get back to the drums."

"I heard a guy from the other company talking to the driver of the truck. He mentioned the Comello quarry, between Piacenza and Cremona, on the Adda River. It had already been shut down then."

"And is it one of the quarries you surveyed?" Dante asked.

"Yes. I remembered it after I got Fabrizio's phone call. You know how these things work, you don't think about something for years and then it suddenly pops up . . . I searched through the documents. In 1989 it had been decided that it would be turned into a dump for the processing of industrial waste. That was still possible under the old law."

"But it didn't happen," said Dante.

"No. It became a wildlife repopulation area." Stanchetti's cell phone vibrated. He glanced at the display but didn't answer. "It's my wife, she's starting to get worried. I really ought to get back home now."

"Just give us the address, please."

Stanchetti jotted it down and practically jumped out of the car.

Colomba got back behind the wheel, entered the information into the GPS navigator, and put the car in gear. They left the center of town and in less than twenty minutes were driving down a country road. "It's not exactly going to be easy to find a bunch of fuel drums in a dump twenty-five years later," she said to Dante, who had the look on his face that meant his brain was spinning especially fast.

"Didn't you hear what Stankfoot said? They never turned it into a dump."

"But the drums can't be visible. Otherwise someone would have removed them. Maybe the same people who put them there."

"There's a way to find them, I'm sure of it. Don't the police have those ground-penetrating radar devices?"

"Sure, we do, and we use them to find buried bodies. But remember, we aren't the police." *Not anymore*, Colomba added mentally.

"We can buy one. Or we can get a metal detector, the kind that treasure hunters use. My father has plenty of money; we can even hire a hundred or so people to help us out."

"While *we* wind up in prison."

"It won't matter at that point."

"Do you think that all the answers are in the drums?"

"Not all of them. But one answer is, for certain."

"To which question?"

Dante didn't answer, just pointed to a sign on the county road, just past a small scattered group of houses. The sign read: FORMER QUARRY OF COMELLO—NATURE RESERVE. The arrow pointed to a dirt road, barely visible in the darkness. Colomba turned down it and slowed the car as it bumped over the potholes. When the road ended, they continued on foot, lighting their way with the flashlight they'd found in the pickup truck. It wasn't hard to identify the gravel quarry: in fact, it was impossible to miss. Now they understood what Stanchetti had been talking about when he mentioned a wildlife repopulation area.

Gravel quarries are located above shallow water tables, and once you stop quarrying, especially if you've dug too deep and you haven't capped the site, the water starts to rise.

The secrets that the Father and his men had sealed in the drums were now buried under millions of gallons of water. The quarry had turned into a lake.

18

The sixth-floor office on Via San Vitale reeked of stale cigarette smoke and the leather of the old red couch pushed against the wall. Listening to the street noises coming in through the glass window panes, Curcio decided that every city had a different voice. Sometimes in the morning with his eyes closed, half-asleep, he had a hard time remembering where he was; he'd try to figure it out by listening to the sounds. Even the light changed, the dawns and sunsets were never the same. But the sounds remained the same.

At ten at night, awake now for twenty hours, Curcio was struggling against exhaustion. He crumpled the empty candy pack and looked under the desk for the trash can, remembering a second later that he didn't have one yet. The office had been readied in great haste, installed in a conference room of the Anticrime Division, until Rovere's old office could be emptied of his personal effects after the state funeral scheduled for that Sunday. That was fine with Curcio: he was in no hurry to sit in a dead colleague's chair, though it would hardly be the first time he'd done it.

Someone knocked at the door. It was a young police officer, fair-skinned, with freckles here and there; on his nose a large bruise was starting to fade.

"Officer Massimo Alberti, sir," he said as he snapped to attention.

"Take a seat." Curcio pointed him to the chair. "I have a few questions I'd like to ask."

Alberti hesitated for a moment, then obeyed, sitting stiffly. "Captain . . . have I done anything wrong?" he asked in a worried voice.

"That's what I'm trying to figure out," Curcio replied. "Deputy Captain Caselli called you the night she escaped from the hospital. We see that from the phone records."

Alberti blushed violently. "Captain, sir . . . I didn't know what she'd done."

"If someone thought you had, you'd be in handcuffs right now," Curcio said sternly. "What did she want from you?"

Alberti stuck a finger in his collar, as if it were throttling him. "She wanted me to look up a name for her in the system." His voice dropped. "The name was Luciano Ferrari. But she didn't tell me why. I didn't know he was . . ." Alberti broke off.

"Dead. I can imagine. You just assumed you were doing a favor for a superior officer, even if she was on leave."

"That's right, sir."

"You realize that you could go on trial for what you did? Especially for not having reported it. You've barely started, and you could already have derailed your career."

Alberti looked down. "I know that, Captain, sir," he murmured.

"Then what did the deputy captain say or do?"

"I didn't talk to her again. They told me that Ferrari tried to kill her."

Curcio shook his head. "You don't talk about investigations currently under way if you're not involved. Why did the deputy captain ask you? She had plenty of other colleagues she could have turned to."

"She didn't tell me, sir."

"You have some idea?"

Alberti blushed again. "I think that . . . she didn't have a lot of interactions with her other colleagues. And that she saw me as . . . harmless."

Curcio scanned him; the young man was anything but a complete idiot. His expression softened and broke into a half smile. "When did you meet her?" he asked in a gentler tone.

"I was ordered to take her to the Vivaro mountain meadows, the day that the boy was kidnapped. Luca Maugeri."

"Who gave you the order?"

Alberti gave him the name of one of his direct superiors and told him that he'd volunteered to help search for Luca and his mother when they were still believed to be lost. He had to guess that the order had come from Rovere, because he'd taken Colomba straight to him.

Curcio smoothed his mustache. "Then did you take her home?"

"Not immediately," Alberti said, relaxing slightly when it became clear that Curcio wasn't interested in him. He took off his cap and set it on his knees. "First I took the deputy captain and Captain Rovere to a local restaurant, where they talked."

"About what?"

"I wasn't present for the conversation, sir. But afterward the deputy captain was evidently quite upset. The following day I was ordered by Captain Rovere personally to take her to the residence of Signor Dante Torre. Then I took them both back to the mountain meadows and after that to a meeting with Judge De Angelis."

"In the district attorney's office?"

"No, in an autogrill. Signor Torre suffers from claustrophobia. You ought to see the place he lives—"

"And the reason for this meeting?" By now Curcio wasn't bothering to conceal his interest.

"I wasn't told. But I believe it had something to do with the kidnapping. Later I drove the deputy captain here, first—" He stopped, embarrassed.

"At this point it would be better if you told me everything."

"The deputy captain had a dispute with Deputy Chief Santini. I believe that . . . they actually fought physically."

"As a result of the meeting at the autogrill?"

"Signor Torre had been unwell. I believe that . . . the deputy captain blamed his state on Deputy Chief Santini."

Curcio let himself slump in his armchair. "Then you drove her home."

"Yes. And that was the last time I saw her. Except for when I went to see her in the hospital." Alberti hesitated again. "Captain, sir . . ."

"I'm listening."

"She wasn't the one who killed Captain Rovere," he said with downcast eyes. "I don't know why she ran. I don't know why Ferrari tried to kill her, but . . . she's innocent."

Curcio sighed. "You can go."

Alberti snapped to his feet, put his cap on his head, and saluted. As he opened the door to leave, he ran almost headlong into Infanti, in shirtsleeves and tie, who was holding a couple of pieces of paper and was about to knock on the door.

"Captain Curcio, do you mind if I bother you?"

Curcio made an effort to remember his name. "Come in, Infanti."

"If I may . . ." Infanti laid the printout of a police report on his desk. "The carabinieri in Modena have received a tip from a street vendor who says that he recognized Deputy Captain Caselli and Dante Torre not far from his stand, while they were purchasing foodstuffs. The deputy captain had red hair, but otherwise the description matches."

Curcio didn't miss the fact that he'd called her "the deputy captain." *Another one who doesn't believe she's guilty*, he noted. "Have you already forwarded the report to the colleagues at the CIS?"

"Not yet. First I wanted to let you know."

"Leave the report with me, I'll take care of it."

"Yes, sir."

Curcio sat staring at one of the two sheets of paper for a good solid minute, his chin in his hands. Then he decided that his residential hotel would have to wait for him a little longer.

According to the code of etiquette of police hierarchies, it was always the lower-ranking official who was expected to go to the office of the higher-ranking official, but Curcio decided he could break the rule for once.

He headed down the central hallway of police headquarters and walked downstairs. There weren't many officers in the building, considering the time of night, and almost none of them greeted him; most of them didn't know who he was yet.

On the floor below, he followed the signs for the CIS and knocked on the third door, the only one where the frosted glass was still lit up, then walked in without waiting for an answer. Santini raised his head from his computer and, when he recognized him, looked surprised. "Captain Curcio!" He stood up and extended his hand. "Your first day never seems to end."

"And I can't imagine what it will be like tomorrow."

"Any problems, Captain?" Santini asked.

"I just wanted to bring you this report sent in by the carabinieri of Modena," he said, handing him the sheet of paper. "A sighting of Caselli and Torre."

Santini took it. "Thanks. You shouldn't have bothered." The surprised expression had been replaced by a watchful one. He knew that that couldn't be the real reason for the visit.

"I wanted a chance to stretch my legs," Curcio said.

Santini scanned the sheet of paper. "This confirms our thinking. That Torre is helping to cover Caselli. Modena is on the way to Cremona, where Torre's family lives."

Curcio sat down, apparently uninterested in what Santini had to say. He started toying with a pen.

"Is there anything I can do for you?" Santini asked.

Curcio smiled. "What was Naples like?" he asked in a tone of idle curiosity.

Caught off guard, Santini went back to his desk and sat down in turn. "Excuse me?"

"What was Naples like when you were there?"

"The Scampia gang war was under way. It was brutal."

"I worked with one of the judges from the anti-Mafia team two years ago." He mentioned the name, and Santini nodded. "He thought quite a lot of you. He said you did a good job."

"Thanks very much." Santini grimaced. "Captain . . . what are you trying to tell me?"

Curcio smiled. "That you and I have two things in common. We both have mustaches, though mine's better-looking than yours, and we're both good cops."

"I do my best."

"Do you?"

Santini threw his arms wide in exasperation. "May I ask you what you're referring to?"

"I think you know."

"I'm not in charge of the Caselli investigation," said Santini. "I just follow the magistrate's orders."

"You're hitching the cart to whichever horse your master tells you," said Curcio, and for the first time his voice was harsh. "But it's the wrong horse. And Deputy Captain Caselli is the wrong target."

"And you figured this out in a single day, sir?"

"The deputy captain was working for Captain Rovere. She didn't just go crazy and decide to barge into the investigation up at the mountain meadows. If Rovere had entrusted her with a job of that kind and she had accepted it, it meant they trusted each other."

"Maybe so. Just as the assignment you mentioned might have sent her around the bend, made her lose her mind."

"Or else someone didn't appreciate the two of them meddling. And that's why Rovere's dead."

"Tell it to De Angelis," Santini said slowly and clearly.

"I'm telling you. Because you're a colleague. And because I know you believe me. Leaving aside the respect you no doubt feel toward De Angelis or your personal dislike for the deputy captain."

Santini struggled to maintain his self-control. "Let me thank you for your suggestion, Captain," he said through clenched teeth. "I'll certainly consider it. Is there anything else I can do for you?"

Curcio stood up. "No, nothing. Thanks for the conversation. Think it over. I'd be sorry to see you go down over this case. We don't have a lot of capable colleagues. Much less with mustaches."

He left the room. Santini sat staring at the door for a few seconds; then he snapped the pen Curcio had toyed with in half and threw it in the trashcan. "Fuck yourself," he said under his breath, but for the first time since that case had begun, he had a bad feeling. It crawled up his spinal cord like an icy millipede. He shook it off and started organizing his trip to Cremona.

19

Colomba had woken up at dawn. She wasn't accustomed to sleeping next to another person, and even if Dante was curled up on the short sofa by the window, she'd been aware of his presence all night as he fell asleep and woke up. She'd dreamed of the Father and the explosion in Paris, her colleagues arresting her, then the Father again, and the silo. At eight in the morning, sick and tired of tossing and turning, she'd gotten up. Dante was still asleep, snoring lightly, his mouth wide open and his face turned toward the window; the roller blinds were pulled up to let in the morning light. He was modestly clad in a tracksuit that had belonged to Wanda's late husband, and it was too loose and too short for him.

Colomba had gotten dressed again in the bathroom, and when she emerged she'd found a note on the kitchen table from Wanda saying she'd be back around lunchtime. She was going to take Valle to look for the things Dante had requested the night before, after he and Colomba had returned from their trip to the quarry. Just how Dante had managed to talk him into helping them again, Colomba couldn't say, but he'd done it.

Colomba had eaten breakfast alone, a meal that consisted of stale zwieback toast with honey and a whole pot of coffee; then she'd started pacing the house, nervous as a lion in a cage.

Dante appeared in his ridiculous jumpsuit, his face pale. He looked as if he'd been reexhumed, more than awakened from a restful sleep. "I can't go on like this," he said. "Is there any coffee in this house?"

"Yes. But not the kind you like," Colomba replied with a tense smile.

"It doesn't matter. I've decided to make the sacrifice. In prison it's going to be even worse, and I'm already going cold turkey like the worst street junkie . . ."

"I'll make it for you," said Colomba. "You go ahead and use the bathroom." She leapt to her feet.

Dante looked at her, baffled. "Everything okay?"

"I'm just sick of doing nothing."

"And you're nervous."

"Of course I'm nervous. Aren't you?"

"No, Wanda has a substantial supply of Xanax. Or maybe I should say she used to."

While Dante was eating his late breakfast, they heard the sound of an engine in the courtyard. Colomba peered out from concealment behind the curtains, gesturing for Dante to keep quiet. It was a flat-bed truck equipped with an electric winch bolted to the deck. The winch was bigger than the one you'd see on a tow truck. The cable, however, was smaller and ended in a pair of hooks connected to two very stout-looking chains.

"Everything all right?" asked Dante, who was sitting with a break-fast cookie halfway to his mouth.

"Apparently someone's making a house call," said Colomba. "But I didn't see who's driving."

The passenger-side door swung open, and Wanda appeared; she didn't get out right away and was clearly worried about how high she was off the ground. The driver came running around to help her. He was a Maghrebi, and looked about fifty, dressed in a gray suit and red tie.

"Come take a look," Colomba told Dante. "Wanda's here with some guy."

Dante dropped the breakfast cookie he'd been about to bite into and peeked out from behind the curtain, moving with exaggerated caution, like a mime portraying a thief. He smiled when he saw the man. "That's Andrea, my father's right-hand man. Sort of his hench-man, and certainly the only friend he has."

"Do you trust him?"

"Yes, but I don't know how much he knows. It's probably better for *you* not to be seen."

"Okay," said Colomba. She went to hide in Wanda's bedroom. Through the door, left ajar, she could easily keep an eye on the front door. The bedroom smelled of Coloniali shaving soap, and Colomba couldn't help but notice other items of men's clothing, as well as the oxygen tank and mask that helped Valle to sleep without suffocating, sitting on one side of the bed.

Meanwhile, Wanda and Andrea had come in. Dante hugged the man and seemed sincerely happy to see him.

"You've put on weight," said Andrea. "Before long you'll look like your father."

"You'd like that. Then you'd have two of us to boss around."

Andrea laughed briefly, then turned serious. "The truck is the best I could find at the construction yard. The cable is eighty feet long, and they assured me it can pull up a couple of tons. But I haven't tested it."

"It ought to work."

Wanda said something that Colomba didn't clearly catch. She might have asked Andrea if he wanted anything to eat or drink.

He thanked her but declined. "I have to get back to the office. But first I have to unload the rest of this stuff." He hesitated and turned back to look at Dante. "Your father asked me to remind you that the offer still stands," he said with a hint of embarrassment.

"What makes him think I've changed my mind in such a short time?"

"He knows you're a fickle guy."

"Not lately . . ." Dante said with a hint of melancholy. "I'd help you unload, but it's probably better for me to stay out of sight."

"I understand." Andrea raised his arms in a sign of surrender. "I'll get going."

He opened the front door, and Colomba moved to keep from being seen through the gap in the door. Her knee bumped against a stack of interior decorating magazines next to the wall, and they fanned out onto the floor. When she bent over to pick them up, she noticed that there was a photo album in the pile, the kind people used to have, with thin paper sheets separating the pages. Feeling nosy but still enjoying herself, she opened it: the first picture, just as she expected, was of a couple getting married in a church, dressed in clothing from the seventies. The woman didn't look a bit like Wanda, but the groom . . . Colomba realized that the man looking seriously at the priest, dressed to the nines in a narrow-shouldered jacket, was a very different Annibale Valle, forty years younger and at least two hundred pounds thinner. The dark-haired woman in a white gown, then, was Dante's mother.

While Andrea unloaded the truck and kept up his bantering with Dante, Colomba sat on the edge of the bed and leafed through the photo album. A couple of black-and-white pictures depicted a seaside city, it might be Rimini or Riccione, with women in one-piece bathing suits and Valle playing beach tennis. Three photos later, Dante's mother, with a big belly, was smoking on the balcony of their home. Then came Dante, lying naked on a blanket, probably six months old. Colomba couldn't wait to show it to him, even though she was a little afraid of how he might react. Perhaps seeing pictures of friends and relatives that the silo had erased from his memory, like the people applauding his earliest attempts to crawl, might come as a bit of a shock. Dante believed that all his memorabilia had been destroyed in the fire, but actually something had survived, something that his father had forgotten to show him. *It wasn't that he forgot*, Colomba realized immediately. *He chose not to.* That explained why the album had been stuck in among the magazines in the only room where Colomba, as a guest, should never have set foot. She imagined that Valle must have hidden the album in a hurry when he'd gone in and come upstairs to announce their arrival.

She went back to the first pictures, started leafing through the album more carefully, and finally saw something that at first puzzled her and then made her blood run cold. She quickly flipped through the pages as the ice spread through her veins but stopped when she heard Wanda's heels clicking toward the bedroom. She hastily put the album back where it was. *This isn't the right time*, she thought. *Not now.*

Wanda opened the door and found Colomba standing by the window, the stack of magazines exactly as it had been. "You can come down now, Colomba."

"Thanks."

"Andrea's waiting outside for me, to give me a ride to where Annibale is. He thinks it's probably best for me not to stay here."

"I think so, too," Colomba agreed.

Wanda hesitated. "Today the police came to ask him about Dante. It didn't turn out like the other times. They were more aggressive. Do you think they suspect he's helping you?"

Colomba shrugged. "I couldn't say, but I do know for sure that they'll find out, one way or another, if we stay here. Today's the last day, I promise."

"I'm a little frightened," Wanda murmured. "At first it seemed like a game, but now . . ."

"I know. Dante and I will deny you had anything to do with it. That's the least we can do. And once they catch us, they're not going to waste a lot of time on you two."

"You talk as if you were certain you were going to be arrested."

"Because I am." She shook Wanda's hand. "Thanks for everything."

Colomba waited until Wanda left, then went back to the living room, where Dante was sitting on the couch. He was looking at three large boxes marked with the logo of an athletic equipment company, arranged on the carpet in the middle of the room. "Father Christmas came," he said.

"Or not," said Colomba. "Let's just say Santa Claus. I've had more than enough Fathers for right now."

She asked Dante to help her, and together they opened the boxes and carefully emptied the contents onto the floor: there was a 10 mm scuba-diving wet suit with a winter hood, a headlamp dive light, a 100-cubic-foot scuba tank, and a portable magnetometer for use as a metal detector.

"Are you sure you know how to use it?" Dante asked.

"It's been three years since the last time, but I think I still remember everything," she replied. "Or would you care to try?"

"I'd be dead before I hit the water."

"Then you'll have to operate the winch." Colomba studied her wrist dive computer, much more sophisticated than the depth gauge she was accustomed to. This one could even calculate the amount of air left in the tank, expressed as time, based on the depth and the ascent time required. She decided to read the instructions from start to finish, because that night her life was going to depend on it.

Because that night she was going to dive into the quarry.

20

At eight o'clock, the Friends of the River was starting to fill up with the evening clientele, younger and more diverse than the afternoon fauna. A number of couples dined there regularly, even on weekdays, while at that hour the elderly habitués were generally heading home, though they occasionally showed up again later for an after-dinner *amaro*, at least the ones sufficiently fit to ride their bikes.

The checkerboards were put away and the tables were set with red-and-white-checked tablecloths, chosen especially by the proprietor because they were reminiscent of the trattorias of days gone by; the scent of sautéing onions began to fill the air, and before long there would be frog's legs browning in the pans, the specialty of the house. The chef, who was writing up the evening's specials on the slate blackboard, was the first to notice the blue lights flashing on the roof of the Alfa Romeo parked out front and the two men in plain clothes getting out of the car. One of them had a salt-and-pepper mustache, a haggard face, and an athletic physique; the other one was short and bald; they came in and headed straight for the counter. The chef decided they spelled trouble, and one of the older men playing checkers made a face, having caught the smell of cops. The Friends of the River had been in operation since the turn of the twentieth century, even if a great deal had changed since then; up until the sixties it had been the meeting place for the so-called Lìggera, the organized crime syndicate of Lombardy, criminals who didn't use weapons, long gone and largely forgotten. How many of the old members of the Lìggera were still in circulation was impossible to say, but the survivors hadn't given up their habit of gathering at that establishment.

The policeman with the salt-and-pepper mustache showed his police ID to the proprietor, who read the name: Deputy Chief Marco Santini. "Good evening," he said. "We're looking for two people."

The bald man pulled two photographs out of his pocket: one was of an attractive woman; the other showed a man who seemed to be malnourished, with the intense gaze of a rock singer.

The proprietor shook his head. "I'm sorry, but I haven't seen them. Are you sure they've been through here?"

Santini put his finger on the photograph of the man. "This is Annibale Valle's son. You know who I'm talking about, don't you?"

The proprietor looked startled, then worried. "I know Annibale very well, but he's never come here with his son. He wouldn't be the one . . ."

"He would," Santini said brusquely.

"He looked different in the papers. Have you asked Annibale?"

Santini stared at the proprietor as if he'd just spewed some awful obscenity. At that moment, a little old man, standing less than five feet, came up to the bar with an empty glass, indicating by gesture that he wanted a refill. He wore an oversized pair of eyeglasses and an equally oversized pair of hearing aids that were almost entirely hidden by the tufts of hair protruding from his ears.

"Just a minute, I'll be right with you," the proprietor said to him. Then he turned back to the two cops. "Is there anything else I can do for you?"

Santini shook his head and reached out for the picture, but he found the old man's hand on top of it. The man muttered something in dialect that Santini didn't understand.

Santini glanced at the bald man. "Did you understand?"

His partner nodded. He'd been born in Brescia, and the dialect around here was similar to his. "He said he'd seen him."

"Torre? When?" asked Santini.

The old man mumbled a few more incomprehensible words, and the cop understood that it had been the day before. Torre had sat down to chat with the old man until a woman with red hair had come in to get him. They'd left with a big fat man he'd seen here regularly, a guy who had money.

Santini looked at the proprietor, who was now quite clearly uneasy.

"I swear I didn't notice. I didn't even see Annibale come in."

"Because the fat man is Annibale Valle, right?" Santini asked.

"Skinny he's not," the proprietor replied, realizing he'd just said too much.

Santini raised one hand to silence the proprietor's protestations, then asked his partner to take down the details of the old man's ID. They'd come to the right place; they'd just come twenty-four hours too late. Soon he'd close that case and he'd be done with lunatics on the lam and little kids. God, the kids . . . They'd started appearing in his dreams.

The two policemen left, and the old man went back with a full glass to the game of checkers he'd left. He discovered that his adversary, as old as he and with hands tattooed with blue ink, had crossed his arms and was glaring at him with contempt. And he refused, despite the bespectacled old man's protestations, to resume the game.

21

Standing atop the truck's deck, Colomba finished attaching the oxygen tank to the BCD, or buoyancy control device, with little more than symbolic help from Dante. She tightened the ballast belt around her waist and slipped into the belt a flat-head dive hammer of the kind used by underwater mussel poachers, and with it a small waterproof flashlight. The wet suit fit her snugly, while the neoprene flippers were half a size too small, but she could tolerate the pinch. She fastened the lamp to her forehead and tried it, blazing away the darkness for a good fifty yards around her.

"You look ready to take on Alien and Predator at the same time," said Dante.

"I hope that won't be necessary," she replied. She sucked on the mouthpiece to check the airflow. It was a little hard to pull, so she loosened the valve.

"Remember to turn on the tank."

"The advice of an expert. Help me get down."

He jumped down off the deck and put his hands around her waist. They were practically embracing for a few seconds, and Dante on impulse really did put his arms around her. "Be careful down there," he whispered, resting his chin on her shoulder.

Colomba responded to the embrace for a few seconds; then she politely disengaged herself. "It's not as dangerous as you think."

"What if you have an attack?" he asked.

Colomba sighed. She preferred not to think about that. "I'd just better not have one." Controlling your breathing is the most important thing when you're hooked up to an air tank.

"If you want, I have a couple of Xanax . . ."

"That'd be worse: I need to be clearheaded."

By the light of Dante's flashlight, they went over to the edge of the quarry lake; in the dark of the night the water looked black as tar. All around them, darkness. On their way in they'd noticed a couple of parked cars using the trees as a lover's lane, but no one had questioned them. Colomba looked at the lake water. The wet suit would protect her a little from the cold, but at the bottom the water temperature would be around fifty degrees, possibly colder. She'd have preferred a dry suit. With her advanced certification, she could certainly have used it, but she would have had to purchase it herself. Leaving aside the fact that a dry suit is harder to find.

"According to the old map," said Dante, illuminating the ground with his flashlight, "the quarry road ran around here. So I'd have to guess that the Father's group came this way with the dump truck."

"And that the barrels are down below," added Colomba. "But it all depends on how they brought them down here and whether the current has moved them in all these years." The body of water was a large one, 1,500 feet long and 650 feet across at the widest point, with plenty of grottos, excavation pits, and caves. Colomba would never be able to explore it all, not alone and not by night. She could only pray that her efforts would be aided by the little bit of good luck she hadn't seemed to be getting, at least not so far.

"Let's just hope that this thing works the way they say it does in the brochure," said Dante, handing her the metal detector. It looked like a foot-long torpedo with a handle along the top and a circle of LED lights near the tip. When Colomba turned it on, the LEDs blinked, changing from red to green, while the device buzzed and vibrated slightly. She'd tried it out at Wanda's house and had had no difficulties finding metal pipes in the walls, but she had no idea what its behavior would be underwater. Dante had set the sensitivity at medium, to keep it from going off at every lost coin.

Colomba tossed it from one hand to the other, then inflated the BCD to ensure that it would hold her up as she swam the first few yards away from shore. The walls of the quarry were sheer, but jagged and very possibly sharp enough to cut.

Wanda's cell phone rang in Dante's pocket.

"Did you leave it turned on?" asked Colomba.

"Just in case of unexpected developments," said Dante. He answered, and Colomba realized that something bad had happened, because by the light of the smartphone screen, he seemed to turn even paler. "I understand. All right. Thanks. Good luck." He ended the call, pulled out the battery, and stuck the phone back in his pocket.

"What is it?" Colomba asked.

"That was Wanda. She was calling me from the bathroom with her cordless. The police have arrived at my father's house. She said that they know we've seen him."

"It wasn't a good idea to call you," Colomba replied. "They'll trace the call."

"How long will it take them to find us?" Dante enquired.

"The dive time of this tank at sixty-five feet, which is the lowest point in the quarry, is about an hour," Colomba replied. "I'd say we'll be done before they can get here. And we'll have enough time to get out of here, too. Unless they're more efficient in Cremona than in the rest of the world."

"Then we'd better get moving."

Colomba let herself slip into the water, which slowly started to seep into the wet suit and warm up with the heat of her body. She swam a few strokes, swung into a vertical position, and then opened the valve to deflate her BCD. She immediately began to sink.

She descended slowly, stopping every ten feet to compensate, holding her nose and blowing. The quarry water, illuminated by the lamp, glittered with green and purple highlights and was clearer than she would have expected, at least from her first sight of the surface covered by bobbing vegetation and rotting branches. She also saw a couple of iridescent pike dart away as she approached, as well as an enormous carp almost a yard long. With neutral buoyancy, ten yards under according to her wrist dive computer, she forgot for a moment why she was diving and delightedly drank in the fantastic panorama. Then she deflated the BCD some more and started descending again, this time without stopping, until she was within little more than a yard from the bottom. She once again adjusted her trim to make sure that the tips of her flippers didn't touch bottom, because they'd kick up silt, making the water murky. The water temperature had dropped sharply, though it was still tolerable. She rotated to light up the wall next to her, which was covered with nudibranchs and tiny clams, then in the other direction, toward the center of the lake, which vanished into darkness.

For a moment she felt tiny in that space and feared that she'd never be able to find what she was looking for in time; if, that is, it was even there. She turned on the metal detector and pointed it downward as she pushed out into open water.

The metal detector almost immediately blinked red, and Colomba felt her heart leap into her mouth. She reached out a hand to touch the bottom, but all she felt was a chain that looked as if it might lead to an anchor, covered with mussels and algae. *You can't count on being lucky on the first hit*, she thought to herself. She went back to swimming, moving in a spiral, and the detector blinked a number of times, leading her to find a wide array of metallic garbage that had nothing to do with what she was looking for. She found a piece of a moped, a gas can, cans that had held bait or food, more chains, metal cables, a pick blade, and even a television set. She wondered who'd gone to the trouble of bringing a TV set all the way out here just to throw it into the water, but she knew that idiots always seem to have plenty of time on their hands.

After twenty minutes or so of fruitless searching, she took a look at her wrist computer. She had thirty-six minutes' worth of air left. Calculating the five minutes it would take to ascend without risking a brain embolism, however unlikely at these depths, she realized she'd have to come up with a better system, and quickly.

She strained to remember the map of the quarry that she'd studied on the screen of Wanda's cell phone—it had fortunately been able to access the Internet, though at an embarrassingly slow rate. Dante wasn't wrong about the access road, but perhaps the Father and his henchmen had driven the dump truck to a different point than the quarry entrance. In fact, considering the results of Colomba's searches, by now it seemed practically certain. But why hadn't they just dumped the drums immediately? Why waste time, with the risk of getting bogged down? She understood as her headlamp lit up the wall in front of her, opposite where she had entered the water: there seemed to be a projection at the base. As she was swimming in that direction, she realized that for thirty feet or so, instead of a sheer drop, there was a gentle slope down to the center of the quarry.

Colomba silently prayed that the Father's fellow soldiers had behaved like soldiers around the world, with or without insignia, and that in order to avoid pointless effort, instead of carrying the barrels down, they'd rolled them down the slope to the bottom, which even then must have been muddy, or perhaps yards deep in water.

She started at the bottom of the slope, swimming slowly in small circles. The metal detector blinked only once, about five yards from the quarry wall. Colomba touched the bottom, finding a hard, compact layer under the silt. She pulled the hammer out of her belt and used it to scrape at the clayey substrate. The water turned murky and the light was blocked by the billowing detritus, but she continued to dig until the tip of her tool hit something elastic.

She slipped the hammer into her belt and went on digging with her hands. She felt the shape of a rounded object and was then able to make out in the mud the upper end of a fifty-five-gallon drum. She realized that it was made of some material that appeared to be heavy plastic, with steel hoops on the exterior. It wasn't a standard fuel drum, therefore, and when she saw a second one and then a third next to it, she realized that she'd found what she was looking for. To mark the spot, she turned on the little flashlight she carried on her belt and planted it in the water pointing straight up, then swam hastily to the far end of the lake, inflated her BCD slightly, and ascended, seething with impatience at each of the two decompression halts that she deemed adequate. As she was ascending she felt a stabbing pain in her upper dental arch and realized that there must be microfractures in her teeth and tiny air bubbles had made their way into them; as they expanded, the bubbles exerted pressure on her roots. The legacy of one of the two explosions she'd survived, no doubt about it.

She surfaced just a few yards from where she'd gone in, and Dante hurried toward her lamp, almost winding up in the water alongside of her.

"CC! You're back!"

She pulled the regulator mouthpiece out and gulped fresh air, almost unable to speak from the pain in her teeth, though fortunately that subsided rapidly. "Yes, I am. You're going to have to move the truck over to the other side."

Dante understood. "So you found them?" he whispered, almost incredulous.

"Yes. They're strange, but they're going to be easier to hook up. Can you get the truck over there?"

"Certainly, even if I have to push it the whole way."

"I'll wait for you on the far shore."

Colomba swam back to the opposite shore of the lake and stopped where she guessed the wall began. She checked her wrist computer: she still had about fifteen minutes of air at sixty-five feet. She'd better not get the cables tangled up.

The headlights emerged from the darkness, and she waved her arms so Dante would know where to stop and turn the truck around. There were fallen trees near the edge of the water; they'd been left to rot where they fell. Dante had a hard time getting around them, but he finally maneuvered the truck into the proper position, with the rear tires close to the water's edge. He pulled the hand brake, jumped out, lowered the tailgate, and climbed up onto the deck.

Colomba watched him work for a few minutes by flashlight; then she heard the electric winch motor start up and the cable start to unspool. Dante let it reel out for a few more yards; then he jumped down, grabbed the two hooks at the end of the cable, and ran through the mud to hand them to Colomba. "What now?" he asked.

"You keep unspooling the cable until you get to the end. It should be longer than I need, but that doesn't matter. I'll guide it through the water and do my best not to get it snagged or tangled."

"And once you've hooked it?"

"I'll start tugging on it and I'll just hope you get the message," said Colomba. "Keep in mind that it'll take me a few minutes to get the winch drum hooked up. If you feel tugs on the cable before it's all paid out, that just means that I'm getting it untangled. If I can't get it done, I'll surface, but I hope I won't have to because I don't have much air left."

"All right."

Colomba put the mouthpiece back in, turned around, and walked toward the center of the lake, struggling a little to haul the end of the cable behind her. Carrying it, she'd reach the bottom much faster, and she'd have to compensate frantically unless she wanted her ears to explode.

Dante climbed onto the deck and started the winch unspooling again. He watched as Colomba's headlamp vanished into the water and thought to himself that he'd have given anything to be able to accompany her and help make sure everything went off without a hitch in this most delicate phase of the job. A job that, now that he thought about it, had actually begun twenty-five years ago, the day he had escaped from the silo and first told his story, hoping he'd be believed.

The cable continued to pay out until the motor halted automatically as it reached the last yard. Four minutes had gone by, and Dante waited, ticking off the seconds in his head. After two more minutes he thought he felt a sort of vibration, and he lowered his ear to the cable to make sure. The vibration repeated itself, rhythmically. Dante understood that this was the signal he'd been waiting for: Colomba had hooked up the winch drum. He went back to the winch controls, but before he could start reeling the cable in he heard a rustling noise next to the truck and the sound of boots sinking into the mud. He whirled around and stared, breathless. Standing by the water, his terrible eyes gleaming in the moonlight, the Father was watching him.

22

Colomba banged her hammer on the cable hooked to the drum, then started jerking at the drum itself again, though it was clear that she was barely budging it. The cable still wasn't moving, and Colomba cursed herself for failing to ask Valle's henchman to buy a couple of underwater walkie-talkies. Unfortunately she had never done any underwater salvage work, and that had occurred to her only after she'd made the first dive. She checked her computer and saw that she had only six minutes of air left. She'd have to go up.

She stuck the hammer back into her belt and inflated the BCD. Halfway through her ascent, she began to feel the pain in her teeth again; it lasted through the entire decompression phase. When she got to the surface, she immediately yanked the mouthpiece out, but she froze before she could yell "Why don't you get moving, you blockhead?" Dante was on his knees in the mud, hands over his face, moaning. Standing behind him was a large, powerful-looking man who was aiming a pistol with an absurdly long barrel at the back of his head. It had a silencer, Colomba realized. When the man shifted his gaze in her direction, Colomba saw his eyes glitter like ice in the light of her headlamp. She recognized him.

"Turn it off," the man Dante called the Father and Pinna called the German told her. His voice sounded like a calm whisper, yet it had carried all the yards of distance that separated them. "Turn it off this second, or I'll shoot him in the head."

"I'm turning it off right now," Colomba panted. "Don't hurt him." She reached her right hand up and pressed the switch. The lakeshore plunged into darkness, and she understood that she was in plain view, with the moonlight reflecting off the lake water behind her, and that the German was probably taking aim and was about to shoot her. Her lungs clamped shut instantly, as the darkness seemed to pulsate with even darker shapes. Colomba could no longer distinguish real shapes from those her mind created. She stepped back instinctively and lost her balance, falling backward, dragged by the weight of the oxygen tank. Her head echoed from the blow, with a blinding stab of pain. Her lungs opened up again, and she gulped down air and water, coughing desperately.

"Get up on your feet," the German said. "Up on your feet, or I'll shoot him."

"I'm doing . . . doing it," Colomba stammered. "I fell over."

"I don't care. You have two seconds to get up. Move it."

Colomba slipped twice on the slimy lake bed, then finally managed to get up on all fours, coughing as she did so. "I'm taking . . . let me take the tank off, otherwise I can't do it," she implored him.

"Get busy."

She did as she'd said and slipped off the BCD with all the accompanying harness. Lighter now, she managed to get back onto her feet. Her eyes were a little better adapted to the darkness now, and she could see the German's gun still aimed at Dante's head. Dante remained helpless, hands over his face, weeping with a prolonged, heartbreaking moan. "Don't hurt him," Colomba said again. "You've hurt him enough already."

"Still, he's alive, isn't he?"

"No thanks to you."

The German laughed quietly, and it was almost worse than hearing him whisper. "Do you really think it's just chance? Come on. Walk toward me."

"And when I get there?"

"Get moving. We've done enough talking."

Colomba realized that the moment she was out of the water he was going to shoot her. The German couldn't run the risk of her corpse falling into the lake and drifting out into open water or sinking. He needed to make her disappear. With the truck and Dante.

Colomba took one step and then another. The water was now down to her knees. "Tell me what you want," she said.

"Just for you to get closer." In the darkness, Colomba saw him move the hand holding the pistol, raising it in her direction. "Come toward me. Just another step," he said.

Now the gun barrel was lined up with her face. Colomba thought about diving into the water and trying to get away, but she knew she wasn't fast enough. And that this could be a quick, merciful way to die. One shot, and it would be over. She wouldn't feel a thing. And most important, she wouldn't face the horror of watching Dante die before her eyes. She was no heroine, and God only knew how much fear she'd experienced in her lifetime. But then and there, at the sight of Dante's desperate weeping, she'd have done anything to console him, anything to save his life. Even if only for a second, the time it would take the German to kill her.

She lifted her leg to take the step that would bring her once and for all onto dry land. Her flipper emerged from the water, bringing with it silt and withered reeds. Colomba noticed everything in that moment, every slightest detail, as if it were all etched in glass. The rustling of the trees, the lapping of the lake water, and Dante's piteous sobbing and the way it suddenly stopped. She saw his head lift and turn toward the man he'd called the Father.

"You're not him, you son of a bitch! You're not him!" he shouted. And he lunged up onto him, grabbing the hand that held the gun.

23

The German pulled the trigger. Colomba heard the puff of the silencer, and the bullet ricochet off the water close by her. But she'd already moved. She ran as fast as was possible with flippers on her feet and threw herself at the German, who had turned and punched Dante, laying him flat on his back, and was now raising the pistol again and turning it in her direction.

Colomba didn't make the mistake of going for the arm with the gun. Instead she lunged straight at the German's chest and rammed her forehead into his face. It felt as if she'd just slammed into a tree trunk. The German didn't even stagger, just jammed his knee into her belly and hit her in the temple with his pistol grip. If Colomba's head hadn't been covered by her wet suit hood, she would have been neutralized by the violent blow, but the grip just slid over the rubber. She rolled across the grass and heard the ground next to her puff twice as the German squeezed the trigger. In the meantime, Dante had recovered sufficiently to sink his teeth into the man's calf, deep enough to draw blood. This time the German sighed with pain; he turned the pistol toward Dante but didn't pull the trigger. As she was crawling over to him, Colomba slid her dive hammer out of the utility belt. Still on her knees, she slammed it down with all her might, tearing a hole in the toe of the German's left boot, shattering the bone within. Then she swiftly raised it again and brought it down on the wrist of the arm with the gun. The German dropped his pistol. Colomba didn't bother to go after the gun but just kept hammering the German himself, with blows to the body, the face, the knees, while Dante grabbed him from behind and tried to shove him to the ground. Together they managed to topple him. Dante held his legs while Colomba pinned his face into the wet lakeshore mud, forcing him to breathe dirt. Shaking with adrenaline and rage, she raised the hammer to bring it down on the back of his head, catching herself only at the last second, altering trajectory just enough to smash into his cheek, which lacerated and sprayed out a handful of teeth and a spurt of blood. The German shouted with a mouth full of mud, struggling like a wounded bear, but Colomba kept his face crushed down with both hands until he stopped moving.

Then she turned him over and cleaned off his face so he could breathe again. She turned her headlamp back on and lit up his badly dented face. She was appalled to see him up close: he was an old man with white hair and a wrinkled nose.

Dante crawled away and covered his face again. Colomba bent over him, without taking her eyes off the German. "How do you feel?"

"I feel like I'm dying."

Colomba put an arm around his shoulder. "No, you're not dying. You were great."

"I can't do this, CC. It's too much. It's just too much."

Colomba squeezed him. "Dante. I still need you. Please don't abandon me now."

Dante panted feverishly for a few more seconds. "What do you need me to do?"

"Help me tie him up. Before he regains consciousness. Otherwise I'll have to hit him again, and this time I'd kill him."

Dante stared at her, his eyes filled with tears. "Well, would that be a bad thing?"

"Yes. It would."

Dante dried his eyes, and Colomba helped him get back onto his feet. "Are you okay?" she asked.

"I've never felt so bad in my life."

"You're a lucky man. Go see if there's anything in the truck we can tie him up with."

Dante limped away, and Colomba felt herself all over to see if anything was broken. It seemed as though nothing was, even though every bone in her body hurt, but she was so overjoyed to have the man of Dante's nightmares right there in front of her, finally rendered helpless, that it almost didn't matter. Still keeping an eye on the German, she bent over to search for the gun he'd dropped. She found it stuck in the mud, barrel first. It was a Glock 19 with a plastic handle.

Colomba unscrewed the silencer, because she didn't know how to aim with one, then pointed it at her prisoner, who was just starting to blink his eyes.

"Who are you?" she asked him.

The man said nothing. He just lay there, breathing hoarsely, his face streaming blood and turned up to the sky.

Dante came back with two rolls of packing tape. "This could work," he said in a slightly steadier voice.

"Tape his feet first, then his hands," said Colomba.

"Okay."

"But don't ever get between me and my line of fire, understood?"

"Got it."

Dante walked over to the German and started wrapping the tape around his ankles. From close up, he realized that Colomba's hammer had driven all the way through the foot and that there were bone fragments glistening in the blood. He turned his head away and stifled the urge to vomit, wondering how on earth the man could keep from crying out in pain.

"Why did you say he's not the Father?" Colomba asked.

"Because he's not. He doesn't move like him, he doesn't walk like him. When I saw him again at the hospital, I missed it. But here I can see."

Colomba felt her head start spinning. "Are you trying to tell me that we've been chasing the wrong man? It wasn't him at the silo?"

"Yes, it was him."

"I don't follow you."

Once he was done with the ankles, Dante grabbed the German's hands and crossed them over his chest. The man put up no resistance and just kept looking at the sky. Dante started binding his hands, too, fearful that he might make some sudden movement.

Realizing his misgivings, Colomba stepped closer and pressed the pistol barrel against the prisoner's forehead. "Be a good boy, eh?" she said.

He remained impassive.

"I told you, he's not the Father. He *is* the man I saw that night, but he's not the man who came in with a ski mask over his head and dark glasses to give me lessons. I think he might be shorter, and he's certainly more powerfully built. When I saw him through the crack in the silo wall, I associated him with the Father, but he was the only human being whose face I'd seen in eleven years of imprisonment. I was just wrong." When he was done binding the man's wrists, he stood up to admire his work. "He didn't take care of prisoners like me. Now I understand that he had another job."

Colomba stared at that expressionless face. "The killer. So all that whimpering you did was just put on for show?"

"Let's say it was, from a certain point onward anyway. As long as he thought I was completely helpless, he wasn't going to waste a lot of time on me." He turned to look at Colomba. "What are we going to do with him now?"

"We aren't going to do anything with him. We need to finish hauling up the drum."

Dante nodded. "Can we do it even if you don't guide the cable?"

"We have no alternative. My tank is out of oxygen, and in any case I'm in no shape to dive again. We just have to pray it doesn't get snagged."

"All right, then, I'll start the winch."

Dante started to climb back aboard the truck, but the night's darkness was suddenly broken by the beams of flashlights. Someone shouted, and the eardrum-shattering noise of a police siren split the air.

The German had wasted too much of their time; the police were already there.

24

Colomba and Dante, shivering from the cold and covered with mud and blood, were searched, and their hands were cuffed behind them. Meanwhile, the cops from the police headquarters of Cremona and Milan swarmed in from the dirt road that ran through the trees, and squad cars were arranged in a semicircle so their headlights could be used to illuminate the scene.

Once the area was safely locked down, Santini ordered his men to give first aid to the bound man who lay on the grass and to call an ambulance.

Colomba thought about how close they'd come to recovering the barrel. Ten minutes, maybe less. After everything they'd done, they'd been screwed just as they were about to cross the finish line. It was the burden of defeat, more than the shame of being arrested, that made her drop her eyes. Dante, absorbed in his thoughts, couldn't get his mind off the idea that he was going to be tossed into a dark cell where he'd never see the sky again.

Santini slouched over to them with his hands in his pockets, without ever having pulled his government-issue revolver. He seemed almost as tired as Colomba and Dante. "Who's the half-dead guy, Caselli?"

Colomba looked up at him and pretended to be unruffled. "They call him the German. He works for the Father."

"That's enough of this Father crap . . . cut it out, Caselli. No one's going to believe that you're as crazy as your friend."

"Then what do you think he's doing here?"

"I don't know. But I've come to realize that I don't care. My job here is done."

Colomba ground her teeth, even as they were chattering with the cold. "That's easy for you to say."

"You should have done the same thing. A long time ago." An officer handed Santini the Glock in a clear plastic bag. "Is this yours?" he asked Colomba.

"No, it's his," Colomba replied. "It's what he used to shoot us. Do a gunshot residue test on his hand, and you'll see."

Santini turned to look at the German, his wounds covered with bandages from the first aid given him by a couple of officers. His foot kept oozing blood in spite of the fact that it was completely wrapped in gauze. "Did you hear what they just said? Is it true that you were trying to kill them?"

"I don't have any idea who these people are," the German whispered. "They attacked me."

Santini asked for the man's ID. Piero Frabetti, he read. "And just what were you doing down here, Signor Frabetti?"

"Taking a walk."

"At night?"

"Please . . . I'm not well. Could you cut me loose, please?" His hands and legs were still bound with the packing tape.

"Maybe later," said Santini. "Where the fuck is that ambulance?" he shouted.

"It's coming, ten minutes," replied the lieutenant from the CIS who was accompanying him, the one who spoke the northern dialect. "There was a major accident on the county road, and all the mobile ER units are busy."

"What a fucked-up city this is," Santini muttered. "Take Caselli away, with her friend. Straight back to Rome, okay?"

"All right. What about him?" he asked, pointing at the German.

"Hand him over to the Cremona colleagues. They'll figure things out."

The lieutenant issued appropriate instructions. Colomba was shivering with cold and anger. "Santini . . . the proof of what we've been telling you is in the lake!" she shouted. "Just reel in that winch! There's a fifty-five-gallon drum attached to it!"

"And what's in the drum, the Father?" laughed Santini.

"It would take you five fucking minutes—"

"That's five minutes too long. *Ciao*, Caselli."

He turned his back on the prisoners and walked over to the lake-shore, lighting a cigarette as he went. His stomach hurt, and all he wanted was to do was get some sleep. But before that a shower, and even before that a glass of something strong. Maybe more than one.

"Are they really going to leave it all here?" Dante asked, bewildered, while the officers were pushing them toward the squad cars at the edge of the trees.

"They'll put guards on the area and wait for the magistrate to arrive from Cremona," Colomba explained. "At that point he'll have the barrel pulled up. Maybe."

"And what will they do with it?"

"It'll be taken to the forensic squad's laboratory and opened up."

"It'll disappear during the trip," Dante pointed out. "Or from the laboratory. And too much time will go by. We need to haul it up now, CC. Before the Father realizes he needs to get rid of all evidence. Which means the children . . ."

"Dante . . . we tried . . ."

Dante looked around feverishly, and his gaze landed on Santini. How had he managed to miss him until now? "We still have one chance," he said, jutting his chin in Santini's direction.

"That's enough talking, you two," one of the cops escorting them warned them.

"Oh, go fuck yourself, penguin," Colomba retorted, and her voice vibrated with an authority so profound that the cop fell silent. Then she told Dante, "Santini is on De Angelis's side."

"But he's not on the Father's side," said Dante frantically.

"Why do you think that?"

"Just look at him. Look at his bowed shoulders, his hands in his pockets. If he was happy with the way things are going, he'd be pounding his chest like a gorilla. Instead he's in a state of crisis. He knows something's wrong." In a loud voice, he added, "Isn't it true that you've figured it out, Santini? Something's wrong. And you're wondering whether someone might not be leading you around by the nose!"

Santini didn't turn around, but Colomba saw his back stiffen. The policemen who were holding Dante jerked him toward the path to the edge of the trees. He put up resistance, and a third officer came over to help his colleagues lift him physically off the ground.

"Maybe you don't even like children, Deputy Chief Santini!"

Dante went on shouting. "But one day, when you discover that Luca Maugeri and Ruggero Palladino died in a cage, you're not going to be able to sleep at night! Because that will have been your fault. Because you didn't have the courage to act according to your conscience."

Santini swung around, tight-faced. "Who is Ruggero Palladino?"

The policemen stopped to let their superior officer talk to the prisoners.

"Another boy who was taken by the Father," Dante replied. "Just like me. With the help of that man tied up on the ground. And I believe there are others waiting to be freed, though I can't be positive of that fact."

"Your kidnapper has been dead for twenty-five years, Torre. You're delirious," Santini said. But once again Colomba noticed that he lacked the brutal certainty he'd once had. Dante was right; Santini was in a crisis state.

"Then why did the German try to kill us?"

"I don't know what happened here."

Dante smiled. "But you do know that the German is dangerous, since you didn't even have his hands cut loose. And if we're right about him, there's a chance that we're right about the children. That's what you're thinking."

"No, I'm just thinking I want to be done with this whole mess," said Santini. His voice was uncharacteristically soft and distant.

"And you *can* be done with it. In the best way imaginable. Have the fuel drum recovered and opened."

Colomba had remained silent to keep from interrupting the communication between the two men. But at that point she could no longer resist. "I know what it means to carry a sense of guilt with you, Santini. I just hope for your sake that it never happens to you, not for something like this."

Santini was about to come up with an answer, but he said nothing because he suddenly caught a glimpse of himself reflected in the eyes of his men. A middle-aged policeman in a trench coat too light for the chilly weather that night, a man his younger colleagues regarded with fear because of his rages and tongue-lashings and whom his older colleagues shunned because they distrusted him. And he realized they were right, because there are all kinds of cops, but the worst kind is the cop who just doesn't care anymore. He didn't care whether they caught the right guy or the wrong one, he didn't care if someone got hurt or died, if the person he sent behind bars was innocent or guilty. Because the only important thing was to archive the case file and not have complications, to "go along to get along," as his mother liked to say. As a boy he used to dream of being the star of one of those scenes you see in the movies, where the cop gets a round of applause from his partners for having done something heroic, standing there bathed in an angelic light, but that character had slowly vanished from his imagination, transformed instead into a drab gray functionary who always knew which side of the table he ought to sit at, who to blame and who to praise. But now he realized that he didn't even care about that anymore, he didn't give a damn about his career. He felt used up and old, hopeless. "You know what you're asking me to do, don't you?" he asked.

"Yes. To do the right thing. How long has it been since you tried it?" Colomba replied.

Santini shut his eyes for a moment; then he turned toward the officers who were searching the truck. "Does any of you know how to use that fucking winch?"

The lieutenant from the north grabbed Santini by the sleeve. "Could I talk to you for a second, sir?"

Santini shook free. "No, you can't. Well? Is anyone going to answer me, or do I have to do it all myself?"

An officer on the truck raised his hand. "I do. My father taught me, on a construction site."

"That's what I wanted, the story of your life . . . Run the winch, and reel in whatever's attached to the end of that cable."

"Yes, sir," said the officer.

"What about them, sir?" asked the policeman who was holding Colomba.

"Let them wait."

The cop who had raised his hand hoisted himself up onto the deck of the truck and started the winch. The cable tautened and rose; the sound of the motor rose in pitch as if it were under strain, until

Colomba was afraid it might be about to seize up. Then the cable started slowly reeling in, hauling its load as it did. The policeman at the controls really did know what he was doing, because he slowed the motor every time he heard it laboring. The other officers were standing around in a semicircle, watching, talking in low voices, intrigued and filled with anticipation. The cable reeled in for about thirty feet; then it stopped.

"It must have snagged on something," shouted the policeman running the winch.

Santini shook his head in resignation. "Put on your gloves!" he shouted.

"What?" asked the lieutenant from the north.

"All of you, put on your gloves and haul on that fucking cable. Get moving. Except for you," he added, speaking to the men guarding the prisoners.

"We're not going to run away, Santini," said Colomba.

"I'm not interested in taking the risk. Whatever turns out to be in your drum, I'm taking you back to Rome, on foot if necessary."

The officers lined up along the cable and grabbed it, jerking and lifting until the drum came unsnagged with a jerk. The men let go of the cable, and a few of them even clapped their hands with satisfaction.

So I got my applause after all, Santini thought to himself, almost amused.

One of the officers closest to the lake put his fingers in his mouth and emitted a shrill whistle when the water began to splash. "Something's starting to surface!" he shouted in his excitement.

The man at the controls slowed the motor, and the barrel, encrusted with algae and mud, slowly slid out of the water, across the beach, and onto the grass, until it came to a halt a few yards from the lake's edge. The winch was turned off, and two officers freed it from the hooks, spattering their uniforms with mud as they did so.

"Do you have anything to open it with?" asked Santini.

"Use the jaws of life," Colomba replied. "There's one on the truck."

Santini gave the order to find it, and the officer who had operated the winch hoisted it off the truck and dragged it over to the drum. It was like a giant pair of pliers connected to a portable air compressor.

Rescue crews used such devices to cut through the metal of crashed cars and free the passengers trapped inside.

Meanwhile, an ambulance had finally appeared at the entrance to the dirt road, and two paramedics in reflective jackets pulled a collapsible stretcher out of the back. The lieutenant from the north went over to them and guided them back to the German, who was quickly examined and strapped onto the gurney. Dante couldn't take his eyes off him. Even now that he knew who he was, or at least who he *wasn't*, the man exercised a morbid fascination on him, like a nightmare made flesh, even stronger than the spell cast by the plastic drum that had finally emerged from the water. The paramedics used a scalpel to cut the tape off his ankles and wrists; then the lieutenant handcuffed the German to the gurney by one wrist and one ankle, just to be safe. In spite of his age and his injuries, there was something about him he found unsettling, and the paramedics clearly felt the same way, seeing that they said nothing about the handcuffing, even though they could have been counted upon to object loudly under normal circumstances. To cuff the German's ankle, the lieutenant had to lift his pants leg, revealing a tattoo on his shin. It depicted a small blue bird that vaguely resembled the Twitter logo; the color had faded over the years.

For Dante, seeing it was like an insect bite that puffed up rapidly, turning into a painful swollen lymph node: all of it inside his head. "That's not possible," he murmured. But it added up, it held the whole story together. *My God . . . that could be the explanation*, he thought.

In the meantime, the policeman carrying the jaws of life approached the drum. He turned on the air compressor and tested the jack, which opened and closed, huffing and puffing like the hand of a robot in an old movie.

Santini went over and inspected the drum by the light of his Maglite. He realized that he was still in time to turn back. He realized that he could still reverse his decision.

"Should I go ahead?" the officer asked timidly.

Santini nodded. "Yes. And watch out for what's inside."

"This is it, Dante," Colomba announced.

But he wasn't listening: he was bent over on his knees, shaking.

"Dante?" said Colomba, trying to get closer to him but held back by the cop. "Let go of me! Can't you see he's not well?"

But Dante wasn't unwell. And when he did look up, Colomba realized that he was laughing so hard he was about to choke. Hysterical laughter that he couldn't hold in. "God, Colomba. The bluebird, 1989, don't you understand? It all fits together."

"What all fits together? And let go of me!" she snapped at the officer.

"An urban legend. I was held prisoner by an urban legend. No, wait. I wasn't a prisoner. I was an artichoke."

"You're delirious, Dante."

"No, I'm not . . ." and he laughed again.

Colomba started to ask him other questions, but her voice was drowned out by the sound of the jaws of life lacerating the plastic drum, producing a large tear at the top. A tremendous stench of rotten eggs spread into the air. The policeman took a step backward in disgust, but without letting go of the hydraulic pliers. He gave the tool one last twist, spilling the fetid contents of the barrel onto the grass. It was a dense, light brown liquid, which seethed on contact with the ground.

"What is this shit?" asked Santini, clamping his handkerchief to his nose. Then he fell silent, because at the center of the stinking puddle he'd spotted something unmistakable, the white of a human jawbone.

25

There were nineteen barrels in the lake, and they were all recovered over the course of a day by the police dive team and subsequently examined by the Cremona forensic squad with the support of their colleagues from the LABANOF (Laboratory of Forensic Anthropology and Odontology) in Milan. Every one of them contained a mixture of sulfuric acid and human remains, though before they could determine the exact number of victims it would be necessary to await the results of the DNA tests; in fact, the acid had left only a few scraps of the bodies that had been immersed in it: mostly teeth, but also fragments of larger bones, kidney stones, prosthetic implants, and traces of fat. The victims' ages ranged from seventeen to sixty; they'd been killed at least twenty-five years ago, and their corpses had been dismembered.

In the meantime, Santini had been forced to give up his plan to take his prisoners back to Rome, because in the wake of the macabre discovery they'd been claimed by the head of the district attorney's office in Cremona, Angela Spinelli, an energetic woman in her early sixties with a short fuse; she'd been alerted to the situation by a call from Curcio, who knew her from the old days, long before they had both gone gray. De Angelis kicked up a tremendous fuss, but to no avail: Colomba and Dante were to be left in custody of the local police, to ensure that the Lombard judicial investigators could be afforded easy access to them. Or to Colomba, at least, because the minute he was marched through the front door of police headquarters, Dante went into an extended fit that Colomba assumed was at least partly faked, though quite convincingly, with head butts to the walls and lots of broken glass. He was promptly sedated and admitted to the neurological ward of the municipal hospital. There he was held under police guard, declared unfit for questioning, and confined to observation and bed rest.

The burden of the interrogations thus fell to Colomba, who did her best to persuade Spinelli and her team about just where the corpses had come from. At first, she was pretty unsuccessful. Her story of long-ago military kidnappers, and of ties to first the bombing in Paris and later Rovere's death, aroused a great deal of skepticism, especially in view of the fact that she was facing charges of being a dangerous psychopathic bomber herself. In her high-security cell, during the short intervals between one interview and the next, Colomba kept wondering what Dante had been talking about with his "artichokes" and "bluebirds"; that is, assuming the words meant anything at all. And she wondered if the answers to those questions would do anything to help her persuade her audience. Probably not, considering Dante's usual thinking processes. Although her situation as a suspect neither improved nor worsened, the German's was plummeting drastically.

The investigators discovered almost immediately that his ID was fake, that he had gunshot residue on his hands, and that a partial fingerprint was also found on one of the Glock shells, proof that he'd loaded it himself and hadn't just found it by accident, if there were anyone willing to believe that explanation in the first place. The German had refused to provide his true identity or offer explanations of any kind, and he'd remained silent, at first in the hospital and subsequently in the prison infirmary. His fingerprints weren't on file, his photo wasn't found in the archive, no relatives had called to inquire about him: a Mr. Nobody, even though he did show a vague resemblance to the identikit Dante had helped put together at the time of his liberation, which was still in the court's files.

Exactly what he'd done, aside from ruining Colomba's dive, began to become clear when his clothing was examined and the investigators found traces of the DNA of a young Roman man and woman who had been found with their throats cut in their apartment: Jorge and his girlfriend. The German's status was therefore officially upgraded to murder suspect and his detention transformed from temporary detainment to full-blown arrest. His new investigatory file was added to the others. Colomba, too, was transferred to the local house of detention, in defiance of Counselor Minutillo's strong and lively objections. Minutillo had flown up from Rome with a demand for her release. Colomba was placed in the special security wing of the prison, among child molesters and corrupt policemen, and she fell asleep instantly without a thought for her unpleasant company. While she was sleeping, the Rome Mobile Squad tracked down the German's nondescript apartment and found, in their search of the place, six false passports from a variety of countries for six different identities. One of those names led the police to a garage in the Tiburtina neighborhood, where they found stacks of unlabeled pharmaceuticals in noncommercial packaging. How had the German procured them, and what were they for? Questioned on that point, the man simply stared at the ceiling.

Four days after the opening of the barrels, while the newspapers were beginning to debate whether the woman at the center of that story was a murderous lunatic or a misunderstood heroine, Colomba was awakened at dawn by the prison guards and hastily marched into the interview room. There she found Spinelli awaiting her arrival.

In spite of the early hour and her weariness, Colomba displayed her usual respect for the investigating magistrates. "At your disposal, your honor," she said.

The prosecuting magistrate ran the back of her hand over her forehead. She, too, seemed tired and worried. "I've come to ask you for your cooperation, and I have to make it clear that, if you choose to accept, we're not offering any kind of deal. My hands are tied, as far as that goes."

Colomba didn't understand, but she nodded anyway. "Just tell me what you need."

"Six hours ago, the Rome Mobile Squad got a tip. A man who says he'd handled a real estate transaction, a property purchase, on behalf of the suspect now in detention whom we know as the German. Before you ask, in this transaction, too, he used a false name."

"What property is this?" Colomba asked.

"A farmhouse near the western bypass road of Rome. The officers of the Mobile Squad entered the property and found ten industrial shipping containers. The containers had been modified with the addition of small entry hatches"—she hesitated—"and the entry hatches had been booby-trapped."

Colomba felt a shiver of horror. "Booby-trapped?"

"With C-4 and detonators: handmade but extremely sophisticated. If the doors are forced or opened in any but the exact right way, all ten of the containers will blow sky high."

Colomba leapt to her feet and grabbed the judge's hand. "They're in there, aren't they?"

The judge didn't pull back, and she nodded to the officer observing the conversation to stay where he was. "We . . . don't know for certain."

Colomba let herself drop back down into her chair. "The children . . ."

"Maybe," said Spinelli. "What we're asking you is to go to the place and provide whatever information you possess to facilitate the work of the rescue squad. It'll take the bomb squad about six hours to finish their work. By then you'll be there, obviously under armed guard—that is, if you give your consent."

Colomba was filled with hope. She did her best to push that hope away, out of fear of jinxing herself, but she couldn't do it. She kept thinking of the children, praying they were still alive. "Of course I'll go, your honor . . . Anything you ask. But it's Dante you need, not me."

Spinelli flashed her a half smile. "He asked for you, Deputy Captain. Your presence is one of the conditions he set for being there. Among other things."

The other things were a Neapolitan coffeepot, a camp stove, and a sack of ground, freshly roasted single-origin arabica coffee from the Torrefazione Vittoria of Cremona, which he had been told was the best coffee roaster in the area. When she was escorted under armed guard to his hospital room, Colomba found him stretched out on the bed drinking his tenth cup with an ecstatic expression. She was handcuffed; he had a male nurse keeping an eye on everything he did. They didn't hug, but they did smile, and Colomba saw that he was beside himself with excitement.

"Did you hear, CC? They've found them."

"They're not positive," said Colomba.

Dante sighed in exasperation. "I am. Trust me."

"I will when you explain to me about the bluebird."

He flashed his sarcastic grin. "Soon. I don't want to talk about it before getting my thoughts organized. And I have to read a boring document in English that Roberto brought me this morning."

"In English?"

"Yes, and as a language, there's far too much of it around, I agree. I'd have already finished if they would let me have Internet access."

"You can forget about that," said the male nurse.

"You see? How are they taking us to Rome? In an armored car?"

"Helicopter."

Dante lost his smile. "Not a chance."

"It's an air ambulance. You'll be asleep the whole way. We'll sedate you here. And you'll wake up at the airport. With me right next to you," said Colomba.

Dante writhed on the bed. "I can't breathe, I need air."

"You'll get plenty of air on the flight, too much, even," said Colomba, tersely. "And try to remember why you're doing it."

Dante continued to writhe for another good minute, sweating copiously. "Okay. But I want to be sedated *now*; otherwise I'll change my mind."

"No problem," said the male nurse. "If that would make you shut up for a minute. I'll go call the doctor."

Dante was sedated, placed in a stretcher, and then loaded onto the helicopter. Boarding with him were Colomba, Spinelli, and three officers from the Cremona Mobile Squad. It seemed to Colomba that the flight lasted a lifetime, but just two hours later she was looking down on the asphalt of the Rome bypass highway as it rose up beneath her and then a ramshackle building surrounded by the earth-tone rectangles of the shipping containers, half-hidden in the trees. It was ten in the morning on the dot when they landed. Dante was brought to with an injection of stimulant. He leapt to his feet as if spring-loaded, running in his dressing gown and slippers straight toward the line of policemen surrounding the building. He was halted by the men of his police escort, handcuffed, and led with Colomba to see the director of operations, none other than Curcio, with his usual rumpled appearance.

"Signor Torre, at last we meet. Madame Judge . . ." They shook hands; then Curcio looked Colomba in the eyes. "Deputy Captain

Caselli, I'm happy to know you, even if you might well wish you were anywhere but here."

"I wouldn't be anywhere else for anything on earth," she replied. "I understand you've taken my case to heart, sir. I've wanted a chance to thank you."

He shook his head. "Wait and see how it turns out before you say that. You're still in a state of detention. Madame Judge, are the handcuffs really necessary?"

"I'm afraid they are."

Curcio shrugged and spoke to Dante. "What can you tell us?"

Dante looked at the containers. They were old pieces of junk covered with graffiti and rust, arranged in an irregular fan shape, each some twenty feet distant from the next. Dante decided that they were even smaller than his silo. Narrower. He felt his breath catch, but the sedative still circulating in his blood placated him. "Have you opened them yet?" he asked.

"Not yet; we're waiting for the bomb squad to run some last checks."

"The young children won't give you any problems," said Dante. "But you'll have to sedate the older boys immediately."

"Why?"

"Because they've grown up in there. And they've learned the rules. You can't leave for any reason whatsoever. You can't even think of leaving. Give them chocolate. That's the reward."

"The reward?" Curcio asked.

"For when we're good boys," Dante explained.

"Understood," said Curcio, trying not to shiver.

"And make sure Ruggero Palladino's parents come. And Luca Maugeri's father. Both of those boys are in there."

"You can't be so certain," Spinelli broke in. "And Stefano Maugeri is being detained under court order. We'd need the permission of the supervisory judge."

"Then send for his sister-in-law, Giulia Balestri." He dictated from memory her address and phone number.

Curcio took note. "If you're wrong, it's going to be a cruel trick to play on them," he said.

"I'm never wrong. Just ask your colleague."

The colleague was Colomba. She smiled. "He's wrong quite often, but he's not this time."

Curcio nodded and handed the sheet of paper with the names and details to Lieutenant Infanti, who turned purple when he saw Colomba. She ignored him, and he hurried away.

Half an hour later, a fiber-optic cable was inserted into the first shipping container. On the monitor they saw that it had been transformed into a minuscule prison, with its own chemical toilet. A filthy adolescent boy with long hair was shaking uncontrollably, standing with his face to the wall, hands clasped behind his back. *Like a school-boy being punished*, thought Colomba.

Dante recommended having a single man go in, without uniform, without weapons. A paramedic with an especially reassuring appearance and a degree in psychology was chosen. He entered the container after one of the bomb squad men cut the detonator wires and pried open the door. The prisoner went on staring at the wall, pretending not to notice. At Dante's suggestion, the paramedic called him "son" and placed his hand on his shoulder. The prisoner screamed and began running in circles in the container until he could be detained and sedated. From an examination of his physical condition, the rescue team was able to determine that he hadn't been given food or water in the past several days.

As Dante had predicted, the younger children reacted less drastically, within the limits of their conditions. Dante recognized the symptoms of autism in three of the younger children and two adolescents, varying in gravity from individual to individual.

The fourth adolescent greeted his rescuer brandishing a piece of wood, but he lowered it immediately when Dante called to him from outside the container: "Stop, Beast!" The boy kneeled to the ground with his head between his hands.

Dante mentally asked the boy's forgiveness and felt filthy inside. Then he broke into tears, as did nearly everyone present and as did many viewers later that evening as they watched footage caught by a person with a cell phone in the adjoining fields.

The boy extracted from the ninth container was Ruggero Palladino, and his parents got out of the carabinieri helicopter just in time to give him a hug before the sedative took effect. The last boy was slightly pudgy, his eyeglasses held together with adhesive tape, and he was strangely calm. Luca Maugeri. When she saw him, his aunt Giulia fainted and had to be attended to by a doctor.

"It's over," Colomba told Dante, hugging him in spite of the handcuffs.

She couldn't have been more wrong, but of course she didn't know that yet.

26

Colomba was taken back to the Cremona house of detention and Dante to the hospital, but their situations were quite different now. Colomba realized it from the number of officers who had gone back to calling her "deputy captain" and addressing her as "ma'am" instead of just "hey, you." Dante noticed the growing number of rubberneckers and fans crowding outside the windows of his hospital room, as the news of his role in rescuing the prisoners began to spread. If anyone had nominated him for the Nobel Prize or for sainthood, there would very likely have been a groundswell of support. There was also a drastic change in the status of Stefano Maugeri, who was released immediately once his son was found alive; there was also a corresponding change in the status of De Angelis, who was promptly and urgently stripped of all authority in the investigation of the Vivaro mountain meadows murder by the Superior Council of the Magistrature, Italy's highest judicial body. De Angelis held two press conferences in twenty-four hours: the first to denounce the decision, the second to announce his retirement from the judiciary to devote himself to a private legal practice; both press conferences were by and large ignored.

The investigations of Colomba and Dante were thus transferred to the Cremona district attorney's office; that office immediately ordered Dante's release and began laying the groundwork to do the same with Colomba once the German's arsenal was discovered, seven days after the plastic drums were opened. The arsenal was found near the Roman farmhouse where the containers had been hidden. Not only were there handguns and rifles of various makes and provenances, there was also twenty pounds of C-4 with the same chemical signature as that used in the bombing that had killed Rovere. Along with it was a floor plan of Rovere's apartment.

If De Angelis had still been in charge of the investigation, he probably would have claimed that the German and Colomba were surely accomplices and perhaps even lovers, but luckily everything had changed. Colomba was released from prison on the morning of the eighth day but wasn't even given time to enjoy a breath of fresh air before she was hastily ushered into a briefing at the district attorney's office. Dante was the keynote speaker. It was going to be held on a sunny terrace. When Colomba saw him arrive in an impeccable black suit and with a cocky attitude, she understood that the audience was going to be treated to quite a show that day.

Dante stopped a few yards short of the table, waiting to make sure everyone was looking at him, smiled, lit a cigarette, and then shook hands all around, announcing his name each time. There were Curcio, Spinelli, her secretary, the forensic archaeologist from LABANOF who had performed the examination of the bones, and a man in his early sixties with a beard and a buzz cut, without a hair out of place. Colomba immediately identified him as a carabiniere. His name was Di Marco, and he was a colonel in the Internal Information and Security Agency, or IISA.

Dante shook his hand with an eager grin. "So they managed to talk you into it," he said.

"I hope this isn't going to be a waste of time," the colonel replied, grimly.

"Actually, that's exactly what you do hope," Dante observed and sat down at one end of the table, sliding to the center a pile of folders that he'd brought with him. "This is a short report that I drew up in the past few days, strictly as a memo. At the end you'll find a short bibliography concerning the principal topics."

Everyone took a copy: it was about twenty typed pages stapled together. Colomba already knew what was in it because Minutillo had given her an advance peek at the document before she was released from jail, to make sure she was prepared. If she hadn't lived through what she'd lived through in the past several weeks, she would have considered it a compilation of idiocies. Instead it all made perfect sense to her.

The man from IISA looked at the headline on the first page of the report and turned pale. It said: PROJECT BLUEBIRD.

❖   ❖   ❖

"Let me remind you all that today's meeting is informal in nature and that we called it to give Signor Torre a chance to express his view of the events now under investigation by this district attorney's office," Spinelli began. "Can you briefly summarize what you think is at issue here, Signor Torre?"

Dante smiled. "In two words? National interest."

"Maybe we're going to need more than two words, in that case," said Spinelli, baffled.

"Let's start with the established facts. You'll find an outline on page two of your document," Dante began in an exaggeratedly affected tone of voice: the only thing missing was a pair of pince-nez glasses to make him look like a professor of days gone by. There was a rustling of pages. "In 1975," he went on, "the Church Committee of the US Senate certified that, beginning in 1950 and continuing at least to 1973, the CIA, with the cooperation of the FBI, carried out a series of experiments on behavioral control and the alteration of personalities by means of such drugs as LSD and barbiturates, physical violence, coercion, and sensory deprivation. The avowed purpose was to create agents capable of obeying orders even in defiance of their own free will, as well as to withstand interrogation. In their defense, they were afraid of the possibility that the Soviet Union might beat them to it," he added ironically. "They were hoping to use the agents against Castro, along with the exploding cigars."

"The Manchurian Candidate," said Roberta, the scientist from LABANOF.

Curcio looked at her in amazement. "You've heard of it?"

"They even made a movie about it," she replied with a smile.

"More than one," said Dante. "But those who have made serious studies of the topic consider that the declared objective was just a cover. It's impossible to force someone to kill if he doesn't want to; you can't make people obey posthypnotic commands like so many robots. And simply paying a professional killer costs less. Altering an opponent's personality, breaking it or deleting inconvenient memories, on the other hand, is far more useful for a government and its henchmen."

"Who were the subjects of the experiments?" asked Curcio, his curiosity piqued.

"First and foremost, thousands of US soldiers, who according to the rules of engagement were all considered to be 'volunteers.' They also used convicts from prisons, patients from hospitals and insane asylums, and unsuspecting citizens selected at random. In particular, among those who were given LSD without their knowledge, there were numerous suicides, acts of self-mutilation, outbursts of violence, and long-term cases of psychosis. We know that in one case all the clients of a house of prostitution were drugged and brutally interrogated, in the sure knowledge that none of them would file a complaint. In another case, a substance that was designed to trigger psychotic episodes was dispersed as an aerosol spray in the subway."

"That's never been proved," said Di Marco.

Dante grinned his sarcastic grin. "True, in part because in 1973 the CIA director, Richard Helms, ordered most of the documents on the experiments destroyed. Other documents were intentionally mis-filed, and finding them turned out to be very challenging, even for the investigators. In spite of that, there are at least twenty thousand pages of documentation in the possession of the US Congress, and they're now declassified and freely accessible thanks to the Freedom of Information Act."

"Might I ask you what any of this has to do with what we're working on now?" asked Spinelli.

"I'm afraid I'm going to have to come to that by steps, if you'll forgive me," Dante replied. "In any case, what the CIA scientists were working on was at first known as Project Bluebird, just like *Sialia sialis*, the state bird of New York; in 1951, however, the project changed its name to Artichoke, because the idea was to 'peel away' layer after layer in the subjects' minds, the same way you might do with the leaves of an artichoke."

"Nice image," Curcio muttered.

"Then the name was changed again to MKUltra, a more neutral term. I believe you know the meaning of the word 'ultra,' Colonel."

Di Marco nodded imperceptibly. "It dates back to the Second World War. The highest level of secrecy."

"According to the findings of the Church Committee, there were more than a hundred and fifty subprojects that fell under the jurisdiction of MKUltra, all of them funded separately."

"Just for the sake of the historical record, did this vast deployment of resources lead to any useful results?" asked Spinelli.

"Not according to the CIA. According to several scholars, however, including Naomi Klein, the results of MKUltra are at the foundation of all modern torture techniques used by special forces around the world."

"Signor Torre," Spinelli replied, "what you're telling us is certainly fascinating and no doubt well documented. But we're talking about a long time ago, in a different country."

"And the project was shut down in 1974," the colonel pointed out.

"In the United States, perhaps," said Dante. "In the rest of the world . . . there are no reliable data. And what information there was has been destroyed."

"In the rest of the world?" asked Curcio.

Dante nodded. "After the Church Committee, the US Congress ordered the cessation of all experimentation on American citizens. But it made no mention of foreign citizens. Yet there was an entire section of the project that focused on experiments outside the United States, and we know for certain that experiments were done all over Europe, even though the only surviving records concern two experiments undertaken in, respectively, France and Canada. The section that operated overseas was called MKDelta." He smiled. "Sorry, but the military lacks imagination."

"Especially when the military is asked to listen to fairy tales," said Di Marco. "Do you realize what you're telling us?"

"Everything I've set forth here is documented."

"But the idea of tying MKUltra to what happened to you is pure conjecture." Di Marco looked around the table at the others; Colomba looked back with all the malevolence she could muster. "Does anyone really believe that the CIA was behind what happened to Signor Torre?"

No one spoke.

Dante narrowed his eyes. "Do you remember what was going on at the time, Colonel? The Western intelligence services feared that Italy was about to be lost to a communist revolution, and they were ready to do whatever was necessary to prevent it."

"It was a terrible time," Di Marco admitted.

"And terrible times demand terrible solutions, evidently."

"However, nothing that you're talking about has been the subject of any judicial investigation," Curcio broke in. "We'd know if it had. The way we learned about other crimes committed by the deviant intelligence services."

"Do you really think we know everything that happened?" asked Dante. "And what we're talking about was a small, controlled experiment, the security for which was run by a few men selected carefully from the ranks of the Italian army, men like Ferrari and Bellomo, under the German's orders. And with only twenty guinea pigs, an assortment of children and adults, isolated, tortured, and stuffed with psychotropic substances by a scientist who called himself the Father, the director of the project, in collaboration with the German. One director whose expertise was security and who may have come out of the intelligence services; another whose area was the scientific aspect, as it were, and who was a civilian."

"We don't have any records showing that Bellomo and the others were in the army," said Spinelli.

"That's understandable if the top ranks of the military—or, more plausibly, *someone* in the top ranks of the military—preferred not to have the record show such a thing. If the German's team really had no links to the army, how do you explain the story that Pinna told Rovere just before dying?"

"Pure delirium," Di Marco replied.

Dante smirked. "Oh, I'm starting to see why they sent you here."

"Believe whatever you like."

"Then how do you explain the barrels? Who put them in the quarry?"

Di Marco said nothing, and Dante took advantage of the pause to study his audience. Their expressions were of bafflement, though also still of interest. The picture that was taking shape was so horrible that they all hoped it wasn't true. It was much easier to live with the idea of a serial killer than with that of a rotten limb of one's own country, capable of imprisoning and murdering innocent children and adults. No one sitting at that table was naive. All of them had seen enough in the work they did every day to lose faith in the human race. But what Dante was suggesting went beyond that; it made them feel suspicious of who might be working alongside them, whom they might be reporting to.

"Signor Torre," said Spinelli after a few moments, "no doubt the theory you're putting forth is fascinating, but it's still nothing but a hypothesis."

"But isn't that an investigator's job? To formulate hypotheses and then test them?"

"Then why don't you just throw aliens into the mix?" Di Marco asked.

"Strange you should mention aliens," Dante said. "Because, you see, after the revelations concerning the existence of MKUltra, there was an epidemic in America of people who swore they'd been kidnapped as children by soldiers and that they only remembered it much later. There are many pages on the Internet about this phenomenon; just search for the phrases 'MKUltra children' or 'MKUltra abduction.' Among them, there are several who claim that the many notorious alien abductions reported were nothing more than a cover for the experiments of MKUltra. Personally, I always assumed they were merely an urban legend. But now I find certain unsettling similarities to what happened to me." He turned to the woman from LABANOF. "Ma'am, have you by chance found something to corroborate my thesis in the remains of those poor souls?"

Caught off guard, Roberta started. "How would you know about that?"

"I saw the look on your face when I was talking about psychotropic substances."

The woman exchanged a glance with Spinelli, who nodded. "We have a great deal of work left to do, but in one fragment of a femur, there was still a certain amount of reasonably well preserved bone marrow. And, as you all may know, it is possible to detect in bone marrow residues of whatever substances were present in the bloodstream at the moment of death."

"Go on," said Spinelli.

"We believe that the victim had been subjected to the repeated administration of a substance similar to propranolol—an antianxiety agent developed in the fifties but that has recently been the subject of study because it seems capable of triggering selective amnesia."

"And that's not all," Dante added, his eyes sparkling. "It can be used for posthypnotic conditioning as well as to eliminate inhibitory brakes. It was one of the substances that the scientists at the CIA were studying in their work to come up with a truth serum."

"But that might be nothing more than a simple coincidence," said Curcio.

"Yes, but there are starting to be a lot of coincidences, don't you think? Certainly, if the German confessed, or if one of the other men in the picture said what he knows, it would all become much easier."

"Have any of them been identified?" asked Colomba.

"Only one, the man standing next to Bellomo," Curcio replied. "We've worked our way through Bellomo's and Ferrari's acquaintances, and he seems to have been a skydiving instructor who died in an accident six years ago."

"So that leaves two," said Colomba. "Including whoever took the picture."

"And we're looking for them, Deputy Captain," Curcio replied. "Just as we're searching for other ties to the German."

"So we still don't know who he is?" asked Roberta.

"Unfortunately, no," Spinelli replied. "But what we do know about him is sufficient to link him at the very least with the kidnappings and the murder of Luca Maugeri's mother. Signor Torre, if what you say were true, why at a certain point would the German and his platoon have killed all the prisoners?"

"Because times had changed and the Italian MKUltra program was shut down," Dante replied.

"If it ever existed," said Di Marco.

"We can always rely on you," Dante sneered. "In 1989, after the collapse of the Berlin Wall, the idea of a Soviet invasion became much less plausible and it became harder to justify the allocation of funds to keep the operation running. The German was ordered to clean house. And a few weeks later, he did exactly as he was told." He lit his fifth cigarette since he'd started talking. "Nineteen guinea pigs wound up in plastic drums at the bottom of the lake. One of them is here, talking to you today. The members of the brigade responsible for the surveillance and kidnapping of the guinea pigs were sent into retirement with generous pensions. The equipment and the pharmaceuticals were destroyed and burnt. We'd never have heard another word about them if the Father hadn't decided to get back into business four years ago, to judge from when the first kidnapping of the new season took place. That is, of course, unless there's a whole set of prisoners in other containers that we know nothing about."

"You said earlier that the idea of a communist invasion is obsolete these days," said Curcio. "Why would the MKUltra program have been revived?"

"I don't believe for a second that it's been revived," Dante replied. "What I think has happened is that the Father has found a new customer. He's working for a private company."

27

Dante lit his sixth cigarette since he'd begun talking, off the butt of the one before. "I believe that the Father went on studying the results of his so-called research over the years and came to the conviction, rightly or wrongly, that one of his guinea pigs, before being killed, had actually benefited from the mix of pharmaceuticals they were injected with. Am I wrong, Doctor, or is propranolol now being studied as a potential cure for a disease that is otherwise incurable?"

"Yes, autism," said the scientist from LABANOF, shaking her head as she returned to the topic at hand. "Though autism isn't a disease. It's more accurate to think of it as a cluster of personality disorders."

"True, you're quite right," Dante admitted with an apologetic smile. "And I don't know whether one of the guinea pigs really was autistic and whether he actually improved before being killed and dissolved in acid or whether the Father is simply a madman. What I do know is that he has resumed his experimentation on prisoners, choosing very specific guinea pigs to work with."

"Were they all sick, Madame Judge, even before the kidnapping?" asked Curcio.

"As of now, only five of the ten prisoners in the containers have been identified. All of them suffered from one form or another of autism or cognitive deficit," Spinelli replied.

"It can't have been a random selection," Dante observed.

"And would the Father have done this just to find a cure?" Curcio inquired.

"*Just?*" asked Dante. "Aside from the possibility that he considers this his life's mission, do you know how much an effective cure for autism would be worth on the market?"

"Billions," said Roberta. "There are at least five million people with autism in Europe alone: an enormous market. But as I was saying earlier, it's a syndrome, not a disease. Autistic patients need speech and learning therapy, not injections. Psychotropic drugs can be used in certain cases strictly to mitigate states of crisis."

"What about the theory that autism can be caused by vaccinations?" asked Curcio.

"Pure idiocy," Roberta replied tensely.

"I believe that the Father has been funded by someone who had a specific interest in having him continue with his experiments. Someone who offered him access to an ideal venue, such as Silver Compass, where he could select his guinea pigs, someone, however, who got tired of wasting his money and two years ago cut off the funds. That's why Silver Compass shut down and the Father started to sell child pornography on the Web to raise money."

"And just who would his financers be?" Curcio inquired.

"Find out who supplied him with pharmaceuticals, and you'll have your answer."

"If he's truly convinced he can find a cure," Spinelli broke in, "why hasn't be made use of a standard experimentation protocol?"

"Because no one would have approved treatment based on his methods, given the fact that he couldn't tell anybody how he got started. And because he wanted to isolate his guinea pigs, the way he did before, and that, too, wasn't possible under normal conditions." Dante shook his head. "Deputy Captain Caselli and I have always wondered why the Father didn't just take street children or abandoned kids. Why go to such extreme risks, why commit murder and stage car crashes? In the context of medical experimentation, the answer becomes clear: he needed to know everything about his guinea pigs, including any potential hereditary defects. He needed to know who the parents were, how they'd lived, what treatments they'd undergone."

"Laboratory conditions," said Roberta.

"Exactly." Dante looked over at Spinelli. "Forgive me if I jump in for a moment and ask questions myself . . . but can you tell me whether the medicines found in the German's cellar storehouse have been analyzed?"

Spinelli nodded. "So far, there have been no matches with pharmaceuticals on the market."

"Maybe they're not on the market *yet*."

"Signor Torre, would you rule out the possibility that the German was operating alone the whole time?" asked Curcio. "The presence of this Father has never been pinned down in the investigations. The German might very well know something about medicine."

Dante shook his head. "I know that you'd rather believe that he never existed, but the Father is still out there," he replied. "He has no men, he no longer has the German to kill for him, he no longer has funding. But he was the one who set the whole thing up, and he's the most dangerous one. He's the one who has to be stopped before it starts all over again somewhere else, with new guinea pigs."

For a few seconds there was silence.

"Are you done?" Di Marco asked rudely. "Because if so, I ought to go back and work on some serious matters."

"I'm done," said Dante. "Thanks so much for your invaluable contribution."

Spinelli held out her hand to the colonel from IISA. "Thanks for taking part."

"It was my duty, signora." Di Marco got up and left without saying good-bye. The others exchanged doubtful and slightly embarrassed glances. Deep down, Dante sighed. He'd hoped to be hailed as a conquering hero, but the outcome, unfortunately, was the lukewarm response he'd actually expected. He'd planted a seed; perhaps something would come of it one day. All of them, magistrates and cops, the next time they found themselves confronted with a new coincidence, a tiny significant match, might be less likely to file it away with a shrug of the shoulders. At least they might stop and think.

He lit another cigarette and felt the urge for a good espresso, followed by a Moscow Mule big enough to swim in. As he was saying good-bye to them all, thanking them for their words of praise—especially the scientist from LABANOF, Roberta, who gave him her phone number—Dante couldn't help but notice that Colomba was remaining at a distance, shut up in her own thoughts, with the grim expression of the very worst times. Yet she'd been in a good mood when she'd arrived earlier that day. And the mood had held for almost the entire meeting. What had happened? He was about to go over and talk to her, but Curcio beat him to it.

The police officer locked arms with Colomba and led her over to the parapet. She gave him a half smile, and he released her arm immediately. "What I just saw was very interesting, though I'm not sure how useful it will prove to be. What do you think about it?"

"I believe it," Colomba replied grimly.

Curcio stroked his mustache. "Even without evidence."

"We fished evidence out of the bottom of the lake. But thanks for everything all the same."

He smiled. "You've already thanked me once, when we met at the farmhouse, but if you really want to pay me back . . . why don't you come by my office one of these days? To talk about your future."

"In the police?" Colomba asked, astonished.

"It'll take a while before all your legal issues are cleared up once and for all, but I'm pretty sure everything will turn out all right. So why shouldn't we do some advance planning?"

Colomba shook her head. "Give me a few more days."

"All right. A car is going to take me back to Rome in a few minutes. Would you care to join me? With Signor Torre, if you like."

"I still have something to take care of here. I have to . . . meet someone." Looking over Curcio's shoulder, Colomba saw that Dante was coming over, and she felt a surge of panic. "I need to go, excuse me." She turned on her heel and hurried out, leaving Dante open-mouthed and feeling hurt. Colomba felt guilty for having abandoned him, but he seemed to read her mind with disturbing ease. She'd have had to lie to him, and that was something she knew she couldn't pull off. Better to just turn and run and apologize later.

The day was cold, and the lights in the shop windows made it clear that Christmas was coming. Colomba walked up the Corso and reached the old city center of Cremona, stopping at three pharmacies along the way, until she finally found what she needed. Then she turned off into a small pedestrian street onto which opened the courtyard of an eighteenth-century palazzo with cobblestones perfectly arrayed in a peacock-tail pattern behind the bronze street door. She rang the doorbell, and a housekeeper ushered her up to the second floor,

through a living room with a fireplace, and down a long hallway lined
with books.

Annibale Valle was waiting for her, sunk in an enormous armchair,
wrapped in a dressing gown that might be big enough to serve as the
mainsail of a brigantine. He was drinking from a snifter of cognac that
practically vanished in his hand. "What do you want?" he sighed. The
only light burning was a small table lamp beside him, which cast long
shadows onto his face.

He doesn't look like him, thought Colomba. *He doesn't look a thing
like him. How could I have missed it?*

"Aren't you happy that Dante and I have been let off the hook?"

He took a sip. "I called him this morning to give him my best wishes.
I invited him to lunch, too . . . I don't think he likes my house. Not
that I like it either, but it was such a good investment. He'll inherit it."

Colomba turned a chair and sat down in front of him, straddling it.
"We're going back to Rome tomorrow."

"Good," said Valle.

"But you asked what I want. Well, before we leave, there *is* something I need you to do for me." Colomba pulled the DNA kit out that
she'd bought in the pharmacy of her pocket. She tore open the sealed
envelope and pulled out the test tube; she extracted the long stick
with a sterile cotton swab on the end. "Put this in your mouth, please."

Valle half-closed his eyes. "No."

"It doesn't hurt. I'm just going to collect some of your saliva."

"No. And you can't force me to."

"I could take it by force."

"Are you willing to beat up an elderly invalid?"

"I'd be willing to beat *you* up."

Valle sighed. "How did you figure it out?"

So it's true, thought Colomba, losing the last crumb of hope that
she might be wrong. "I found the family photo album that you'd hidden at Wanda's house. The one you claimed you burned."

A sad smile wrinkled his face. "I could never bring myself to destroy
it. They were the last memories I had of him."

"Of Dante."

"Yes." He took another drink. "I had resigned myself to the fact that I'd lost him. In prison . . . I didn't even care anymore that no one believed me. Then my lawyer came to tell me that he'd been found. That he'd run from his kidnapper, who had kept him in a silo. That my son couldn't wait to see me. And I believed in the miracle."

So did I, thought Colomba. *We all did.*

"They gave me a nice suit to wear, and they took care of all the bureaucratic red tape to get me out in a hurry," Valle continued. "Word had already spread through the prison. For the first time the other convicts looked at me with something other than contempt. I was no longer . . . the child molester, the killer of kids. Someone actually gave me cigarettes, someone else gave me chocolate . . . I felt . . ." He shook his head. "I can't even begin to tell you how I felt. They took me to the hospital in a civilian car, without handcuffs. I knew that he'd look different, older. It had been eleven years. I'd last seen him as a child; now I'd be meeting him as an adult. But I didn't care." He coughed. "I went on believing in the miracle until I saw him. He shouted 'Papà!' and hugged me. But I knew."

"You knew that it wasn't him," said Colomba in a whisper.

"No. It wasn't Dante. It wasn't my son."

28

Valle poured himself another glass. He gestured toward Colomba with the bottle, but she shook her head coldly. "Go on."

"If you insist." Valle licked his lips. "The boy kept talking about things that Dante had done when he was little. He didn't get a thing wrong. Only he wasn't Dante."

"But you said nothing."

"What would you have done in my shoes?"

"I'd have told the truth."

"So I could be sent back to prison even though I was innocent? I protected him! I gave him a roof over his head! And I loved him . . ." A burst of coughing forced him to break off; then he added in a subdued tone, "Or I tried to love him . . ."

"You sent him away."

Valle shrugged. "He was starting to notice that there were differences between what he remembered and reality. They upset him. Sooner or later he would have figured out that something wasn't adding up."

"And he would have ruined your life," said Colomba contemptuously.

"He would have ruined *his* life. Suddenly he would have found out he was . . . nothing."

Colomba gazed longingly at the bottle of cognac, now regretting her rejection of a glass. But she'd rather have drunk poison than touch anything in that home. "He's much more than *nothing*," she murmured.

"Maybe now he is. Thanks in part to me," said Valle.

"No one ever had the slightest doubt that Dante was your son?"

"No. They all fell for it, judges and cops. Bodini had put Dante's name in his suicide note. And back then, people didn't do DNA tests. It seems like a century ago . . ." Valle stared at Colomba. "I could have reported the two of you to the police before you even got to the lake. I could have stopped you."

"So why didn't you?"

"Because I was sick of waiting for someone to find out the truth. You have no idea of what it's like to carry a secret like that inside you."

"I don't have any sympathy for you," Colomba said harshly.

"No, of course you don't." Valle turned the glass in his hands. "You're the avenging angel, come to right all wrongs. What was in the album that alerted you?"

"The pictures at the beach," Colomba replied. "They show your son bare-chested. He had a birthmark on his chest that looks exactly like the one you have on your face. The Dante I know doesn't."

Valle nodded. "Good job. And did you also figure out why they would do such a thing? Why they would make him believe that he was my son? That's something I've never been able to figure out. However hard I tried. There's not a good reason on earth."

There is one. To prove it could be done, thought Colomba. *With drugs and torture. A successful experiment.* But all she said was: "I don't care if you understand. In your fashion, you were an accomplice." Once again she pulled out the stick with the cotton swab for the sample. "Now please put this thing in your mouth, and let's get this thing done."

Valle took it. "Then what?"

"Your DNA will be compared with the human remains fished out of the lake. To see if one of those corpses belongs to your real son." Colomba stepped closer to him and talked to him, her face just inches from his. Her eyes were the color of a windstorm. "And you'd better hope there is a match. Otherwise you'll just go back to being the one guilty party."

Valle hesitated again; then he quickly put the stick into his mouth.

"That's good," said Colomba, taking it and placing it in the test tube.

"Are you going to tell Dante?" asked Valle.

"No, you're going to tell him."

Valle grabbed the armrests. "You're insane. I can't do it."

"Dante loves you, God only knows why. If he hears it from you, it won't be as hard for him. And in any case, I'm not offering you a choice." Colomba stood up. "Get your ass in gear."

Valle wasn't capable of covering the distance on foot, and he refused to drive. Colomba had to call a taxi to cover the few hundred yards from there to the Hotel degli Artisti, the fashionable, centrally located hotel where Dante had reserved two rooms. Colomba had already gone by that morning before the meeting to take a shower and put on the clothes that Minutillo had picked up for her from her apartment. In prison, she'd had to make do with what she'd been wearing at the time of her arrest and the underwear she'd been able to purchase at the commissary.

When Dante opened the door to his room, he was ready to scold Colomba for disappearing after the meeting, but when he saw Valle he forgot all about that. "Papà, has something happened?"

"The two of you need to talk," said Colomba.

"About what?" asked Dante.

Colomba didn't answer. "Call me when you're done if you feel like it, okay?"

She left, doing her best to appear untroubled, but when she entered her room she grabbed a pillow and shouted all her frustration into it. She felt like breaking something or running down the street as fast as she could. She made do with three sets of push-ups and sit-ups; then, covered with sweat, she flopped onto the bed with a bottle of beer, which she drank while channel surfing. She wasn't hungry. She counted at least four different daytime talk shows where the topic was the prisoners in the containers, and appeals were being made to try to identify the nameless ones. Colomba wondered whether the parents of some of them were simply pretending not to recognize them, to avoid having to take them back, with all their baggage of issues and maladjustment. She also wondered whether she'd judged Valle too harshly, even though right now the only person she cared about was Dante. How would he take it?

After about half an hour of pointless programs watched with a distracted eye and not even a smidgen of her brain, she heard the door across the hall slam shut. Thinking that was the signal that the conversation was over, she hastily put on her shoes and ran to Dante's room. She knocked. "Everything all right?" she asked. "Come on, let me in so we can talk it over."

The door swung open, and Colomba was surprised to find herself face-to-face with Valle, who was scrambling around, trying to get up onto his feet, up off the floor that was sticky with coffee and cigarette ashes. Dante had shoved him aside and burst out of the hotel.

29

Dante was walking at a brisk pace away from the center of town.

The cellar door, he was thinking. *That damned door.*

He'd chosen a direction at random, and now he was walking down the tree-lined boulevard leading to the iron bridge over the Po River, at the edge of town. It was a road he knew well. He remembered walking down it dozens of times with his real father to get to the first newsstand, which stood half-hidden behind the plane trees. There his father had bought the daily newspaper, and he would always get a special treat, a pack of soccer trading cards.

Except that obviously it wasn't true.

The cellar door, holy Jesus, he thought again.

As a boy, he had always stopped in front of one of the houses along the boulevard, which had a strange shape midway between a castle and a minaret, with an enormous iron spider on the facade. He'd always thought a wizard or a monster might live there. It had both scared him and attracted him.

But no, actually, he'd never done that.

Sometimes he'd ride that stretch of road on his bike, before they put in the bike path. He remembered the first time he'd ridden without training wheels, his mother running behind him, clapping her hands.

But that, too, was an illusion. Like everything else he thought he'd done or seen before the silo.

Yet the sensation of freedom from his first real bike ride seemed real to him; he could feel it in his body. Perhaps it really had happened, but in another city, in another world, where the woman who had held the back of the seat and called out "Good boy!" was still alive. His real mother—deleted a piece at a time by the Father—though he couldn't even remember what her face looked like.

Maybe it was all fake. Not only his childhood, but his memories of the silo, too. He'd never run away, he was still inside, and he was just imagining all this.

Maybe I'm dead.

At that thought, it seemed to him that the whole world began to unravel and fade around him, that his own body began to become insubstantial. Unable to go on walking, he stopped and leaned against a fence. He pushed his back against the bars: they were real. He could feel them through the fabric of his trench coat. He grabbed on to that sensation, allowing it to flow through him, until he was finally able to move his hands again. He stuck them into his pockets in search of cigarettes; he lit one.

I should have realized, he thought. *From the cellar door.* Now, only now, did he understand that that had been the first sign that there was something wrong with his memories, the first wrinkle in a past that had been constructed for him. The mental equivalent of stepping off a stair that doesn't exist.

When he'd gone home to the place where he thought he'd grown up, with a man he'd believed was his birth father, newly released from prison, he'd been convinced that in the kitchen he'd find a door that led down to the cellar pantry by way of a steep, narrow stone staircase. He even remembered the color of that door: red. A faded red through which you could see the grain of the wood. In winter, terrible drafts pushed through that door, partially blocked by a roll of cloth that gathered dust, but in the summer it was nice to lie on the floor in front of it and feel the cool breeze caressing his face.

The only thing was: that door wasn't there. It couldn't be there, because the apartment of his supposed father was on the fourth floor of an apartment house. If there had been a red door, it would have opened into the neighbors' bathroom. But Dante still continued to perceive its presence whenever he was in the kitchen. He could feel it right behind him, as if it were just a hair outside of his line of sight and someone was moving it every time he turned around to look for it.

Now that he thought about it, though, the door had only been the first of a series of signals. The courtyard that seemed so cramped, his bedroom that was the wrong color. Where he remembered blue-striped wallpaper that looked like a huge tent, he'd found a white wall that his supposed father told him had always been white. All of them signals that he'd ignored. Just as he'd failed to realize that his escape had been far too easy. When he'd struggled with the German on the banks of Lake Comello, it had been clear that the man was monstrously strong in spite of his age. He and Colomba had only barely managed to force him to the ground. Twenty-five years earlier, the malnourished child he had then been could *never* have caught that same man off guard and escaped. The man had let him go; that was the only explanation. Even what Dante had always considered the most heroic moment of his life had never existed.

The Father and his platoon had seen to everything. The false escape, Bodini's fake suicide, the fire: Dante was living proof that their system worked. They wanted him out in the world, to test him in the field. He'd started walking again, but now he froze in place, crushed by an intuition too horrendous to be a product of his imagination. *The other boy*, he thought. The one he'd seen before the German killed him. Who could he have been but the boy whose place he had taken? The real Dante Valle, who would never become Dante Torre, who would never play blackjack in Dubai, would never know the taste of a Bellini at Harry's Bar, never drink Kopi Luwak coffee and consider it proof of the existence of God. When he'd described the boy in the other silo, he was describing himself. No one had ever found him, because no one had ever thought he was missing.

He saw a taxi go by with the dome light illuminated, and he hailed it on impulse. When he told the cabbie where he wanted to be taken, the man objected to the distance but took the fare all the same.

Dante threw himself into the backseat and watched the landscape go streaming past him without trying to catch any of the details, his face pressed against the glass. They immediately left the boulevard and pulled onto the fast county road that ran through the small towns between Cremona and Mantua. The unbroken walls of apartment buildings soon became small clusters of low houses, with cafés displaying Mokarabia and Segafredo coffee signs, churches with small playing fields next to them. Then solitary houses, open countryside. When it began to get dark, the first real farmhouses appeared, the first white metal silos, the first fields with round hay bales. When they reached the turnoff for Acquanegra, Dante gave the driver detailed step-by-step directions. He knew the road very well; he'd taken it a hundred times at first in pilgrimage, and then never again for twenty years and more. Those were his own memories, from after his escape or, really, his release.

At sunset he told the taxi driver to pull over onto a dirt road that led to the ruins of a farmhouse built around a large courtyard, the windows boarded up and moss covering the roof tiles.

"Are you sure you want me to leave you here?" asked the driver.

"Yes. This is the right place," Dante replied, paying the fare.

"If you need to go back, there aren't any cabs around here."

"But there's the train," said Dante. "There was back in my day, anyway."

"I don't know if it runs anymore. Anyway, the town is in that direction." He pointed the way. "It's a long way to walk."

"I like to walk."

Dante got out of the cab and went over to the farmhouse with a knot in his belly; behind it an enormous swollen sun was sinking out of sight. The walls were covered with graffiti and the tags of local crews, obscene phrases and slogans glorifying Marco Pantani, the great local racing cyclist who had died tragically young. The stink of irrigation ditches and dead leaves. The smell hadn't changed.

I'm home, he thought. *The only home I've ever had.*

But maybe it wasn't a home. Maybe it was the womb from which he'd been reborn after eleven years of gestation. Before then, nothingness.

He walked over to the courtyard entrance and put his eye up to a crack in the large wooden door, which was chained shut with a padlock. Inside, he saw only junk and trash, more graffiti, and vines climbing the walls. To the left was the door to Bodini's house, where he could still see the marks of the fire, black brushstrokes on the stones. To the right was what had been Bodini's mother's apartment, uninhabited after her death. That was where Bodini had killed himself, on the ground floor. From where he now stood, Dante couldn't see the stables. He remembered the mooing that had come from outside the silo wall, the bleating of the calves.

He walked around the outside wall of the farmhouse until he found himself standing on a cement platform cracked by humidity and the passing years, roughly the size of a soccer pitch. The silos had once stood there, his and the one that had housed his matrix, his twin. Both silos had been demolished fifteen years ago by a new mayor, sick of witnessing the pilgrimages of local youth, who came to tell each other horrible stories about the place. Stories about the ghost of the boy in the silo, a ghost that appeared on nights with a full moon if you uttered his name, a sort of Candyman of the lower Po Valley. When he'd heard that the silos had been leveled, Dante, who hadn't gone back there since he'd left Cremona, spent a whole day trying to decipher his feelings. He'd felt violated, somehow, though he couldn't say why.

The platform still bore the marks of the silos' circular bases, marks that were almost black against the gray of the cement. Dante went to what had been his silo, still feeling the weight of the walls around him. He saw his bed again, the bucket he'd used to defecate and urinate. He remembered exactly where everything had been. He squatted down where he'd used to read the fragments of text brought him by the Father, to study his lessons. He heard the sound of an engine and realized that a white panel van had pulled up next to the platform. Dante assumed it must be a local farmer, or else a man hired by the town government to keep away the horror tourists who still came at night in search of cheap but powerful thrills.

He raised his good hand in greeting. "Don't worry, I was just leaving," he said.

The man at the wheel didn't move. By now it was almost dark, and Dante couldn't see him behind the glass.

It was that very quality of stillness that he started to find unsettling. He waved his hand again. "I'll leave! I haven't broken anything."

He got down off the platform, on the opposite side from the panel van; he meant to take the long way around, through the tall grass, and follow the path back to the road. He didn't care if he got all muddy.

The panel van's horn honked briefly, and he thought that the man at the wheel had waved at him.

Dante didn't react until the horn honked again and the man repeated the gesture, unmistakably this time. The driver wanted him to come over. After a moment in which Dante dragged his muddy feet purposefully across the cement of the platform, he cautiously approached the car.

When he saw who the man at the wheel was, Dante tried to run, but it was already too late.

30

At first Colomba wasn't worried, or at least not very worried. Unable to get in touch with Dante because they had both ditched their cell phones when they first went on the run—a situation that Colomba now found tremendously frustrating—she waited for him to come back, going to check his room every ten minutes or so. As evening drew on, she called Minutillo, hoping in vain that Dante had at least left word with him. Finally she wrote a note and left it on the door of his room, telling him that she was going to eat dinner at the Osteria La Bissola with Roberta from LABANOF and explaining how to get there.

She reached the restaurant at eight that evening. It stood next to a Romanesque church and featured a first-rate paella that was hardly in line with the local culinary tradition. But Colomba merely picked at her food, anxious as she was about Dante and the reason she had come there tonight. Which was to give the forensic anthropologist a sample of Valle's DNA and tell her everything she'd discovered. She wished she could have informed Dante first, but that hadn't been possible, and it made her feel guilty, as well as afraid that she'd be taken for crazy. Roberta, however, took the news well. After a moment's bewilderment she told her she believed her and assured her that she'd give the sample to the team biologists and guarantee complete confidentiality. Or at least, until the results were available, whereupon she'd have to hand them over to the prosecuting magistrate.

"Is there any chance that you're wrong about Signor Valle, Colomba?" Roberta then asked her. They'd been on a first-name basis since Colomba had called to arrange to meet and Roberta had invited her to dinner.

"Not a single chance," Colomba replied. "He admitted it. And if you ask me, he's been wanting to spill it all to someone for a long time now."

Roberta speared a piece of chicken with her fork and chewed it slowly. "I've worked on a lot of horrible cases in my career, as I have to guess you have in yours, but this goes well beyond. How is Signor Torre?"

"Not well."

"I'd be surprised to hear he was. If you see him, tell him I'm very sorry to hear it."

Colomba smiled. "He prefers not to be pitied."

"But I don't pity him," Roberta said. "Quite the opposite. He has a very effective way of reasoning, and I find him quite attractive, even if he is skinny as a nail. On another topic, I think it's only fair for you to know that the prosecuting magistrate is requesting authorization for a new examination of the bodies from the Paris bombing."

When she heard the Disaster mentioned, Colomba's lungs clamped suddenly shut, as always. "Are they reopening the case?"

"Spinelli is trying, but it's not easy. From what I understand, aside from your testimony and that of Signor Torre, there is no objective evidence concerning the group that supposedly aided the German, either from the eighties or from now. The connections are all . . . shall we say . . theoretical. Do you think that the American intelligence agencies will cooperate?"

"No," Colomba replied gloomily. "Neither will the Italians. You saw for yourself the way that buffoon reacted during the meeting."

"That came as no surprise to me," said Roberta. "That's how they always are."

"Have you had dealings with them before?"

"In the past I've been asked to analyze the bodies of suspected terrorists," Roberta explained. "And I've never been able to get a speck of information out of them. Communications are always one way. After all, they are the *secret* services, aren't they?"

"Right. If there's one thing they know how to do, it's stonewall," Colomba observed. "There are nineteen dead and ten kidnap victims, and that's not counting the victims in Paris and the murders that the Father and the German committed in Rome in just the past few days. Still, everyone's clamming up."

Roberta took a sip of her sangria. "Today I saw the cop who arrested you."

"Santini?" Colomba was stunned. "He's in Cremona?"

"Yes, I saw him check in to the hotel where I'm staying, the Ibis. I usually go back and forth from Milan, but tomorrow morning I have a very early meeting with the Forensic Squad, and I'd like to get a good night's sleep."

"And what is he doing here?"

"He didn't tell me that." Roberta flashed her a conspiratorial smile. "I think Spinelli is grilling him. She couldn't get to De Angelis, but Santini doesn't have the same kind of connections."

"For someone who spends all her time in the lab, you sure know a lot," Colomba commented.

"Actually, I don't spend a lot of time in the lab when I'm here." Roberta smiled. "I spend my days at court, meeting with local experts and prosecutors. And I have to tell you, I find that to be much more exhausting."

The proprietor came to their table to ask if there was anything else he could bring them; they ordered coffees and asked for the check.

"How's it going with the identification of the bodies?" Colomba inquired.

Roberta shot a glance over at the neighboring table to make sure no one was eavesdropping while she talked about corpses; it was the kind of dinnertime conversation that could ruin someone else's meal. "We've identified the names of missing persons who might have the same ages as the subjects whose remains we've recovered," she finally said. "Now we're going to try to contact the relatives and get DNA samples from them for comparison, even though I can't say how many of the remains in the barrels are going to offer us any identifying details. By the way, I'll need a sample from Signor Torre, in order to cross-reference our data."

Colomba nodded. "It would be nice to find out who he really is."

"Don't get your hopes up. It's been a long time. Just as it has for those poor souls at the bottom of the lake. If we manage to identify two or three, we can consider ourselves lucky."

"Aren't you being a little conservative?"

"At LABANOF we have almost a hundred nameless corpses in our coolers, and for most of them we have more than just a tooth that's been marinating in sulfuric acid." She smiled. "I have a few colleagues who might tell you that I'm just an incurable optimist."

When Colomba got back to the hotel at ten, she found a little knot of reporters and photographers waiting for her in the lobby: a rumor had circulated about where the two main characters behind the macabre discoveries in Lake Comello were staying. The flashes blinded her, but even more befuddling was the feeling that she was at the center of attention, something she wasn't used to, something she didn't like one bit. She refused to answer any questions, and instead hurried up the stairs. She found that the Post-it was gone from Dante's door. She heaved a sigh of relief and knocked, but there was no answer.

She went back downstairs, and a straggling photographer took pictures as she hurried over to the reception desk.

The clerk on duty greeted her with an apologetic smile. "We tried to send them away, signora, but they keep getting back in."

"I'm not here about that," she said brusquely. "My friend, Dante Torre. Can you tell me if he's in his room, or has he gone out again?"

The concierge checked on his computer screen. "I'm afraid he's checked out."

At first, Colomba didn't understand. "Excuse me?"

"He paid his bill in full and left."

"And he didn't leave a message for me?"

"No."

Colomba shook her head. "I don't believe it. That's not like him." However upset he might be, he'd never have just dumped her like that. "Who did he speak to?"

"The manager. Shall I get her for you?"

"Yes, thanks."

The concierge vanished into the rear, and after a while the manager called her name. She was a stern-looking woman, about forty.

"Signora Caselli . . . is there some problem?"

"Yes. Did you see Signor Torre leave? Did he seem to you to be"—she hesitated, searching for a word that didn't exist—"normal?" she concluded, realizing that it was a word poorly suited to Dante.

"I really couldn't say. And anyway, our guests have a right to their privacy . . . try to understand."

"You know who I am, and you know who he is, right? And the reason we're here in Cremona?" said Colomba.

The manager sighed. "Yes, ma'am."

"So don't talk to me about privacy. Did you or did you not see him?"

"No, I didn't. He settled up over the phone and gave me his credit card number. It was about nine this evening."

"And the things in his room?"

"He gave instructions to have them sent to his address in Rome. He even paid extra for the service."

"No way," said Colomba. Her heart was in her mouth, and she felt her chest constricting with anxiety. She forced herself to breathe normally.

The manager stared at her with a worried look on her face. "Signora . . . I assure you that's exactly what happened."

"And are you sure it was actually him on the phone?"

The manager hesitated. "I think it was. We hadn't actually ever spoken before."

Colomba galloped upstairs to her room and pulled out the folded sheet of paper that served as an address book in case of an emergency. She found Spinelli's number but stopped just before dialing it. She'd have to tell her that just before leaving, Dante had fought with Valle, and the prosecuting magistrate was unlikely to share her concern; Dante wasn't a minor, after all, and he wasn't considered an endangered witness, because he'd already told what he knew and it hadn't led to the identification of any culprit. And even if Spinelli agreed to send the carabinieri out in search of him, Colomba would have to sit in her hotel room and wait for news, without knowing whether they were out looking or not, much less what steps they were taking. And the Father would learn all about the search efforts, Colomba felt certain.

She hung up the receiver of the room phone by her bed. She'd have to find another way, and right now only one possibility was taking shape in her head. *I'm insane even to consider this*, she thought. But it was an effort she'd have to make.

She asked the receptionist for the address of the Hotel Ibis and discovered that it was just a twenty-minute walk away. It took only fifteen for her to get there, and she managed to get the room number by pretending she was expected.

Santini opened the door in a tank top undershirt. He needed a shave, and he reeked of sweat. When Colomba told him what she wanted, he let out the first wholehearted laugh he'd had in quite a while. But then he let her in.

Meanwhile, Dante was slowly regaining consciousness. The last thing he remembered was the panel van's window rolling down, then darkness. The same darkness that now pressed in on him, a darkness that smacked of the taste of fabric and the smell of his own breath. Then someone pulled the hood off his head, and Dante saw where he was.

He started screaming.

31

Santini listened to Colomba's story, sitting on his single bed and pol-
ishing off the twenty-two-ounce "bomber" bottle of beer he'd bought
at the hotel bar. The hotel room reeked of cigarettes, even though the
CIS detective had left the window ajar. "Maybe your boyfriend really
did go home," he said in the end.

Colomba shook her head, in irritation. "I don't believe it."

"Because he didn't say good-bye?"

"If he really was so upset that he ran away and forgot his manners,
he would have forgotten to pay for the room, too," said Colomba,
forcing herself to curb her temper. "He has an old school code of
conduct, and I believe he would have paid for my room, seeing that
he reserved for the two of us."

"You can't be sure of that. People aren't always predictable, especially when they're under stress."

"I've seen him upset before, terribly upset, and I know what to
expect. No, that was someone else calling, pretending to be him."

"The German is in prison. He was the dangerous one."

Colomba shook her head. "No, the Father is the dangerous one.
And he's still out there."

"Show me a single piece of evidence that he exists."

"All I know is that Dante believes in him and that he's been right
from the very beginning, from the Vivaro mountain meadows, from
the disappearance of Luca Maugeri. And if you'd listened to him," she
added, making no secret of her anger, "you wouldn't have come off
looking like the complete asshole that you did."

Santini let himself sink back against his pillow. "You have a nice
way of asking a favor, Caselli."

Colomba pulled over the only chair in the room, turned it around,
and sat down in it, straddling it. "I'm not asking you a favor."

"Ah, no?"

"I'm asking you to do the right thing."

Santini sighed in exasperation. "Don't be ridiculous."

"But it *is* the right thing. And even if you don't believe that, it's better than sitting here drinking and crying over your troubles."

Santini closed his eyes. *Of all things I could choose to do, why is it that lately I've always been choosing the stupidest option available to me?* "Let me make a few phone calls, and let's see what happens," he said. He felt like laughing again.

It took more than just a couple of phone calls, but finding Dante's trail in a city as small as Cremona was easier than expected, in part because a couple of Santini's subordinates, whom he treated like doormats, pitched in to help. After quickly marking trains, buses, and car rentals off the list, along with hospitals, the city morgue, and other hotels, they managed to track down the taxi driver who'd picked Dante up on the tree-lined boulevard. When they reached him by phone, the cabbie told them all about the farmhouse where he'd left him.

Around midnight Colomba and Santini pulled up outside the farmhouse in Santini's government car. They examined the place by flashlight before making their way around back to the cement platform.

"Is this where they held him?" asked Santini.

"Yes," Colomba replied. "Though the silos are gone. But what did he come here for?"

"A nostalgic outing." Santini looked around: there wasn't a light in the darkness other than theirs. "He's not here. And without a cell phone he couldn't have called another taxi. He must have left on foot."

Colomba waved for Santini to light up the surrounding area. "Or else someone picked him up. A car came through here recently," she said, looking at the tire marks in the soft dirt.

"A panel van," Santini corrected her, and he knew what he was talking about. "But it might just have been a farmer from around here."

"Bring the light over here," said Colomba, pointing to the cement of the platform.

Santini did as she asked, highlighting a number of dark strips. "Dry mud. Someone wiped their feet off."

"Not just *someone*: Dante. And he wasn't wiping his feet off. Come over here."

When Santini did, he saw that the strips were actually letters and numbers traced out with the sole of a shoe. "EH29" he read.

"A partial license plate number," said Colomba. "So you still think it's all pure chance?"

Santini sighed and pulled out his cell phone.

While Santini was calling his office, Dante reawakened in his prison, and this time he didn't faint immediately. *I was given something,* he realized, sensing that his thoughts were crawling along like snails. *Enough tranquilizer to calm down a horse.* Maybe injected directly into his neck, because it ached.

Whatever it was, the drug was working. Not only did it slow him down, it also made it almost tolerable to be shut up in a narrow, rectangular space, twenty by ten feet, with all the openings closed off. It was illuminated by a green child's night light tucked away in a corner; the walls were covered with insulation and wooden boards. There was a Formica counter with a sink, cabinets, a table and chair, and a bunk bed. Dante was flat on his back on the lower bunk, and there was a collar on his neck, made for a big dog, padlocked and fastened to a metal cable that was welded to the headboard of the bed. He tried to tug at it with hands rendered insensible by the tranquilizer, but the ring didn't budge and the bed turned out to be anchored to the floor.

While trying to figure out just how much play the cable had, Dante moved too suddenly and the collar jerked at his throat. It wasn't much of a jerk, but he still felt he was being suffocated and the surge of adrenaline wiped away the effects of the drug. Once again, the walls around him seemed to narrow in as if about to crush him. He opened his mouth to yell for help, but he couldn't do it. As he was passing out once again, he had one lucid thought. Of Colomba.

She knew, he was sure of it. She was coming to get him. He just
wondered whether she'd be in time.

"No license plate," Santini told Colomba. They were still at the farmhouse, fighting against the cold and damp. No van registered had a
plate that began or ended with the letters and numbers traced in the
mud, he explained. Only cars, and there were vast numbers of those.

"Either Torre got the number wrong," said Santini "or else *we're*
wrong. For all we know, someone was here the other night, maybe
playing Battleship in the mud."

Colomba shook her head. "No. It was him. This is how he does
things."

Santini lit a cigarette. "You think you might be a little too confident?"

"I told you before, I know how he thinks." But did she really?
Maybe she just hoped she did, because it was the last thread tying her
to Dante. "Can you call the highway patrol?"

"There aren't any video cameras here."

"But maybe the panel van pulled onto the highway. We know the
time frame, and we know a part of the license number. That's more
than enough. They can just look in their system."

Colomba was referring to Safety Tutor, a speed camera system that
recorded the license plates of vehicles passing through toll gates and
sent the data to the processing center in Settebagni, where it was analyzed to catch speeders. The police could get into the database, but
there were so many search requests for wanted criminals and stolen
cars that if you wanted a fast response, it required either a formal
request from a judge or else an inside contact. Santini had one.

At two in the morning, as they were waiting along the county road
in a bar and tobacco shop that stayed open late for truckers, Santini
got his answer. And when he hung up, Colomba saw that he'd lost the
weary, indifferent expression of the past few hours. "Okay."

"Okay what?"

"Okay, you were right."

Colomba immediately dropped the stale piece of pastry she'd been
trying to choke down. "Did they find the license plate?"

"Yes. And it's a white Fiat Ducato panel van. But according to EUCARIS, that license is registered to a Fiat 500 that was sent to the crusher." EUCARIS is the European Car and Driving License Information System.

"So it's stolen. Where did the camera film it?"

"Around Bologna, then Florence, and then in Rome. It left the highway two hours ago, at an off-ramp from Via Salaria. After that we lost it."

"Someone took Dante to Rome. That's where the Father is," Colomba muttered under her breath.

"Caselli, we need to sound the alarm."

"No," said Colomba decisively. "The Father would hear about it."

"How?"

Colomba shook her head. "He killed Rovere because he knew he was on his trail, and he sent the German to kill Jorge as soon as he was released from prison. He's getting firsthand information."

"Do you think he's one of us?"

"Either that or he has someone like you on salary. In fact, until just recently I assumed it actually was you, or else De Angelis." Colomba chewed on her lips. "Or both of you."

"It's not me, and as far as De Angelis goes, you don't have to worry now that he's quit."

"Are you sure?"

"Listen, I worked for him, and not just for a couple of days. There's nothing he wouldn't have done to further his career, and he did favors for anyone he thought could do favors in return. But he's no murderer. Nor is he the accomplice of a murderer." He shrugged his shoulders. "And even if he wanted to pass information to the Father, because maybe he doesn't really understand who he is, he wouldn't be able to do it anymore. The colleagues all steer clear of him now. So you don't have to worry."

Colomba shook her head without a word, and Santini understood that she was at a loss. It was the perfect time for him to throw in the towel, but he didn't do it.

"Listen to me, Caselli," he said in a reasonable voice. "We can sound the alarm but keep it to a minimum. We'll just report the van as stolen and nothing more. No matter how much inside information the Father is getting, he can't know everything. And this information would come directly to my office."

"Which you trust implicitly, right?" she said angrily.

"The way you're thinking now, there's no one I can trust. And you might even be right. But working alone, we're not going to get anywhere."

Colomba chewed on her lip for a few more seconds. "How long did it take you to get up to Cremona?"

"Four hours. Using the siren."

"Let's see if we can take less time to get back." She stood up. "Have them start looking for the van, while we go to Rome."

32

Dante's third reawakening was a terrible thing; or perhaps it was the fourth, he couldn't exactly remember. Previously they might have given him enough tranquilizers to knock out a horse, but this time he'd basically undergone a chemical lobotomy. He was shaking uncontrollably, and in his head a carousel of overlapping, interchanging images kept spinning, merging one into the next. Some of them came from his past, others from his nightmares, but they all seemed equally real. He was plummeting into hell, he was still in the silo, he was running from an invisible enemy, he was in the restraining bed back in the clinic, on the glassed-in terrace of his home as it went up in flames.

He was dead.

No, he thought. *I'm still alive. He still wants me alive.*

He tried to sit upright, and once again the collar choked him, but this time without triggering another attack. What it did instead was help him get back to the present; it reminded him of where he was. A prisoner in a hole, buried alive. The drug that made it hard for him to think worked this time: he didn't pass out, and he didn't scream.

In an attempt to control the spasms, he swung his legs off the bed. His shoes had been taken, and the cold from the floor seeped through the cloth of his socks. The floor seemed to be made of plastic, and it sounded hollow. Whatever place they were holding him in, it wasn't an apartment; maybe it was another shipping container. With his good hand he grabbed the padlock on his collar. He couldn't see it, but he recognized it by feel: a Master Lock with a forty-digit dial. Sixty-four thousand possible combinations. If he could try a different combination every twenty seconds, it would take him more than three hundred hours to try them all. And something told him that he didn't have three hundred hours. Maybe not even thirty. He used to know a trick to do it faster, he thought desperately. He just had to fish that trick out of the sewer he now had in place of a brain.

Little by little, a violent surge of nausea had risen inside him, and now he knew he could no longer keep from vomiting. He looked around from something to puke into and he saw . . .

A metal bucket.

Like the one in the silo. He'd come back.

He grabbed it and vomited bile. For a long minute he was lost. Then he came to, curled up on the bed, an acid taste in his mouth, trying to convince himself that the silo no longer existed, that he had been a free man for twenty-five years, but he knew he was lying to himself. His imprisonment had never ended. It had only been expanded to include the whole world, and now it had been shrunk again to the size of a jail cell. At that moment a section of the wall in front of him swung open, and Dante discovered that he had been looking at a carefully disguised door. He finally understood where he was: in a camper or a large trailer. The amber light of a streetlamp slanted in toward him.

Don't look out the door, his voice as a child said to him. *It's against the rules. You'll be punished.*

He resisted the impulse to shut his eyes. He glimpsed what looked like a packed-earth courtyard and, in the distance, what seemed to be aluminum roofs. Next to the door was a man in his sixties whom Dante had seen before: he was the driver of the panel van, the one who had taken him at the farmhouse and who had given him the first injection. He'd recognized him instantly, even though he'd been much younger in the photo that Colomba had found in Ferrari's apartment. He was one of the German's men, sitting on the truck with his combat boots hanging around his neck, the one making the thumbs-up sign.

The man withdrew immediately, and the door frame was filled with another figure. A tall, skinny man, wearing a factory worker's jumpsuit, with heavy gloves and a full-face ski mask. His eyes were covered by a pair of mirrored sunglasses.

So many years had passed, and the body was no longer the one he remembered. Skinnier, more hesitant in his movements. But when he came in and the other man closed the door behind him, he tilted his head to one side as if to observe him from another viewpoint.

That movement, more than anything else, ensured that Dante recognized him.

This time it really was the Father.

The bad news came just after Florence. Santini had nodded off, hanging off his shoulder belt, while Colomba drove with the window partway open, a stream of wind battering her face. Santini's cell phone rang, and he grabbed it with his eyes still closed. "Yes," he muttered. "Did they check?" he added faster. "No, forget it." He hung up.

"The panel van?" Colomba asked, her guts and her back both aching from the tension.

"Yes." Santini rubbed his eyes. "They found it near the Foro Italico. Empty. They must have changed cars, but there's no way to know what they're driving now because there are no video cameras there. And I doubt that was a coincidence."

Colomba pounded the wheel. "Fuck!"

"We can send the Forensic Squad to see if they can find anything," said Santini.

"The Father would find out, and we don't have the time."

"Caselli, we don't have anything left."

Colomba heaved a deep sigh. "Listen. The Father pulled that ruse at the hotel to give himself more time, and we need him to keep thinking we're further behind than we are, otherwise Dante's dead."

"More time for what?" Santini asked.

"Whatever it is, it's nothing good for Dante," Colomba replied with a quaver in her voice. "But if we put out an APB, he's going to know everyone's after him. He's the murderous monster, the boogeyman who steals children. Thousands of tips will pour in, and one of them could be the real thing. So he'll disappear, but before he does, he'll get rid of Dante. We need to keep a low profile until we're truly desperate."

"Caselli, I'm already desperate," Santini said. It seemed as though he really was, and his exhaustion couldn't have helped. "This isn't the first kidnapping I've worked, and there's one thing I've learned: finding a hostage is a long process, and you can't do it without a team."

"*We're* the team."

Santini shook his head. "We're not enough."

"We have our brains. And we know everything about the Father. All we have to do is figure out what he's doing now." Colomba grabbed a bottle of water and drained the last gulp, then tossed it onto the backseat. "Let's start with the kidnapping. How did he know where to find Dante?"

Santini lit a cigarette. Colomba put up with the smoke; they'd argued it out in the first mile. "He followed him from the minute he left the hotel," Santini replied. "In fact, the minute he left the hospital."

"Dante is convinced that the Father was watching him earlier than that."

"Since when?"

"Since the day he escaped from the silo."

"I don't know if that's true, but I can guarantee you he didn't escape," said Santini. "They let him go."

Colomba glanced over at him for a moment, stunned, then turned her eyes back to the road. "Why?"

Santini lowered the window to flick out cigarette ash. A small whirlwind formed. "You go to all this trouble to create some kind of clone of another person; well, don't you want to see how it behaves? They were road-testing him."

"According to Dante, they were shutting down the project," Colomba said, unconvinced.

"And by pure chance he's the only one who got away?"

Colomba realized that Santini was right. She hadn't really thought about it because she'd instinctively tended to believe Dante's version. "If the Father really was watching him, how did he do it, in your opinion?"

"The usual things. Bugs in his apartment . . . ambient surveillance," Santini replied. "And of course, seeing that this is a medical experiment, I'd have kept an eye on his charts, his exams, so I could keep track of how he was doing."

Colomba was suddenly struck by an idea, and she swerved slightly, even though at 110 mph. "The clinic!"

"What clinic?"

"There's a sheet of paper with some phone numbers in my jacket," Colomba said, ignoring his question. "Dial Valle's number and put it on speaker."

"How about next time you let me drive. I'm tired of being your secretary," said Santini, but he did as he was told.

Valle's rheumy voice filled the car. "Who is this, and what's happening?" he wheezed.

"It's me, Caselli."

"What's happened? Is this about Dante? Is he in trouble?"

Is he really worried about him, or is he just putting on a show? Colomba wondered. "No, he's not in trouble. I just need to ask you a quick question. Do you remember the Swiss clinic where you sent Dante?"

Valle coughed. "Yes, of course I remember."

"What was it called?"

"Can't you just ask him?"

"What the fuck was it called!" Colomba yelled. Santini jerked in his seat.

"Eiche. It was called Eiche . . ." Valle spelled out the name. "It was in Erlenbach, near Zurich. On the lake."

Colomba gestured to Santini to write it down. He pulled a pen out of his jacket pocket and wrote on a utility bill he found in the glove compartment.

"Why there?"

"What?"

"Why did you send Dante there? How did you find it?" Colomba was shouting again.

"Someone recommended it."

"Who?"

"I can't remember."

"You can't remember something that important?" If she'd had him within arm's length, she would have strangled him.

Valle's breathing became even more labored. "Someone at the hospital. Christ, it's been twenty-five years!"

"Someone who?"

"I can't remember! Will you just tell me why—"

Colomba turned off the speaker with a flat-handed slap to the control on the steering wheel.

"Why are you fixating on the clinic?" asked Santini.

"For two reasons," she replied as she checked the GPS device to see how long it would be till they reached Rome. At least half an hour. She passed a truck that pulled over to let her pass when it saw her flashing roof lights; there had been no need to turn the siren on, because there was no traffic. "First: the Father is a doctor, or a scientist who has some connection with the medical field. He deals in drugs and was in charge of treatments for the Italian MKUltra."

"That story doesn't really convince me all that much, Caselli."

"Well, you'd better *get* convinced, because it's the only one we've got right now. Second: for four years after his liberation, Dante was locked up in this Eiche clinic. If the Father wanted to know how he was doing, that's where he needed to go. And just possibly it was he who arranged to have him sent there in the first place through an accomplice."

"Do you think he might have been one of the doctors?"

"That's what I'm hoping. Maybe he wasn't in charge of him directly, because Dante might have recognized him, but I wouldn't be a bit surprised if he was in the room next door. Or maybe he just took a stroll through the ward every now and then, taking advantage of the pliability of his colleagues."

"You're stumbling around in the dark, you know that, don't you?"

"Do you have anything better in mind?"

Santini thought it over for a few seconds. "No. Still, even if it turned out to be true, Eiche is a Swiss clinic. To get staff lists from twenty years ago, we'd need an international letter rogatory. And even if we did have the lists, I doubt that next to the specialties of each physician we'd be likely to find the word 'kidnapper.'"

"The Father is Italian. Dante said he had no particular accent. And a German accent is hard to miss. In eleven years, some word in his native tongue would have slipped out. And believe me, Dante would have remembered."

Santini shrugged. "There can't be many of them, and they'd be easier to check, but still, we don't have the lists."

"Check the clinic's website."

While Santini was searching on his smartphone, Colomba rummaged desperately in her memory. She knew there was something she was forgetting. Something Dante had told her . . . She was exhausted, goddamn it, and her brain wasn't engaging.

"Nothing," said Santini. "Maybe we got the name wrong. No, wait a second . . . There's a page in German . . ." He looked over at her. "You won't believe this, but I speak German."

"You won't believe *this*, but I don't give a flying fuck. What does it say?"

"That the clinic went out of business ten years ago. We can skip the headache of finding a prosecuting magistrate for the letter rogatory."

At the words "prosecuting magistrate" Colomba had a sudden satori, a blinding illumination. "Dante had to obtain a certificate that he was in full possession of his faculties," she exclaimed triumphantly. "He must have submitted an expert report from the clinic."

"It should be part of the transcript," Santini pointed out. "If there's a name, we can put it in the system and see what comes up. But if he's Swiss, we'll have to work with the police there or else Europol."

"In the meantime, let's get a copy of the court decision."

Santini looked at the dashboard clock. "It's five in the morning, a little early for the clerk of the court."

"In small cities things are much simpler. On the same sheet of paper, you'll find Spinelli's cell phone. Call her."

Santini objected. Spinelli had treated him like crap, and he doubted the judge would listen to them. In the end he did as he was told, though, and sat listening, open-mouthed, as Colomba buttered her up and begged her to help them, in violation of all imaginable rules and regulations. Except one: the overarching law that demanded she do anything possible to save a human life.

Twenty minutes later, an astonished clerk of the court of Cremona was dragged out of bed by a phone call. Luckily, he had a copy of the keys to the archives.

33

The Father stood looking at Dante without speaking for a few seconds; then he walked over to the table and sat down at the only chair. Dante was again seized with a wave of tremors, and he grabbed his legs with his left arm. With his good hand he continued to jerk at the lock, convulsively.

"Hello, Son," said the Father. "It's nice to see you again."

His voice had changed. It was faint, weak. His pronunciation was murkier too, less crisp, the way it is when old people begin to have problems with their teeth. Dante wouldn't have recognized it as the voice of the man who had held him prisoner. Still, it somehow rang familiar. "That's enough . . . of this . . . bullshit," he stammered. He was shaking. "You're not my father."

"I raised you. I made you what you are. Isn't that what fathers do?"

Dante shook his head, continuing to tremble. His thermometer had skyrocketed, but the drugs in his blood were struggling to keep his soul tethered to his body. "You're just . . . a sick monster. And you turned me into a . . . monster, too. You should have died long ago."

The Father went on staring at him. "You've become stronger, but you always were strong. I've watched grown men fall apart and turn into nonentities after just a few months. They stopped reacting, quit fighting back, and just waited for death to come. Not you. You made it all the way to the end of the treatment."

"You killed . . . them," said Dante as he continued to decipher that sense of familiarity. The man before him was the Father, but it was as if his persona had been overlaid on that of someone else. "And you buried them . . . in the lake."

"It gave me no pleasure, believe me," the Father explained. "But it was necessary. The history of the world is made up of sacrifices, some small, some great."

"What about the children that . . . that you put into the shipping containers . . . were they sacrifices, too?"

The Father shook his head. "Dante, Dante . . . how can you fail to understand? I was their only hope of recovery. The damage that you and Colomba have done is incalculable. I'm going to have to start over from scratch in some other country. And I just pray that God will let me live long enough to see the results."

Colomba? Why is he calling her by name? Dante delved into his memory. But it was fragmentary and vague. "I just pray that God decides to make you die."

"I'll be remembered, Dante. As a pioneer. All will be forgiven. And know that I never did any of it for myself. I was never chasing glory. What I do is a gift to the world."

Dante was too exhausted to continue that debate. "Why—" He stopped; the tremors were so violent that they prevented him from uttering the words. "Why am I here? What do you want?"

"I missed you, Dante. I wanted to talk to you. And I wanted to give you a gift."

"I don't . . . don't want anything from you."

The Father leaned toward him. "Don't you even want to know who you were before I let you be reborn?" he asked.

Dante got the impression that he was smiling under the ski mask.

When the proprietor of the Gold bar and tobacco shop on Corso Francia in Rome raised his shutters at six on the dot, he found himself looking at a couple with an exhausted and dangerous appearance. The woman especially, with a feral glare in her bottle green eyes. He imagined that they were a pair of criminals and considered not opening the door at all. Then the man with the mustache slapped his police ID against the glass.

"Move your ass," the man said from the other side of the glass.

The barista opened the door with a smile. "Forgive me, it's just that I've been robbed twice."

"I'll take that as a compliment," Santini commented.

Colomba pointed to the sign on the door that read: FAXES AND PHOTOCOPIES. "Does your fax machine work?"

"Yes, of course it does," the barista replied.

"What's the fax number here?"

The barista provided the number and then went to prepare their order—two double espressos and a grilled ham-and-cheese sandwich—while Colomba called back Spinelli and gave her the fax number to give the clerk of the court so he could send her the documentation.

"I'm going to have to open a file on the disappearance of Signor Torre," said Spinelli.

"I'm begging you to wait, I just need time . . ."

"I'm required to do it, it's my fiduciary duty. But no one can criticize me for waiting until office hours. Nine thirty."

Colomba understood that that was the final deadline. "Thanks. I'll try to make that do."

"Don't thank me," Spinelli said before hanging up. "We'll probably both get into deep trouble for this."

Colomba gave the cell phone to Santini, thinking to herself that she didn't care what happened to her once she managed to find Dante. And she cared even less what would happen if she failed. Chewing on a mouthful of grilled ham-and-cheese sandwich, Santini quickly typed a text on his phone.

"Should I be worried?" Colomba asked, eyes narrowed.

Santini swallowed. "About what? About this?" He turned the screen toward her, showing her the text he'd just written.

I won't be able to come pick you up, Stellina. It's work. Give my apologies to your mother, too. Kisses to you, Papà.

"You have a daughter?" Colomba asked in amazement.

"Part-time, I do," he replied. "What's the matter? Do you think people like me have no right to reproduce?"

She shrugged. "I just had you pegged more for home, office, and ass kissing, mostly I guess."

He nearly crushed the cell phone in his fist. "I can't wait for this whole case to be over so I never have to lay eyes on you again."

The barista leaned over the counter. "Excuse me . . . a fax is coming in, and I think it's for you."

Colomba and Santini hurried to the fax machine, which stood on a shelf in the tobacco products sales booth. It was a race to see which of them could grab the first emerging sheet. Colomba won by default. It had nothing on it but the emblem of the court; she crumpled it into a ball and threw it into the trash.

"If you need anything, just let me know," said the barista, clearly intimidated.

"Yeah, sure," Santini replied brusquely.

Colomba crumpled up the second sheet as well and tossed it into the trash. "I hope they don't send us the whole text of the decision . . ."

"When we get the names, I'll forward them on to my office. Is that all right with you?" asked Santini.

Colomba nodded. "I'm thinking that we could also compare them with the names from Silver Compass. That was the support center for children with problems where Ruggero Palladino went, along with half of the others who were being held prisoner in the shipping containers."

Santini looked at another sheet of fax paper, and this time he placed it on the shelf. On it were the names of the judge and the clerk of the court who had drawn up the document. Those might prove useful.

"I know that Spinelli has had the place under investigation, but for now nothing has emerged. Most of the people who worked there were well-meaning volunteers. It's going to take time."

Santini crumpled up another sheet of paper after quickly scanning it: it was all legal boilerplate. "The undersigned," "the above-mentioned," and so on and so forth.

There was a pause in the transmission; then came a sheet that didn't have the typewritten text of the court. On the top right was a logo that depicted a stylized oak tree and, beneath it, the name EICHE KLINIK.

"Here we go," said Colomba.

It was the expert evaluation by the physician in charge of Dante's case, who vouched for his recovery. Luckily, it had been translated into Italian. The evaluation was five pages long, and the signature on the last page was that of Dr. Maja Hutter.

"A woman," Colomba noted with disappointment. She'd hoped to hit a bull's-eye the first time, even though she knew the Father would never be so reckless as to risk exposure.

"Maybe she has a deep voice."

"Dante wouldn't have fallen for that," Colomba replied, though she'd thought the same thing for a few seconds.

"Anyway, I'll have her tracked down," said Santini, pulling out his cell phone.

But the fax still wasn't finished. Another page came out. The heading on this one was WISSENSCHAFTLICHE AUSSCHUSS, again with the clinic's logo. Colomba showed it to Santini. "What does that mean?"

He answered with the cell phone pressed to his ear. "Hunh. Wait a sec, Wissenschaft . . . Wissenschaft . . . 'science' . . . it's a 'committee of scientific advisers'!" Then he started speaking to his subordinate, who answered in a weary voice.

The fax emitted another soft beep and then turned itself off. Colomba took the last sheet that had just come out of the machine. It was a list of the members of the scientific advisory committee. When she got to middle of the list, she felt all her blood drop into her feet. She staggered and was forced to lean against the glass front of the sales booth.

Santini covered the mouthpiece with his hand. "Are you feeling sick, Caselli?"

She shook her head and put her finger next to the name, incapable of speaking. When he saw it, Santini hung up, even though his underling was in the middle of a sentence.

The Father came back into the camper, this time carrying something bulky in his arms, wrapped in a length of cloth. He set it down on the table and stood there, saying nothing. He had left immediately after telling Dante what his gift would be, to let him savor the idea.

Dante sat up on the bed, resting his head against the wall. He was shaking less now, though he was weak and had a hard time breathing. His heart was racing in his chest. "Have you brought me another gift?" he laboriously got out the words.

"No, not exactly. We could say that this one is a gift for me," the Father replied. He tugged open the wrapping and pulled out a cardboard file folder, a tourniquet, a bottle of hydrogen peroxide, and a syringe. Then he let the cloth drop to the floor, and Dante saw that the bulky object that he'd had difficulty carrying was an old hand-operated professional paper cutter, a sort of hinged scimitar with a wooden handle, connected to a metal base. They were used in printing plants to square reams of paper or trim the edges of books.

When he saw the razor-sharp blade, Dante shivered. "A gift for you?"

"Proof that you're the man I think you are." He pushed the table toward Dante's bed until its legs almost touched him. Then he pulled up the chair and sat down. Now the two of them were less than a yard apart, the length of the chain. The Father had calculated that Dante still couldn't reach him, just the table. Just the paper cutter.

"What am I supposed to prove to you?"

"Your strength of will," the Father replied. "And your determination." He picked up the cardboard file folder. "In here is everything I knew about you when you were chosen. What I learned about your parents: where you lived, where you went to nursery school . . . everything that there can be to know about a four-year-old boy."

"I was six when you took me," Dante objected, feeling an urge deep inside to shout and rave. He controlled himself by studying the profile of the man in the ski mask, the shape of his head, of his neck. He wasn't wrong. He knew who he was. And that made him stronger than he'd ever been with respect to the Father or the thought of him. He was no longer an anonymous phantom, no longer a shadow from the past.

"I'm afraid not. You were four and a half, to be exact," said the Father. "You've forgotten nearly everything about your first few years in the silo. That was necessary to make sure your story matched up, you understand? We spent almost thirteen years together, not eleven like you thought. Like I made you believe," he added with a hint of satisfaction.

"Thirteen years," Dante murmured.

"But maybe after you learn who you really are, you'll remember that, too. Who can say? I'm eager to find out. But first"—he pointed to the paper cutter—"first you have to pass this test. The last one. The most difficult. Sacrificing a part of yourself."

Dante felt his stomach knot up. "Speak clearly."

"I want your bad hand."

Dante was frozen in shock. "You're insane," he whispered after a few seconds.

"Truth has a price, Dante," said the Father. "You've always known that. And what I'm asking you now is a small price. Without that hand but with your name, you'll be much more complete than you are now."

"No."

"Don't be afraid. I'll help you do it the right way."

"I'm not afraid, I just don't want to give you the satisfaction."

The Father nodded gravely. "The choice is yours. But I'm going to give you one more minute to make up your mind. Then I'll walk out of here and I'll never come back. You'll lose your last chance to discover what has been denied you for your whole life, your identity." He leaned over him, though never crossing the security line, the safe distance. "Are you really willing to give that up?" he added. And even though the Father was doing his best to speak in a neutral voice, Dante detected pride and pleasure.

"You're enjoying yourself, aren't you?" he asked.

"I'm only doing what's necessary."

Dante shook his head. "You pretend to be a scientist, and maybe you were one in a certain period of your life. But now you're nothing but a sadist with a sick lust for power. The suffering of your victims excites you. You take pleasure from it. And you just want to use me for the last time."

"You still have twenty seconds." The Father touched his forehead with his begloved hand. "I have a stopwatch in here."

"Do you really not realize what you are? Or are you lying to yourself, too?"

"Ten seconds." The Father tried to wipe his mouth, forgetting that he was wearing a ski mask. "You won't feel a thing, I guarantee. Or not much pain, anyway. I'll help you to hit the center of the joint." He pointed to the syringe. "You'll use anesthetic. And then I'll stitch you up. The way I used to when you'd cut yourself in the silo. You remember?"

"You may even believe you're doing the right thing."

The Father shot to his feet. "Time's up. I expected something more from you," he said. He strode toward the door, but Dante called him back.

"Okay," he said.

The Father froze to a halt. "Okay? Are you sure?"

Dante had turned even paler. "Let's do it. The bad hand just reminds me of you. At least I'll finally get rid of it."

The Father again tried to wipe his lips. His hand was trembling slightly. "Good boy . . . good boy."

He came back and sat down at the table. He took the tourniquet and tossed it to Dante.

"Tie it just below the elbow."

Dante took off his jacket. "You've been watching me all these years?"

"I've been keeping tabs on you," the Father replied. He grabbed the bottle of hydrogen peroxide and sprayed some on the blade, drying it with a rag.

"I always knew it," said Dante.

"I know."

"Just as I always knew you'd come get me again. It was just a matter of time." Dante started to undo his shirt.

"Get moving," the Father ordered, stroking the edge of the blade with his begloved fingers.

Dante pulled off his shirt. "I thought about having a location-tracking chip implanted, but there are none that can actually fit under your skin the way they say. If they are going to be found by a satellite they're the size of a cigarette pack, and you have to change the batteries frequently."

"I know that, too," said the Father impatiently.

"I realized that I'd have to be able to take care of myself if it ever did happen. I'd have to be able to open any lock if I wound up being imprisoned. I spent years studying locks." He looked at the Father. "And studying padlocks, too," he added.

Dante grabbed the collar and hurled it to the floor. Then he lunged forward, overturning the table. The paper cutter tumbled onto the Father's legs, making him shout in pain.

Dante in his turn fell onto him and grabbed him by the throat, even though it was with his half-numb hands. "If you use the lock-up points on a padlock, then the possible combinations drop to eighty, did you know that? Eighty. It takes half an hour. I can do it blind-folded if I need to." He clamped his hands around his throat with what little strength remained to him.

The Father groped for him, trying to lay hands on him, but the gloves just slipped off Dante's body.

"No, you didn't know that, did you? You don't know everything. You're just a little man behind a big mask. Like the Wizard of Oz you like so much."

The door swung open, and the man who had kidnapped Dante came running in, brandishing a billy club. Dante let go of the Father and grabbed the file folder. He pulled it open. Nothing inside but blank pages. He dropped it just before the truncheon came swinging down and caught him on the temple. He dropped to the floor. The club hit him in the ribs. Something creaked, and he fought to keep from losing consciousness.

The Father's voice arrived from an infinite distance. "Don't kill him!" he shrieked. "And don't let him pass out!"

The man with the truncheon grabbed Dante and pulled him onto the bed. Pinning him to the mattress with one knee, he pulled out a handful of plastic zip ties, the kind riot police carry, the kind you can't get off without cutting them. He used them to tie Dante's wrists behind his back, then he bound his ankles together, too. They were so tight that they blocked his circulation.

Last of all, he put the collar back on him. With his hands bound, Dante had no way to reach the padlock.

The Father got laboriously to his feet. His legs hurt. "I don't know whether to be proud of you or offended. Perhaps both."

"Liar," Dante said under his breath. "Storyteller. Piece of shit. Coward."

"No. I told you the truth. I've never known who you were."

Dante snickered. "Thanks."

"For what?"

"I've been obsessed with you my whole life. And I think I've even felt a certain love for you, in spite of what you've done to me. But now that I've seen you for what you are, you've broken the spell, you've freed me. Even if you keep me locked up in here, I'll be freer than I've ever been before."

The Father quivered with rage. He turned toward the man with the billy club. "Go get the bulldozer," he ordered.

"Should I leave you here alone?" the man asked. It was the first time Dante had heard him speak.

"He can't do anything to me now."

The man left. All Dante could think was: *Bulldozer? What are they going to do to me?*

"You understand why I can't leave you alive, don't you?" said the Father. "But I won't just abandon you. I'll be with you to the very end." He pointed to the ceiling. "There's a webcam up there. I'll watch you. This, too, will have value."

"What value?"

"I'll be able to watch the reactions of a claustrophobic as he's being buried alive. Something people imagine but that no scientist has ever watched in real time."

Dante tried to say something, but his throat had completely shut down. He writhed and jerked, trying to get loose from the plastic straps, but all he did was cut his flesh. His wrists began to bleed.

"Farewell, Son," said the Father as he opened the door.

"I know who you are!" Dante shouted. "I know who you are! I just recognized you! You came to my hotel."

The Father stopped. "I so wanted to see you up close," he admitted. He pulled off the ski mask. "I wanted to see my creation."

The sharp-hewn face of the pathologist Mario Tirelli appeared.

34

Colomba rinsed her face with the ice-cold water in the bar's bathroom. She'd had a minor attack, earlier. For a moment she'd stopped breathing, and she'd slammed her fist into the cigarette counter, injuring her knuckle. She'd have kept slamming her fist, just for the pleasure of the pain, if Santini hadn't stopped her. Santini. Who was doing the right thing, while she was no longer thinking rationally.

Tirelli.

She couldn't believe it, but she knew it was true. She thought back to the time at the mountain meadows, when Tirelli had seemed not to realize that the murderer's knife blows had been too accurate and clean to be the work of a jealous husband in a violent frenzy. Tirelli, who usually noticed if a comma was out of place.

Because he knew it had been the German.

And at the hospital, when she had asked him to check into Silver Compass. Secretly, because she trusted him

And he decided to have me killed. He decided it at that moment.

He'd known all about the investigation at the public health clinic, and he'd ordered Montanari killed, too. Colomba had asked *him* for the doctor's name, him of all people. He must have had himself a good long laugh.

And then there were the names he'd used. Tirelli liked old movies and TV shows. Zardoz . . . Colomba remembered that Leonard McCoy, the account name on the virtual credit card, was a doctor on an old TV series her mother used to watch when she was a kid. *Star Trip? Star Trek?* Yes, that was it. He'd made fools of them all, but especially her.

She had been his mole, his number one confidential informant.

Idiot. If anything happens to Dante, it'll be your fault.

She shut the faucet so forcefully that she bent the plastic pipe; then she dried her face and left the bathroom.

Santini was waiting for her outside the door, and he walked with her out onto the sidewalk. Now there were other people in the bar: early risers, construction workers and factory workers for the most part.

"Did you find the number?" Colomba asked.

"Here you go," Santini replied, handing her his cell phone with the number already entered.

The sleepy voice of Anzelmo from the Ministry of Justice's Special Internet Crimes Division answered on the fifth ring. When he realized that it was Colomba who was calling, he was speechless for a few seconds. What should he say to her? Congratulate her for having been cleared? Or tell her to go to hell because of the internal investigation he'd been put through on her account?

Colomba beat him to it. "I need a favor."

"You're joking, right? Do you know how much trouble you got me into—"

"The Father's taken Dante," Colomba interrupted. "With you, there's only three of us who know it. If word gets out, he's dead."

"Why?"

"Because the Father is Tirelli."

"The pathologist? Have you lost your mind?"

Colomba gestured to Santini, who took the cell phone. "This is Deputy Chief Santini; we know each other."

"Yes, Deputy Chief, sir, but what on earth is going on?"

"What Caselli just told you. Now, either you help us, or hang up and forget we ever spoke."

Colomba took back the phone. "I need you. Anyone else could be involved or just too close to Tirelli. You don't have anything to do with it, I understood that at the public health clinic. Unless you're an Oscar-worthy actor, but I'm willing to bet against that possibility."

"Caselli, you need to report him," said Anzelmo, befuddled.

Colomba ground her teeth. "Wake the hell up, Anzelmo! Do you really not understand why I can't do that? Tirelli knows half the police of Italy; hundreds of colleagues have worked with him, all over the country. He's a venerable institution. As soon as he gets word that we've figured it out, he'll dispose of Dante once and for all."

"But what can I do?"

"Locate his cell phones. And find the phone records."

Anzelmo decided that he really was in deep shit this time. If he refused, he might turn out to be responsible for a man's death, while if he accepted he ran the risk of another internal investigation and a suspension. But if he refused and then remained silent, he'd have the worst of both options, and he didn't feel like being a rat spy. "Give me the numbers," he sighed.

Santini smoked a cigarette while they were waiting. Colomba stared into the empty air.

"Would you ever have thought it?" asked Santini.

"No. It still seems unreal to me."

"What are the chances that we're wrong?"

"Zero. Fuck. Not a single chance."

The cell phone rang ten minutes later. It was Anzelmo, with bad news. "Tirelli has had his phones turned off since yesterday. They read as being at his home. I tried calling him on his landline."

"Are you insane?"

"I would have thought of something if he'd answered. I work with him. Or I used to . . . But he's not picking up. If you ask me, he's not home."

"He left his cell phones behind, but he's not there," said Colomba angrily. "He's still with Dante."

"I sent you the phone records," Anzelmo said. "Maybe there's something useful in there. I'll be waiting at home, all right?"

Just then, the barista stuck his head in with a stack of paper. "These are for you."

Colomba grabbed the pages out of his hand and scanned them rapidly, sharing them with Santini. They were printouts of an Excel spreadsheet that contained, aside from the numbers of the phone calls made or received, the names of the individuals called and the location of the cell tower that the cell phone that had been called was connected to. They started reading from the bottom, then from the top, and in just minutes it was clear that they were completely at a loss. Tirelli had made only work calls to colleagues and friends they both knew, to restaurants, to his sister, who lived in Milan, to the taxi dispatch number, and not much more. Nothing that could be considered even remotely suspicious. Or maybe everything could be considered suspicious, but they had no way of checking it out in such a short space of time. For the past twenty-four hours, nothing. No calls. Colomba threw the stack of paper to the floor in a burst of fury.

"Shit! We're just wasting time!"

"We can still find him," said Santini. "But we have to stop trying to do it all ourselves. In ten minutes we can have half the cops in Rome helping us."

"And one of them will call Tirelli! I know it, and you know it."

Santini grabbed her arm. "It's the only chance we have. I'll do it even if you don't agree to it, at this point."

She shook loose. But without the vehemence she might have used until recently.

I'm no better than he is, she thought. *It's partly my fault that Dante's risking his life.* "It's impossible that he hasn't made at least one small mistake," she murmured.

"The only mistake he made is that he's completely insane. That aside, if he's been out there for all these years, there has to be a reason. He's probably never made a compromising phone call in his life."

"Oh, no, he made them, all right," said Colomba. "It was Tirelli who phoned all the children's mothers, introducing himself as Dr. Zedda. The German did the dirty work, but his voice is too distinctive, maybe his vocal cords are damaged . . . He can only whisper."

"Could Tirelli have another phone?"

"No, he was using Skype."

Santini and Colomba stared each other in the eyes, both thinking the same thing. "Shit!" they exclaimed in unison.

Dante heard the sound of the bulldozer grow outside the camper until it became deafening; then the first crash knocked him to the floor, so that the collar almost hanged him. He pulled himself to his knees, his head against the foam rubber mattress that reeked of his acrid sweat. There was another crash, this time not as violent but more prolonged.

They're crushing me, he thought, crazed with terror. He'd tried to wear through the plastic ties by rubbing them against the headboard of the bunk bed, but it was too smooth and the plastic was too tough: all he'd managed to do was make his wrists bleed even more profusely. He tried again, shouting and spewing insults at the man who was watching him via the webcam. There was a part of him that wanted to fall silent, to avoid giving that man any further satisfaction, but that was the rational part of his mind, shoved aside by the animal howling to be set free.

Another crash, but once again the camper remained intact. But it shifted on its wheels, creaking. The bulldozer was slowly shoving it.

Where? Where? shouted the Beast in his mind.

He understood when he felt the camper tilt toward the wall to which he was tethered. Dante rolled across the mattress and banged his head against the bunk bed above him, as the camper leaned over onto a forty-five degree angle, creaking and screeching. The table slid down the floor, the doors of the small cabinet on the opposite wall flew open, and a plastic trash bag tumbled out, ripping open as it hit the floor. A rat emerged from the garbage and started scampering wildly in circles, squeaking. The camper keeled over even farther, and Dante hit his forehead against the headboard; the resulting cut started streaming blood. The cabinet fell off the wall and burst apart at the seams; the plywood covering one of the small windows broke away. For an instant Dante saw the morning light through a film of blood and had a flash of irrational hope. *I can get out that window if I can only reach it*, he thought. *I can save myself.*

Then the bulldozer gave another shove and the camper slid downward, landing after a drop that lasted just a fraction of a second. The light from the small window was blocked out by a shadow that shot up from below like a reverse guillotine; the floor returned to an almost horizontal position. They had tossed the camper into a pit, into utter darkness. With his last glimmer of lucidity, Dante just hoped he'd die in a hurry.

✻   ✻   ✻

The idea that had occurred to Colomba and Santini was very simple. In order to connect to Skype, the Father must necessarily be using a smartphone or a PC, and that fact reminded them that Tirelli had a laptop he always carried with him when he visited the scenes of various crimes. Both Colomba and Santini had seen it dozens of times. The laptop had a flash drive he used to connect to the Internet. Anzelmo identified it and tried to pin down its location: unfortunately, it, too, was turned off. That didn't mean that the PC wasn't connected to the Web, just that it was connected in some other way: an Ethernet cable, for instance, or else by Wi-Fi. Some computers had an internal GPS locator in case of theft, and it was possible to find out where they were if you knew the access code. But Anzelmo didn't know it, and in any case he seriously doubted that Tirelli would have activated it.

The cloud, he thought to himself. He connected to the server at the Institute of Forensic Medicine. Tirelli had a shared folder on that server to which he uploaded his expert reports, and it updated automatically whenever his computer was connected to the Internet. The folder had updated twenty minutes ago. Anzelmo, sitting at his computer in his underwear, high-fived himself and then tried to figure out where Tirelli, without even realizing it, had connected from.

Colomba and Santini were back sitting in the car, ready to take off the minute they got an answer.

"Even if we do find out where his PC is," said Santini, "that doesn't necessarily mean that Tirelli's anywhere near it. And if he is, it might not mean Torre's there, too."

"I know. We only have one shot. If we get this wrong, we'll do what you say," Colomba replied.

"If we get it wrong, we might be too late. Are you sure you're willing to take on that responsibility?"

Colomba shook her head. "No."

"But you're going to take it anyway."

"Yes."

"I'm glad I'm not in your shoes," said Santini.

Two minutes later, the phone call came in from Anzelmo. Tirelli's PC was connected to the Wi-Fi of a long-term parking area for campers and recreational vehicles.

35

Via Pontina was the regional highway that ran from the EUR section of Rome to the little beach town of Terracina. The long-term RV and camper parking facility was located on Via Pontina just outside of the Rome beltway. It was a small facility, just twelve acres, nearly all of it covered with sheet-metal canopies under which the vehicles were parked in long orderly rows. A sign at the front gate—which opened automatically, powered by an electric motor, once you punched in a code on a keypad—announced that due to construction work currently under way, vehicles could be dropped off and picked up only between ten in the morning and six in the evening, instead of the usual hours of seven to midnight. "We apologize for the inconvenience." Perhaps that was why many of the parking spaces were empty, and it could also explain the appearance of general decrepitude. In the distance, in a fenced-off area invisible from the road, a bulldozer was moving piles of sand, pushing them into a large hole in the ground. Next to it, a cement mixer was turning, beside a stack of cement bags.

At seven in the morning, on the stretch of road overlooking the vehicle storage facility, the truck traffic was already intense, while pedestrians were virtually nonexistent. The watchman, a fifty-year-old Romanian who spoke Italian poorly and in general didn't talk much at all, was sitting in the guard's booth next to the front gate. He was alternately watching the screen connected to the two video cameras trained on the road and the television set showing an old movie. The watchman's name was Petru, but he was generally known as "Dumbo" on account of the cauliflower ears that were a legacy of a short and inglorious career as a boxer; his orders were to keep people out and turn a blind eye to whatever his boss was doing on the far side of the parking area. Illegal construction, maybe. Or maybe he was burying toxic waste. Something nasty, but Petru didn't care. He was paid *not* to care.

The intercom buzzed. On the screen, Petru saw a man and a woman; he had a mustache, she had red hair. They buzzed again. Petru pushed his chair over to the window, opened it, and leaned out. "Closed!" he shouted.

The couple outside didn't seem to hear. The man buzzed the intercom again. Petru sighed, got up, and left his booth, shivering in the cool morning air. In the booth he had a little electric heater that he kept turned up to maximum. "Till ten, we closed. There's sign!" he said, walking over to the gate.

The woman reached her hands through the bars and slammed him toward her and against the gate, banging the nose he had broken in his last bout as a professional, when some guy ten years younger than him had flattened it and shoved it practically up onto his forehead. The man pulled out a pistol and stuck it in his face. In his other hand he held a cop badge and ID.

"Open up," the woman ordered.

The Father was sitting in one of the abandoned trailers about thirty feet from the excavation. When a customer left a vehicle or trailer—usually relatively worthless—and vanished, the storage facility would clean it up and try to sell it. If it was too old and beat up, it was simply hauled to the edge of the parking area, to what was known as "the elephants' graveyard." The trailer the Father was sitting in was one of them, and it still bore the marks of the family it had belonged to: the walls were dotted with decals of children's cartoon characters, and in one corner a wooden cradle sat gathering dust. The Father's computer was wedged atop the kitchen sink, and on the screen streamed the images of Dante's dying torments, beamed in through the Wi-Fi network.

The Father stood watching, in silence, without moving a muscle in spite of the ache in his legs. Observation was the essence of the work he did, the art he'd honed over decades of unbroken experience. When he imagined himself, he saw an unblinking eye, capable of reading every secret, whether kept by the living or the dead. In his other line of work, which he had built as a sort of house of reflecting mirrors, he used only a fraction of this skill of his, but it had already been enough to elevate him well above the average level of his competition, so careless and imprecise, so incapable of paying attention to details. His cover occupation gave him a sense of peace. The material he was working with was inert now, devoid of any twitches or rebellions. There was no battle of the wills when it was time to insert a thermometer into a cadaver's rectum or extract a heart from a chest cavity. The struggle had already taken place elsewhere, and what was laid out on the autopsy table was the loser's remains. By studying the causes of death, the Father was actually searching for traces of the life that had been abandoned there. The marks of habits, dietary preferences, hidden vices and sins. He sniffed at the scents, he caressed them bare-handed. When no one was watching, he kissed them to savor their tastes. But there was nothing that could truly chase away every last shadow, let him know everything. Each time he was forced to stitch up a corpse and relinquish it to the morgue, the Father felt as if he were being asked to give up a fascinating book he'd only just begun to read.

It wasn't until he went back to his *real* life that his senses sharpened and he felt rejuvenated. Because the secrets of a live and reactive mind were infinitely greater than those of a slab of meat just starting to decompose. It was a constant clash with the uncertain and the unforeseen; there were no clearly marked roads. His subjects could rebel against him or love him, let themselves die or try to kill him. At first, that is—until he'd finally shaped them into their definitive form, the form he had decided upon.

Dante had told him he felt power in domination, but the Father rejected that accusation. He was simply an artist who loved his work, because at the highest levels, art and science both aspire to beauty. To the absolute.

He brightened the screen a little. The battery-powered lamp inside the camper continued to work, as did the webcam, but it wasn't as powerful as the Father would have liked. Part of Dante's face was in shadow now, and he couldn't see his expression as clearly as he would have liked. All he could glimpse was his mouth, open in an attempt to gulp down the air that was beginning to be in short supply.

When the first load of sand was dumped onto the camper, Dante began battering the back of his head against the wall, maybe because he hoped to lose consciousness. But he'd soon run out of strength. He'd almost stopped moving entirely, aside from the spasms in his legs. Still, he was conscious, and his eyes were open. The Father was saddened that he couldn't look into them.

He shifted his gaze from the screen to his camper's window. About thirty feet away he saw the bulldozer, halted at the edge of the pit. The driver was staring at him, awaiting instructions. His name was Manolo; he'd been with the Father from the very beginning. Chosen by him personally, not the dreck that the German recruited. Even if he'd put away enough money to live very well, the Father had held on to the long-term parking facility he'd inherited from his parents.

With a sigh, the Father decided that the time had came to say farewell to the last vestiges of the most productive and astonishing period of his life. He caught Manolo's attention and gestured for him to cover up the hole.

Santini handcuffed Petru to the desk. Colomba leaned toward him. "Where's Tirelli?"

"Who?" asked Petru.

"Old man. Skinny. Long hair."

"Not know," Petru replied.

Just then, the sound of the bulldozer's engine revving higher came from a distance. Instinctively, Petru turned to look in that direction.

"He's there," said Colomba, heading for the door.

Santini started after her, but that's when Petru caught him off guard. Until that moment, the Romanian had put up no resistance, but now he rose to his full six foot three inches and ripped the desk apart. A two-foot chunk of wood dangled from the handcuff; Petru brought it down on Santini as he was still turning around. Santini managed to dodge fast enough to avoid the blow to his face, but the sharp chunk of wood drove into his thigh and nearly ran it through. He collapsed to the floor, clutching his leg and screaming in pain, unable to grab his weapon.

Petru had acted without thinking. He just wanted to run and get away. Now that he'd injured a policeman, all the more so. If they caught him this time, it wouldn't be like before. He wouldn't get out again. He'd die in prison, just as his brother had. He charged straight at Colomba, who was standing in front of the door, windmilling his enormous fists. She stepped lightly aside and bashed him hard in the face with the swivel chair Petru had sat in all night long. One of the wheeled legs caught him right in the Adam's apple, and the Romanian fell to his knees, both hands clutching his throat, suddenly red from the struggle to breathe.

Colomba kicked him in the face. Petru raised his hands. Colomba kicked him again, wounding his eye, then rushed over to Santini and pulled the keys to the handcuffs out of his pocket. Santini had unfastened his belt and tied it above the wound, applying pressure to stop the blood, which was spilling out in copious amounts. In the meantime, he cursed in a low voice.

Colomba unlocked Petru's other handcuff, and this time she fastened it to a metal pipe, jerking her prisoner's arm until he slithered the proper distance. "If you try to get out of here, I swear I'll kill you."

Petru turned his swollen face downward and remained seated on the floor.

Colomba went over to Santini. "Are you going to die?" she asked.

"No, I don't think so."

"I'll leave him with you. Call the others, okay?" She slid Santini's handgun out of his holster and ran outside.

Santini breathed slowly, doing his best not to pass out.

Colomba headed straight toward the noise of the bulldozer that reverberated through the metal canopies. As she walked past the last row of parked vehicles, she found herself in an area that looked more like a junkyard than a long-term parking facility. There were dented carcasses of campers and rusted trailers, broken picnic tables, skeletal beach umbrellas, tangled knots of cables, charred firewood, broken camp chairs. At the edge of that area was a field where sparse yellowed grass grew among the scrub and the tree stumps. Back toward the fence that separated the parking area from an adjoining untilled field, she saw the bulldozer, which was dumping a bucketful of sand into what looked like a long ditch.

Into what looked like a grave.

Colomba leveled her arm and aimed her gun at the driver. "Halt!" she shouted. She was twenty-five feet away from him.

The driver took shelter on the floor of the bulldozer's cab. Colomba watched as the door cautiously opened, letting the barrel of a weapon protrude. She lunged for the shelter of a camper spangled with tiny flowers, just seconds before the first burst of automatic fire. It was a Kalashnikov, a weapon that before now Colomba had only seen displayed on evidence tables as confiscated goods, never being aimed at her with intent to kill.

The bullets chopped away the corner of the camper as if it were made of paper, and Colomba huddled into a crouch. Under normal circumstances, she would have awaited the arrival of reinforcements, but she couldn't, not without getting some news about Dante's condition. She tried the camper's door handle. The door opened easily.

She dived inside, hoping to find a better vantage point from which to aim at the man on the bulldozer and catch him off guard. She realized she'd made a mistake when she glimpsed a movement behind her out of the corner of her eye. She barely had time to whip around before he'd slammed his laptop into her face, twisting it two-handed like a baseball bat.

Colomba lost hold of her gun and felt something breaking in her mouth. Then she saw nothing, heard nothing; she stopped breathing, her lungs two empty sacks.

"I swear I didn't want to do it, Colomba," said Tirelli and lifted the computer again. "I've always been fond of you."

Colomba jerked her head away just in time, and the computer shattered onto the floor. The pain of that movement restored control of her breathing. She reached out and grabbed Tirelli's wrist; he'd lunged forward and lost his balance. The wrist was thin and frail. She yanked it toward her, and Tirelli fell upon her, as if into an embrace. He tried to struggle, but his strength was nothing compared to Colomba's; she wrapped him in her grip, glaring at him with blood-sheened eyes.

"Where's Dante?" she whispered. She was having difficulty moving her mouth; something crackled in her jaw like broken glass.

"It's too late for him, Colomba."

She tackled him onto the floor. He was as light as balsa wood. She climbed on top of him and let blood and saliva from her shattered lips drip onto him. "Where."

"In the hole."

Colomba got to her feet and retrieved her gun. She was seeing double. "Get up," she muttered.

He obeyed. She got behind him and braced her left arm around his throat. "Walk," she said.

"What are you trying to do?" asked Tirelli.

She squeezed, he fell silent. She forced him out the door, out into the open air. The man on the bulldozer saw them, and, as Colomba had hoped, he held his fire.

"Tell him to drop his weapon," Colomba ordered. She'd have done it herself, but she couldn't: the pain every time she uttered a word was terrible.

"He won't do it. Survival comes first, Colomba."

"Tell him."

He obeyed.

The man on the bulldozer got to his feet, still holding the rifle, but no longer aiming it in their direction. "I'll go away from here!" he shouted.

"No," Colomba murmured.

"She says no, Manolo," Tirelli shouted.

"I have to go away from here! I don't want to have anything more to do with this bullshit."

"No," Colomba whispered again.

"Be reasonable, Colomba," Tirelli said.

"No," she said again.

The man on the bulldozer seemed to understand. He suddenly jerked the rifle up. Colomba did the same thing, over Tirelli's shoulder. They both fired at almost the same instant. Half of Colomba's bullets hit their target. Manolo fell backward off the bulldozer, tumbling onto the tread.

Two of Manolo's shots passed through Tirelli's chest and hit Colomba in her left side.

She felt as if she'd been run through with needles of ice. She let Tirelli drop but managed to stay on her feet. She looked down at him, sprawled on the ground, his chest ripped open at the sternum. The blood had pumped out in gushing spurts and was now forming a broad puddle beneath him, as he alternated between rapid panting and breathlessness.

The Father was dying, and he knew it. Someone would lift him up off the ground and cut him open on a metal autopsy table, and they'd study him the way he had done with hundreds of men and women, some of whose lives he had been responsible for ending.

But they wouldn't understand, the Father thought with his last spark of life. They'd never understand who he'd been. No one would understand his dream.

The last thing the Father saw before dying was a pair of terrible green eyes.

36

Colomba staggered unsteadily away from the Father's corpse. At a certain point along the seemingly endless path, she let her pistol drop, and she herself almost fell to the ground.

When she got to the edge of the pit, she realized that there was an entire camper buried in it. She could see only part of the crushed roof, and through it she could see a heap of sand. If Dante was in there, he was dead. He had to be.

Colomba jumped down onto the camper. It was less than a yard down, but the effort was almost enough to make her pass out.

The bullets actually served as hemostatic plugs, but she was still losing blood, and the pain in her face had become monstrous. She dropped down into the opening and landed on the pile of sand, sliding down the side until she reached the far end of the camper, the only part still clear of detritus. Grains of sand got into her throat and eyes. She coughed, and the pain was so bad that she wept. She wept in great racking sobs, entirely forgetting where she was until she could finally lift her head and saw a human figure illuminated by a dim green night light. All that emerged from the sand was part of his chest and his head.

Dante was tied up with a dog collar, and he was desperately stretching toward her, trying to make it across the sand but unable to move.

"CC," he said in a voice that seemed to come from beyond the grave. "I knew you'd come."

Colomba crawled toward him and hugged him tight, without speaking. When the first responders arrived, that's how they found them.

EPILOGUE

It took two months before Colomba and Dante recovered from their injuries and their imprisonment. In those two months, the investigation into the Father, known by his everyday name of Mario Tirelli, continued, though without clearing up all the mysteries that the case had raised. Whoever his contacts and financers might have been, he hadn't written their names down anywhere or confided them to a living soul. Any relations he might have had with the CIA or the Italian army were categorically denied, and the only thing worthy of note in that connection was that a retired Italian general blew out his brains with a collector's piece, a pistol from the Second World War. According to his personnel files, he had been the commanding officer of the barracks where Bodini had served before leaving the service and becoming, for many years, the only guilty party in Dante's kidnapping.

There were more suicides. The managing director of the foundation that had run Silver Compass turned on the gas in his apartment, killing himself after stabbing his wife to death. Murder-suicide, the investigators decided, even though there were newspapers that theorized murder-murder, plain and simple.

A few weeks later, a man turned himself in of his own accord at a carabinieri barracks, saying that it was he who had originally taken the photograph of the German's little platoon and now he was afraid he might be killed. He had no evidence to support his claim. He said that he had been enrolled in the platoon by the German himself, that he did not know the German's real identity, and that the only part he had played was that of supplying food for the prisoners. The only contribution he offered to the investigators was an explanation of the shoes hung around the neck.

"It was our nickname, 'Two Shoes,'" he told Spinelli during an interview. "Because we had our feet in two shoes, Italy and America, get it? And the rule was that if we did something that might attract the attention of the authorities, we just needed to tie together two shoes on the scene of whatever we had done, so whoever it concerned would get the message and cover us up."

Whether what he was saying was the truth or merely the fantasies of one of the many lunatics involved in the case had not yet been established. Digging into his past, the investigators learned that he'd been dismissed from the armed services because he was a drug addict. The man said that was a decoy, a cover-up.

The German was still in jail, keeping his mouth closed, and not much progress had been made in figuring out who he actually was. No one came forward to identify him, aside from a number of people who had met him in any of his numerous fictional identities. Since not even his nationality was known, he was given books and periodicals in a number of different European languages, and he seemed to read and comprehend them with equal facility.

In the meantime, an American pharmaceutical company was accused of having supplied experimental medicines to Tirelli, and the CEO defended himself by claiming that the pharmaceuticals had been stolen and the theft had been properly reported to the authorities. He suspected a case of industrial espionage and was disconcerted to learn the deplorable uses to which they had been put. The fact that the founder of the company was one of the chemists who had taken part in Project Bluebird in the 1950s could only be viewed as an unfortunate coincidence.

Colomba and Dante remained in constant contact. He regained his tranquility before she regained the use of her jaw, and he persuaded her to spend Christmas Eve with him at one of his favorite spots: the Bagni Vecchi of Bormio, a thermal spa and hotel in the province of Sondrio where Dante liked to go for massages.

The room was virtually all glass and looked out onto the outdoor swimming pool, fed by hot springs; Colomba and Dante dove into that water with immense pleasure on December 23, looking out over the snowy panorama, enjoying the contrast between the icy wind and the heat of the water.

Colomba's scars had almost disappeared, and anyway the other guests swimming alongside had other things to look at than the marks left by bullets that had come to rest just a sixteenth of an inch from her kidney.

Dante floated on his back, his mouth still filled with the taste of the green coffee he'd filled his suitcase with. He considered it to be the queen of regenerative herbal infusions. "Any news from Santini?"

Colomba lifted her head out of the stream of hot water pouring out of a pipe above the edge of the pool. "He's back on regular duty. He says he still walks with a limp, and as far as he's concerned, he doesn't want to see either of us for the next millennium."

"If you talk to him, tell him the feeling is mutual." He sprayed water out of his mouth like a little boy. "What about you? What have you decided? Going back into uniform?"

"I don't know yet. Curcio seems like a good guy, but . . ." She shook her head. "I'll consider it, anyway. I still have a few more days of convalescence."

"Well, I've decided to keep my name."

Colomba smiled. "Well, that's good to hear." Among the human remains in the plastic drums, a match had been found to Annibale Valle's DNA. That had given rise to a legal nightmare, a labyrinth through which Minutillo was trying to find his way so that Dante, the *living* Dante, could find grounds to avail himself of a court order that authorized him to use his mother's surname, a mother who was no longer his, a surname that was no longer his. In the end, Valle had offered to adopt him and Dante had accepted. Legal proceedings were already under way.

"If I had decided to change my name, I would have picked Leo. What do you think? Or Leonidas."

"Why not Rambo?"

Dante snickered. "Or else do like Prince, you know, and have no name. Just call myself by a symbol."

"A coffee bean."

"Something like that. But then I realized I was used to Dante." He went over to the hydromassage and let the water slide down his back. "I mean, also because my real name . . . what are the odds I'll ever know that?"

"Better than the odds you had of ever getting out of that pit alive," Colomba pointed out.

Dante sprayed her. "I hate you when you're such an optimist."

She grabbed the side of the pool and hoisted herself up. Dante tried not to look; half the men present were staring, though.

"I'm going to get a shower," said Colomba. "See you at dinner."

"Okay."

Dante let himself fall back into the water and floated on his back until he heard the sound of his new cell phone ringing. The sound was coming from the pocket of his bathrobe, lying by the side of the pool. He swam over and grabbed it without leaving the water. The screen said: "Unknown caller."

Dante hesitated. Since his recovery he'd received hundreds of phone calls from people who wanted to track down a relative, give him their best wishes, or insult him for some unknown reason. So he'd changed his number and given the new one only to his closest friends, and they all knew that he didn't answer to unrecognized numbers. But he was on vacation and he was feeling benevolent. He took the call and asked who it was.

A male voice without any particular regional accent replied. "Are you the man who calls himself Dante Torre?"

"Who's speaking?" Dante asked again.

The man on the other end of the line seemed to hesitate. Then he said, "I shouldn't be phoning you. You aren't even supposed to know I exist. But I couldn't help myself. Not after I heard about you. About what happened to you. I just wanted to tell you that I'm happy you're all right. It was a shock for me to learn that you were still alive."

At first, Dante assumed that it was just another of the many nutcases who had tormented him over the years, and he wondered how this one had managed to find his phone number. But there was a sincerity in the man's voice that prevented him from hanging up. "And just why should you care?" he asked.

After another pause, speaking quietly as if he were afraid someone might hear him, the man replied, "Because I'm your brother."

Dante heard a shuffle and click—then just the sound of his own breathing.

AUTHOR'S NOTE

I changed a few abbreviations of Italian law enforcement and armed forces agencies in order to afford myself greater freedom in my descriptions of the way they operate, and I also took certain liberties with unit headquarters, barracks, addresses, and other such details.

I've taken even greater liberties with the geography and topography of Rome and Cremona. The building where Santiago lived doesn't exist, any more than Lake Comello exists, though the lake I described does resemble a body of water not far off that I visited and studied. The Vivaro mountain meadows were also adapted as needed. In other cases, however, I limited myself to changing the names, but the places are real and recognizable.

If you wish to know more about MKUltra, there are plenty of books, among them *The Search for the "Manchurian Candidate": The CIA and Mind Control: The Secret History of the Behavioral Sciences*, by John D. Marks, and *Mass Control: Engineering Human Consciousness*, by Jim Keith, as well as a vast fount of information online. There are, of course, people who say it's all nonsense, but you be the judge. The Italian branch of the experiments, at any rate, is pure speculation on my part.

I'd like to thank my editor, Carlo Carabba, and my agent, Laura Grandi, for having worked closely with me in the final phases of writing this novel; without them, I never could have done it. I also thank Giulia Ichino for having been the first to read it; Emanuela Cocco for the fact checking; Licia Troisi for explaining how you dive in a wet suit; Dino Abbrescia for his advice about campers; the managing editor of Mondadori Fiction, Fabiola Riboni, and the editor Paola Gerevini for their careful handling of the text; and Yulia

Buneeva and Piero Frabetti for their invaluable pointers. Also, great thanks to my magnificent English translator, Antony Shugaar, and the team at my American publisher, Scribner, most especially my editor, Rick Horgan; his assistant, David Lamb; and art director Jaya Miceli. Last of all, I'd like to thank Sabrina Annoni for stubbornly encouraging me.

And, of course, you readers, for this trip we've taken together.

ABOUT THE AUTHOR

Sandrone Dazieri is the bestselling author of eight novels and more than fifty screenplays. *Kill the Father*, the first in a planned series featuring Colomba Caselli and Dante Torre, is his UK debut.